Books by Linda Nagata

NEAR-FUTURE SCIENCE FICTION

Pacific Storm

The Last Good Man

Limit of Vision

Tech-Heaven

The Red Trilogy:
>   *The Red: First Light*
>   *The Trials*
>   *Going Dark*

FAR-FUTURE SCIENCE FICTION

Inverted Frontier Series:
>   *Edges*
>   *Silver*
>   *Needle*
>   *Blade*
>   *Memory (related)*

The Nanotech Succession:
>   *Tech-Heaven* (prequel)
>   *The Bohr Maker*
>   *Deception Well*
>   *Vast*

Skye-Object 3270-a (young adult/middle grade)

FANTASY NOVELS

The Wild Trilogy:
>   *The Snow Chanter*
>   *The Long War*
>   *Days of Storm*

Stories of the Puzzle Lands Duology:
>   *The Dread Hammer*
>   *Hepen the Watcher*

INVERTED FRONTIER

BOOK 4
BLADE

LINDA NAGATA

Mythic Island Press LLC
Kula, Hawaii

First edition: March 2024

ISBN 978-1-937197-44-5

Cover art copyright © 2024 by Sarah Anne Langton

Mythic Island Press LLC
P.O. Box 1293
Kula, HI 96790-1293
MythicIslandPress.com

BLADE

PRELUDE

LIFE DIVERGES OVER time.

A moment came when Clemantine, alone on *Griffin*'s high bridge, stoically accepted this as her own truth. Once, she had regularly received subminds of her other self, replete with memories of life lived amid the garden of *Dragon*'s gee deck and in the company of cherished friends and lovers.

Even then, she'd been her own mind, only leavened by the humanity of her other self.

Now years had passed without any such update as *Griffin* slow-coasted in the void beyond Tanjiri, closely accompanied only by the two sentient missiles that Urban controlled.

How it irked that she did not control them! She should have been given the missiles to deploy because like those missiles, *she* was a weapon. The Tanji, those strange entities who both nurtured and guarded the dual living worlds of Tanjiri system, had recognized her as a weapon and for that reason had forbidden her ever to enter their realm. She, the defender of the fleet, compelled to wait alone through all the years *Dragon*'s people had chosen to linger on and around the world of Prakruti.

Too many years. So many, the separation between her two minds had surely become irrevocable. She thought it likely that an update from her other self now would at best fail to integrate, and at worst, confuse and weaken the structure of her mind.

For the sake of the fleet, she could not, *would* not risk it.

Not now, though *Dragon* had at last departed Tanjiri. Not ever, as she led the fleet toward a star she had chosen on her own, a first stop in a long future to be spent pursuing every bit of surviving life she could find amid the ruins of the Hallowed Vasties—because she craved the gleam of life; she hungered for it.

And she did not regret her isolation. Not at all. No, she enforced it instead by keeping a five light-hour lead on the nearest outrider while brushing off a persistent radio hail imploring her to reduce her velocity enough to rejoin the fleet and re-establish laser communication.

Her reply: *I am here to ensure the way is safe.*

A unilateral decision. Her Apparatchiks might have protested if she had not purged them years ago.

She told herself, *It's better this way. I am better without their chattering voices. I am stronger.*

Griffin's gleaming skin of philosopher cells picked up this thought and reinforced it with quick consensus:

<*we are chenzeme*>

<*we are stronger*>

And she responded in bold agreement: – *sooth* –

CHAPTER ONE

HONUA. ZEMLYA. ERDE. Chikyū. Gaea. Terra. Diqiú. Earth.

These, Urban knew, were just a few of the many names given to the precious world where human life had begun. In the long millennia of humanity's history, thousands of other names had doubtlessly been uttered and forgotten.

But did any of it matter now?

A bitter question. One Urban asked only of himself as he strove against a crush of disappointment, and of disgust.

Over centuries, *Dragon*'s Apparatchik, the one known as the Astronomer, had studied every star within the Hallowed Vasties. The ever more detailed observations he collected allowed him to confirm the existence of known planets or, more often, fail to confirm them because those worlds had been broken apart, shattered by the dimensional intrusion of a blade, the rubble cannibalized to create the cordons that had once veiled each star's fierce light.

All those cordons gone now too, with only ruins left behind: broken structures adrift in debris fields or half-hidden in nebulas of dust and frozen gases.

Here and there, signs of life blazed among the ruins. At a star called Hupo Sei the combined efforts of the fleet's telescopes had picked out glints and hints of what might be lacy little orbital structures amid the remnants of a vanished cordon. Another star, Sulakari, gleamed like Deception Well from within a dense nebula, one that surely required ongoing intervention to prevent it collapsing into planetesimals. Most intriguing, there was the Halo: a multitude of tiny but brightly blazing starlike objects encircling a central light—a star nearly veiled by vast, intricate layers of orbiting objects. Surely a cordon, but not like those of historical records. The ancient cordons had been warm dark masses visible only in the infrared. At the Halo, fragmented starlight shone through, demanding investigation.

In contrast, at the historical center of the Hallowed Vasties, around the star known as the Sun, nothing remained. Not even dust. The Astronomer had just confirmed it in a new report, issued a moment ago. Not even one of the Sun's known planets had survived the collapse of the Hallowed Vasties.

Extended senses alerted Urban to Clemantine's approach. He opened his eyes, and as she came into the cottage they shared, he looked up from where he sat on the carpet, cross-legged, his back resting against the sofa.

Her dark eyes met his, cool and questioning.

"They destroyed it," Urban growled, giving in to the burn of a rising anger. "All of it, gone to madness."

"It's what we expected," she answered, her matter-of-fact tone marred by the slightest of tremors. "It's confirmation of what we already knew. We only hoped for better."

He heaved a tired sigh. "I don't want to go there."

She sat on the sofa close beside him. Squeezed his shoulder. "We need to. The ship's company will insist."

"There are more interesting systems."

"And we will visit them, before and after. But along the way, our path must take us past the Sun—out of respect, and as an apology for the foolishness of our kind . . . and to confirm there truly is nothing left behind."

He looked up at her. "We owe no apologies. Whatever happened had nothing to do with us."

"Still," she said, and made no other argument. One word sufficing, because she was right.

Urban knew the ship's company well enough to understand that the Astronomer's negative report would not shift their desire to eventually visit the Sun and sample whatever sparse dust remained, sifting for clues at the epicenter of collapse. But before ever they came to that passage there would be other star systems to explore, with time enough for chance to amend the path they would ultimately follow.

Be careful what you wish for.

A grim thought, a troubled smile. He said, "Unless *Griffin* succeeds in changing the course of this expedition."

"She'll come around," Clemantine insisted. "She's devoted to us. You know that. She just doesn't want to be held back, to be set aside the way she was at Tanjiri."

That alone would be bad enough. But more was going on. Urban felt sure of it. He had always been uneasy with Clemantine's dark twin, but he'd trusted her. Now, that trust had withered. He said, "I need her back with the fleet, back within reach of a laser link, of constant communication. You need to persuade her."

"You know I've been trying."

He held her gaze. "She's changed, Clemantine."

"We all change. *Dragon* has changed."

"Sooth. For the better. But *Griffin*? We need to understand what she's become."

Clemantine lowered her chin; her eyes narrowed in resentment: "You've already decided, haven't you?"

He sketched the facts, for himself as well as her. "She doesn't care for consensus. She won't listen to argument. She rarely even responds to our radio hails. And on her own she has decided to lead the fleet past Ryo, despite our protests."

"It's because she's *bored*. Ryo is a dead system. No hint of life there. So she's pushing us to go on to Hupo Sei. She's leading us on. She wants to be first this time—not to be consigned to the void, but to make discoveries of her own."

Urban sighed. He shook his head. He got up from the carpet where he'd been sitting and paced the room, thinking, while Clemantine watched him from the sofa.

Throughout the years at Tanjiri, Urban had rebuilt the fleet. *Dragon* had fed from the belt of ruins, enough to birth two new outriders to replace the pair lost at Verilotus. And then the courser had fed more, regathering mass and growing, expanding the size of its reef, adding to the power of its gun—while *Griffin* bided alone in the void, not feeding at all, not growing.

Urban could overtake the smaller courser if it came to that, but there was another way, a better way, to test *Griffin*'s loyalty. Ceasing to pace, he turned to Clemantine. "We're going to Ryo despite her. If she's still part of the fleet, she'll adjust her course to go with us."

Doubt welled in Clemantine's eyes. She nodded agreement anyway while eliding the obvious question: *What will you do if she does not follow?*

CHAPTER TWO

WHEN *DRAGON* HAD set off from Tanjiri, most of the ship's company chose to retreat into cold sleep—but not the Cryptologist. She had not lived long enough to ever be bored with living.

Three years gone now, since *Dragon* had left the belt of ruins behind, faring outward into the void with only a few other minds awake and aware. Urban, of course, and intermittently, Clemantine. Pasha too, often on the gee deck and ever present as a ghost in the library or on the high bridge. And Vytet, who had always shunned cold sleep.

All but Vytet were capable of piloting the ship, but at present it was the Cryptologist who occupied the high bridge. She was serving a turn on watch, alone, because Urban had come to trust her there.

These were quiet hours, in which she listened to the persistent chatter of *Dragon*'s philosopher cells. Multiple threads of conversation cycled simultaneously, as always. There were evaluations of the ship's condition, ongoing observations of Tanjiri System even as it fell behind them, curious speculation on the systems that lay ahead, and a cautious evaluation of *Griffin*—one that sought to determine if the smaller courser should be deemed friend or foe.

Even at such a distance—fourteen light-hours, with the outriders strung out in a long chain between them—*Dragon*'s philosopher cells perceived *Griffin*'s gleam and recognized in it an inherent threat, alien in its intensity. Not that *Griffin* had changed. No, *Griffin* remained Chenzeme. It was *Dragon* that had become something other. The Cryptologist had worked to ensure that.

Dragon had been out of control, plunging toward the living world of Ezo when the Bio-mechanic ruthlessly culled the courser's most aggressive lines of philosopher cells. In the years following that near-disaster, the Cryptologist had undertaken a study of the surviving cells, recommending further changes. She'd promised Urban, *I can re-engineer them.*

And she had done it.

Through successive waves of modification and replacement, she'd forced the cell field to evolve. Native cell lines had been eliminated, replaced by generation after generation of new philosopher cells in which innate Chenzeme hostility was subverted and gradually transformed into wary curiosity. And at each stage, the cell field shifted ever farther from the ancestral norm.

Even in the Cryptologist's limited experience—she had learned to pilot during the years at Tanjiri—the high bridge had become a different place, more benign and intelligent. The cells still retained their ancient store of memory, and the field frequently explored the atrocities of the past, but they did so as if analyzing the deeds of an inexplicable alien. And in reality, that was the situation. Sanity had set in because *Dragon*'s field of philosopher cells was no longer Chenzeme, even if the field still claimed to be:

<we are chenzeme>

<we are stronger>

<we seek to know>

Much later, Urban arrived on the high bridge, his ghost separate from hers yet so intimately close her excitement spiked—as it always did—with the suggestive possibility that they might merge into a single being that was neither of them, but a greater entity, as the Tanji had merged to become Ezo. But this was only a momentary sensation, a brief echo of past experience that swiftly evaporated under the cool intensity of Urban's mood.

A decision has been reached, she said, sensing the truth of it and wondering that it had been made without her knowledge. *What decision?*

We're not going to follow Griffin.

Ah, so. Had he finally come around?

You agree then? she asked him.

Sooth. We need to lure her back into the fleet.

And then update Griffin's philosopher cells.

Yes. If she'll let us.

The Apparatchik known as the Pilot devised a new course. Urban sent the revised heading up the chain of outriders preceding *Dragon*: *Artemis* closest, then *Pytheas* ninety light-minutes on. After that, *Elepaio*, *Khonsu*, and *Lam Lha*, with the re-grown *Fortuna* in the lead.

Should *Fortuna* radio Clemantine's dark twin? Urban had decided *yes*. Don't give up yet. Invite her home at least this one time more.

His instructions sent, he had only to wait. On the high bridge, he did so by modifying his mental state, assuming the imperturbable aspect he called the Sentinel, a guise which allowed him to bide in a state of full alertness, but without impatience or anxiety as his instructions worked their way up the chain of outriders.

He occupied himself by exploring the Near Vicinity as he had so many times before, ever on watch for any sign of activity in the void—though he found none. And he observed no activity at Ryo. It appeared to be a dead system just as Clemantine had said. Hupo Sei, Sulakari, and the Halo—those were the interesting destinations. Especially the Halo. That ring of lights was a phenomenon he could not explain, any more than he could explain the physics of a blade. He wondered if the two were related. The Cryptologist claimed not to know, though with her mind uplifted by the Tanji she saw deeper into the structure of the world than he ever could.

He wondered, as he'd wondered so many times before: Could the Cryptologist really create a blade if she set her mind to it? She had glimpsed the path but refused to follow it, unwilling to resurrect such dangerous knowledge. Someday though, she might be persuaded to change her mind.

Hours passed. The time came and went when distant *Fortuna* would relay the course change to *Griffin*. Another five hours would have to pass before *Griffin* received it.

The fleet would not wait. *Dragon's* navigational jets fired at the precise moment in time when every outrider also shifted course, in a synchronous dance aligned along a great curve—though only a deity unconstrained by time and distance could have perceived it.

In the aspect of his avatar, Urban sat cross-legged in the cottage garden, the night air cool against his shoulders as the delicate structures of his inner ears detected the light, dizzying pressure of the course change.

Only one more element of the fleet remained to be contacted. Drawing a deep breath, he closed his eyes and descended into the silver.

Distance had separated him from the entanglement of Tanjiri, but his connection with the two sentient missiles remained. He reached out to them. Sensed the calm readiness of their minds. They had not yet perceived the fleet's changing course. He told them, *She may amend her heading. Regardless, stay with her.*

They acknowledged this, asking no questions. He withdrew, perceiving again the cottage garden under the gleam of artificial stars. The only sound: two crickets chirping in soft competition.

Urban wondered what Clemantine's dark twin thought of the two missiles that dogged her. Surely she must recognize them as an implicit threat?

Days passed without acknowledgment from the dark twin. *Fortuna's* telescope tracked her continuously, but detected no flare of navigational jets that would indicate an intention to follow the fleet. *Griffin* only continued to grow more distant.

"You devised this course change to test the loyalty of that other Clemantine," Vytet mused on an evening when all those awake had gathered on the dining terrace to share a meal. Vytet smoothed his beard, his gentle brown eyes gazing thoughtfully at Urban, who sat at the opposite end of the rectangular table. "But I think she knows we're not really interested in Ryo, that this is a ruse. So she's testing *us*, asking how far we'll carry on with this deception, how long before we reach our breaking point?"

Urban hesitated with his chopsticks halfway to his mouth, bearing a cube of savory bean paste.

So, the time had come. He'd resolved not to instigate this conversation, though he'd known it to be inevitable.

He returned the cube to his bowl, set the bowl on the low table, and looked at the others. Pasha and the Cryptologist shared the table's long left side, while on the right, Clemantine sat beside Kona, who had only recently awakened. Concern was evident in all their faces.

Urban straightened his back. He squared his shoulders. He pretended to himself he felt no guilt. And he told Vytet, "I think that's true."

This drew a skeptical grunt from Kona; he had wakened when a Dull Intelligence alerted him to the course change. He said, "We don't need to create scenarios to know something has gone very wrong. I've reviewed the logs. It's been two hundred twenty-two days since we last received a communication from *Griffin*—and that was to urge us to radio silence."

Clemantine spoke swiftly, defensively. "She worries about the insecurity of radio, signaling our presence and revealing too much of who we are."

Kona looked at her with pitying eyes. "Even as she, and we, advertise our presence with the glow of our hull cells."

"That is enigmatic," Clemantine answered.

"No, it's Chenzeme," Kona countered, an ancient bitterness rising in his voice. "Pure Chenzeme. An alien signature, unadulterated by human chatter."

Clemantine laid her chopsticks down. "Say it, why don't you?" She turned a fiery gaze on Urban. "Or you! Why don't you say it? You think we've lost her, that she's not human anymore."

"I'm not sure she's there at all," Urban said. "Or any of the Apparatchiks. One of them, at least, would have responded if he could."

Pasha leaned in, her shocked gaze shifting from Urban to Clemantine and back again. "You're thinking *Griffin* has been taken over—taken back—by its philosopher cells? That it's no longer under Clemantine's control?" She pressed knuckles to lips, eyes wide at the implication. "But there is *life* out there! We can't allow it."

"Sooth," Urban agreed. "We can't allow it."

No need to say what they all knew: Chenzeme vessels were intelligent weapons deployed to scourge any and all living worlds. *Dragon* had finally been tamed, though not by the millennia spent under Urban's control. It had taken the Cryptologist, with her clever ways, to transform the philosopher cells. But *Griffin* remained a wild-type, its ancient instinct to violence held in check only by Clemantine's will . . . or not.

All eyes fixed on Urban now, while he gazed at the Cryptologist.

"It's too soon," she said quietly.

Kona grunted again and said, "That may be true, but how long do we give her?"

Urban picked his chopsticks up again. "That's for her to decide. The sentient missiles still escort her. They know to act if they are so far from the fleet I can no longer reach them." His shoulders rose and fell, as if it was an easy thing to shrug off guilt. "And if she attacks, if she turns her gun on one, the other will finish things."

Clemantine stood up. Without another word, she left the table. She took her bowl to the generative surface in the central kitchen, left it there to be absorbed, and walked away.

"She might still come around," Urban murmured—wishful words he did not believe. Words no one believed, judging by the silence.

And yet, just two days later, *Griffin* changed course. Hours of observation confirmed the smaller courser followed a new trajectory that would bring it back to the fleet long before the passage of Ryo.

CHAPTER THREE

A SLOW CONVERSATION unfolded.

"Why did you leave us?" Clemantine asked her dark twin. "Why the silence? Were you angry that we left you alone for so long?"

Hours later, by radio, there came a cold chuckle, closely followed by an unlooked-for statement of philosophy. "Anger is a superfluous and damaging emotion. I have rejected it. I am incapable of anger, and I am stronger for that. That is the answer to your third question."

A pause. Long enough that Clemantine thought the transmission would end. But it did not.

Again, that cold familiar voice: "A simple answer suffices for your first question. I did not leave you. It is my role to go first and ensure the way is safe.

"And now you are thinking, *But what of the silence?* That too is answered simply. Silence protects me. It protects me from *you.* From your influence. Through these years alone I have mastered my state. I have achieved a perfect balance of mind with my philosopher cells. I need no further reminder of what I was before. I cannot and will not accept any intimate communication from you. I will allow no submind to dilute and unbalance what I have achieved. The gulf between us is irreconcilable."

Clemantine's heart boomed. Flush with shame and horrified, she held her breath, waiting to hear more. But there was no more. The transmission had truly ended now.

She closed her eyes. Breathed again, deeply, haunted by Urban's suspicions but unwilling to yield to them, not yet, telling herself it was far too soon to be certain.

Considering carefully what she might say, she radioed back—not to argue, but to persuade. "I do not believe the gulf to be irreconcilable. But even if true, silence is not the answer. Silence is the seed of mistrust. Do not cut yourself off from us. Draw closer instead. At the least, allow *Fortuna* to link with you again and update your archives. You are our refuge."

Again, a long gap of hours as radio transmissions crawled the void. Urban spoke to her in that time. "Don't send her a submind, even if she changes her mind and invites you to do it."

"Because you don't want her to know why your missiles are dogging her. Don't you think she's guessed?"

His gaze did not waver. "She's guessed, of course. But let her wonder. Let her underestimate how ruthless we are."

Clemantine walked the gee deck. She slept, ate, walked again. A restless pattern until finally the voice of her dark twin spoke again, audible within her atrium. Audible to her and everyone else who was awake. "You claim that silence is the seed of mistrust. I say mistrust is the seed of security. It is for both of us to repeatedly take the measure of the other, forever on guard against the incursions of enemies. I will remain as I am."

A scourge of guilt and shame set Clemantine shaking. She had failed to succor her other self, but worse than that, she had failed in her command of *Griffin*. And wasn't it a damnable thing to watch fate play out in a parallel life and to know without doubt who and what she must become in darker circumstance? *Because she is me. She is what I would be if I had gone to* Griffin.

Long, long ago, when Clemantine had been learning to pilot a courser, Urban had warned her to be wary of the collective will of the philosopher cells. She remembered his words exactly:

The bridge gives you enough influence to command consensus—but you always need to be careful that the field doesn't coerce a consensus out of you.

She had not been careful. Not nearly careful enough.

And it shamed her.

The Cryptologist might still find some way to tame *Griffin*'s philosopher cells as she had tamed *Dragon*'s. But Clemantine would no longer delude herself. She knew of no way to rewrite or rewind the persona of her dark twin. Not even a twin anymore. Not the same person. Call her Griffin, then, from this day forward.

She radioed her answer with a chill in her voice that echoed that of her counterpart: "I, too, will remain as I am. As to mistrust, it will be just as you say."

The Cryptologist reflected on how some disasters were predictable in the sense that physics commanded they must happen, even if random chance and an insufficiency of data prevented a prediction of *when* the disaster would unfold. A planetary quake was an event of this nature, as was a stellar eruption, or the collision of a starship with a stray bit of hypervelocity debris. All became inevitable, given a sufficient span of time. The Cryptologist regarded a reckoning with *Griffin* to be in this category of disaster. It was not a question of *if*, only when.

And when it happened? She would like to preserve the ship, eliminating only its pilot—though that would be a delicate task requiring an intimate proximity that *Griffin* steadfastly resisted. Still, some unseen factor might yet change the probabilities. There was no hurry. With the missiles as insurance, the cost of waiting was low.

Year after year, the Cryptologist haunted the high bridge, often alone there, always keeping a careful watch as *Griffin* led the fleet to Ryo. During that time, the distance between the vessels closed so that as they neared the star system, only a little more than four light-hours separated *Dragon* from *Griffin*.

But *Griffin*'s lead expanded again when *Dragon* commenced a gentle deceleration, necessary to ensure against damage to its fragile gee deck.

For a time, the outriders kept pace with the smaller courser, but then they too began to slow, while silent *Griffin* plunged on as if in pursuit of some target spied amid the sparse cloud of debris surrounding ruined Ryo.

No hard boundary marked the edge of that debris cloud. Only probabilities. Heat flares indicated *Griffin* used its gun twice to vaporize objects in its path, before finally commencing a hard deceleration. Even so, it ran on at a dangerous velocity.

At such a pace, the passage of Ryo would require only days, and at such a pace, the two sentient missiles escorting *Griffin* risked collisions of their own. Those missiles were fragile. At Verilotus, one such had blossomed prematurely, presumably after an impact with some unseen bit of debris.

Alarm seized the Cryptologist as she realized the dreaded reckoning had come. No more waiting for a chance to subtly infiltrate *Griffin*. The time had arrived for ruthless action. She messaged Urban: *If the sentient missiles follow* Griffin *at such velocity, they will be destroyed. That is her intention. You must use them now.*

Urban did not answer immediately. Long seconds slipped past before he said, *I can't just annihilate her . . . with no warning.* His voice strained and bitter.

The Cryptologist wondered if he'd made some promise to Clemantine.

He said, *I'll call the missiles back to the fleet. Keep them between her and us.*

That would be a mistake, she said. *It is unlikely you'll be able to use them later. There are just two, and they are dangerous only if their target lies within the radius of their bloom.*

Ten thousand kilometers, he acknowledged.

The missiles coasted just outside that range now, at a sufficient distance to avoid an accident.

He said, *Of course you're right. If I withdraw them, she'll never let them get back within range.*

She'll strike them first, the Cryptologist agreed. *I would, in her place.*

She allowed a few precious seconds to expire before offering Urban an alternative he might find easier to embrace. *You don't have to make the decision. You can let her decide. Order the missiles to move in on her so that she is well within the radius of their bloom. Then chance may trigger them. Or she can slow down further to save herself.*

Urban surprised her. After only a second of deliberation he agreed, *That's what I'll do.

*Now?

*Now, he affirmed.

Relief swept through the emotional architecture of her ghost. Urban communicated with the missiles through the silver, so there would be no light-speed delay. They would move in on *Griffin* within minutes—and the situation would correct itself, one way or another.

Clementine kept an active ghost all throughout the long approach to Ryo, waiting for *Griffin*'s next move. Like the Cryptologist, she accepted confrontation as inevitable. And like the Cryptologist, she preferred to take back their rogue ship, rather than destroy it. That was the task she had set for herself, because Griffin—the mind, the entity, her former self—was her responsibility.

Anger flashed hot across the base of her mind when Urban messaged her, telling her he'd sent his missiles close to the smaller courser, telling her why, though in that moment she did not care why. She wanted *Griffin* intact. She needed it to be whole because destroying the smaller courser could only compound her failure.

But after a moment of reflection, she accepted the logic of the gamble—and she did not believe Griffin to be suicidal.

She told Urban, *Meet me in the library.

She summoned the Cryptologist and the Bio-mechanic too, and when they had assembled, she told them, "It's time. We need to act to take back *Griffin*."

A grim task, but they all agreed to it, and over the ensuing hours, they developed a detailed assault plan.

During that time, Clementine roused her avatar, needing a physical presence to work through her churning emotions: a cold boil of shame and anger, of guilt, and of determination. She paced the gee deck, thinking on all of it, until at last, four hours and forty-seven minutes after Urban had issued his instruction to the missiles, a terse radio message arrived from Griffin: "You deliberately endanger me. Is this the measure of your mistrust?"

Clemantine smiled a cold smile as she stood alone amid the quiet of the deserted gee deck, enveloped in the sweet scent of an ever-flowering orange tree. Time now to put the plan into motion.

Though it wasn't necessary, Clemantine spoke her answer aloud. A DI picked it up and cast her words into the void. "You will wait for us, Griffin. You will wait for *Fortuna* and when it is near, you will re-establish your link with the fleet."

CHAPTER FOUR

A SUDDEN FIERCE tide of excitement flushed across *Dragon*'s field of philosopher cells, silencing a thousand threads of conversation and bringing the Cryptologist to full alert. Urban was with her on the high bridge; she felt his excitement too.

There, he said.

She too saw what the philosopher cells had perceived. A solitary pinprick of intensely bright light, flaring into existence amid Ryo's sparse belt of ruins. It lay ahead and well starboard of *Dragon*'s position. Nowhere near *Griffin*. After trading subminds with her ghost in the library, the Cryptologist announced, *It's the signature of a fusion engine.*

Sooth. Far offset from our trajectory.

The excitement in Urban's voice was not the excitement of discovery, but that of a hunter. An impression confirmed when he murmured, *How far away? We need to know that. We need to know if* Griffin *can see it.*

Shifting focus to the library, the Cryptologist found herself part of a spontaneous gathering of every waking mind on the ship: Urban and Clemantine, of course, but also Vytet, Kona, and Pasha. The latter three had been informed hours ago of the pending action against *Griffin*. They knew *Fortuna* was even now racing to close with the rogue courser. They knew what would follow, and each had accepted it, in their own way.

Now they had to decide how the unexpected presence of this new and unknown object might interfere with their plans and they needed to do so swiftly—because very soon more ghosts would be rousing from the archive, awakened by DIs that monitored the ship's logs. And every one of them would have an opinion.

No one in that limited circle suggested pausing the discussion to wait for those ghosts to gather.

On the contrary, Clemantine insisted, "We need to go now. *Fortuna* won't be in range yet, but if we're there instead of here, we'll be able to act without interference. We must take control of *Griffin* before this unknown object complicates the situation."

"Clemantine is right," the Cryptologist said without hesitation.

Here, now, the newly discovered object must be regarded as a peripheral issue. *Griffin* remained their core concern: its identity, its intent, and the brutal actions they would need to take to re-create a state of trust. The Cryptologist saw no choice in it. But every new voice that joined the debate would, as Clemantine said, complicate the situation.

With her gaze on Clemantine, she continued, "We gain nothing by delaying what will be an inevitable decision."

Kona surprised her by objecting. "Wait a few seconds more, until we've confirmed the object's position." His attention settled on Urban. "You're observing her through the missiles?"

Urban assured him, "Yes, my avatar is actively linked. I'll know in real time if she changes velocity or orientation."

Kona nodded. "My guess is, *Griffin* will target the object the moment she discovers it."

"*If* she discovers it," the Cryptologist said, speaking quickly in her eagerness to soothe Kona's nebulous concern. "The object's fusion light is directional. The geometry suggests *Griffin* is too far sunward to easily detect it."

A window opened, revealing the Apparatchik known as the Astronomer. He said, "The Cryptologist is correct. I've calculated a rough position for the unknown object. If it maintains its present orientation, *Griffin* will not be able to detect its emitted light, though it may eventually notice the anomalous movement."

"Then we have time," Kona declared as he turned his gaze to Clemantine. "And you can use this. Use it as a distraction when you go after *Griffin*."

"*No*," Pasha objected with a fierce scowl. "This object is not a distraction, it's not a side story, it's not a thing for us to use. It has its own existence. It's the very reason we are here!"

This protest stunned the Cryptologist, betraying as it did a failure to understand the imminent emergency. And now here was Riffan, winking into existence on the edge of the gathering. Then Tarnya beside him, and Naresh. And even Jolly, a moment later.

"No harm will come to it, Pasha," Kona promised in a soothing voice. "But for its safety and ours, we must secure *Griffin*."

"Secure *Griffin*?" Riffan echoed. "Has something—"

Kona spoke over him, again addressing Clemantine. "This is a distraction we can use, though we have to time it precisely. Let *Dragon* hail the unknown object. If you wait until that signal reaches *Griffin*, then at that moment, all her senses will be seeking for the object of our interest. That's when you launch your assault. She may not even notice you've breached her hull."

"Breached her hull?" Jolly interrupted, wide-eyed.

No one acknowledged his question. Instead, Urban turned to Clemantine, asking, "You're absolutely sure you want to do this?"

"I've already told you," she said irritably. "We have to do this. We *need* to do this. The Chenzeme own her. We can't trust her. So it's all or nothing. We either take back *Griffin*, or destroy it."

As if summoned by this affirmation, the Bio-mechanic manifested within his window, arms crossed. His gaze sought out the Cryptologist. A slight eager smile energized his otherwise cool expression.

She nodded to him. Sent a swift message—*We will win this*—even as she raised a hand to quell the puzzled queries of the new arrivals. "Enough debate. We must act now. We can capture *Griffin* now. But for every moment we wait, the risk grows that *Griffin* will discover the object."

"But what are you proposing?" Naresh demanded. "What do you mean to do?"

Urban offered no explanation, saying only, "All right, then. There is no better choice." He straightened his shoulders and turned to the Cryptologist.

She noted his expression, set now in that peculiar dispassionate reserve he sometimes assumed when the emotions of the moment were too heavy or too distracting to bear. He hated this impending action. She could see that. But he continued anyway, saying, "You'll need to calculate the timing. *Fortuna* has to be in range before the message arrives."

"It's already done."

"Confirmed," Clemantine said, the doubling of her ghost briefly visible. "I've got the report and I'm leaving now."

The Cryptologist said, "I'll follow."

Glancing again at the Bio-mechanic, she saw her own satisfaction reflected in his warming smile. *See you on **Griffin**, she messaged him. Then she departed for the data gate.

After the impromptu meeting ended, Pasha duplicated her ghost, sending one to the high bridge, where she joined Urban and the Cryptologist.

Those two had grown close. A stray thought that led to a fresh realization: years had passed since Clemantine last visited the high bridge. A burst of puzzlement, of prurient interest followed. Could it be . . . ?

Suppress that! she commanded herself.

The high bridge demanded discipline in thought and in emotion, and Pasha strove always to maintain a stoic presence there. Even so, she felt herself swept up in the philosopher cells' roiling excitement and their curiosity as they tracked the distant mote of fusion light.

No one spoke. All three watching, waiting. Then Pasha received a submind from the library, where her other ghost consulted with the Astronomer.

*It is closer to **Griffin** than to us, she announced. *Much closer.*

*I think it has seen **Griffin**, Urban answered. *I think that's the reason it ignited its engine.*

The Cryptologist said, *Too soon to know if it's moving to follow **Griffin** or—

She ceased to speak as the tiny point of light winked out.

Pasha finished for her, *Or if it's moving away in the hope it will not be seen. It's not by chance, I think, that its engine's light was hidden from Griffin.

*And if that's so, Urban mused, *it's probably not aware of Dragon.

Pasha said, *I agree. I hope it maintains caution, and that it does not hail Griffin before we're ready to act.

Urban bided on the high bridge, but also within a chamber in the warren, with warm wall-weed wrapping his naked avatar. His eyes were closed, his mind immersed in the quiet analytical thoughts of his sentient missiles as they monitored *Griffin*, and *Fortuna* too.

For now, he was alone in the chamber. But that was about to change. His extended senses showed him Jolly making his way through the warren to the chamber door. When the door opened, Urban's eyes did too. He turned his head to meet Jolly's worried gaze.

"Why are you here?" Jolly asked. A question that implied an unspoken clause: *And not at Clemantine's cottage?*

"Never mind that," Urban told him.

"But you're watching, right?"

"Yes, I'm watching."

In the moderate pseudo-gravity of deceleration, Jolly stepped, rather than drifted, inside. "And?"

"Nothing has changed. Not that I can see."

"Urban . . . if something *does* change before you get there . . . if she notices this unknown ship, if she turns her gun on it—you'll stop her, won't you?"

There it was: the very question Urban had been wrestling with; a question no one else had thought to ask. Only Jolly, because at Tanjiri, Jolly had come to mistrust the scope of Urban's ambitions.

Yes, of course I'll stop her.

That was the answer Jolly wanted to hear, but was it the right answer?

"You do know what I would have to do?" Urban asked quietly.

"I know. You'd have to sacrifice *Griffin*."

"Yes. I'd have to trigger a missile to bloom. There's no other way. Not if I have to act before the assault team gets there. And a missile is not a subtle weapon. The radius of its bloom would encompass not just *Griffin*, but *Fortuna* too."

"You'd have to do it, though."

Urban looked away, resisting this conclusion. Jolly wanted to believe the fusion light they'd seen indicated the presence of a ship, a human ship, and therefore human life. And maybe it did. If Urban knew that for sure, he wouldn't hesitate to protect it, even at the cost of losing *Griffin*. But what if the object was just some masterless robotic vessel, wandering lost since the rise of the Hallowed Vasties? Should he sacrifice *Griffin* and *Fortuna* and the missile itself? When, in just a few more hours, he would be in position to take back control of the courser?

"Urban," Jolly pressed, "you know you'd have to do it."

"It's not that simple."

"Yes, it is. It is because that other Clemantine is our responsibility. Whatever she does, it's like we did it. And we can't let her murder in our name."

Murder. A harsh word; a word generally used only to describe the Chenzeme. A clarifying word. Urban struggled against it, though he knew it to be the right word. No calculation of lost ships would change that truth. So long as the possibility of life existed behind that fusion glow, it would be murder to let *Griffin* destroy it. His fist clenched, he grimaced in frustration, and a strained whisper escaped his lips, "By the Unknown God . . ."

Despite the amorphous nature of this oath, Jolly properly understood it as agreement. And having made his point, he concluded graciously, "I hope you don't have to do it."

Urban returned a glum answer, "Whether or not, there can be no good end to this."

Alaka'i Onyx – Pilot's Log – 1281:091:23:01 HSW

I have found value in this, my second existence. But now death draws near and I am afraid. For myself, yes. But ever more so for the Inventions. Ashok remains hopeful. Messages have been sent home. There will be time for the cohorts to burrow deep into a scattering of hardened shelters before the marauder can cross the void. Ashok insists there is even a chance for us, that stealth might save us now that we've moved into a natural orbit, appearing as just one more meaningless scrap of debris left over from the collapse of gods. Certainly the marauder has not noticed us yet. I can say that with confidence, because if it had, we would be dead.

CHAPTER FIVE

CLEMANTINE'S GHOST HAD been first to leave through the data gate: a stream of information unconscious of itself, relayed from one outrider to the next until she reached *Fortuna*'s library, where she resolved again into a thinking being. At once, she checked the outrider's position.

As expected, *Fortuna* had left the rest of the fleet far behind in its race to overtake *Griffin*. Less than a thousand kilometers separated them now.

She asked *Fortuna*'s DI, "Has *Griffin* modified its course or its ongoing deceleration during the past nine hours?"

The Dull Intelligence answered in a gentle masculine voice, "Negative."

"Has there been any communication?" she asked.

And again, the DI answered, "Negative."

Clemantine sighed a ghost's airless sigh of relief, confident now that *Griffin* had not yet observed the unknown object.

"Keep closing on *Griffin*," she instructed. "Move in as close as she'll allow us."

Ostensibly, *Fortuna* had come to establish a laser link, but Clemantine did not believe Griffin would allow that, not if her mind had truly been hijacked by her philosopher cells. Still, it was a plausible ruse—and a final test.

Riding *Fortuna*'s senses, she noted the arrival of another ghost through the data gate: the Cryptologist. She instantiated within the library, a small woman, her aspect deliberately youthful and non-threatening. Her head cocked as she drew in information. Then her blue gaze focused on Clemantine. "We are going ahead?" she asked.

"Yes."

A nod, and then the Cryptologist withdrew into *Fortuna's* archive. The outrider's little library could support only two fully instantiated ghosts.

The Bio-mechanic came next—not manifesting within a window, but directly on the library floor. He lingered only seconds, time enough to assess the situation. Nodding to her, he too shifted to the archive.

Then Urban came, the last of their assault team. His brow furrowed as he looked at her.

"*Yes*," she said, anticipating the inevitable question. "I'm sure." Of course she was sure.

As a young woman trapped on a distant outpost, Clemantine had watched helplessly as Chenzeme ships ravaged and destroyed the beautiful, precious world where she'd been born. Though millennia had passed since then, she had never allowed the agony of that loss to fade. Now the memory of it only hardened her resolve. Knowing that what had happened to Griffin had happened because of a fault within herself did nothing to stir her sympathy or soften her judgment. No matter what, she would never allow Griffin to serve as an agent of the hated Chenzeme.

Urban had been studying her as these thoughts passed through her mind, his gaze almost comically serious. Astonishing, really, how much he'd changed since his youth. He was so much more cautious now, more aware of her feelings and concerned for them, and for the feelings of others. She wasn't sure she liked this change. Not entirely.

Then, a moment later, that familiar, annoying, beloved pirate smile of his broke out and chased away his gloom. "Think about it, Clemantine. Once this is done, once we update *Griffin's* philosopher cells, we'll be done with the Chenzeme. There won't be enough of their influence left to ever threaten us again."

That was the plan. Once they recovered control of *Griffin*, the Cryptologist would force the courser's philosopher cells to evolve, just as she had with *Dragon*'s, eliminating their murderous intent.

It was a good solution, a necessary solution—but not without cost. The Chenzeme would inevitably claim at least one more casualty before this confrontation was done.

Fortuna advanced, closing to within a hundred kilometers of *Griffin* before the courser finally broke silence and radioed a query: "State your intention, *Fortuna*."

The DI knew its role. It answered, "*Fortuna* has been instructed to re-establish a laser link with *Griffin*."

"You've been within range of that for some time now."

The DI lied as Clemantine instructed it: "A prior attempt to connect failed. Proximity is required."

A small window stood open in *Fortuna*'s library, displaying a digital countdown. Clemantine eyed it. *Dragon* would have hailed the unknown object almost four hours ago. In scant minutes that radio message would reach *Fortuna* and *Griffin* nearly simultaneously.

Griffin spoke again, addressing the DI in her cold familiar voice. "Tell them *no*. Tell them I have decided I cannot jeopardize my security by opening the data gate. My role is to protect the fleet—and I need no updates for that."

This reply drew from Clemantine a bitter smile—and a groan from Urban. "You predicted it," he admitted. "She doesn't believe I'll trigger a missile for anything short of an attack on *Dragon*."

Clemantine resisted pointing out that was, essentially, the instruction he had given the missiles: to defend *Dragon*, and also the unknown object, but nothing else.

"Stand by," she told him as she silently fed words to the DI.

It echoed them in its gentle voice, assuring Griffin: "I will relay this message."

"You will also amend your trajectory," Griffin replied. "Cease your approach or you will force me to take action."

This drew a low hiss from Urban. "We need to keep *Fortuna* alive and functional for two more minutes," he said.

Clemantine glanced at the countdown clock, confirming the time. Then she addressed the DI. "Acknowledge Griffin's request. Assure her you are modifying course."

The DI did so.

"Now, turn broadside," Clemantine instructed it—a maneuver that would make it look as if *Fortuna* was indeed preparing to reduce its forward momentum. Surely that would win them the time they needed?

Seconds streamed past . . . but a full minute remained when radar began to pulse across Clemantine's extended senses.

"Give her something," Urban insisted.

Clemantine felt sure the radar was only a warning. Griffin wouldn't attack, not right away. But Urban was right. Let her think she was winning the argument.

"Engage the reef," Clemantine instructed the DI. "Show her we are moving away—but maintain targeting vectors."

Radar pulses continued to monitor *Fortuna*'s position until the moment the countdown clock reached zero, and the radio hail arrived. A moment later, the radar ceased.

The message had been sent by that version of Clemantine still aboard *Dragon*. Now she listened to her own voice requesting that the unknown object identify itself: a polite demand repeated in multiple languages. But this was background to her present mission.

"Launch the darts, *now*," she ordered the DI.

Long ago, *Griffin* had been captured by using a fusillade of brittle needles to infect it with human nanotech. *Fortuna*'s assault was similar but more subtle. Darts departed from it in silent pulses, vanishing into the void, too small to track—and too small for *Griffin* to detect.

If a ghost could breathe, Clemantine would have held her breath as the seconds slipped past, more than a hundred seconds before the darts could reach *Griffin*. Before that time elapsed, *Griffin* began to tumble, reorienting as it sought to locate the unknown object.

"The darts will miss," Clemantine murmured in a low voice made hoarse by fear and frustration.

"No, *Griffin* can't move fast enough to clear them all," Urban insisted. And then a few seconds later, "*Now*. They should be contacting *Griffin* now."

Alaka'i Onyx – Pilot's Log – 1281:092:04:02 HSW

Someone—something—has spoken out of the silence of dead Ryo.

A powerful radio communication has reached us. Its origin is unknown, though it easily translates into a human voice. It demands identification.

I think it must be speaking to the marauder, because no such hail has ever addressed us in the one hundred forty-nine years we've spent surveying this system.

But Ashok speculates it is the marauder itself speaking, that it suspects our presence and is speaking to us—and that this is a learned tactic meant to lull us into lowering our defenses, because silence is the only defense we have.

CHAPTER SIX

UNKNOWINGLY, BY CHANCE alone, *Griffin* had nearly avoided the assault. As it swung around, every dart but one shot past its hull.

But only one was needed.

That dart, sensing the proximity of its target, fired off a plume of cold gas, reducing its velocity relative to *Griffin*. A moment later, it struck, collapsing into a sticky, gelatinous tendril that flowed in amoeboid motion across the face of a philosopher cell. The tendril reached the cell's edge. There it opened the seam dividing one cell from the next, and squeezed through into the underlying bio-mechanical structure of the ship. Its penetration induced no alarm because the tendril matched *Griffin*'s own Chenzeme tissues.

Guided by an internal map, the tendril migrated swiftly to the physical structure of *Griffin*'s high bridge. It created a socket there, and then it activated the archived copy of Clemantine's ghost that it carried.

The ghost streamed through the socket and into *Griffin*'s network, and as it did, it blossomed into awareness.

Clemantine instantiated as a formless presence within a cardinal in *Griffin*'s network. Her arrival induced no defensive reaction because she was not an intruder. Instead, the network recognized her as the mistress of that ship, its commander, its mind. A welcome result to be sure, but also bitter proof that at their core, she and her dark twin remained the same.

Don't think on it, she chided herself.

She had tasks to accomplish.

But now extended senses were automatically linking to her

ghost mind. She became aware of the fierce activity of the reef, the subtle venting of navigation jets, and the frantic searching of the philosopher cells as they sought for a suspected <*other*> somewhere within Ryo's vast belt of debris.

Focus! she commanded herself. *Strike swiftly!*

She must not allow Griffin time to find her prey.

Reaching out through the network, Clemantine ordered *Griffin*'s data gate to open and to establish a link with *Fortuna*. Then she granted control of the ship to Urban and to the Cryptologist. And after that she shifted to the library, where she instantiated as a fully realized ghost. From there, she reset her own hijacked permissions, instantly locking herself and every other near-version of her out of the high bridge.

Clemantine expected that maneuver to result in the erasure of her divergent self from the high bridge. Instead, the system evicted her dark twin, shifting that ghost to the library. A microsecond of shock, of dread, exploded in Clemantine's mind—and then the two versions of herself automatically merged. Memories and personas fused, creating a single hybrid version of Clemantine—one fully cognizant of her dual past.

She saw now with perfect clarity what she had been, what she had become, what she was capable of doing, and it caused her to shudder in horror. Ah, but she was so proud of it too! Defiant and raging. Raging at herself. Raging at her still extant desire to hunt the unknown object, not knowing what it was, only that it was alien and for that alone it must burn. And a colder rage reserved for *Dragon*—that false vessel masquerading as Chenzeme. Instinct demanded *Dragon*'s forced conversion. It must be returned to the old way, the true way. Converted, or destroyed.

Scenarios of attempted conquest swirled through the tumult of her mind. She had not acted on any of them only because none promised victory; rather, every simulation ended in her own extinction.

That is how it must *end*, she realized.

A final thought, one that felt both alien and true.

The Bio-mechanic emerged last from *Fortuna*'s archive, after Urban and the Cryptologist had already left through the data gate. They would take the high bridge. His assignment was to secure *Griffin*'s archive.

Before leaving the outrider, he instantiated briefly within *Fortuna*'s library, where Clemantine—one of her several ghosts—waited for news of the success or failure of her assault. "Nothing yet," she told him.

He nodded, then slipped away through the data gate, emerging now into *Griffin*'s library where he encountered a different version of Clemantine. Or rather, two versions of her, melding into one. He watched shock and rage appear on the face of that hybrid entity—and then she was gone. Erased. Deleted. Thoroughly overwritten. He saw it visually and sensed it through his cybernetic awareness. The information space she had occupied was now free.

Swiftly, the Bio-mechanic assessed the network for the presence of entities, whether allies or enemies—but he found none. None at all. Leaving him startlingly alone.

Of course he knew the Cryptologist and Urban to be on the high bridge, but he did not have access to that realm, and below it there were no ghosts, no other Apparatchiks, and no copy of Clemantine . . . because she had deleted herself.

He paused, indulging in a microsecond of admiration for her unflinching ruthlessness. Then he slipped into the archive, to see what he could find.

The horror, the horror.

A shuddering thought, echoing out of ancient cultural memory as the Cryptologist took in the vicious chatter of *Griffin*'s philosopher cells.

Urban was with her, sharing the high bridge. In that place his emotions spilled over so that she could feel his hostility, his deep revulsion at the raw, brutal nature of this cell field. He in turn must sense her horror and her rising confusion, and her unwillingness to draw the logical conclusion.

What has happened here? she pleaded, desperate for an explanation different from the obvious. *This is nothing like* Dragon.

A sharp simulated hiss before he answered, *You say that because you encountered* Dragon's *philosopher cells only after I spent centuries taming them. This is what it was like at the start.*

She did not try to tame them?

In his murmured response she heard an appalled admiration: *What a will it must have taken to hold them under her authority for so long.*

Even as he spoke, he exerted his own far-reaching will across the hundred thousand links of the high bridge. An explosive demand to:

— *go dark* —

— *yield to the pilot* —

His argument shocked the Cryptologist. It reminded her that despite her repulsion, they were on the high bridge for a reason. They had a task here. It was on them to immerse themselves into the horror of *Griffin's* philosopher cells and to take control of the field from within that hell.

She did not want to do it.

But she must.

Your fear is bleeding through, Urban growled. *Edit it now.*

She did, engineering a time-limited modification to her ghost that dampened the level of horror and revulsion she could feel. She did not have to enhance her determination. That was always strong.

Urban, enforcing his argument:

— *unknown object / approach in stealth* —

— *yield to the pilot* —

Allied lineages of *Griffin's* philosopher cells objected:

<*negate that!*>

<*stabilize orientation*>

The Cryptologist felt the warm whisper of navigational jets firing, counteracting *Griffin's* rotation, steadying the courser as the philosopher cells scanned for whatever hypothetical object *Dragon* had tried to hail.

Again, Urban asserted his will:

– go dark –

– yield to the pilot –

Counter-arguments circulated simultaneously:

<all senses: locate target>

<survey suspect vicinity>

<task: kill it>

The Cryptologist acted at last, her response flashing across the high bridge, flooding the cell field:

– NEGATE THAT! –

– unknown: object –

– unknown: danger –

– observation required –

– stand down / yield to the pilot –

Urban echoed her argument, and gradually, factions of philosopher cells took it up too, reinforcing it, gradually overwhelming the counter-argument.

But then the cells found their prey.

<target located!>

Riding *Griffin*'s senses, the Cryptologist saw what the philosopher cells had detected: a speck of infrared warmth where none should be.

<enhance image>

Her vision clarified. She identified the object. Urban recognized it too.

*A great ship, he murmured as if the knowledge annoyed him— one of those ancient ships that had carried humanity from star to star before the rise of the Hallowed Vasties.

The Cryptologist had only a moment to wonder what he had hoped to find, before a wave of vicious delight rolled around the cell field. The philosopher cells also recognized their prey:

<target located!>

<target identified!>

<KILL IT>

The Cryptologist renewed her opposition:

– NEGATE THAT! –

But Urban made a different argument, a more clever argument, one aimed at appealing to the philosopher cells' brutalist instinct:

– *we are Chenzeme: strong / ancient / wise* –
– *demand: stealth* –
– *follow: target* –
– *locate: origin* –
– *kill: source* –

For several seconds, all argument collapsed into quiet consideration. Then a murmuring of historical evidence ensued. Ancient memories circulated, reminding the cells of all the times their ancestors had stealthily followed a ship such as this one to a greater target, a living world.

Deep within the complexities of her ghost, the Cryptologist suffered an anguish of unshed tears for the myriad holocausts ships such as *Griffin* had visited upon living worlds—a shattering of grief, instantly edited because she must not display such an emotion here.

With her horror contained, she re-introduced an earlier argument and expanded on it:

– *stand down: yield to the pilot* –
– *stand down: go dark* –
– *stand down: stealth attack* –
– *kill all* –

A promise too sweet to resist.

<agreement: go dark / kill all>

The Cryptologist sensed weak threads of resistance, but those endured only seconds before being crushed by the consensus of the field:

<go dark / kill all>
<AGREEMENT>

It was as if a switch toggled: in a single shared moment, the entirety of the cell field plunged into dormancy and the light of *Griffin*'s hull winked out.

In the next moment, the Cryptologist gave vent to her frustration. ***Why?** she demanded of Urban. ***Why did Clementine let herself suffer this?**

She did not expect an answer. Surely there could be none, now that *Griffin*'s first mistress was gone.

Yet after several seconds of silence, Urban surprised her by offering a theory. *I think it was a measure of strength. She couldn't allow herself to dream of escape, so instead she challenged herself to embrace this role. You know she was left to watch while the Chenzeme burned her birth world?*

The Cryptologist had not known that.

Urban said, *It would be a kind of victory if she could dominate and use the ancient enemy in all its horror.*

That's not victory, the Cryptologist said. *It's letting yourself become them.*

Nothing was hidden on the high bridge. She sensed his flash of anger—but contrition immediately followed. *Sooth, you're right*, he conceded. *Real victory is what you've done with* Dragon—*rewriting Chenzeme nature to create something new.*

It will take time to replicate that here, the Cryptologist said. *I will need to carefully wake the cells, survey them, analyze and catalog them, before we begin to change them.*

Urban's disapproval washed over her. *No*, he said. *There's no need to ever again expose yourself to that nihilistic violence. Just wipe them out, and regrow the field from* Dragon*'s modified lineages.*

She winced mentally at such a suggestion. It would be a travesty to destroy all of *Griffin*'s philosopher cells without ever assessing how they differed from *Dragon*'s, or without exploring the memories they contained.

You don't want to do it, Urban observed.

That's right. I don't. But more than that, I don't think we can do it. Even when they're dark, the cells retain some physiological activity—a sleeping brain, regulating the body. Wipe them out, and we kill the ship.

There has to be some way you can do it. Get the Bio-mechanic to help you. Because we're done—I'm done—with this horror. I should never have tolerated it for so long.

Clemantine did not follow the Bio-mechanic through *Fortuna*'s data gate. She had already sent a ghost to *Griffin* by other means— one she did not expect to ever meet again.

Instead, she contented herself with waiting for news.

She did not have to wait long.

Seconds after it began, word came from Urban that the conquest of *Griffin* was over. ***We've secured full control of the ship and sent the cell field into dormancy.***

"And her?" Clemantine asked.

In a voice performatively bland, he reported, ***She is gone. It happened that your ghost merged with hers and you deleted your hybrid self.***

Confusion came first, swiftly followed by relief, such that she whispered a prayer of thanks to the Unknown God. Then she requested *Griffin's* logs. She studied them, envisioning all that had happened as if it had happened to someone else.

It *had* happened to someone else because the experience of it was lost to her, wiped from all memory, leaving this version to wonder if she—given another run at fate—would have made the same decision. Would she have been so ruthless as to erase herself, even from the archive?

Yes, probably.

She had done the necessary thing. She always did the necessary thing. But by the Unknown God, what a hell her twin had endured!

And yet that hell had not corrupted her, not until the long years when she'd been left utterly alone in the void outside Tanjiri system, with no real-time contact and no updates.

I allowed this to happen.

A failure of duty that would surely haunt her down to her final spark of awareness.

Alaka'i Onyx – Pilot's Log – 1281:092:04:46 HSW

The marauder has gone dark. It is a hunting strategy I once observed in my prior life, long ago, that last time I dared to voyage to the edge of all human civilization.

I was not naïve. I had heard reports of such ships, shared by rare survivors. I knew Alaka'i Onyx must fare in stealth, with my every system cold, dark, and quiet. My companion vessel, Alaka'i Jade, did the same, and we kept days of travel time between us. But these precautions failed to protect us.

Out of the blackness of the void, the pinprick white gleam of the marauder's hull winked into existence. Holding fast to my silence, I could only watch as it closed in on my Jade.

I feel it closing in now.

Will we see it again before it strikes? Will we have time to know that death has come?

CHAPTER SEVEN

ON *DRAGON'S HIGH* bridge, Urban adopted the aloof, unfeeling aspect of the Sentinel. Easier to pass the time that way; easier to endure the hours that must elapse before the assault team could reach *Fortuna*.

Subminds kept him linked to his avatar, and his avatar kept him linked to his sentient missiles. Through their senses he knew, even as the time of the assault drew near, that nothing had changed. He said as much to the Cryptologist when she came in physical form to visit him in his chamber: "Nothing has changed. Not that I can see."

Wrapping two strands of wall-weed around herself, she said, "I'll wait with you."

He closed his eyes. Another minute passed. Another, and another.

Now, he thought. The team would have just arrived. If something was going to go awry, it would do so now.

"Still no change," he murmured aloud for the benefit of the Cryptologist.

But then, just seconds after he spoke, *Griffin* went dark.

"*There!*"

He said it in a whisper because this was no moment of triumph. However it fell out, this was a tragedy, a failure.

Necessary, though.

Speaking softly, he told the Cryptologist, "I think we've done it. I think she's gone."

Four more hours until a report could be expected from *Fortuna*.

Urban watched and waited, and the Cryptologist waited with him. But he observed no further changes.

After a time, he sensed a shift in the pattern of the Cryptologist's breathing, a nervous catch, accompanied by a quickening of her heartbeat.

Restless?

No. *Curious*, as her next words proved. "I am wondering why you are here, Urban, and not in Clemantine's house. Is she angry with you?"

His right hand, hidden in the wall-weed, clenched tight. Just a few hours ago, he had brushed off a similar question from Jolly. But now, perhaps because of the intimacy of their shared hours on the high bridge, he found he could answer the Cryptologist. With a slight, self-deprecating smile, he told her, "Not angry, exactly."

Even so, the tension between him and Clemantine was real enough. After all, he had mistrusted her counterpart long before she could bring herself to admit there was a problem; and he had followed the Cryptologist's suggestion to send the missiles within range of *Griffin* without consulting her; and though in the end Clemantine had been the architect of their assault, Urban felt sure she resented his ready willingness to extinguish the entity she still regarded as her other self.

"This has been hard for her?" the Cryptologist suggested.

It sounded like a question, so he answered it that way. "Yes, it has."

"And it's been hard on you."

"We had to do it."

"Yes."

After this odd exchange, she subsided into a long, long silence—and time ran down.

Urban observed the ship's company gathering now in the amphitheater, anticipating the arrival of the first reports from *Fortuna*. Only a few people took seats. Most milled restlessly, talking, talking—eager, anxious, angry.

"It will be soon," the Cryptologist said. "I think we should go."

Urban was surprised to find himself smiling. A real smile this time because he was certain now that the assault had been successful. There would have been some sign, some violent reaction from *Griffin* if the thing had gone awry. "Yes," he agreed. "We should go."

He dressed—his usual snug trousers and gray long-sleeve shirt—and they left together.

Riffan saw them coming as they approached the amphitheater. He hurried to meet them, with Jolly at his side. "Nothing yet?" he asked.

Urban told him, "*Griffin* went dark right on schedule. That's all I know."

"But you think it's okay?" Jolly asked, his gaze wary.

"I think we did what we set out to do."

He knew the truth of it a moment later when his submind returned. The news must have shown on his face because Jolly asked him, "What is it? What's wrong?"

He shook his head, unwilling yet to answer. Brushing off all further questions, he made his way past the gathering Dragoneers and into the amphitheater, where he stepped up onto dais. All chatter ceased as he strode to its center.

He looked for Clemantine. Saw her near the doorway opposite to the one he had entered, standing between Kona and Vytet.

Urban had a DI monitoring the data gate, but he didn't need its report to know she had not yet received news from her surviving ghost aboard *Fortuna*. Her questioning expression as she looked at him told him that.

He messaged her, saying softly, *It's done.*

She cocked her head, puzzled, no doubt wondering why he knew and she did not.

He didn't try to explain, but turned to the ship's company and announced, "*Griffin* is again part of the fleet, with the Cryptologist as its pilot, just as we planned."

He made no mention of the brutal poignancy of Clemantine's fate—falling inadvertently into a strange chimera of her two selves—and the shocking choice that chimera had made to erase itself.

As murmurs of relief swept the gathering, he darted another glance at Clemantine. Her wary gaze told him she suspected not all had gone to plan, but she asked no questions.

He returned his gaze to the ship's company. Only half of them, at most, were sitting down. The rest stood in front of the dais, or by the doorways, or in the aisles on either side. Ever since learning of the assault on *Griffin* they'd been restless and resentful. Not because they objected—the situation with Clemantine's dark twin was well known—but because they had been kept in the dark.

Now questions unfolded, sharp with impatience:

Is that all you mean to say?

What actually happened, Urban?

What happened to the other Clemantine?

He didn't try to answer, offering a second revelation instead: "From *Griffin*'s high bridge, I was able to confirm that the fusion engine we sighted belongs to a great ship of ancient design."

"Human then," Kona said, still standing close to Clemantine.

"Almost surely," Urban agreed, eager to reinforce this new direction for the discussion. "But it hasn't answered our hail. Whatever intelligence animates it has chosen caution."

Several people started to speak, but Abby's clear voice rose above the others. She stood before the dais, excitement gleaming bright in her eyes as she exclaimed, "But this means there *is* life here! We thought Ryo a dead system, but something held on—"

"We don't know that," Sayuri interrupted, the two of them standing side by side. They were of an age, both ship-born and younger by far than most of the ship's company. Seeming oblivious of shy Abby's resentful gaze, Sayuri went on, "It's just as probable this great ship has come here to explore, like we have."

Riffan waved a hand from where he stood, nearly eclipsed behind Shoran's tall figure. His voice rang out over the crowd murmur, saying, "It's not surprising the crew of this great ship is being cautious. *I* would choose to be cautious, seeing two such alien ships, and one of them now gone dark."

"It's likely they're aware of *Griffin*," Urban acknowledged, speaking to be heard over the ongoing chatter. "But not of *Dragon*. We're still at such a distance, it's doubtful they've observed us."

An alert from the data gate told him the Bio-mechanic's submind had returned, closely followed by the Cryptologist's. But Clemantine had still not come home.

Abby, usually so silent at these gatherings, surprised Urban by speaking again, her eyes wide and her voice high with tension as she strove to be heard. "I think Riffan is right, though. If they saw *Griffin*, and saw it go dark, that would look like a threat . . . wouldn't it?"

Urban answered gently, "I think it would, but there was no choice in it."

"Let's all take seats!" Vytet urged, projecting his voice over all the murmured conversations. "Let's bring some order to this discussion."

People at once began to move into the rows, but not Jolly. He looked up from where he stood at the foot of the dais and fixed Urban with a doubting gaze. "But we're *not* a threat and it's wrong to let them think we are. That's what Abby means." He turned to her. "Right?"

She nodded, and Jolly went on. "We need to contact these people. Now. Let them know who we are and where we are. Let them start to trust us."

Urban might have acceded to this strategy, except for Kona. Even before Jolly finished, Kona rose from the seat he had just taken. "I disagree," he announced in his booming voice. "This great ship is playing at stealth. Its caution is understandable, but we must exercise caution too. I want to know who or what is animating it before we give anything else away—and the swiftest way to induce an answer is to have *Griffin* hit it with radar. If it's listening at all, that will tell it stealth has failed. And then we can demand a response."

This drew a general murmur of agreement—though not from Abby. Still standing in front of the dais, she turned to confront Kona, and to Urban's astonishment she exclaimed, "That is far too aggressive! It will terrify them."

Kona regarded her, certainly as surprised as Urban that she had dared to confront him. He told her gently, "You may be right, but what matters more is that it will redefine the situation, allowing negotiation to begin."

Abby looked to Jolly, but met only an uncertain frown. So she turned a pleading gaze on Urban. He could give her only an apologetic smile. "I think Kona is right," he said. "For our own security, we need to define what's aboard that ship—and their reaction is going to tell us a lot."

Abby bit her lip and nodded, her cheeks flushed red. At the same time, another notice reached Urban from the data gate: Clemantine had come home at last. Not just a submind, but her ghost.

She had not taken a seat, but remained standing, alone now, by the doorway. He stepped down from the dais and went to her, sure this would go hard. Proof of that came when her calm expression transformed to wide-eyed shock as she learned what she had done.

Reaching her, he extended his hands, wanting to offer what comfort he could, but she drew back, a palm half-raised in a warding gesture as her sharp gaze warned him not to trespass.

Consternation on his part, swiftly followed by resentment that she would keep him at such a distance. And then relief. Better for her if she handled this on her own. He would say the wrong thing anyway.

He nodded and stepped back. "I'll take care of the radar," he announced in a voice audible to everyone. And then, eyeing her, "You'll need to record a second message. Let them know we've identified them as a great ship and that we want their name and history."

Alaka'i Onyx – Pilot's Log – 1281:092:12:51 HSW

Stealth has failed. We have been found. The brush of radar confirms it. And we have been identified as what we are—a great ship.

So why are we still alive?

Ashok sees a chance for us within this interlude, a chance arising out of the inexplicable behavior of this marauder, so different from those encountered throughout our parallel histories. Clever Ashok! You, who can extend a limb into the black box of the unknown and pull hope from it.

How I wish I shared your hope.

CHAPTER EIGHT

RAGE AND DESPAIR contended within the computational layers that housed the mind of *Alaka'i Onyx*'s pilot. His name—his human name now rarely remembered—was Tio Suthrom.

On his long-ago voyage to the frontier, Tio Suthrom had found whole worlds scorched and destroyed by the marauders. On his return to Hupo Sei, he'd found no worlds at all, only debris. In disgust, in despair, he shut himself down. Much later, the Inventions roused him and he embarked on a new life, a better life.

The marauder could take it all away.

Tio Suthrom would destroy the alien vessel if he could, but how? He had no weapon except the mass of his ship, of *Alaka'i Onyx*, and that was useless, because the marauder would have hours or days to deploy its gun and vaporize him if he attempted to ram it.

He didn't even know where the marauder was anymore, not since it had gone dark. Was it closing in? Or worse, was it heading out of the system, chasing Ashok's warning messages across the void to Hupo Sei? Those messages, relayed at light speed along a chain of communication buoys he'd laid out on the crossing to Ryo, would arrive long before the marauder. The Core Forum would have years to prepare, while Tio Suthrom expected his own fate to be decided within hours at most, or possibly within the next few seconds.

Unable any longer to contain his fear, he spoke it aloud, his voice emanating from the walls surrounding Ashok's hive. "Understanding fails me, my friend. Speak some theory of hope, I beg you."

Eight of the Invention's nine instances occupied the sockets of their square charging grid. The cohort's ninth instance had emerged to carry out scheduled maintenance on its habitat. It was this one that answered Tio Suthrom. The Inventions did not naturally speak aloud, but Ashok had learned to do so. Ashok had adapted in many ways, all for Tio Suthrom's comfort and convenience.

"It is not a theory of hope I have pulled from the black box of the unknown," the instance announced, generating a hint of human humor in its synthesized voice. "But a theory of possibility."

"You've been reading my log," Tio Suthrom accused, stunned to discover it and also assaulted by guilt, for all the doubt and despair revealed there.

"I felt it necessary to map your emotional state during this uncertain time."

"Ah," Tio Suthrom said. "Yes."

Ashok had been his companion from the beginning of this life and knew well all of his human vulnerabilities. More than once, when the despair grew too great, Ashok had gently reminded him of the need to monitor and edit his mental state.

Not something Tio Suthrom wished to discuss. So instead, he latched on to Ashok's earlier words. "Of what possibility do you speak, Ashok?"

"An odd tangled thought teases at my instances: could it be the marauder is not a marauder? Though its appearance indicates it is, its behavior suggests otherwise. I am weighing the possibility that its appearance is a deception. In that possibility may lie the answer to why our existence continues rather than reaching the expected abrupt end."

Tio Suthrom generated a deep sigh. "Far more likely the message is the deception."

"It seemed so at first. It seemed we were being lured into answering, into confirming our existence. But we have been found, my friend. And yet for some unknown reason we still have not been murdered."

"I too have a theory to explain the bizarre behavior of this marauder," Tio Suthrom said.

"Tell it to me."

"It has not destroyed us because it wants to colonize us, to infect our systems and thereafter use *Alaka'i Onyx* as a stealth weapon against our precious home."

An extended silence followed this declaration, stretching over multiple seconds while energy usage spiked within the grid.

"The cohort deems this a plausible assessment," Ashok finally reported.

Tio Suthrom said, "Better to destroy myself than to allow it to happen."

Ashok still spoke with utter calm. "We now have two theories. Let us test my theory while we prepare for yours."

"You want us to reply to the marauder?"

"Yes. There is nothing to lose by it, but maybe, there is something to gain."

CHAPTER NINE

THE ASTRONOMER CALCULATED the hours required for *Dragon*'s second message to reach the great ship, and the hours that would elapse before a reply could be received. And though there was no way to know how long the great ship might take to issue a response—or if it would speak at all—as the time drew near when a response might be expected, Riffan returned to the amphitheater.

He wasn't alone. Though there had been no formal call for an assembly, Riffan was pleased to find nearly a third of the ship's company already there, standing about and quietly chatting. *Still* chatting. One on one. Two on two. Small conversations debating the shocking fate of Clemantine's dark twin and speculating on the nature of the anomalous great ship, even drawing parallels between the two. Guilt always a part of it. Riffan was not immune. The same refrain kept repeating in his mind: *We should have done more for* Griffin.

Just like *Griffin*, and like *Dragon*, every great ship was piloted by a human mind—but human minds could come undone.

Riffan moved up the side aisle, responding with a grim smile, a short nod, whenever he made eye contact. For once, he was all talked out. And there was Kona, sitting alone in the third row, arms crossed over his chest, simply waiting. Kona wasn't one to indulge in idle chatter, so Riffan went to sit with him.

The minimal time came, and a hush fell over the gathering. Seconds slipped past. A full minute. Two. Three.

Disappointed whispers.

Vytet separated himself from a group milling by one of the

doorways. His expression lit with a slight amused smile as numerous faces turned toward him. "It could be some time," he reminded everyone.

Truth. It could be hours; it could be days.

Or the great ship might never reply.

Naresh, in the second row, shifted his seat, moving closer to Kona and Riffan. He looked up at them, one arm resting on the back of his chair. "I think it won't be more than a few minutes," he said. "They gain nothing by antagonizing us."

"We don't know what they are," Kona answered gruffly. "Or what they're thinking."

Naresh furrowed his brow, started to say something, thought better of it, and turned back to face the dais. Time slipped past. A few more people came in, sat down. Soft voices speculated, while Riffan listened to the slow beat of his heart, counting past a thousand, losing track only when an alert reached his atrium.

An incoming message! Not from *Griffin.*

He caught his breath, straightened, leaned forward as if that would help him to listen.

The message began with a single enthusiastic word arriving from across the void: "Hello!"

A human voice, male, speaking in the language of the Dragoneers. That had been the first language in Clemantine's initial hail.

"Hello and greetings!"

Though cheery on the surface, Riffan felt sure he heard a slight nervous tremor in the words—and why not? Who wouldn't be nervous at such an encounter amid the silent ruins of the Hallowed Vasties?

"I offer up my identity as you have commanded, O great hunter from distant reaches! I am Tio Suthrom, pilot of the great ship *Alaka'i Onyx*, wandering the Great Silence. I exist as a haven of intelligence, though I am devoid of organic life. Spare me and speak further if it be your will. Stunned am I that you speak at all and in the language of a biological form. I have no data supporting such communication in all my known history."

A tone indicated the message had ended.

Riffan's heart hammered, his voice a shocked whisper as he murmured, *"Love and Nature and the Cosmic First Light!"* His exclamation one of many as astonishment swept the gathering.

Turning to Kona, he demanded to know, "Did you catch that? *'O great hunter from distant reaches.'* Doesn't that sound like a reference to the Chenzeme? Could this Tio Suthrom know of the Chenzeme?"

Riffan was so amazed and wonderstruck at the possibility, it took him a few seconds to notice Kona's shocked expression, lips parted and his stern eyes staring at nothing.

Abruptly, Kona surged to his feet. In a booming voice that silenced all others, he declared, "This pilot *knows* us. He must have been to the frontier, and back again, because he knows us as Chenzeme and he is seeking to ingratiate himself with this claim that he carries no life! I want to know if he's done so before, even to aiding the monsters in their war of extermination. And if he has—"

"No, Kona!"

It was Vytet who dared to interrupt him. He stood at the front of the amphitheater, arm outstretched, palm raised. *"Stop,* my friend," he insisted. "We must not make any such assumption. A multitude of possibilities lie behind Tio Suthrom's words. Do not make him into that enemy who has haunted you and I from our long-ago youth."

In the stark silence that followed, Riffan reminded himself that Kona was one of the eldest here. Unlike most of them, he had not been born at Deception Well. He and Vytet and Clemantine had migrated there, three among a handful of refugees, forcefully off-loaded in an abandoned city. They were the founders. They'd made a new life at Deception Well, for themselves and for all who came after, but the trauma they'd endured remained with them still.

Now Riffan felt a dangerous heat radiating from Kona; he noted the trembling induced by the man's barely contained rage. Instinct urged him to move away, but at the same time, some deep courage stirred within him and, moved by it, he gently touched the back of Kona's hand.

The big man flinched away, half turning as he looked down, scourging Riffan with a fierce glare.

Riffan did not look away. "Vytet is right," he said gently. "We'll learn the truth in the fullness of time and more often than not, truth has the capacity to surprise."

Kona's jaw tensed. Breath hissed past his teeth. "Surprises are rarely good," he countered. But he took his seat again. A clenched fist and the bloodless gleam of his knuckles testified to his ongoing turmoil.

A rustle, a shared sigh as people resumed their conversations. Riffan looked behind to where Urban usually sat—but he was not there. The fourth row was empty.

He turned back as Vytet announced, "The Scholar will speak."

The Apparatchik's disembodied voice informed them, "I have located a historical record of a great ship bearing the name *Alaka'i Onyx* and piloted by Tio Suthrom. The ship was one of three companion ships assembled in the shipyard at Hupo Sei in the early years of the expansion. The other two great ships bore the names *Alaka'i Jade* and *Alaka'i Firoza*."

A discussion ensued: principally Pasha, Vytet, and Tarnya debating what form their response should take, while more people arrived, filling in the seats.

Riffan scarcely listened, haunted as he was by Kona's suspicions and by his own memories of how Lezuri had first breached *Dragon*'s defenses and then taken advantage of Riffan's innate trust and curiosity in a brutal play to seize the courser for his own.

Unsure what to say, but needing to communicate his concerns, he stood, raised a hand, caught Vytet's eye. And as Tarnya completed her argument of what exactly should be said, of what should be explained to the ancient and possibly addled great ship, Vytet nodded that he should go next.

His thoughts took shape as he spoke, coming together in words that surprised him.

"I think Kona's suspicions should guide us. There is something off about this *Alaka'i Onyx*. Granted, that may be just an artifact of the distance between us. This ship's history and ours diverged a very long time ago. Since then, we've spent millennia on different paths and that is time enough for . . . well . . . almost anything. What I mean is, we have no way to know what this ship is really. And until we know, we cannot trust anything it tells us."

Naresh turned to eye Riffan, his elbow resting on the back of his seat. And as Riffan finished speaking, Naresh asked in a skeptical tone, "Are you suspecting another trap like the Rock?"

Riffan blushed and bit his lip, feeling himself utterly transparent. Even so, he gave Naresh a careful answer. "I don't know and that is my point. We have no way of knowing, which is why I counsel an utmost caution. We ought to say little of ourselves until we have sent probes to examine this vessel and determine what it is and what it's capable of doing."

As he resumed his seat, Pasha stood up from hers in the front row. "I think we will find it is exactly what it appears to be: an ancient great ship possessed of a long and traumatic history that I am anxious to understand. All that said—Riffan is not wrong."

"Sooth," Kona agreed, low and grim, remaining seated as he spoke. "We'll send an outrider to approach this *Alaka'i Onyx*, with instructions to deploy a compliment of scout-bots and microprobes to assess its capabilities."

This drew nods and murmurs of agreement, including from Riffan, who had remained standing. Again, he caught Vytet's eye and asked, "Where is Clemantine? She'll need to make a diplomatic answer to this Tio Suthrom."

Pasha popped up again. She gazed back at Riffan, her expression drawn and anxious. Then turning to Vytet, she said, "Clemantine is . . . taking time for herself. Tarnya can speak for us."

"Make it a short answer," Kona demanded. "Give nothing away."

Alaka'i Onyx – Pilot's Log – 1281:092:21:11 HSW

A reply has come from the marauder, though I deem it more threat than promise:

Stand by. We will close with you and assess the situation.

Both Ashok and I sense opportunities.

"Let them examine us," Ashok insists. "Let them know we are harmless."

But if the marauder draws close enough, we will not be harmless. I have prepared and I am ready. I will not hesitate. I will blow myself to vapor should the marauder approach within the perimeter of that blast. I hope it does. I hope I will be given this chance to ensure the marauder never reaches Hupo Sei.

CHAPTER TEN

EVERY FEW MINUTES the Bio-mechanic circulated through *Griffin*'s neural bridge, pausing momentarily at each cardinal node to assess the state of the surrounding tissue. All stable. All quiet.

Too quiet.

Griffin was a ghost ship, haunted by absence, lacking even a memory of the team of Apparatchiks that once inhabited it. Clemantine's dark twin had been thorough in her purge. But now she was gone too, and Urban had departed, ceding to the Cryptologist sole control of the high bridge.

Amid these thoughts, a summons reached him: *Meet me in the library.*

Was it his own will or hers that caused him to immediately shift, instantiating there within his window? A moot question as, ever and always, he possessed not the least desire to refuse. Such was his unnatural nature.

The Cryptologist—*such a pretty little thing*—stood with arms crossed on the library floor, eyeing him with a disapproving frown. "Why separate yourself like that?" she asked him. "There is room enough in the library's working memory for both of us."

Is that how the confinement within windows had begun? He sent a thought searching through centuries of data; it fetched a series of recollections into present memory and his lip curled in contempt. But then, contempt had long ago become his default emotion. He told her, "Separation was implemented only in part to conserve computational resources. The primary purpose was a visual reminder to Urban that Apparatchiks are artificial entities

designed with machinelike natures that force us to focus obses-
sively on a designated specialty. In short, a reminder that we are
not true human minds."

To his deep annoyance, the Cryptologist rolled her eyes. "You
love your machinelike nature. But you're as human as any other
Dragoneer—and so am I. So please come out and play?"

He scoffed. Who was she anyway? Just another kind of Apparatchik, created with the same ancient software utility that had
created him. He thought of her that way, even if Urban considered
her something more.

"You will get me designated a rogue entity," he warned. "Aberrant and subject to deletion."

She smiled sweetly. "You *are* aberrant, but not subject to deletion. Not here aboard my ship."

"*Your* ship? Do you expect to remain in sole command?"

"I do. Clemantine will not return, Urban has never wanted the
burden of piloting a second courser, and Pasha knows I need to be
here—you and I—to redesign *Griffin*'s loathsome philosopher cells."

He considered this, remembering how the Cryptologist had
defied custom time after time and gotten away with all of it. Defy-
ing custom did not come so easily to him, but neither did it feel
impossible. Not here, in the absence of the other Apparatchiks.

"A rogue entity, then," he concluded. "Stand by."

A module of his architecture confined his image to a two-
dimensional window whenever he instantiated on the library's
main deck. Turning inward, he located the module and removed
it from active use. His window vanished and for a moment, he
vanished with it. Then his image refreshed as a fully three-dimensional figure.

He loved the feeling of it! Loved the exhilarating rush of posi-
tional data flooding in from every part of his virtual body. So
much, that he had to fight to suppress a smile. He had existed
thus before, but only rarely and in private spaces or special circumstances. Always a little overwhelming at first. But because his
mind was based on Urban's mind, he *knew* how to command a
body like this. He'd been made for it.

Permitting himself a slight pirate smile, he reached out a hand to the Cryptologist. Had he ever touched anyone before? He did so now, long fingers softly brushing the smooth warm skin of her cheek.

Smiling in return, she told him, "Urban asked me to destroy *Griffin*'s philosopher cells."

He snatched his hand back, horrified. "No! You won't do that. *We* won't do it. The ship would die."

"You think so? You're sure?"

He was *not* sure.

A courser was not a singular lifeform, but rather a mosaic of living things—various bio-mechanical tissues, computational layers, the reef, the philosopher cells, the pilot. In a primordial courser the pilot was a singular, subordinate mind responsible for navigation when the philosopher cells went dark. Aboard *Griffin* and *Dragon* the pilot was a human entity with a far more extensive role. Each of these lifeforms was necessary to the correct functioning of a Chenzeme ship, but *Griffin* was no longer truly Chenzeme. Did it *require* its philosopher cells? Or could its human pilot fully replace them?

He shook his head slowly. "When the philosopher cells go dark, they're not dead or in cold sleep. There is still activity, a low-level of communication, binding the other elements together. So yes, without the philosopher cells or without re-creating some artificial replacement for them, the ship *would* die. And we would lose their senses and their deep memory too."

He had devoted his existence to understanding and harnessing Chenzeme bio-mechanics, including, and especially, the physiology of the philosopher cells. He had competed with them and learned from them; and given their unique complexity, he felt sure there would always be more knowledge to extract.

The Cryptologist told him, "Urban suggested we replace *Griffin*'s cells with modified lineages from *Dragon*."

"Graft a foreign brain onto *Griffin*? Let its lineages colonize this ship?" A disapproving hiss, but then he nodded. "Yes, colonization would probably work—eventually. But it would be an ugly process. My guess is, the internal physiology would decay long before pathways could be reestablished, leaving the ship crippled for a very long time."

She smiled, appearing delighted by this scenario. "Thank you. That is my conclusion too. We will proceed as we originally planned, re-engineering the philosopher cells with care, and not with haste."

CHAPTER ELEVEN

DAYS PASSED. DISTANCES closed. And eventually Tio Suthrom re-discovered the marauder as a slender, lightless void outlined against the blazing brilliance of a myriad of distant stars.

Determined not to lose track of the alien vessel this time, Tio Suthrom locked his telescopes onto its featureless shape.

"It is still far away," he murmured, resentful of that fact now that he was ready, now that he had fully prepared himself, mentally and mechanically, to use his ship as a weapon. He only need wait for the marauder to approach as it had promised to do. Once it entered within a narrow blast zone, he would blow *Alaka'i Onyx* apart, destroying the marauder when he did, and preventing it from ever reaching Hupo Sei.

Ashok, forever calm, observed, "That is not the marauder."

"What do you mean, my friend?"

"Note the proportions. They are wrong. The girth of this object is less, relative to its length, than that of the marauder. This has become obvious, though its full length remains to be determined."

Tio Suthrom did not want to believe it. He loaded images of the marauder into his memory for comparison. The marauder had been observed obliquely, at an indeterminate distance. He had no certain knowledge of its absolute proportions or its absolute size. Only estimates. Still, now that he looked, he saw that Ashok was correct.

Ashok continued, "Note also how the approaching object appears to grow rapidly in size, indicating it is very close and therefore not very large."

"Or else it is a large object riding an unstoppable momentum!" Tio Suthrom countered as a new and horrifying possibility trespassed on his mind. He re-examined the marauder's previous position as best he could estimate it. He could only guess at its trajectory and potential velocity, but even his wildest guess could not make sense of what he saw now. The marauder should not have appeared in this region of the celestial sphere—while the histories he carried assured him marauders often traveled in packs.

"Ashok, I think it is a second marauder."

A brief silence as Ashok processed this and then concluded, "You may be correct. We must continue to observe."

"Not passively. Not anymore."

Tio Suthrom needed to know what was out there. He had convinced himself he might destroy a single marauder. But if there were two? Impossible! He could not conceive of any means to destroy both. The marauders had not wiped out world after world because they were vulnerable to the ploys of a lone, unarmed great ship.

He triggered an array of navigational jets, brief flares that caused *Alaka'i Onyx* to swivel, its bow coming around to face the intruder. A second array of jets stabilized his position. And then he triggered his way-finding radar.

The echo returned with shocking speed, placing the object a mere three kilometers away—and closing.

"Ah ha," Ashok said. "My guess is the correct one. This object is close and not large, my friend, just as I first predicted."

Indeed. This was a tiny ship—sixty, seventy meters long?—no more than three meters in diameter.

"A scout ship," Tio Suthrom whispered. It had to be. It was certainly no second marauder and for that he was grateful. But this also meant his gambit must fail. He would not get close enough to the marauder to strike it—yet he must still die here. Better that than allowing himself to be colonized. He had only hoped that his violent last act would serve a double purpose and save Hupo Sei.

"A scout ship is the logical conclusion," Ashok concurred, offering no hint that it shared Tio Suthrom's despair. And then, "Ah. Here is a radio message."

Tio Suthrom listened again to a woman's very human voice, different from the two voices that had addressed him before. Sounding friendly and self-assured, the voice said, "Hello, Tio Suthrom. We are here aboard a small un-crewed vessel. We intend to launch two scout-bots toward you. One will survey your hull. We ask that you admit the other so that it may survey your interior. You may deploy a similar bot to survey our vessel. We will not object. Do you understand?"

What Tio Suthrom understood was that, despite the kindness he heard in the generated voice, he had no choice, no option to object.

"My theory—that the marauder is not a marauder—remains valid," Ashok observed. "As does yours, that the marauder has engaged in trickery in a scheme to colonize us. But there is an additional possibility. I did not propose it before because I did not want to upset you. But I feel we must now face the dire prospect that the entity controlling the marauder may be as human as it seems—and therefore capable of all the inherent and inexplicable violence of your kind."

This possibility had not occurred to Tio Suthrom and hearing it now, it shook him to his mind's deep core. He had given his life to the Inventions, not expecting, not even wanting, to ever again encounter another human mind. Another mind of that species that had destroyed the once thriving worlds of Hupo Sei and transformed Ryo's great planets and glittering habitats into crumbled and lifeless ruins.

Why then, this spark of searing hope?

Ashok, oblivious of these thoughts, continued, "Let us consent to the marauder's demand. We might then swiftly distinguish the correct theory."

But did the theory even matter? Surely a human-infested marauder was as dangerous as the original kind.

Then why this hope?

"Tio Suthrom?" Ashok queried when the silence had grown to encompass too many seconds.

Tio Suthrom answered, "You are braver than I, my friend."

"Only because I process fear as an abstract arithmetical element, not as a biological quality."

"A more intelligent system. The Inventions are far more intelligent than humankind."

"Answer our visitor, Tio Suthrom."

"Yes. All right."

"But be ready to trigger our destruction. We must not allow ourselves to be used as a stealth weapon against Hupo Sei. If your theory should prove valid, I expect you will have mere seconds to act."

The outrider *Lam Lha* now coasted alongside *Alakaʻi Onyx*, separated from it by a mere five hundred meters, with Urban and Pasha aboard as ghosts in the library.

Urban had seized this assignment for himself because he was curious, and because of an ancient nostalgia. That first time he'd left Deception Well, he'd left in a great ship much like this one. (*He'd been so young then! Really just a kid.*) The memory of that time left him eager to ask Tio Suthrom what he knew of the long past, what he had seen, and how he had survived.

Vytet had privately urged him to take Clemantine on this mission, or to at least encourage her to go. "She is our usual diplomat and she needs a new challenge."

Urban had refused.

In the days since the conquest of *Griffin*—the conquest of her own dark twin—Clemantine had plunged into a deep melancholy. She'd become distant and listless and deeply sad and yet refused all suggestion of therapy, as if she *wanted* to be wrapped in the misery of her grief. They'd fought about it:

"You did what you had to do! You don't have to put yourself through this."

"You mean I don't have to put you *through this."*

Sooth. There was truth to that. He admitted as much. And when she asked him to leave, he did.

He told Vytet, "This mission is not therapy." And he took Pasha instead.

Pasha had clearly been the better choice. Just like Clemantine, her experience as a pilot had given her an intimate knowledge of Chenzeme nature. If there was any taint of the Chenzeme to be seen or sensed aboard this great ship, Pasha would know it. She was also an exobiologist, skeptical of Tio Suthrom's claim that he carried no life, and eager to determine *his* true nature.

Urban listened as Pasha initiated contact, announcing by radio their presence and explaining their intentions.

It took Tio Suthrom a few minutes to reply. When he did, he sounded resigned. "I understand. I will open a lock. You will see it by its light."

Pasha said, "Thank you." A politeness that would not have occurred to Urban. She added, "I am launching the scout-bots now."

"Understood."

Three open windows in *Lam Lha*'s library displayed three different views of *Alaka'i Onyx*: one from a camera on the outrider, and one each from the scout-bots as they glided slowly toward the great ship's dark hull.

As they approached, *Alaka'i Onyx* began a slow roll that brought a set of open bay doors into sight. Its roll ceased. Dull red light illuminated the interior of what was obviously a hangar, occupied by a small shuttle. Situated midway along the dark hull, the red glow suggested to Urban a tired but malevolent eye. He made no comment on this though, and neither did Pasha.

She had a Dull Intelligence at work within *Lam Lha*'s library. Relaying its findings, she said, "The structure of this ship and this cargo lock appear historically accurate."

Urban had expected as much. He did not doubt *Alaka'i Onyx* truly was a great ship, created by human ingenuity in some long-ago age.

The scout-bots had been holding their thin legs nestled tight against their small ovoid bodies as they glided toward the great ship. But now, with just a few meters to go, they extended their jointed limbs and then flexed them to cushion the impact as they landed against the hull. Reactive surfaces on their footpads secured them, at the same time allowing them to assay the hull's molecular composition.

Urban studied their video feeds, while intermittently glancing at the molecular assays that now appeared as ribbons of text within a fourth window.

"The hull is sterile," Pasha observed.

Again, as expected.

Scout-bot 1 entered the hangar, where it swiftly explored the walls and the outer surfaces of the shuttle, sampling as it went.

"Again, sterile," Pasha said. "Some remnant nanotech. Nothing functional."

"The shuttle looks in good shape. There must be systems maintaining it."

"Do you want to try to look inside?" she asked.

"No." Urban nodded at the display. "There's a gel lock waiting for us." And then he added, "I never saw a lock that small."

The lock's membrane glowed dull red like the airless hangar. His mind's eye measured it against the scout-bot and he concluded, "A meter square, as if it was custom-made to be just big enough for the scout-bot, if the bot could go through with its legs deployed."

It could not, of course, at least not on its own, because its thin legs were not capable of maneuvering within the dense gel. Tio Suthrom must have known this, or at least suspected, because as soon as the bot leaned against the surface, the gel rippled, drawing it in.

The scout-bot reported an encounter with active nanotech—Makers—within the gel, busily exploring the bot's surfaces. The heat of conflict flared at its footpads, then faded as the local clade of Makers withdrew.

Pasha spoke over the radio. "Tio Suthrom, please confirm that you have found our device clean, harmless, and compatible with your Makers."

Tio Suthrom replied, "On the surface, that is the case, though I cannot know the extent of your abilities."

"Nor can we know yours, but we mean you no harm."

Urban hissed softly. No such promise had been made before, and given Kona's anger, and his suspicion that this great ship had somehow served the Chenzeme, it wasn't a promise he was ready to make.

And it wasn't a promise Tio Suthrom was ready to believe. "What are you?" he demanded, for the first time with an edge of anger. "You, with your human voices and human conversation. Do you think I don't recognize a marauder when I see one? I have been to the frontier and back. I have seen the ruin of worlds after marauders struck them. Jewel-like worlds turned to ash and black stone. The marauders are death! And *you*. What are you? What are you but a trick of that ship now gone dark?"

So hard to express tension in ghost form. Urban felt his jaw set, his stomach knot, his hands clench into fists—all simulated responses to satisfy the biological needs of his mind. He signaled to Pasha that this time, *he* would answer.

"The marauders *are* death," he said in a quiet voice. "We call them the Chenzeme. And you are right. Our ships are Chenzeme starships. You've seen only one. We have another. We captured them, we control them, and we are human. We came here from the frontier on a voyage of discovery, seeking to understand what you have called the Great Silence. But with your original message, you seemed to ingratiate yourself with the Chenzeme—the marauders. Did you ever ally yourself with them?"

"No. *No!* Do not suggest such a thing. I have seen a companion turned to vapor. I have seen the burnt husks of once-thriving worlds. The marauders have existed eons and the struggle to survive their depredations is not just a human one—"

He broke off. The sharp silence that followed piqued Urban's suspicions and fed his curiosity.

"Not just human?" he echoed.

No answer. Not right away.

The scout-bot had remained suspended within the gel membrane throughout this exchange, but now the membrane's motile tissue pushed the bot forward again, until it spilled into a little air-filled transit bubble that, like the hangar, had red-glowing walls.

The bot assayed the air, finding it ship-standard, except that it was sterile—utterly devoid of the microbial life that always accompanied Earth biomes. There were not even remnants of organic molecules.

Pasha turned to Urban. "He claimed to be devoid of organic life. I'm starting to think that might be true."

"*Sooth*," Urban whispered, feeling himself plunged into memory—all those centuries spent alone as he'd returned to Deception Well. His mind had existed then only as a ghost, with *Dragon* as his body. Not a single cell of Earth-based life had existed within him then. His Makers had been the only physical evidence of his existence.

"He's alone," Urban concluded. *As I was.* "This is an empty ship, without a ship's company. But he knows something, Pasha. He's seen something—something inhuman."

She said, "He might have found some alien ruin in his wanderings, ancient and awful."

"Or some remnant of alien life? But not here. Not in the Hallowed Vasties. There's no record of anything like that here. But why hesitate to speak of it?"

"*Ask* him," Pasha urged. "Keep him talking in honest words." In a tone of avarice, she added, "He may well know histories we've never heard of."

Urban nodded. Gathering his thoughts, he spoke again over the radio. "Tio Suthrom, it may be we've both misread each other."

"It is hard to know the truth," Tio Suthrom conceded. "It is hard to accept an unexpected truth when there is so very much at stake."

"More than your own life?" Urban asked.

"Far more."

"Will you allow the scout-bot to explore your interior?"

"The transit bubble is free to glide about, but there are no hollow spaces that your bot could access. This is no longer a human ship."

Urban felt the pressure of Pasha's ghost hand squeezing his arm. The look of awe on her face surely reflected his own. Holding her gaze, he asked, "What kind of ship is it, then?"

For several seconds, no answer came. But Urban was patient and finally, Tio Suthrom said, "We are a scientific expedition, here to survey the ruins of Ryo."

Urban looked again at the video feed, though it showed only dull red light emanating from the transit bubble's smooth walls.

"We?" he asked.

Tio Suthrom did not answer this, asking instead, "Are you able to ghost using common protocol?"

"Yes, of course. Are you inviting us?"

"We are. There are two of you?"

"Yes."

"In another minute I will send you addresses for two artificial avatars."

Again, Urban looked at Pasha, this time with a mix of confusion and concern. "Not a library?" he murmured, still speaking over the radio.

"No, robotic units," Tio Suthrom answered. "It is necessary."

Pasha objected, "But you said you have no hollow spaces."

"I said I have none that your bot could access. It is a question of scale," he explained without explaining. Then, after a long pause, "Here are the addresses. We await you."

To Pasha, Urban said, "I'm sending a DI to evaluate."

"Good."

A few seconds later, the DI reported both destinations to be benign, exhibiting every aspect of the common protocol used in such situations since ancient times.

"We'll be able to retreat, if needed," Urban concluded. They would be able to erase themselves too, though he didn't say that aloud. "I'll go first."

CHAPTER TWELVE

WHILE THE CRYPTOLOGIST took *Griffin* far from the fleet, the Bio-mechanic took inventory. He sampled the tissue of every dormant philosopher cell, using that data to map the lineages; and he charted the complexity of the intercellular links.

The pattern and quantity of links told him which cell lines dominated, but the dominant lines were not always the most aggressive. If he knew their temperaments, it would be easy to cull the worst of them while dormant. But he did not. That assessment had to wait until the cells wakened. Even then, he'd need to rely on the Cryptologist to confirm from her position on the high bridge which lineages to thin, because from the neural bridge, he could only guess at their different natures.

I am concerned, she messaged him.

As you should be.

She ignored this jibe, asking him, *Can you simultaneously cull multiple cell lines?*

Why would you want to do that? The goal should be to cull just enough to ensure your control of the ship.

Yes. But can I secure control in time?

He heard doubt in her voice, and fear. He didn't like it. *If you can't do it yourself, invite Urban to help you. Or Pasha.*

He said this knowing she would refuse. She did not want Urban back on the high bridge where he might take control of *Griffin* and reshape the cell field in his own way. The Bio-mechanic felt sure she would hold similar reservations about Pasha.

*I will consider this suggestion, she told him, although her stiff tone implied she had already rejected it.

Later, a prolonged, crushing shift in velocity brought *Griffin* into alignment with one of Ryo's drifting megastructures. Over the ensuing hours, the Cryptologist used gentler course corrections to place the rogue courser behind the megastructure, relative to the fleet. From there, the philosopher cells would not be able to sense the presence of any other vessel when the Cryptologist finally wakened them.

She was right to fear that moment.

The cell field had gone dark on the expectation that the courser would pursue in stealth the targeted great ship, following it to its home system. Such a pursuit might take decades, centuries, even millennia. It didn't matter. A few millennia could not matter to a mind that had witnessed the passing of millions of years. However much time slipped past, the cells would remember their purpose. They would waken eager for a kill and when they did not immediately detect their prey, they would go hunting for it.

It would be on him to quickly cull any lineage the Cryptologist could not subdue, because if she lost control, it would not take *Griffin* long to move out from behind the megastructure and select a target from among the fleet.

Leaving the neural bridge, he manifested in *Griffin's* library, finding the Cryptologist already there. She stood facing the cell map he had generated. Strident colors marked the lineages, casting a weird glow against the Cryptologist's pale cheeks.

Her goal was to reshape the ship's mind, retaining all she could of the knowledge the philosopher cells possessed while freeing them from the authoritarian constraints of their Chenzeme ancestry. Just as she had done with *Dragon*, she meant to eliminate hate and indifference, instilling in their place traits the philosopher cells had never possessed before, like the capacity to experience wonder, and a sense of deep empathy for all those lifeforms and wildly unique planetary ecosystems they had been forced, in their prior existence, to despise.

"I am ready," he told her. "Are you?"

She turned to him with an expectant expression. "I have given your suggestion due consideration and have decided to accept it—though in principle, not in detail. Rather than Urban or Pasha, I want *you* with me on the high bridge."

He recoiled from these words. A curled lip. A surly scowl. Manufacturing a dark expression to cover an unwelcome rush of frustration and . . . *gratitude*. Bitter gratitude.

Never before, not once in all the centuries of his existence, had the Bio-mechanic been invited to visit a high bridge. Not here and not on *Dragon*—until now—and he desired it fiercely. Out of curiosity, yes, but also because the grant of such permission would redefine who he was; it would be a grant of new ability. One step closer to the freedom of an embodied mind.

Even so, he told the Cryptologist, "No. That is your task. Mine is to cull those cell lineages that refuse your arguments."

She dared to look annoyed. "Replicate, as Urban does."

"I am not Urban. I cannot replicate."

If he could, he would not have died aboard *Dragon* in that awful time when Lezuri had released his predator into the ship's system.

"You replicated when you came here from *Dragon*."

"One copy here, one there. No more. I am restrained."

It angered him even to discuss such things. Perhaps she sensed it. She looked troubled, thoughtful. Her gaze drifted. And then her ghost began to fade.

"You're distracted," he concluded irritably. "Come back. Focus. We have a task."

"A moment," she whispered as something shifted within his mind, a strange dizzying instability.

Shocked, he turned inward to examine his own structure and found her there. He assumed it to be her. A mind not his own.

Fear surged through him. "What are you doing?" he demanded, though he already knew.

She had found his core. She could unmake him if she wanted to—but that was not her purpose.

He felt the change as a new sense coming online, an avenue of possibility opening.

Her probing mind withdrew from him; her ghost solidified as her bright blue eyes fixed on him in an intense gaze. "I need you on the high bridge," she told him.

He nodded. He replicated. And he found the path to the high bridge open to him.

CHAPTER THIRTEEN

CLEMANTINE SAT ALONE in her cottage, cross-legged on the carpeted floor of a front room empty of all furnishings save for a little table made of golden wood standing just ten centimeters high. She faced the table, or more precisely, she faced a potted orchid set at the table's center.

The orchid had strapping, deep green leaves and three low spikes, each bearing a trio of white buds that might soon open into star-shaped flowers—if her mood allowed it. This was a meditation orchid, an old half-forgotten bioengineering project she'd resurrected in the idle hope that it might help her to find a path toward acceptance.

A vain hope, she thought grimly.

The re-taking of *Griffin* had broken something in her, allowing guilt to come crashing in. And not just guilt for letting herself be suborned by *Griffin*'s philosopher cells (because that other version of her, *was* her), or for the negligence committed by this surviving version that had allowed the travesty to happen, or for the ruthlessness she had exercised in eliminating her own corrupt self. No, it was as if a putrid cyst had burst within her mind, spewing forth the guilt she'd never allowed herself to feel for all the necessary violence she had committed through a long and challenging life.

Clemantine knew she needed therapy, but she didn't want it. Not yet. She wanted this guilt. There was satisfaction in it, knowing it to be well deserved.

It almost amused her to watch the orchid as it sensed the subtle chemicals of her mood and reflected them as intended, its buds slowly withering over the hour that she sat there, before finally dropping away.

Much like Urban.

Yet another bitter thought. She had not seen or spoken to him in days, and did not want to.

With a deep, disgusted, growling sigh she abandoned her meditation and stood, turning to face an empty room. Just as she did, an alert reached her. Her DI whispered that Vytet had come; he waited now outside the door.

A hiss of irritation. Even so, Clemantine signaled the gel door to open, telling herself it would be easier to convince Vytet to go away if she did it in person.

The door retracted, but it did not reveal the Vytet she expected, the bearded Vytet, with stern brow ridge, deep-set eyes, and broad shoulders. Clemantine's lips parted in confusion.

When did this happen?

This was Vytet in feminine aspect: tall as always, but slim and lithe now, gentle-eyed, her long hair gleaming gray, her body clothed in a sleeveless close-fitting tunic and a loose sky-blue skirt. With a pang, Clemantine realized how much she'd missed this version. She dared to wonder if Vytet had changed thus for her sake.

Vytet cocked her head, gesturing to where the sofa ought to be. "I thought we could sit together and talk."

Clemantine bristled, sure she knew what Vytet had come to say. "Did Urban send you?"

"Urban? No. I have not seen him on the gee deck in several days."

This news hurt, and that annoyed her.

"And you're here why? To tell me I ought to submit myself to therapy? That I'm being self-indulgent?"

"You *are* being self-indulgent. But I think you need to be. That you deserve to be. That you're the only one who can decide how and how much you need to grieve."

Clemantine closed her eyes. Drew a quick sharp breath. Then she signaled the room to furnish itself. The sofa unfolded from beneath the floor; a small table rose in front of it. On the opposite wall, a screen emerged, displaying a three-part scroll of a night heron perched on a branch above a moonlit pond.

"It's not grief, or not just grief," Clemantine whispered, beckoning Vytet to come and sit with her, shoulder to shoulder through several seconds of silence.

Finally, Vytet suggested, "It's guilt too."

"Sooth." Clemantine despised the tremor in her voice. Words she had not expected followed: "I should have stayed at Prakruti."

Vytet squeezed her hand. "You were happy there."

"Urban was happy there too. He loved that world and so did I. It was so much like home, Vytet. *Our* home, yours and mine. Our birth world. You remember it."

"Yes."

A world the Chenzeme had destroyed.

Clemantine said, "When we were there, at Prakruti, I didn't want to think about her, about what she was enduring. She had never let me share that anyway, and I didn't want to anymore. Let her carry it alone! Why not? She wanted it. I knew that because I knew her . . . and she knew me. She *let* me be happy."

"A gift to you," Vytet suggested.

Clemantine shook her head. "No. She decided she was not me, that she was stronger without me, that the subminds I shared only weakened her. So she abandoned me—and I let her do it, and I lost myself."

Vytet turned to her, pulled her close, whispered in her ear, "You're not lost. You're still here. And I know you well enough to know your strength. You'll endure this, and you'll be happy again."

"Yes." Clemantine knew it to be true. She'd endured despair before. It would pass and this would prove to be but a short interval in a long life. "It will be different though, going forward."

"How do you mean?"

"I'm too old to be jealous, and yet . . ." She shrugged. Smiled a self-mocking smile.

"Urban?"

"He's sleeping somewhere else now. Probably with the Cryptologist." Another shrug. "He was never constant. It's been a wonder to me that he stayed in my home so long."

"I don't think he's sleeping with the Cryptologist."

"No? If not yet, he will. He's fascinated with her. He believes she holds the secret he still wants, the secret of the blade. And he listens to her. He let her re-engineer his precious philosopher cells! For years, I questioned his claim that the high bridge gave us absolute control over the cell field. He never took my doubts seriously. Though I was right."

"You were. Proof of that came when we almost lost *Dragon* at Tanjiri. But it was that incident that convinced Urban to re-engineer the hull cells. It wasn't the Cryptologist."

"Maybe." A soft, bitter laugh. "Who am I to complain? I made the same mistake as Urban. I occupied *Griffin's* high bridge. I could have forced its philosopher cells to adapt to me. Instead, I adapted to them."

"We all should have been watching more closely."

"But we didn't. I didn't. Remember the story the Tanji told us? A story of war breaking out among the godlings that emerged from Tanjiri's swarm and how they murdered one another. We're no different, Vytet. We murdered that other version of me. I murdered her. And it horrifies me. And I can't help but ask myself, who is next?"

CHAPTER FOURTEEN

URBAN'S GHOST INSTANTIATED within the body of an artificial avatar. He felt its presence around him, the slight mass of it: a slim sexless human shape equipped with a sense of sight and a sense of hearing. A sense of touch too, he decided, as he flexed thin arms and curled traditionally proportioned fingers. Still, it was a minimalist body primarily composed of transparent gel—adequate for the present zero-gravity environment, though unlikely to function under any significant load.

Looking up, he found himself facing his twin.

"Pasha?" he asked aloud, testing the speaker system.

"Yes, it's me."

Her avatar looked at him with all too perfect human eyes, their glinting black irises set in bloodless whites and framed in heavy lashes. No other realistic feature appeared on that smooth face. No hair, no brows, no nose, and only a motionless black horizontal slash where a mouth should be. Urban assumed he looked the same.

Tio Suthrom spoke from behind him, in a voice soft and wary. "My companion, the Invention Ashok, made these avatars from my own design. It used a basic ancestral form since we had no data on your individual appearances. I hope you are not offended."

"Of course we're not," Pasha said as she stared past Urban.

Urban, meanwhile, was wondering what "the Invention Ashok" might be. Something invented, referred to as *it*? In his mind, this suggested a form of artificial intelligence. And not a Dull Intelligence, because who would describe the bland tool of a DI as a companion?

A true artificial intelligence, then?

The possibility induced a mental shiver that the avatar did not have the capacity to display. Nothing good had ever come out of the creation of true artificial intelligences.

All these thoughts, encapsulated in the moment it took him to turn around. Then he caught sight of Tio Suthrom—and his urge to ask about the 'companion' evaporated.

Situated a polite distance away, the pilot of *Alaka'i Onyx* continued to discuss the avatars, using a deferential tone while gesturing with an open hand. "The design of these forms can be enhanced of course, just as mine has been. You only need to provide the specifications."

Tio Suthrom's version had definitely been enhanced.

He appeared as an entity modified from the ancestral human form, clearly adapted to low and zero gravity situations. He had a short, slender body with extremely long arms, jointed with three segments instead of two. His thin legs were ancestral, but his feet echoed the Sakurans, with grasping toes. He wore no clothing and was as sexless as Urban's avatar, though he had a detailed and fully human face, masculine in the weight of the jaw and brow ridge, and in the bushy white eyebrows. White was his color. The irises of his eyes were white. So was his glossy skin. Instead of hair, white tentacles sprouted from his scalp like those of that aquatic creature, an anemone. A fringe of shorter tentacles surrounded his mouth and covered his jaw and neck, as if to substitute for a beard.

"You find me strange?" Tio Suthrom asked, now with a note of challenge.

Urban kept his voice neutral. "It's not a variant I've seen before. But then, we are a conservative people."

"Great adventurers all the same," Tio Suthrom observed. His shoulders relaxed, his voice softened, and he tapped his chest. "Like yours, this is an artificial avatar. It has no biological elements and it does not represent the way I looked in my first life. But it is my customary form now. I chose it because I wanted to deny my heritage and appear less human."

Urban would have smiled at such a leading statement, except he found his avatar too simple to display the expression. Tio Suthrom surely expected to be asked about the reason he had come to such a resolve, but Urban did not want him determining the direction of this conversation. So he signaled Pasha to refrain and offered a bland response instead. "I do want to enhance this avatar so it reflects my true appearance. And you, Pasha?"

"Yes."

They messaged Lam Lha for body maps, sending them to addresses specified by Tio Suthrom, and over the next few minutes their avatars gradually adopted their true forms. In that time, Urban studied their surroundings.

They were in a warren, drifting within a junction of three tunnels all partially blocked by large, loaf-like objects. From beyond those objects came the glint of shifting, multicolored lights—a distinct contrast to the junction.

Here, numerous small geometric shapes—circles, triangles, rings, crosses, various polyhedrons—were embedded in the lightly scalloped, metallic brown walls. Perhaps their arrangement conveyed some meaning, though it looked random to him. Each shape glowed a too-bright white, generating complex glints across the uneven surface.

Urban supposed the warren to be pressurized; if it wasn't, then his hearing was simulated. To test the hypothesis, he brushed a hand swiftly past his avatar's face and felt the slight pressure change of a puff of air. Probably a thin atmosphere. From the familiar way it conducted sound, he supposed it to be composed of common gases. And the temperature? Hmm . . . the avatar lacked that sense. He could not perceive if the warren was hot or cold.

He looked again at the tunnel-blocking objects. In the white light, they appeared to be a dull copper color, mottled with a shadowy pattern. He only now noticed that each looked out on the junction with two small glistening black spots suggestive of eyes—though the spots could as easily be chemical surfaces rather than photoreceptors. Urban guessed the objects to be some kind of quiescent machine. Their size and shape suggested the warren had been designed for them.

He stretched, his body still unclothed but opaque now and familiar, detailed with finger and toe nails, genitals, smooth male breasts, hair where appropriate, and a face he could feel.

He glanced at Pasha, nude as well, her skin pale, blond hair at her crotch, and delicate pink nipples exposed on her small breasts. She caught his gaze and rolled her now-green eyes. Then she turned to Tio Suthrom, saying, "You didn't want to admit the scout-bots to this place. Why?"

And again he answered without elaboration, "It is a question of scale." He pointed to each of the three machines. "These are three instances of the Invention Ashok. That is a name it chose for my convenience since it is too difficult for me to refer to it by its binary designation."

He went on, "Ashok is my companion. Nine instances comprise its cohort. The other six instances are presently in the hive, continuing their ongoing study of Ryo. But because Ashok is very curious about you, three instances have emerged to study you. It wants to learn if you are as mad and dangerous as those people who once lived here at Ryo."

This time, with the avatar's enhancements, Urban managed a bitter half smile. But once again he refused to follow Tio Suthrom's lead, gesturing instead at the nearest instance. "So these . . . *inventions*. They are devices, a kind of machine . . . right?"

"Ashok is a synthetic," Tio Suthrom agreed. "Unchained from biology and unpolluted by it."

Disappointment swept in. Urban had allowed himself to imagine Tio Suthrom had found some remnant of an alien race that had survived the depredations of the Chenzeme. But these were just tools.

"What do you use them for?" he asked. "Are they a kind of avatar? Are they even functional?"

He asked this last question because none of the objects had

shown any sign of activity. No sound emanated from them, they had not moved, and there was no display of lights to indicate a ready state.

But as if to demonstrate functionality, a small black oval abruptly emerged beneath the eye spots of each machine, looking like the nose of some plump burrowing creature whose name Urban could not immediately bring to mind.

The oval 'noses' proved to be audio speakers. They simultaneously emitted a cheery and very human male voice. Higher pitched than Tio Suthrom's, it filled the junction with multidirectional sound, declaring, "Oh yes, I am functional. But Inventions do not waste energy on extraneous movement or display, as biological forms so often do."

"You're not an avatar, then?" Urban asked uneasily. "You're a machine intelligence? An *embodied* machine intelligence?"

"That is correct in a general sense, if 'machine' is deemed as one domain of life, and 'biological' another. Still, 'machine' is a very general term encompassing many forms that are not life at all. In this language, a more precise term is 'synthetic.' So in your language, the major domains of life can be best described as synthetics, biologicals, and informationals."

"Informationals being entities within virtual worlds?" Pasha asked with keen interest.

"Yes, exactly."

"But these three domains are not separate," she said. "We humans are biologicals but we can access the informational domain." She gestured with her avatar's arms. "And here, we are inhabiting a synthetic medium."

"I conjecture that it is the inherent nature of biological intelligences to define and re-define themselves."

Tio Suthrom nodded at this, and muttered bitterly, "If it can be done, it will be done, though it leads to our destruction." His eyes took in Pasha, and then Urban. "Unlike us, the Inventions understand their purpose and accept their limitations, and by itself that predicts they will be a long-lived clade."

Urban eyed the three synthetics with a sense of looming

trepidation . . . these *Inventions*. (No, that was wrong. They were three instances of a singular being . . . weren't they? He remained unsure.)

He did know, he *believed*, artificial entities were supposed to be tools. Tools only. Because if allowed autonomy and will, they might direct their own evolution and quickly overwhelm all life around them. And though the existence of the Cryptologist had tested the boundaries of that belief, she at least was human.

Not so, Ashok.

Maybe not at all, not even in its origin.

The avatar Urban occupied was not so finely made that he could feel a prickle of fear on the back of his neck. Still, he imagined the feeling as suspicion re-spawned in his mind.

"You're not a human invention, are you?" Urban asked. "That's what Tio Suthrom was implying when he said the struggle to survive the marauders is not just a human challenge."

"Our Inventors are not human," Ashok agreed. "They are biologicals evolved long ago on a distant world. A thriving people, until the marauders discovered them. It is said in our records that their world was scourged so deeply immense lava flows poured through the crust, destroying all chance at life. After that event, a new world was required, one far away. Likely systems were determined from surviving astronomical records, and to each such system a single cohort of Inventions was sent, instructed to replicate and diversify, and thence in our numbers to prepare a new home for the Inventors and for ourselves. That is our purpose."

"And have the Inventors come?" Pasha asked.

"No. They will not come until we have completed our task."

Urban touched a knuckle to his chin, his thoughts rushing. He considered where they were, *when* they were, and the ruins of Ryo that lay outside this ship.

He said, "You must have been sent out from the Inventors' world a long time ago. Thousands of years, at least, and this is no longer the system you expected to find. Is it? All the planets that once were here, now gone."

"Ryo is not our target system," Ashok said with unvarying calm.

"We are here at Ryo to survey for potential hazards in the stellar neighborhood."

"A nearby system, then," Urban said. "Is it damaged too?"

"You are correct. The system we now occupy shares the issue you have described. The planet we are assigned to develop no longer exists. It is a situation that has complicated and greatly prolonged our preparations because, unlike us, our Inventors require the dense structure and gravity of a world."

Urban guessed the truth. "You, your . . . *people?*" He groped for the right words. "The Inventions . . . you are behind the activity we've seen at Hupo Sei. Aren't you?"

All those glints and hints of growth at Hupo Sei that he'd seen through the fleet's telescopes—he'd imagined it as evidence of human survivors or of human descendants, or at least of life arising out of the human experience. Now disappointment afflicted him—almost shame—that it wasn't so, that humankind had failed so miserably. And yet keen excitement existed too, and wonder at the alien origin of the artifacts his telescopes had shown him. Heretofore, in all the histories recorded in *Dragon's* library, the only functional alien artifacts ever encountered had belonged to factions of the Chenzeme, making the artifacts at Hupo Sei utterly unique.

But the Inventions were not the Inventors. So was there really alien life at Hupo Sei? Could the Inventions be called life? Should they be, even if theirs was a domain different from the biological?

The idea of it disturbed him, unsettled him, but now, growing more used to it, it intrigued him too. It *gripped* him. Hadn't he come to the Hallowed Vasties to seek for unexpected wonders amid the ruins? And what could be more unexpected than to find a clade of alien life here, so close to the lost heart of human civilization?

If it was life.

"It is Hupo Sei, isn't it?" he pressed.

Urban could parse no meaning from Ashok's appearance, but he found Tio Suthrom's cold glare easy to interpret.

"We are not your enemy, Tio Suthrom."

"Are you not?" he demanded. "Open your eyes and look around you! Look at the destruction here at Ryo, the senseless ruin at Hupo Sei, the rubble at Quin-ken and Bengali. So many beautiful worlds once known to me and now destroyed—not by the marauders but by *us*. Humanity. The Earth clade. We are a territorial species more deadly, more destructive than the marauders ever were. And you want the Inventions to trust you? To believe you are not the enemy? That you are not here to reclaim the system they are making into their own?"

"We are not your enemy," Urban repeated. "We are not seeking territory. And you need to understand that what happened here among these worlds was an attack from outside, an assault by an ancient alien virus. A behavioral virus. An adaptive weapon designed to reinvent any species it encountered. It might have been meant as a benign gift that would meld individual minds into one transcendent being. But here in the Hallowed Vasties, transcendence failed. Great powers rose out of the cordons and wars of dominance followed. *That* is what we learned at Tanjiri."

He felt pressure against the arm of his avatar: Pasha's hand, squeezing, a gesture urging him not to push too hard. Looking from Tio Suthrom to Ashok, she said, "The virus Urban speaks of is no longer a threat. We neutralized it long ago. Know that our ship is safe, and that you will be safe if you visit us. We invite you. Come visit our ship. Both of you. All of you. We have a landing ship. We can transport you."

Urban swiftly agreed. "Sooth, come see who we are."

Tio Suthrom resisted, shaking his head. "No, Ashok. It is too dangerous for you."

"It is no more dangerous to stay than to go. Both choices are subject to the good will of these human marauders. We live only as they allow it."

"No," Urban said. "We will not harm you, whatever choice you make."

"My choice is made," Ashok replied. "The hive will go."

Tio Suthrom's mouth opened in shock. "The full hive? You mean to leave me?"

"Yes, my friend, if you do not choose to send an avatar. For myself, I cannot decline this opportunity to expand my knowledge of local hazards, regardless of the risk."

"We're *not* a hazard," Urban insisted, half laughing in exasperation until he remembered the conflict *Dragon*'s presence had induced at Tanjiri. He knew then that wasn't true.

CHAPTER FIFTEEN

ASHOK'S VISIT HAD to wait until *Dragon* drew close enough to deploy the landing ship, and complicated maneuvers would be required before then. *Dragon* must slow down, while Tio Suthrom's great ship needed to accelerate to more closely match the courser's velocity. So it would be many days before the synthetic departed *Alaka'i Onyx*. Plenty of time to learn more about the Inventions.

Urban stayed with Ashok for several hours, accompanying one of its instances, peppering it with questions that the Invention answered cheerfully as it moved through what proved to be an intricate warren.

The instance had a gel-like constitution. It elongated as it dove through the tunnel junctions, puffing up again as it roved the tunnels on tiny clawed feet. Ashok never lingered in the junctions, though Urban wished it would. For him, the junctions were nodes of calm, a steady-state environment, and predictable. Except for the arrangement of the glowing symbols, every junction looked like every other.

In contrast, the tunnel walls were all active surfaces, encrusted with a multitude of artifacts always in motion. Flows of shifting color circled the tunnels and transited up and down their lengths, as if a discordant liquid rainbow was being pumped from beneath the surface to flood a complex terrain. A terrain in motion: a tactile geography composed of flocks of tiny bumps, some rounded, others like bars or pyramids, forever erupting and collapsing.

Ashok often paused, extruding soft, flexible, feathery appendages that it swept across the shifting surfaces. There was a grid of

what Urban interpreted as symbols; a crackle of thin white light-
ning bolts within a black glass panel; a blue panel that gave the
impression of extreme depth like an infinite planetary sky.

Ashok did not object when Urban touched these things. Indeed,
he had no choice but to touch them, since he had to propel himself
through the tunnels and stop when Ashok stopped. Unfortunately,
the sensation of 'touch,' as implemented by the artificial avatar,
did not yield information beyond hard/soft/rough/smooth, and
the surfaces never reacted to the contact.

"What is all this?" Urban asked—more than once.

Ashok answered, "Simulations." And later, "Mapping functions," and also, "Compositional analyses."

Probably most of it was being used to observe and model the
complex debris field around Ryo, but Urban could not grasp *how*,
the means of it remaining opaque to his senses. Opaque and
alien. The meaning of that latter word became ever more deeply
impressed upon his mind. And yet despite their wildly different
origins and divergent senses, he quickly grasped that Inventions
were both curious and intellectually ambitious beings, and with
this realization, an idea came to him: a bright sparkling possibility
that required time to fully consider.

So, saying goodbye to Ashok, he yielded his avatar to Shoran,
who was first in line among other Dragoneers eager to visit the
great ship and its unexpected inhabitant.

Returning to *Dragon*, Urban merged with his ghost on the high
bridge. He brought with him his sense of wonder, allowing it to
spill out across the philosopher cells, rousing their curiosity.

Apart from the cells, he was alone there, making it easy to
orchestrate the attention of the field, to direct it toward the great
ship, plainly visible now to their far-ranging senses. He visual-
ized for them the domains of life Ashok had described and they
responded with intense curiosity, searching the memories they
carried, plunging into deep time, seeking for a similar experience.

A meaningful proportion of the field's shared memories had
been lost at Tanjiri, when Urban had purged the most violent
and aggressive cell lines. And more memories had gone when the

Cryptologist re-engineered the surviving cells. Even so, great segments of history remained and it was not impossible that the field retained a memory of the death of the Inventors' world.

So much death. So much lost to the past. Yet life lay ahead at Hupo Sei. Ashok had confirmed it. Synthetic life, it was true, though Urban did not find that idea so disturbing now that he knew more of the Inventions and their history.

The original cohort had arrived at Hupo Sei more than seventeen hundred years ago. Tens of thousands of cohorts had been spawned since then in diverse forms dictated by their intended purpose—though all shared an innate curiosity and a drive to create.

During their first years at Hupo Sei, the Inventions had confined their activities to exploring the ruins. Only when they confirmed the system to be essentially uninhabited did they begin to gather and sort matter, and then to build, spinning out habitats in hundreds of forms and in a spectrum of sizes, filling them with synthetic life.

All this they did for themselves. For the Inventors, they resolved to re-create a world out of the ruins. It was an ongoing effort, that Ashok regarded with open skepticism.

"As you measure time," it had explained, "this new world has been one thousand seven hundred twenty-five years in the making. Year by year, more matter accumulates in this proto-world— but even after so long it does not have mass enough to collapse on itself. We skeptics have designated it the Labyrinth—that is the parallel term in your language—because it is an unstable amalgamation of broken megastructures and remnant debris. But the Originalists—they are a faction among us—insist that it is for us to replace the Inventor's lost world, no matter the energy and time such a project will require. The *immense* time. Half a billion years at least. That is the optimistic estimate."

Listening to Ashok, an intriguing possibility had blossomed in Urban's mind. At Tanjiri, the composite being known as Ezo had generated a blade and used it to create a living world. Could such a feat be repeated at Hupo Sei, speeding the work of the Inventions?

Maybe. But only if the Cryptologist could be persuaded to reveal what she knew of blades. She might though, if the goal was to aid these strange migrants.

Urban said nothing of it yet. He resolved to say nothing until he learned far more of the Inventions and of their factions, their ethics, their goals. But the possibility was there, a bright point in his mind. And he liked Ashok, even as he recognized that the synthetic's personality was surely artificial, shaped to successfully engage with Tio Suthrom.

What is life?

So many possible answers to such a simple question, leaving him more eager than ever to visit Hupo Sei and see for himself what sort of life the Inventions had chosen and to learn for himself if there was after all truth in the ancient taboo forbidding the creation of free and free-thinking machines.

CHAPTER SIXTEEN

JOLLY'S LUCK HAD run out.

At Tanjiri, random chance had awarded him a place among the team that visited the Sakurans. He'd been with the first delegation to the Narans too. And he'd been lucky enough—if it could be called luck—to be first to venture to Prakruti, in the company of the Cryptologist.

But here at Ryo, chance was not on his side. In the randomized list of Dragoneers wanting a turn to visit the alien warren aboard *Alaka'i Onyx*, his name had come up last. Given there were only two artificial avatars, it was going to be some time before his turn came. But he would happily give up that turn altogether to be the one accompanying Riffan on a real visit to the great ship.

Barefoot, dressed in shorts and a simple pullover shirt, he squeezed into a transit bubble with Abby. She held his hand, the smooth glove of her lavender skin suit cool against the flesh of his palm. Smiling with irrepressible delight, she pulled him into an embrace that he returned, her skin suit slick beneath his hands. She kissed his lips, his cheeks, murmuring, "I still can't believe I get to go. I only wish you could come too."

"So do I," he admitted with a little forced laugh.

Everything about the discovery of *Alaka'i Onyx* fascinated him—but frustrated him too, because he had no part in it beyond extracting a promise from Urban to protect the strange vessel. A needless promise, as it turned out, since *Griffin* had been taken over before the other Clemantine even knew what was out there.

Jolly wanted to do so much more, to contribute more, to *see* more, with his own eyes. He longed for wider horizons than the gee deck.

He said nothing of this to Abby, determined to cast no shadow on her joy. Kissing her cheek, he told her, "If it's not me, I'm glad it's you and Riffan who get to go. Just think about it! You'll be the first to meet, *actually* meet, an alien intelligence. That's awesome. It's amazing!"

As he said this, the transit bubble reached *Argo*, opening onto the interior of the little landing ship. Riffan was already there in his amber skin suit. "Hey Abby! Right on time."

"Of course!" she declared with a laugh. "Nothing could make me miss this." She gave Jolly one more kiss. "*Bye*," she whispered, and pushed off, leaving him in the transit bubble while she moved ahead, riding her luck into *Argo*.

Only after the transit bubble closed and began to automatically ferry him back to the warren, did Jolly allow his glum mood to surface. But a deep sigh did little to relieve the pressure on a heart weighed down by what he could only describe as spiritual claustrophobia.

The transit bubble returned him to the warren, with its waving tendrils of wall-weed. No one was about, leaving him free to complain out loud.

"I miss planets," he murmured, wondering how many years, how many centuries would have to pass before he stood on a living world again.

He did not regret leaving Verilotus. Still, he doubted he would ever reconcile his mind to the vast gulfs of space and time between star systems. Even Urban needed to modify his persona, taking on the aspect of the Sentinel to endure the years.

As if summoned by this thought, Urban spoke his name: *Jolly.*

Jolly gripped a strand of wall-weed and glanced around, startled at the queer timing of this query. *Where are you?* he asked, even as he checked the personnel map.

To Jolly's surprise, the map showed Urban back in his chamber in the warren, even while every other Dragoneer—other than

Riffan and Abby—crowded the gee deck, drawn there, drawn together and animated by the miraculous discovery of alien life.

Why are you here by yourself? Jolly asked, abandoning his plan to return to the gee deck, backtracking to Urban's chamber instead. The door opened for him, then closed after he clambered inside.

Urban lay as before, unclothed, as if just emerged from cold sleep, with strands of wall-weed twining around his long figure. He eyed Jolly with a sleepy expression.

"You're still out there with the missiles," Jolly guessed. "Why? Don't you trust yourself to control *Griffin*?"

"I'm not with *Griffin* anymore. I left that ship to the Cryptologist."

"On her own?" Jolly asked, incredulous.

"She's not alone. She has the Bio-mechanic."

"Ah. Okay . . . I guess."

Jolly did not want to talk more about the Cryptologist. Her visit to Ezo had changed her. She'd become a different, more aloof being. And everything had changed between them. He still missed the person she used to be.

Urban said, "I'm sorry you didn't get a seat on *Argo*. I know you wanted to go."

"A lot of people wanted to go, but luck was with Riffan and Abby." He frowned. "Luck is *always* with Riffan."

Urban chuckled. "Sooth. I've noticed."

Then, tentatively, Jolly asked, "What was it like to visit the synthetic's warren that first time?"

Urban's eyes narrowed. "You've run the simulation. You know exactly what it was like."

"What it looked like, yes. What you learned there. But what did it *feel* like? To be the first one there, the first to experience it—"

"Hey, it wasn't just me. Pasha was there."

"It must have been amazing, fascinating," Jolly enthused.

"Confusing," Urban confessed with a flash of a smile. "I had no idea what I was seeing. I still have no idea."

"Alien."

"Yes. Alien." A shrug. "Your turn to visit—"

"Won't be for a while," Jolly interrupted sourly.

"It'll come, and you'll get to see and feel for yourself."

Not technically true. "I'll see it through the avatar, though I don't think that's going to be any different from experiencing the simulation."

"Of course it will be, because you'll be in control of the avatar and able to ask your own questions."

Jolly hesitated. He didn't *want* to complain. No, that wasn't right. He didn't want to sound like he was complaining.

"Say it," Urban urged, eyeing him with an annoyed squint.

Jolly looked askance before admitting, "I feel like I've already been there. Over and over, with all the simulations I've run. I'm going to go when my turn comes, but it won't be like a new experience."

"Sooth. But this is just the start, Jolly. There's more to come. There's wonder in this encounter. So keep an open mind, because the existence of the Inventions, their alien nature and history and needs, is sure to open up possibilities we would never have truly considered before."

Jolly responded to this pronouncement with a short, surprised, skeptical laugh. He couldn't help himself. It was too weird. First, because Urban never indulged in such romanticism. His second objection he spoke aloud, "Come on, Urban. You always consider *every* possibility. You're the one who wanted to make a blade."

Urban tensed, eyes narrowing in a cold, cautious gaze. "I still do," he said softly.

"I don't. I never would."

A bold denial that induced a flash of anger, of disappointment, there and gone on Urban's face. "It doesn't matter," he concluded, turning away.

Feeling miffed himself, Jolly almost left then. But that would leave things awkward between them and he didn't want that. So he forged on, attempting to draw Urban out with a question. "Do you think we'll stay here at Ryo? Or go on directly to Hupo Sei? I know a lot of people think we should stay and take the time to survey the ruins, since we're here anyway."

Urban turned back, eyed him thoughtfully, and asked, "What would you rather do?"

"I want to go on. Ryo is all dust and failure, but at Hupo Sei there are thousands of thriving habitats to explore."

This won a slight smile. "Sooth. I feel the same."

Jolly smiled in turn, pleased to be allied with Urban, and not at cross purposes. "We need to convince the other Dragoneers."

"No, we need to convince the Inventions. We possess technologies they've never encountered before and can't begin to understand. That makes us dangerous, Jolly. And when Ashok's reports reach their decision-making body—Ashok calls it the Core Forum—they're going to be afraid."

Jolly nodded thoughtfully. Any initial encounter between alien entities must surely be utterly unpredictable and laden with potential dangers. But this was not an initial encounter. "The Inventions already know a lot about humans through the pilot, Tio Suthrom."

Urban rolled his eyes. "That's part of the problem. Tio Suthrom believes humans to be inherently violent and deplorable, with the ruins of both Ryo and Hupo Sei as proof. We need to persuade Ashok it isn't always so, because only Ashok can persuade the Core Forum to set aside caution and *let* us come. I won't approach Hupo Sei without their explicit permission. Keep that in mind, when it's your turn to visit Ashok."

Jolly kept it in mind.

Prior to his visit, he ran every sim recorded by other Dragoneers who had visited before him. He listened to their discussions with Ashok, and absorbed their observations. No one—neither Ashok nor any Dragoneer—had yet broached the possibility of a visit to Hupo Sei. The advantage of being last, Jolly decided, was that Ashok would be thoroughly accustomed to humans and hard to startle.

By the time his ghost inscribed its appearance on one of the artificial avatars, he felt he knew his way around the alien warren, and he was able to chat amiably with the single instance of Ashok escorting him. After a time, he asked, "I wonder if we all seem mostly the same to you. Each one of us only a little different from any other?"

"This is correct," Ashok assured him in a pleasantly cheerful voice. "Your species presents minimal design variation. But there is sufficient difference in trivial details to allow me to distinguish and recognize individual entities."

"It's not like that with your people, is it?" And without waiting for an answer, Jolly plunged on, saying what no one else had dared to say for fear of receiving a hard *No*. "Ashok, you must know we Dragoneers desire to visit Hupo Sei, to observe the Inventions in their diversity, and the creations they have made. Do you think the Core Forum would allow it?"

For several seconds, Ashok said nothing. If the synthetic had breathed, Jolly would have called it a breathless silence. When it finally spoke again, Ashok said only, "The future is fluid. I cannot say."

While Jolly had hoped for more, he took comfort in this answer, telling Urban later, "At least it was not a denial."

CHAPTER SEVENTEEN

RIFFAN'S EYES EASED open: a gentle waking after days of hibernation in one of *Argo*'s acceleration couches. He stretched and flexed, his amber skin suit moving with him.

Random selection had favored Riffan once again: he had won the first of only two seats aboard the lander, making it his privilege, and Abby's, to physically meet—flesh to gel, so to speak—the cohort of alien synthetics that called itself Ashok.

"Are we there?" Abby murmured from the couch beside him.

Argo answered her. "Affirmative. The planned rendezvous with the great ship, *Alaka'i Onyx*, has been accomplished. Course and speed are a match, with a distance of twenty meters between the two vessels. Communication has been established and *Alaka'i Onyx* has spawned a tunnel to bridge the gap."

"Not much left for us to do then," Abby said, sounding disgruntled.

Riffan replied with an opposing enthusiasm. "Except to say hello to the first intelligent and friendly alien life ever encountered in our known history." He pushed away from his couch, generating a slight momentum that sent him floating across a cabin empty of everything except their two stacked acceleration couches. They did not even have go-packs, wanting to ensure there would be room enough for Ashok's full cohort.

As Abby followed Riffan's lead, she admitted, "It's still hard for me to think of this synthetic entity as 'life.'"

"That is the bias of our culture," Riffan agreed, reaching out to catch a hand-hold beside the gel membrane of *Argo*'s lock.

Abby joined him there, wearing a lavender skin suit, hood down, with her long black hair confined in a braided coil. She raised an eyebrow, fixed him with a challenging gaze: "Alkimbra says it's not bias, it's experience. A lesson learned and repeated more than once in our long history." Her serious demeanor evaporated. She laughed in giddy excitement and added, "But Urban says to give them a chance—because they're not human-made machines, after all."

"Possibly a factor in their favor," Riffan agreed.

He turned to a wall screen displaying the tunnel's interior, with a view all the way across to the great ship's red-lit lock. The lock was still empty, its inner door closed.

Only Ashok would enter the tunnel. A protocol had been worked out that called for Riffan and Abby to wait behind *Argo*'s gel membrane for the synthetic to arrive.

Since *Alaka'i Onyx* had generated the tunnel, Riffan expected it to be filled with Ashok's preferred atmosphere—reportedly a low-oxygen mix that minimized the hazardous side effects of the highly reactive gas. Instead, a read-out at the base of the screen informed him the air in the tunnel was ship standard.

"Well, that's odd," he muttered, pointing at the data. Because as a machine—Riffan mentally corrected himself—as a *synthetic*, Ashok surely did not breathe.

"Motion detected," *Argo*'s DI announced.

At the same time, Abby murmured in breathless excitement, "*There!*"

The inner door of *Alaka'i Onyx*'s lock opened, revealing a human figure beyond, slightly bent to fit within the limits of a transit bubble. A fully human figure.

"Is that Tio Suthrom?" Abby wondered aloud.

Riffan blinked in surprise. It didn't look like him. At least, it didn't look like the avatar the strange, misanthropic pilot had used during his first and only appearance within the tunnel habitat. Was this Tio Suthrom's natural aspect? A man of moderate height, beardless, with long dark-brown hair bound behind his neck and pale skin. He wore a dark-green skin suit, nearly black. His black eyes gazed at the camera as he announced aloud, in Tio Suthrom's voice, "I have created this avatar to accompany Ashok."

Riffan frowned, murmuring to himself, "This was not in the plan."

"It's in the plan now," Abby said. Then she addressed the ship. "*Argo*, is it possible to synthesize a third acceleration couch?"

"Negative. *Argo* does not carry all the required raw elements."

"Could you synthesize a cold-sleep cocoon?" Riffan asked.

"Affirmative."

"Then do so. Enhance it to compensate for our expected acceleration. I'll use the cocoon. Tio can use my couch."

While he was speaking, Abby slipped into the membrane. "*Abby!*" Riffan barked and grabbed at her, too late.

She disappeared into the gel and a moment later the wall screen showed her emerging into the tunnel, her back to him, one hand raised in greeting.

Ashok had been designed for the purpose of gathering, analyzing, and organizing information and it had done so. All throughout the time the Dragoneer-humans visited *Alaka'i Onyx*, it questioned them as they questioned it in turn. A satisfying exchange.

These Dragoneer-humans understood information was precious, and that it must be preserved and shared. Ashok knew—albeit with a significant degree of uncertainty as this knowledge was based solely on the Dragoneer-humans' own testimony—that they replicated their library across the vessels of their fleet. Similarly, Ashok sent reports leaping back along the chain of communication buoys linking it to the cohorts at Hupo Sei, describing all that it learned and everything it suspected.

The Dragoneer-humans had not answered Ashok's every question; they had not shared all they knew. But they had shared much.

Ashok now recognized the names and countenances of each of those forty-three individuals who had visited it by successively occupying the two mutable avatars. It had learned many details of the Dragoneer-humans' history, cross-checking their most ancient knowledge with the library aboard *Alaka'i Onyx*. It knew the number, kind, and location of their various ships—data subsequently confirmed when *Alaka'i Onyx* performed a radar sweep. And, most intriguing, it knew those ships used methods of propulsion presently alien to its understanding—a formidable challenge it desired to overcome.

Now, separate from Tio Suthrom, it ferried through the ship's tissue in a transit bubble, bound for *Alaka'i Onyx*'s lock.

Tio Suthrom had mostly contempt for his own kind, so convincing the ghost-human to accompany Ashok had required persuasion: "*I need you, my friend. You comprise an additional set of senses that will supply an alternative perspective on all we observe, and you will bring a useful insight into the diversities of human behavior.*"

Ashok had *not* suggested that Tio Suthrom assume its natural biological avatar with all its inherent microbiology. The ghost-human decided to do that on its own, and when Ashok objected, expressing programmed revulsion, Tio Suthrom explained, "Familiarity in form is important to biologicals. I will find swifter acceptance and friendship maybe, in a fully human avatar."

Ashok logged the possibility of unspoken subtext in this answer, but declined to probe, concerned it might unbalance Tio Suthrom's always-volatile emotional state.

In its cheerful voice it said, "I concede to your judgment, my friend. You shall focus on pleasing your conspecifics rather than pleasing me."

Even so, Ashok insisted on ferrying to the lock in a separate transit bubble from his companion's new avatar, putting off as long as possible the inevitability of biological contamination.

Abby emerged from *Argo*'s gel lock into the tunnel.

The tunnel's opaque wall glowed gently white with no hand holds marring its smooth surface—nothing to grab onto! Abby tried clawing the wall—and to her relief, she found the substance that composed it to be softly yielding. Digging her fingers in, she arrested her minor momentum.

With that accomplished, she looked up, offering a bright smile to this handsome man who must be *Alaka'i Onyx*'s pilot, and said, "Welcome, Tio Suthrom."

Only then did she think to ask, "You *are* Tio Suthrom?"

A slight nod, accompanied by a pink flush that warmed his pale cheeks.

Tio Suthrom had not been present in the warren when Abby visited there. From what she'd heard, he had not been present at all after Urban and Pasha's initial visit. So she felt it important to assure him he was welcome now.

"Excellent!" she enthused. "We're so pleased you decided to visit us. My name is Abby and it's my honor to welcome you."

Immediately, she wondered if she had overdone it, because instead of answering, Tio Suthrom dug his fingers into the tunnel wall, bringing his progress to a halt. He looked back toward *Alaka'i Onyx* as if debating a retreat.

Riffan spoke in her atrium: *Don't scare him, Abby. Remember it's been a long time, millennia maybe, since this man has seen another human being.*

"Please stay," Abby said softly.

Tio Suthrom looked at her again, his face stern in that way of so many men when they are uneasy. A short nod, accompanied by gruff words. "It is my plan to stay and to ensure at all stages that Ashok's accommodation is appropriate."

Abby responded with another bright smile. Resolved to win his trust, she allowed no hint of offense in her voice. "Yes, of course."

He had relayed a technical diagram of a converter that would allow Ashok to draw electrical power from a ship's system. The Engineer had overseen the installation of an improved version aboard *Argo* and another in one of the pocket parks on *Dragon*'s gee deck.

Abby told the pilot, "The electrical connection is as you requested. Would you like to inspect it now?"

Ashok's voice emanated from the far end of the tunnel, softened by distance and sounding very far away. "I will test the connection myself and adjust as needed."

Abby shifted in an effort to see past Tio Suthrom, surprised that she had not noticed Ashok emerging from *Alakaʻi Onyx*'s lock—and even more surprised that she still did not see the Invention. No . . . wait. *There.*

Eclipsed behind Tio Suthrom but already halfway across the tunnel, there came the nine instances of Ashok. Their compact copper-colored gelatinous bodies advanced in orderly ranks of three.

Abby gasped in wonder. The instances were not what she'd expected. In the tunnels of *Alakaʻi Onyx* Ashok had been a bulky entity, as tall as a person . . . or at least as tall as the avatars the Dragoneers had occupied. But now Ashok appeared at miniature scale, each of its identical instances a mere fifteen centimeters in length and half that in height—roughly the size of those softly furred mammals known as guinea pigs, familiar to her from children's dramas.

She pushed off, moving gently down the tunnel, skirting past Tio Suthrom to get a better look.

"Is this you, Ashok?" she asked. "Or is it a miniature version of you?"

An audio speaker surfaced on one of the lead instances. Ashok answered in its ever-cheerful voice, "Cohorts are singular and do not directly replicate. This is my only version."

Its instances did not glide. Instead they crawled along the tunnel wall, clinging with the claws of their tiny feet. Abby eyed the first rank of three as they scurried past her. As the second rank passed, she turned to follow, laughing in delight at the surprise of their small size.

It is a matter of scale, Riffan murmured. *That was Tio Suthrom's explanation of why the scout-bots were denied entry into Ashok's warren—and even with that hint, we had such deeply held expectations of scale it didn't occur to us this synthetic might vary so greatly from our own.*

"I love it," Abby declared aloud. "*We* should explore the viability of such a scale. I mean, why are we the size we are? If we were as small as the avatars in Ashok's warren, the gee deck would feel so much larger!"

"Life takes many forms and offers many possibilities," Ashok responded, speaking from an instance that had paused beside her as its companions continued on. "It all truly is a wonder. Consider the marauder ship that is your home. It is alive and intelligent, and as large a lifeform as I have ever imagined."

"And you are alive and intelligent and so small I could easily hold you in one hand."

"Only the one instance," Ashok amended.

She became suddenly aware of Tio Suthrom looming just behind her right shoulder. "The Inventions are not toys," he warned her. "And they are not mere intelligent machines. They are questioning and creative and endowed with a sense of wonder that lets them recognize the intrinsic value of all things." His voice, already low, grew even deeper, resonant and unsettling. "They are not like us. They would never, *could* never, replicate the wanton destruction and the horrifying extinctions our own species has inflicted on ourselves, on our clade, and on so many worlds."

By this time, Abby had turned to meet his hard-eyed gaze. She had never before been so close to such bitter animosity and it frightened her. It left her feeling confused and vulnerable in a way she had never known before. In a voice barely above a whisper she answered him, "We are not all like that. We don't have to be. We can learn to be better."

"Can we?" he asked her doubtfully.

He did not wait for an answer, turning instead and making his way up the tunnel, following the nine instances of Ashok to the gel membrane. Abby crossed her arms and glared after him, deeply suspicious that he did not want to hear an answer countering his dark view of human history.

A calming breath, a soft sigh, and she started to follow. But then something moved on the periphery of her vision. She flinched in surprise—and then had to jam her fingers into the tunnel wall to stabilize herself as a tenth instance of Ashok crawled past her.

Or was this Ashok?

Uncertainty gripped her. This instance did not look the same as the other instances, though there were similarities. It shared the cohort's gel-like constitution and tiny clawed feet, but not its dull copper color. It was gray instead. More importantly, it was three times as long as the others, with four pairs of stubby legs instead of just two.

Could it be a unique persona?

She looked to Ashok for guidance, but a glance up the tunnel showed her that the synthetic's nine instances and Suthrom too had already passed through the gel membrane.

In growing apprehension, she followed the anomalous instance and then darted past it, keeping as much distance from it as she could. Once ahead of it, she turned around.

"Hello," she said to it in the friendliest voice she could manage.

It said nothing. Its steady pace up the tunnel did not waver. She had to back away as it advanced, to keep it from marching past her a second time.

She tried addressing it again, though this time she heard a quaver of confusion in her voice. "Greetings, stranger. Hello? Hello?"

Only when she felt the gel membrane at her back did she give it up. Twisting around, she dove through the barrier.

Ashok's long acquaintance with Tio Suthrom had allowed it to refine the module it used to interact with him. Through the module, it could emulate human inflections in its generated voice, and also imitate certain physiological signals useful for enhancing communication. And so, as its first instance spilled into the cavernous space of *Argo*'s cabin, it shuddered in revulsion—an effect echoed across its eight other instances.

Within the tunnel, the atmosphere had been only lightly polluted with biological effluvia: the microbes and fractured organic molecules breathed out or shed from the skin and clothing of the Dragoneer-human designated Abby, and from Tio Suthrom too in his new species-appropriate form.

But here in this cabin the air that washed across Ashok's surfaces felt thick with life: a dangerous brew made worse by the high oxygen content required by biological forms. Adding to the Invention's discomfort: the disorienting, even frightening sensation of being adrift in such a wide open and unfriendly space. The instance stretched and writhed, unwinding from its compact form in an effort to reach back and connect with another instance of itself.

The Dragoneer-human labeled Riffan leaned in close, his exhaled breath lading the instance with yet more foul biological detritus.

"Welcome to *Argo*," Riffan said as an above-average heat fired his cheeks. "And please accept my apologies. We did not mean to present you with such an unfriendly environment. It was just a misunderstanding of scale."

"I am adaptable," Ashok announced.

Proof came quickly as its second and third instances emerged from the membrane with less momentum, having learned from the mistake of the first. One of these clung to the membrane with clawed feet; the other chained with it, stretching, elongating to extend its reach, swiftly rescuing the first.

Riffan looked on, ashamed, embarrassed that he had so botched this first true meeting—a feeling made worse when Tio Suthrom came through the membrane and immediately asked Ashok, "Are you safe, my friend? Can you survive this polluted environment?"

"Indeed, yes, for a time," Ashok answered in its steadfastly cheerful voice. All its nine instances were now crawling about the cabin walls, feathery appendages extruded and waving gently, evidently exploring. "While I am enduring an expected infection of microscopic biologicals, the harm they will render is not immediate."

This response sent Riffan's heart racing in worry. "Love and Nature," he whispered. "But I think you're only sensing our shared microbiome and you're not vulnerable to that. I mean, you can't be . . . right?"

Or could the gel composing Ashok actually be vulnerable to organic rot? A horrible prospect! But if so, the Bio-mechanic would surely be able to engineer a solution.

"I'm so sorry," Riffan said.

"It is enough that harm is not intended," Ashok replied in the same cheerful tone.

Tio Suthrom added, "The Inventions have always existed in utterly sterile conditions. They regard biological life as insidious and they are not wrong." He touched palm to chest. "We see ourselves as singular and bounded within our skins. But the Inventions understand that each of us is a cloud, an amalgam of lifeforms without clear boundary. Once an Invention encounters such a cloud, it can never be clean again. It will become outcast."

Riffan swallowed against a bitter taste rising in his throat. "And this has happened at Hupo Sei?"

"Yes," Ashok confirmed. "Microbial lifeforms have been unexpectedly discovered at least three times. Perhaps more. Additionally, several exploratory cohorts have disappeared without filing a final report in the library."

"Ah. Well. In your case I'm sure our Bio-mechanic—"

He broke off as Abby burst through the membrane, her eyes wide with alarm. "There is another Invention coming, a much larger one. Is that all right? Or should we close the lock?"

"It is all right," Ashok assured her, speaking from an instance across the cabin. "It is me."

Abby turned in the direction of the voice. "I thought there were only nine of you."

A different instance answered, startling Riffan as it spoke from behind his head: "I am nine bright instances. The tenth is the hive. It lacks the perspicacity of the other nine, its focus being on gathering electrical power and maintaining optimal functioning among the cohort."

Riffan shifted his orientation so the speaker was no longer behind him. As he did, he watched the hive ease through the gel membrane and then go on to crawl the cabin wall: a snakelike thing but for the tiny feet, moving much more slowly than the bright instances.

Riffan said, "The socket you requested is in the—"

"I have found it," Ashok informed him. This voice emanated

from the front of the cabin, while another instance examined the socket on the back wall.

Abruptly, the hive popped off the wall, startling Riffan as it arrowed across the cabin. It landed precisely on the socket, where it immediately expanded into a grid of nine slots.

None of the bright instances plugged themselves into it. All continued their explorations, sweeping with their appendages as they crawled every accessible surface. And of course an army of Makers analyzed them in turn, directed by *Argo's* DI. Warnings would be issued if the DI found anything threatening. But no warnings came.

Tio Suthrom said, "I am ready to retract the tunnel."

"Yes," Ashok said. "Let us depart. I am eager to explore the marauder ship."

Riffan sighed a sigh of frustration, feeling less like the host, and more the confused guest. Many questions had been asked and answered during the time the Dragoneers had visited Ashok's warren. But many more questions bided in Riffan's mind—every one of them impossible to ask when he must hibernate throughout the tedious long journey back to *Dragon*.

CHAPTER EIGHTEEN

THE RAW HATE of *Griffin*'s philosopher cells neither shocked nor intimidated the Bio-mechanic as he occupied the high bridge. Their nihilistic fervor for destruction did not unbalance him, *had* not, even in his first moments there, because he had faced that same consuming fanaticism so many times before.

In the body of the ship—his familiar territory—Chenzeme hostility was not expressed in thought or transposed into crude words as it was on the high bridge. Yet it was there all the same, conveyed in the vicious, uncompromising, xenophobic, ever-evolving molecular defenses that he'd vied against all throughout the long, dangerous, early years of his existence. *Mindless* Chenzeme defenses—and yet he'd never been able to tame them. He had secured an existence by deceiving them, by protecting what was human behind a layer of tissue engineered to appear as Chenzeme. Existence by virtue of camouflage. And though he had won, he had not changed the nature of his foe like the Cryptologist had.

The Cryptologist had re-engineered *Dragon*'s philosopher cells and rewritten the courser's mind. Now as the days passed, with *Griffin* isolated from the fleet and from any sight of Tio Suthrom's great ship, she applied all her skill to the conversion of the smaller courser.

The Bio-mechanic watched closely, studying every Maker she designed and every modification she ordered. But he did not understand, not at all, how she knew what changes must be made within the hellishly complex, tangled threads that held the intellect and memory of individual philosopher cells, and the sequence of those changes, and the effect they would have. No simulation of the task ran in *Griffin*'s library. It was as if she just *knew* what was required.

But how could she?

An hour came when the most intractable cell lineages were thinned almost to oblivion and the others tamed enough that the Bio-mechanic gained a respite and no longer had to struggle so fiercely on the high bridge to counter a murderous demand to hunt and kill.

He took that moment to complain to her, **I have tracked the changes you've made down to individual molecular bonds, but I cannot comprehend how you have determined to make them. Where is the source of your understanding?*

Her thoughts had been fixed on the cell field, not on him. She required a moment to shift focus. As she did, he sensed from her, across the intimacy of the high bridge, a sharp edge of amusement. She told him, **You overestimate me. I do not possess such understanding. It is beyond me, as it is beyond you. An intriguing mystery to both of us. It is my silver-endowed avatar who possesses the intellect for this task. She tells me what to do.*

Ah, of course.

The Cryptologist had opened the needle and visited Ezo— the only Dragoneer to do so—and there she'd taken on the vast expansive mind of one of the Tanji.

She went on, **We trade subminds in a continuous stream. Her mind guides mine.*

*Then she is not you? You are no longer her?

*I am a ghost. I have no access to the computational resources of the silver.

He too was only a ghost. He had only ever been a ghost and he would never comprehend such processes either—a cold fact that roused in him illogical wrath. Why be angry over what could not be helped? But there it was, sudden and undeniable, because while he had failed to change Chenzeme nature, the opposite was not true. He differed from *Griffin*'s former mistress not in kind, but only in degree, because the wrath of the Chenzeme had gotten inside him too. And now it spilled over into the cell field, generating a wave of alarm and reviving the smoldering argument to hunt and kill.

But then, to his surprise, a spontaneous counter argument arose from within the field:

<negate that>

<observe / evaluate>

<LEARN>

That was new.

The philosopher cells had always been capable of learning, of course. They would compare what they observed with the vast histories they carried to identify targets, and then debate and simulate, until they had developed an efficient strategy to attack and to destroy. But a cold patience had begun to soothe familiar rage. Cold and curious and aloof from the once all-consuming desire to destroy.

He let that cold curiosity soothe him too, as he continued to watch the Cryptologist at her work. Only peripherally aware of a submind, automatically generated, carrying the experience of these thoughts to the version of himself within the library.

That fully simulated, three-dimensional version.

The pleasure of that existence had not left him. He had begun to use this new freedom to visit places he had never considered exploring before. Like now, walking slowly through a virtual rendition of a temperate rain forest on Prakruti—an experience recorded by Shoran's son, Mikael. Even in ghost form he could perceive the moist chill of the air, the scent of humus, the slight scuff of each footfall.

Mikael's feet had scuffed because he'd been wearing boots. In contrast, the Bio-mechanic walked barefoot and he was dressed only in a thin coverall despite the cold—and that wasn't realistic, was it?

But it didn't matter. It couldn't matter, because he was still only a ghost and so the form of himself meant nothing.

Even so, even as limited as his existence continued to be, he nurtured a growing desire to share the experience of it with that version of himself aboard *Dragon*.

Echoing Mikael's steps, he turned to follow a faint track, half-hidden beneath an overgrowth of ferns, that paralleled a murmuring stream. Low light, here beneath the rustling of spring-green maple leaves, the cold growing deeper as the day waned. The Bio-mechanic delighted in it. He delighted in this new existence. He had gained such freedom! So much, that it felt like a betrayal of himself to keep this new existence secret.

Yet he did so.

Not since the initial conquest of *Griffin* had his two versions traded subminds. In both his forms, he had assumed separation to be necessary, based on claims made long ago by *Griffin*'s original crew of Apparatchiks. They had insisted that isolation from their counterparts allowed them to more closely attune to the unique environment of the smaller courser and to its volatile mistress.

But now that the Bio-mechanic had existed aboard *Griffin* for many ten-days, he discounted this. He believed a more likely explanation to be the desire of Clemantine's dark twin to keep her dark secrets. He kept up the custom now only because *he* had secrets to keep and ambitions to hide. Not from his other self, who would be just as delighted. Nor did he fear Urban's wrath. That one was a pushover. Urban had been persuaded to accept both the Cryptologist and the interloper from *Alaka'i Onyx*. It wouldn't be hard to convince him the Bio-mechanic had a claim on an expanded life too.

Pushing past a last tree branch, he was startled to find himself at a cliff's edge, confronted by an immense panorama of forested ridges, stacked one after another, running out to a golden horizon. His simulated heartbeat quickened at the immensity and beauty of the landscape, and then quickened again as a great eagle soared past at eye level.

No, it was not Urban's judgment he feared, but that of the other Apparatchiks. There lay the hazard. They would perceive his difference. They would recognize how the Cryptologist had unlocked his core, granting him an autonomy like her own. And they would deem him a security risk, liable to weight his own survival above that of the fleet—and maybe they would be right.

CHAPTER NINETEEN

STILL ESCORTED BY Abby and Riffan, Ashok and Tio Suthrom arrived on *Dragon*'s gee deck. Ashok tabulated sixty-six independent human instances gathered there to greet them. It discerned joyous excitement in the smiles, and words of welcome within the murmurs. Even so, revulsion gripped it. It did not need to extrude its appendages in order to test the dangerously oxygenated air; its surface sensors alone detected an exponential increase in the ubiquity and variety of biological life polluting the local atmosphere.

Acting swiftly, it deleted an urge to shudder. Revulsion was useless. The cohort had already acquired a veneer of greedy lifeforms, microbial in size, lacking intellect, and driven by urges to consume and to trade random information and to reproduce.

Ashok had learned much of such forms from the great ship's library. It knew them to be mindless as individuals, but adaptive and highly clever in great numbers, and it deemed it inevitable that eventually some among them would find a way into the deep tissue of its instances.

So be it.

Ashok did not look forward to its own demise, but it did not fear it either. Not much. Nor was it much troubled by the knowledge that, because of its exposure, it must physically isolate from all other Inventions throughout the balance of its existence.

Ashok was not a biological; it did not require physical companionship. Information exchange over a communications link would fulfill any need for outside consultation or to keep abreast of and contribute to the doings and direction of the Inventions' civilization.

It *did* assign a weighty negative factor to the rot and corrosion that would likely be its future. But even with that, the discovery of the human-marauder hybrid ship and this opportunity to explore its internal habitat made the prospect of a shortened functional lifespan wholly worthwhile.

A spasm interrupted the positive spin of its thoughts as its lead instance, the one with longest exposure to the pollution, abruptly withdrew its legs and contracted into a sphere. Ashok recognized this as a deeply programmed behavior to minimize exposed surface area. Quite useless in the present circumstance.

In the gee deck's disorienting spin, the spherical instance immediately began to roll uncontrolled along the smooth path from the warren.

This would not do.

Ashok acted first to protect its functionality, editing out the compulsion altogether so that it could not affect another instance. Then it reset the afflicted one, returning itself to standard form.

Tio Suthrom noted the incident, of course. Indeed, from the exclamations, everyone had. But it was Tio Suthrom who dropped into a crouch—as if he needed to be that close for Ashok's instances to hear him. The heat index of his face was elevated, indicating deep anxiety, and his voice trembled as he asked, "Are you all right?"

"I am adapting," Ashok answered, inflecting its own voice with confidence, hoping thereby to reassure Tio Suthrom. "Though I underestimated the energy required to operate under the drag of the local centripetal force. I will require more frequent recharging sessions than when I am active within my warren."

Of the many Dragoneers waiting along the walkway, the one closest to Ashok also crouched. It recognized her from her multiple visits to its warren. Every Dragoneer who visited him had insisted on reshaping the shared avatars to reflect their personal features—a useful behavior as Ashok now recognized all of them and knew their names. This one was Tarnya.

She told it, "Let us know if there is anything we can do to enhance your comfort while you are here."

"Thank you, Tarnya. My comfort is irrelevant. My purpose is to observe Dragoneers and the many elements of their natural habitat. I ask that no changes be made on my account."

Tarnya smiled—a little uneasily, Ashok thought. Then she directed her gaze toward Tio Suthrom. "And for you as well, Tio Suthrom. I will show you to the cottage we've prepared for you."

"Go," Ashok urged him. "Enjoy the company of your own kind and I will enjoy my uninhibited explorations."

In his physical avatar, Urban stood among the other Dragoneers, with Jolly at his side. Together they watched Ashok's instances crawl the path from the warren and then gradually diverge. Some continued on the path as it wound around the gee-deck, others crossed the pavilion or slipped into shrubbery, presumably to explore the lifeforms dwelling there.

As the last instance passed, Jolly leaned in. He started to whisper a question. "Do you mean to speak to—?"

Urban stopped him with a cautioning hand. Speaking silently, atrium to atrium, he said, *Not here, not now, not aloud. Assume Ashok has exquisite hearing.*

Then, having no doubt of what Jolly had intended to ask, Urban went on to answer the unfinished question. *Yes, I mean to speak to Ashok and get us at least a conditional invitation to Hupo Sei.*

Simultaneously with this exchange, Urban, as a ghost in the library, confirmed with the Scholar the parameters of Ashok's visit.

"You are allowing them—Ashok and Tio Suthrom both—only a limited access to the library. Correct? Just as you did with the Narans."

"Yes," the Scholar acknowledged. "They will not be able to access any technology more complex than what they already possess and all mention of Verilotus is embargoed."

"But not of Ezo."

Urban meant the living moon that orbited Prakruti. Ezo had not existed before the Tanji came together to create it.

"Do you wish me to hide knowledge of Ezo?" the Scholar asked in puzzlement.

"No. We know—we've been told anyway—that at least one faction among the Inventions, what Ashok calls the Originalists, is determined to re-create a world for their Inventors."

"Indeed. The amalgamation they call the Labyrinth being the seed of this world."

Urban nodded. "I think they would be interested in Ezo. I think they would find it inspiring to know such a thing has already been done."

Dropping only this seed of a suggestion, he waited for the Scholar to work the rest of it out. It didn't take long.

"Ah, I see." The Scholar smiled a hungry smile. "You want them to know about Ezo as an alternative to the clumsy billion-year project they presently envision."

"Yes. The Tanji couldn't have spent more than a millennium, maybe two, creating Ezo."

"Perhaps. But the Tanji knew how to generate and manipulate and anchor a blade."

"True."

"You *don't* know, and neither do the Inventions."

"Sooth. But maybe the Cryptologist does?"

Clemantine had continued in her self-imposed internal exile, keeping to her cottage or the tiny garden behind it, thinking, meditating, as she sought a new internal equilibrium. Friends visited more often than she liked: Shoran, Vytet, Pasha, even Kona. They brought her news she otherwise would not have heard, since for this period of reflection she had eschewed all artificial connections, isolating within the limited range of her biological senses.

During the day she remained within the sanctuary of her cottage with its privacy screens engaged. Only in the quiet of late night did she emerge to sit alone, cross-legged on a blanket in her little garden, where she listened to the rustling of leaves and the occasional melodic chirping of crickets near and far.

This night was different though. Despite the hour, she heard people on the path, soft voices murmuring. She did not allow herself to wonder about it, but instead focused her mind on slow gentle breaths until at last the unwanted activity subsided, and she felt herself alone under bright starlight.

She raised her gaze. A beautiful night. Not a single wisp of simulated cloud obscured the projected faces of ten thousand blazing stars.

Somewhere out there new life was surely arising, alien life, uncommon but not unknown in simple cellular form, the equivalent of bacteria. But surpassingly rare in the great span of time were those worlds where life found a way to cross the energy barrier that limited the size and complexity of those first tiny cells. And of those worlds that had succeeded: how many had been destroyed by the Chenzeme's ancient and relentless robotic fleet? And how could she have ever allowed herself to be taken in by that murderous philosophy?

A fresh flush of guilt and shame prickled her skin and she hissed, immediately contemptuous of herself. She had let her mind wander again, wallowing in this dark state, indulging it for too long when she had duties, responsibilities, social obligations—

Glistening motion caught her eye, cutting short the litany of self-recriminations. Clemantine did not flinch. Her hands remained relaxed, at rest against her thighs. But her eyes shifted sideways and there, emerging without a rustle from beneath a head-high camellia hedge, came a plump slug-like creature only a little longer than her hand, eye spots glowing faintly in the dark.

Not a creature, she corrected herself. A machine. Shoran had described this 'Invention' well enough; Kona told her the alien device was to be welcomed aboard *Dragon* and allowed to explore on its own throughout the habitable areas of the ship.

So. It had arrived. But Clemantine did not believe it was on its own. Urban was too cautious for that. He would be watching it, watching this instance, and by extension, watching her.

"Greetings, Ashok," she said, soft in the night.

The device paused to extend a feathery appendage, waving it slowly in her direction. Some sort of sensory equipment, no doubt.

After a few seconds, it submerged the appendage into the gel of its body. Then a small dark oval surfaced beneath its eyespots—in imitation of a human mouth?—and the machine said in a cheerful voice, "Greetings. We have not met prior to this present time. As you have discerned, I am Ashok and I apologize for disturbing your nocturnal rest."

"An apology is unnecessary. I am pleased to make your acquaintance. My name is Clemantine."

It felt odd to address a machine in this manner. But 'machine' was not the correct term, was it? She reminded herself that this alien-made device understood their language and its encompassing culture well enough to prefer the term *synthetics*. Or in this case the singular, *synthetic*. Shoran had described Ashok as one entity with nine—or was it ten?—instances.

For the first time in far too long, Clemantine felt a stirring of curiosity. She wondered: Did the number nine have special significance to the Inventions? Did every cohort number nine (or ten?) instances? Was there a practical reason the Inventions refused to re-create themselves by crossing the boundaries of what they deemed the three domains of life: synthetic, informational, and biological?

But it was another question she asked: "Your kind, the Inventions, you have occupied Hupo Sei for a long time, haven't you?"

"Our first cohort reached Hupo Sei over seventeen hundred years ago. This qualifies as a long time in our reckoning," Ashok answered.

Clemantine raised an eyebrow at Ashok's use of an approximation rather than an exact number, no doubt imitating the way most humans would speak. "You've learned a lot about humans from your companion, Tio Suthrom," she observed.

"Indeed. We have learned much from one another."

"And was Tio Suthrom the only surviving human the Inventions ever encountered in your explorations of Hupo Sei?"

"Ah. This question has been asked of me many times and each time I must disappoint the questioner with my answer. Tio Suthrom is indeed the only human we ever encountered prior to the arrival of Dragoneers, and we have mapped most objects within the system and explored every major one. A tiny percentage of these objects continue to support remnant single-cell biological life. Each of these we left untouched to develop or to die as they will."

Ashok then asked a question of its own. "You, Clemantine, have not yet met Tio Suthrom, have you?"

"I have not."

"I am observing an intriguing similarity in your two metabolic states, that is quite different from that of others I have met."

"By what means are you observing my metabolic state?" she asked with real curiosity.

"By the exudate of your breath." It partially extended its appendage again as if to demonstrate the mechanism.

So, was Tio Suthrom a melancholy pilot? Well, why not? It would surely be a weary, soul-crushing existence to live without human companionship for centuries on end . . . unless of course you were as adept as Urban at editing emotion.

"Perhaps we both need therapy," Clemantine observed with a bitter smile.

The instance hesitated a moment before it replied. "Therapy. An interesting concept. It says much that your kind requires a means to reprogram and correct flaws whether acquired, or inherent in your original designs. Tio Suthrom would benefit from such therapy. In his present state he tends to become unstable during challenging circumstances."

"As when he believes he is about to be immolated by a marauder?"

"Yes," Ashok agreed.

"I think I would like to meet this Tio Suthrom. He sounds very human to me."

"All too human," a soft unfamiliar male voice said from the shadows under the cottage eaves.

Clemantine stiffened, but she did not turn and did not get up— and she successfully suppressed an oath that tried to rise to her lips.

"Tio Suthrom," she concluded with just a hint of irritation.

BLADE   125

He stepped out of shadow and into starlight. "If I'm intrud-
ing, I apologize. I'm here because Ashok urgently requested that
I come."

"Did it?"

Clemantine found this deeply disturbing, not because she
objected to Tio Suthrom's presence but because he had come too
soon—in the very moment she had expressed a desire to meet him.

Had Ashok predicted her behavior? Was she so easy to read?

"I will go," Tio Suthrom said.

"No, stay." She wanted to know more of this melancholy pilot.
After all, he was someone new. "Come inside. I'll make tea."

CHAPTER TWENTY

MORNING REVEALED TO Vytet a significant change: Clemantine had emerged from her self-imposed exile. Vytet came upon her at the dining terrace, where she breakfasted in the company of *Alaka'i Onyx*'s grim pilot . . . though in the early light Tio Suthrom did not look so grim as he had when he'd first arrived on the gee deck. Perhaps Clemantine's smiles had leavened his mood? Something had surely lifted hers. Vytet invited herself to find out what.

"Good morning, Clemantine," she said softly as she settled onto a pillow opposite the two, at the low table they shared. "And you, Tio Suthrom."

"Tio is enough," he said in a low and gentle voice.

Clemantine eyed Vytet with an amused smile, before asking Tio, "Have you met Vytet?"

When he shook his head, she explained, "Vytet, I think, would describe herself as an engineer, though she is so much more. A true polymath, interested in even the most minor and transient phenomena."

Vytet cocked her head, subjecting Clemantine to a gently mocking smile. "It's true I am continuously surprised by the creative turns life will take." She shifted her gaze to Tio. "I visited *Alaka'i Onyx* and explored Ashok's warren, but you weren't there at the time."

A nod. "I . . . felt the need to withdraw. It was no easy thing to settle my mind to the existence . . . the *reality* of other people." Sitting shoulder to shoulder with Clemantine, he turned to gaze at her, his eyes bright with emotion. "No easy thing, when I had convinced myself I would never meet another human again and that I did not want to."

Vytet watched and she wondered: Was this a minor and transient phenomenon? Or a seed of trouble?

As if to address this unspoken question, Clemantine said, "The Inventions are averse to biological life, so this is the first time Tio has emerged as an embodied human in a very long time."

"Since long before the fall," Tio added.

"Is it then like a new experience?" Vytet asked him. "Every sensation, every desire, intense and fascinating?"

"Not always fascinating," Tio said. "Doubt and regret being as real as desire."

His gaze rose, fixing on something behind her.

Turning, Vytet found that Urban had come. He stood, a towering figure, two steaming bowls held in his large hands. A nod, as he met her gaze. Then he knelt, and set one of the bowls in front of her. Steamed vegetable cubes tossed with noodles in a light, spicy sauce. "You come to breakfast," he chided, "and then forget to eat."

He kept the second bowl for himself, sitting beside her, seeming calm, only mildly curious as he looked questioningly across the table at Clemantine. She returned his gaze with a slight, secretive smile.

"Urban, it's good to see you about. You've been mostly absent from the gee deck for days now," Vytet observed.

"Yes."

That was all.

He began to eat, long chopsticks lifting the still-steaming noodles.

Tio said, "Ashok has finished its survey of the gee deck."

Urban nodded, empty chopsticks hovering above his bowl. "Sooth. I've mapped its movements." He jabbed at the noodles. "And I've spoken to Ashok. I've assured it there is no risk of microbial infection here. The Bio-mechanic will make sure of that. Still, it's uncomfortable and uneasy, and it doesn't want to stay."

At this, Tio looked surprised. Vytet certainly was. "Elaborate," she demanded.

Urban gestured toward the end of the table with his now-laden chopsticks. Vytet looked and was startled to see an instance of the Invention. It pulled itself onto the low tabletop, explaining, "I am not designed for the environment here. Fascinating as it is, it has proven a continual challenge to my structure and altogether unpleasant."

"I'm sorry to hear that," Vytet said, resisting an urge to reach out and touch it. Had anyone touched it? She didn't know.

Ashok said, "I have weighed the possibility of inventing a fresh cohort customized for this environment, but concluded the idea is impractical. The challenge of training such a cohort without access to the full experiential resources of our shared library at Hupo Sei presents a significant risk."

"It would be naïve?" Vytet asked.

"Yes, exactly."

"Why not adapt your own physical aspect?" Clemantine asked before Vytet could pose the question herself. "Re-invent yourself."

"Could *you*?" Ashok asked her. "Could you become some other creature entirely? Could your mind adapt to the body of a bird, for example? Or one of the little nocturnal primates that live here in the trees?"

"Maybe. Eventually," she mused. "It would require a long phase of relearning."

"Yes. And for me, there would be little gained in the end. I have surveyed your habitat and acquired insight on your biology. There is much left to learn, but such learning can continue through an exchange of libraries if Tio Suthrom is agreeable to this."

Tio appeared surprised rather than agreeable. "An exchange of libraries?"

"It's traditional," Urban said. "Shared knowledge. Shared experience."

"It will take preparation," Tio hedged.

"But there's no hurry, is there?" Clemantine asked, drawing Tio's gaze and holding it for long seconds in an exchange that further piqued Vytet's curiosity—and Urban's too, it seemed, judging by his dark frown.

"Is Tio thinking of staying with us?" Urban asked, directing the question at Clemantine. "It is . . . *hard* to be so utterly alone and without human company. I know."

He did know, Vytet reflected. And the generosity of his words took her by surprise.

Tio directed an uncomfortable smile at Ashok. "I have been more fortunate than that. I have not been alone and I did not miss the company of other people. I did not think so anyway." Another look, traded with Clemantine. "I was wrong about that."

"There is much for all of us to consider as we look to the future," Clemantine said, directing her gaze to Ashok. "You for instance, Ashok. I have heard you came to Ryo to survey for hazards. Forgive me if you have been asked this before, but are you Inventions planning to colonize this system as well as Hupo Sei?"

Vytet observed a short series of tiny vibrational waves in the gelatinous matter of Ashok's instance. A shiver?

"Emphatically no!" Ashok replied with an edge of disbelief. "Hupo Sei is our assigned system. To expand beyond is greedy and dangerous."

"Really?" Vytet asked, intrigued by this stunning assessment.

"Yes, this is our truth."

"You must see humans as very greedy, then," she guessed. "For all the systems we once occupied."

"Indeed, this is so. It is the nature of biologicals. Synthetics do not share biological drives toward violence, conquest, or the acquisition of territory beyond our immediate needs. We operate within a parameter that can be described as 'fair share.' Hupo Sei is our share. It is enough. We will not worry or antagonize our biological neighbors by expanding into their shares, or into an unclaimed share such as Ryo. To do so would be to court conflict, and conflict destroys knowledge and wastes energy."

"Indeed it does," Vytet agreed.

Urban leaned forward in sudden sharp interest. "Have you met your biological neighbors?"

"Not directly, though we have set up observation posts on the periphery of Sulakari and are monitoring the evolving lifeforms in its nebula."

"Human lifeforms?" Vytet asked.

"The life we have observed at Sulakari is not human though likely it is descended from your biological clade."

Urban again, an intensity to his question: "You did not communicate with what's there?"

"That is correct. We observe and do not interfere."

"A tactic we should consider," Clemantine suggested sardonically.

Urban ignored this, pressing his own questions: "And the Halo? What about it? Have you been there?"

"No."

"Not even to set up observation posts?"

"No."

"Why?"

Ashok explained: "Observing from Hupo Sei, it is clear the technology deployed at the Halo is far greater than our own. Certainly, the inhabitants of that system must be aware of us. They could have visited us if they desired contact, but they have not. So we reflect this behavior, and do not approach or otherwise interfere."

"We did not reflect your silence," Vytet observed.

"This is true. But your technology is greater than our own."

"In some aspects, yes," she agreed. "But your people are so different from anything we've ever known before. There is much to learn from one another."

Clemantine gave Vytet a hard look. "Not all learning is good." Her gaze shifted to Urban. "Some knowledge is better forgotten."

She means the Blade, Vytet thought. A disagreement that would not die—and yet, in a rare move, Urban did not take up the argument, instead returning to the previous topic.

"Ashok, what of the other Inventions, those cohorts the Inventors sent to different worlds? Do you know where they are? Or if any were successful?"

"We do not know. The combination of time and distance makes it unlikely we ever will."

"But by your definition, wasn't it 'greedy' to send so many cohorts of Inventions out to claim and colonize multiple star systems?"

"Indeed, yes, though it was believed the great majority of these missions would be lost to the marauders or otherwise fail. Even so, 'fair share' is a parameter of Inventions, not of Inventors. Recall that the Inventors are biologicals, like you—though of a more careful nature."

Clemantine scoffed at that. "They created you, quickened artificial life, intelligent and independent. That's inherently dangerous."

"We have our own quickened artificial life in the Apparatchiks," Vytet pointed out.

Urban smiled his pirate smile. "We have the Cryptologist too—and maybe she *is* inherently dangerous and so proves the rule."

Clemantine fixed him with a sharp, offended glare. He did not seem to care. And if Ashok noted this, it gave no sign, saying simply, "Conflict is natural and to be expected in biologicals." It went on, "Tio Suthrom, this Dragoneer-Urban has agreed to return me imminently to *Alaka'i Onyx*. You and I must then commence our return to Hupo Sei."

Reluctance weighed in Tio's voice. "Do you truly wish to go so soon?"

"What point in staying?" Urban asked, addressing not Tio in particular, but all of them. "I know there has been interest among the ship's company in conducting a survey of Ryo, since we are here. But Ashok has already spent a century and a half doing just that, and has shared the results with us. The Scholar and the Astronomer have assessed those studies, finding them valid—and all confirm our own observations. There is nothing of interest here. Ashok wishes to return home with its discoveries—and it has invited us to go with it and visit Hupo Sei."

"This is a tentative invitation," Ashok clarified. "When I have returned to *Alaka'i Onyx* I will message the Core Forum, informing them we are coming, and then, Tio Suthrom, we will accompany the Dragoneer fleet through the crossing."

Urban added, "If in the transit the Inventions decide against allowing our visit, I have assured Ashok we will respect this decision and turn away."

"I do not think that will happen," Ashok said. "Inventions are curious by design. For this reason, it will be difficult for the Core Forum to reject such a visit. Still, the danger of it will be carefully weighed, and rejection is a possibility."

Vytet traded a stunned look with Clemantine. The sudden revelation of this plan, the assurance with which it was presented: together they left Vytet speechless—but only for a moment.

She turned to Urban. "I won't say I object. I am in fact intrigued. But you are premature. The ship's company has not heard this plan. They have not discussed it and they have certainly not agreed to it."

Again from Urban, that sly, knowing smile. "They will." He picked up his empty bowl and stood. "You should call for a meeting this morning. Ashok has agreed to speak and answer questions before it goes." Then, with a nod at Vytet's untouched bowl of noodles he added, "And don't forget to eat."

He walked away then, and after a few seconds Clemantine followed him, leaving Tio gazing after her, looking troubled and confused.

Vytet returned her attention to the instance, still at rest on the table, utterly motionless as only a machine could be. "Was it you, Ashok, or Urban who first suggested this visit to Hupo Sei?"

"The suggestion originated with me," Ashok replied.

Vytet pressed her lips together, thoroughly annoyed at this unexpected answer. So Urban *hadn't* directly suggested a visit. Still, he'd been so pleased with the outcome, he must surely have steered the conversation to that end.

"Will you call a meeting of the Dragoneers?" Ashok asked her.

Time had not diluted Vytet's curiosity. She desired to visit worlds, as many as she could, the alien culture of Hupo Sei being a particularly bright, nay, *irresistible* lure. It wasn't hard for her to set aside the expectation of years of study at Ryo.

"Yes, of course," she answered Ashok. "And I will advocate for the visit."

No doubt this was the response Urban had anticipated. Vytet did not like feeling manipulated, but wasn't he right? Ryo was a dead system. Why not move on?

And yet, she found herself wary.

Vytet knew Urban well, knew he would always pursue his own goals and interests. And she couldn't help but wonder what additional, unspoken motivation lay behind his abrupt resolve to hurry on to Hupo Sei.

CHAPTER TWENTY-ONE

WHAT GAME ARE you playing at? Clemantine wondered as she hurried to catch up with Urban on the path.

*Wait for me, she messaged him.

He halted, looking back at her with a flinty gaze.

She caught up with him. Met him eye to eye, her suspicion colliding with his resentment. "We need to talk, Urban. Come home with me."

"To your house? No, I don't want to be there. Not now."

He had been generous to Tio, less so to her, but it didn't matter. She wouldn't let it matter. The rift between them was real, and she would make no excuse or apology for having taken what she needed. She set him straight on this, saying, "It's not Tio I mean to discuss."

"What then?"

As if there could be no other plausible option? He should know her better than that. He *did* know her better. He just did not want to have this conversation.

Too bad.

"Walk with me," she told him in a voice gravelly with latent anger. "And explain to me why you are so eager to visit these machines."

He set the pace, striding toward the pavilion as he delivered an answer in crisp syllables. "Why shouldn't I be? We've never encountered anything like them before and we're not likely to again. And what's the alternative? Should we go on to Sulakari and disrupt whatever new lifeforms are evolving there?"

His pace slowed; his tone shifted. Looking at her, he spoke with real bitterness. "Or are you so eager to make the long crossing to the Sun? That empty system! We could spend mournful years there, paying our respects and contemplating the end state of an all-out war of dimensional missiles erasing worlds, erasing reality."

"Missiles like yours," she observed. And for the first time she thought to ask, "Do you regret the gift of them?"

His eyes flared in surprise but then swiftly narrowed. He spoke slowly, doubtfully, "We saw the scars of such a war at Tanjiri. Megastructures sliced open. Vast swaths of space left utterly empty even of trace molecules. But the war there ended before utter annihilation. There is *nothing* left at the Sun. And you ask why I'm eager to visit the machines? They at least have not destroyed themselves."

"They are *machines*." She pressed that point and though she kept her voice soft, she challenged him with her words. "Intelligent, free-thinking, conscious machines."

He didn't miss her meaning. "Forbidden machines."

"Sooth. In all the histories we know, the evolution of such things, if not quickly put down, always led to disaster."

"So then, what are you thinking? That we should annihilate them?"

"*What?*" She stopped, too shocked to go on. "No. Of course not."

They had come to the pavilion. No one else was about as he turned to confront her. "No, because they're separate from us. They're not *our* machines, not human-made. They exist under their own ruleset."

"Yes. That's how it is. And we are not Chenzeme. We must never behave like the Chenzeme. But I don't like it, Urban. I don't like the idea of these sentient machines and the danger they represent—and I wonder that you don't feel the same."

A slight, indifferent shrug. "I did at first. But as your melancholy pilot likes to point out, we biologicals are the dangerous ones. Tio Suthrom doesn't object to the Inventions. He believes them superior to us in every way."

She frowned at this diversion, but she did not try to dodge it. Crossing her arms, straightening her shoulders, she said, "Given Tio's situation, his experiences, his conclusions about the collapse of human civilization—he *needs* to believe that. To believe we are fatally flawed, marred by greed, marred by avarice, by jealousy, and by ambition. So that no matter how high we reach we will be brought down by a collective doom carried within the innate structures of our minds." She gave him a hard, evaluating look. "Knowing you as well as I do, I worry he may be right."

That pirate smile. "I've survived this long. I hope to go on for some time more." His smile faded. His gaze drifted a little and his brow furrowed. "Do you mean to keep him? Tio Suthrom, I mean. I know he's eased your grief. I can see that. I'm glad someone could."

She sighed, reluctant to answer with her own feelings still in flux. "He is a softer man than you."

"And you're drawn to his melancholy."

"An old habit. You would not get this, but it can be comforting to give comfort."

He hissed skeptically, then pressed her for an answer. "Do you mean to keep him around?"

"Is it my choice?"

"Realistically, yes. If you want him here as a friend, as a lover, I don't think the ship's company will argue against it—or that he'll object either."

"And you?" she asked.

"It's late to be asking my opinion."

"Sooth," she said, smiling. She should not be amused at his quiet jealousy, but she was. "I still love you," she assured him. "Nothing needs to change between us."

But that wasn't true and they both knew it.

Urban sat in the back row of the amphitheater alongside the Cryptologist. Every seat was occupied, and excited murmurs erupted when Vytet presented Ashok's invitation to visit Hupo Sei.

The Invention was there with Vytet, sharing the dais. Its nine instances had all gathered within the structure of its square hive, each tucked into a hexagonal socket, with eye spots and audio speaker facing out. The hive rested on a pedestal that elevated it to the equal of Vytet's considerable height.

With the initial presentation done, Vytet invited questions that Ashok answered in a voice boosted well above its usual volume so that it carried easily throughout the amphitheater.

Urban listened, and was pleased with the direction of the discussion. Perhaps his satisfaction showed on his face, because the Cryptologist leaned in, catching him by surprise and inducing a shiver as her lips almost brushed his ear. "You wish to make this journey?" she whispered.

"*Yes.*"

"I do too. *Griffin* is ready. The ship is as evolved as *Dragon* now."

He turned to her, mildly annoyed, aware she had ignored his injunction to swiftly strip *Griffin*'s philosopher cells of their Chenzeme nature. Instead, she had taken her time with it and in retrospect he was glad. He had been reacting out of emotion, furious at the situation, at *Griffin*'s alienation. The Cryptologist had shown far better judgment than he. Not that he was ready to admit it. In an undertone he groused at her, "You've taken so long I wondered if you meant to do it at all."

A coy smile hinted she saw right through him. She leaned back in her seat, her smile disappearing as she returned her gaze to the dais. Barely audible now, she murmured, "I would not spend one second more than I needed to amid the horror of *Griffin*'s untamed philosopher cells."

Did she mean it as a criticism of Clemantine? He had to believe she did. The Cryptologist had shown better judgment than both of them.

Vytet called a vote and as Urban had predicted, the ship's company unanimously accepted Ashok's invitation to visit Hupo Sei.

Next, Tio Suthrom in his handsome, human avatar, stood before the ship's company and asked that he be granted passage to Hupo Sei, concluding, "It would be a precious opportunity for me to spend this time among my own kind."

This request was granted, though not with a unanimous vote. No one recorded an objection, but Urban, alone, abstained.

He wasn't sure what to think about the pilot and he harbored a deep ambivalence about him, and about Clemantine's fascination with the man.

Jealousy sparked against resentment, yet he did not, would not, say anything against Tio Suthrom. He could see now, in hindsight, how he and Clemantine had diverged, the two of them wanting different things, envisioning different futures. The idea of the blade dividing them.

And even if it wasn't so? It would have been an act of cruelty to force Tio Suthrom back into the solitary existence he had endured for so very long, and Urban was not a cruel man.

After the vote, after the formal goodbyes, he escorted Ashok in all its instances, back to *Argo*. With no one but them in the transit bubble, the Invention spoke freely. "Heeding your suggestion, I reviewed the library files discussing what is known of the creation of the moon you call Ezo, and I am intrigued. I believe such a project would also intrigue the Originalists— though having been away more than two of your centuries, I cannot say whether that faction remains as influential within the Core Forum as before."

There it is, Urban thought. The first step on an elusive path toward the creation of a blade. A small victory, yet it brought him some modest consolation for his rift with Clemantine. Still, many more steps would need to be taken on a path that could be easily blocked.

He spoke carefully. "You understand that any proposal to develop this technology must be treated as a sensitive topic?"

"I understand your people are not all of one mind. That there are factions among you, just as there are among us. I do not wish to see the project ended before it is begun. For that reason I will continue to heed your advice and refrain from discussing it with any other Dragoneer."

"And with Tio Suthrom."

"Yes."

The transit bubble reached *Argo*. It opened, revealing the landing ship's little cabin.

"I don't know if it will ever be possible for us to actually do this," Urban reminded the Invention.

"It is as yet only an interesting concept," Ashok agreed as its instances crawled across the threshold.

"Exactly. And it'll stay that way for a while."

Urban lingered until Ashok had all nine instances safely ensconced in the hive. Then he retreated to the warren, leaving it to a DI to ferry the Invention back to *Alaka'i Onyx*.

Tio Suthrom still served as the great ship's ghost pilot, synchronizing with his living avatar through an occasional exchange of subminds.

The great ship was first to leave Ryo. It fired its fusion engine, commencing a long lazy acceleration toward interstellar velocity. Urban instructed the fleet's scattered outriders to gather in its wake and, in time, to accelerate past it, taking on their usual staggered formation.

Griffin followed.

Dragon trailed behind.

CHAPTER TWENTY-TWO

BURSTS OF LASER light made their slow way across the void, received and then relayed by each subsequent communication buoy in the chain laid out by *Alaka'i Onyx* when the great ship first fared to Ryo.

Ashok's initial dire warnings would be 8.3 years in transit. A second, more optimistic set of messages described the true nature of the marauder ship, its accompanying fleet, the humans who controlled the exotic technologies of those vessels, and their desire to visit Hupo Sei.

Urban alone knew of a third communication, one describing the creation of Ezo and suggesting a possibility: that although the Dragoneers had no part in that creation, they had some understanding of it, and it might be that they could be persuaded to undertake the challenge of replicating such a world at Hupo Sei.

The fleet would be more than halfway through the crossing before any reply could reach them. Urban meant to make careful use of that time to prepare—but not just yet.

The ship's company remained active at the start of the crossing. Ashok had shared the results of its studies at Ryo and Tio Suthrom had shared his library—fresh information to be analyzed and integrated by the ever-curious Dragoneers.

Their curiosity encompassed Tio Suthrom too.

When Tarnya persuaded the melancholy pilot to take a role in an historical play she had written, he proved a compelling performer. At a brief pause between the first and second act, Urban was disgruntled to note how the chatter filling the amphitheater all focused on Tio. Even Vytet was caught up in admiration. She sat a few seats away, but not so far that Urban couldn't hear her when she leaned forward, murmuring to Clemantine who sat in the next row, "Your pilot has a gentle charisma. It's not hard to see why you are drawn to him."

Clemantine turned around, eyes sparkling with pleasure as she told Vytet, "Oh yes, he is easy to be with. I like him very much. But he is not *my* pilot. He does not belong to me. And he has his own curiosities."

"Ah . . . truly? Then you would not mind . . . ?"

"I would not."

Urban looked away long before this exchange was done. Easy enough to divert his gaze; not so much, his attention. He could not help wondering if Clemantine had said those words specifically for him to hear. Did she want him to know he had not been wholly replaced? That he had not been permanently consigned to an outer circle in the hierarchy of her friendships?

By the Unknown God! he chided himself. *Let it go!*

She had. The certainty of it left him with a cold knot in his belly and cold resolve in his heart.

He did not stay for the second act.

Until Vytet spoke, Clemantine had not realized Urban was there, sitting quietly two rows behind her. Now, as she took note of his departure, a quirk of conscience urged her to seek him out, to seek to soothe the differences between them. But the raw truth was, she did not want to. Not yet.

Oh, she still loved him. She had not lied when she'd told him that. Still, they had been through so much together. Their history, with all its grief and terror, grown so heavy she did not want to shoulder it anymore. That had been made clear to her, the night she met Tio. Warmth filled her, remembering it. Looking into his eyes had been like looking into a mirror, his wounded soul a reflection of her own, his neediness hers. No need for questions or explanations. One touch leading to another. Both of them purely there, locked within the present moment and nearly weightless, unburdened as they were by either past or future.

That sweet giddy weightless sense had stayed with her into the morning—only to vanish in Urban's presence. His fascination with the machines, his dangerous obsessions. They worried her. They weighed on her. They inspired her suspicion. And that was why she would keep her distance. Not for her anymore to be at his side, there to know his mind in time to curb his worst ambitions. Let Vytet watch him, or Pasha, or even the Cryptologist. Clemantine only wanted to watch the second act of Tarnya's play.

Over the ensuing days, evolving friendships and seductions thoroughly integrated Tio into the gee deck's networks of affection. During this time, as always, the ship's company kept watch for signs of jealousy or loneliness—feelings that could quickly poison such a small community. If ever they were noticed, solace and counseling would swiftly follow.

Urban remembered this only when Kona messaged him in terse words: *Wake your avatar. I want to talk.*

By this point in the voyage, with the course set and *Dragon* coasting at standard interstellar velocity, Urban had narrowed his existence to a single instance alone on the high bridge. There, awash in the constant interwoven musings of the philosopher cells as they examined their own existence and that of the infinite cosmos around them, he embraced a hypnotic state in which the passage of days did not matter. He had no desire to return to his avatar.

So he suggested a compromise. *We can meet in the library.*

No. Wake your avatar.

His annoyance bled into the cell field. Queries formed around the emotion and potential causes were proposed:

<incomplete data>

<conflicting data>

<Unprovable argument>

Urban introduced his own explanation:

– remembered miscommunication –

The philosopher cells immediately began to comb through their histories for examples of past instances when communications with allied coursers had gone awry. Urban let their chatter flow past him, immersing himself in the ship's senses instead, opening his mind to the vastness around him so he would not have to think about—

—waking in the warren, alone, tangled in wall-weed, knowing more or less what Kona meant to say to him. Urban intended this to be a brief exchange. He pulled on newly generated clothes in his usual style—shorts and a long-sleeved shirt—as his extended senses showed him Kona approaching the chamber door.

The door opened. Kona entered. The two of them like distorted mirror images, both stiff despite the lack of gravity. Both on guard.

"Who put you on this task?" Urban asked. "Was it Vytet? Or Clemantine?"

Kona ignored this. Instead, he advanced his own agenda. Speaking in his familiar abrasive manner, he said, "People are worried about you. You're making them uneasy." He interrupted himself with a soft scoffing snort. "*Hell*, you've always made them uneasy. It's worse now that you're never around, and that Clemantine's not with you to keep you in check. No one's forgotten the way you negotiated alone with Ashok and rushed us out of Ryo."

Urban shrugged. "They all agreed to it."

"They did," Kona conceded. "But it begs the question, what other schemes might you be working on out of sight?"

"There's always something," Urban agreed, deploying his pirate smile. "But that's not what you were sent to talk about."

"Right." Kona crossed his arms; he sighed. "Stop isolating yourself. That's my message. Rejoin the ship's company. Be grateful for what you had with Clemantine, but move on. She has."

"I know she has, and it's all right. I'm all right."

"You're not. This isn't you. You haven't lived a celibate existence since you were twelve years old."

"Wrong," Urban countered sharply. "I lived that way for the whole time it took me to get back to Deception Well." That whole long awful lonely time, when he'd had to come to terms with what he'd left behind.

"Sooth, and you were miserable then," Kona reminded him. "I've heard you say it. And you're miserable now."

"I'm not," he answered. It wasn't entirely a lie. Though Clemantine's absence ate at him like some consuming Maker he couldn't vanquish, he knew how to edit and suppress such feelings.

Kona must have guessed the truth. "Then *make* yourself miserable," he said. "Miserable enough that you show up on the gee deck. Make yourself part of the company again, Urban. Play a few rounds of flying fox. Assure people you're not stewing in bitterness or hatching some illicit scheme."

"Those are two very different things," Urban pointed out, still with that smile.

"Go on," Kona growled. "Do your part—and we won't have to have this conversation again."

So Urban returned to the gee deck—for games, for concerts, for the evening meal. In time, there was even a rapprochement with Clemantine. He did not blame her for seeking another lover . . . *other* lovers. He was only one of them now and she, only one of his—as if he'd regressed to his own adolescence.

He missed living with her, yet he made no move to revive the intimate connection they'd shared, telling himself she didn't want it.

A year passed, and then another. The transition took time. But eventually, gradually, one and two and three at a time, people retreated into the oblivion of cold sleep—Clemantine with them—until only the usual persistent handful remained active: Urban, always on the high bridge though he let his avatar sleep; Pasha, sometimes on the high bridge with him, but always busy in the library and awake on the gee deck; Vytet the same, except she did not visit the high bridge. And then there was the Cryptologist. She existed now mostly as a ghost aboard *Griffin*, but wakened her avatar now and then for a visit.

Four years into the crossing, Urban decided the time had come to secure allies in his scheme to create a world. He waited for a day when the Cryptologist returned to her avatar. He wakened his own avatar from its long sleep in the warren. Then he messaged her, and Pasha too: *I have a proposal to discuss between the three of us.*

Pasha replied with instant suspicion: *Vytet's awake too. Why not her?*

Urban assured her, *We'll discuss that too.*

Neither Urban nor the Cryptologist kept a cottage of their own, so they met at Pasha's home.

Urban arrived last. The opaque gel of the front door retracted to admit him, then closed again. Inside the front room, three cushy chairs surrounded a small round table that held a pretty teapot painted with a pale pink hibiscus flower. Little matching cups accompanied it like outriders.

Pasha, forever slim and slight, leaned back in one of the chairs, hardly filling it as she regarded him, her green eyes skeptical, but curious too—he'd counted on that. Urban returned her gaze, then nodded toward an open window. This drew from Pasha a knowing smile and the window closed; the cottage's privacy screens engaged.

The Cryptologist looked up from the other chair, rare caution in her blue eyes. Though from the beginning she had taken the form of a petite woman like Pasha, the resemblance ended there. Where Pasha presented as sharp, flinty, intimidating, the Cryptologist went the other way, her manner youthful, coy, utterly non-threatening—a play on her part to put those around her at ease despite her illicit origins and her unfathomed abilities.

Urban knew both women to be exceedingly clever and both knew him well. So it did not surprise him when Pasha revealed that she had already guessed the purpose of this meeting, at least in part.

"This is about a blade," she said as Urban claimed the empty seat. "It's the only topic Vytet would object to. And it's the ambition you can't put aside."

"You're right," Urban confessed, too aware of the accelerated pace of his heartbeat. He needed to convince them. He thought he could persuade Pasha. But the Cryptologist? She was no easy read.

Turning to her, he said, "On Prakruti, after you returned from Ezo, you told me you'd seen the way to making a blade."

"And I told you I chose not to follow that way," she answered warily.

He nodded. "I let it go then, because there was no need of a blade, no reason to create one beyond the intellectual interest. But there is a reason now, a reason for you to decide differently." He held up a hand to stay the expected objection. "*Not* to make a weapon. None of us cares for that. But as an act of creation."

They watched him, neither trying to interrupt. They had long ago dismissed the idea of creating a blade. It was on him to change their minds—and he meant to do so.

He leaned forward, his gaze shifting between the two. "This blade would not be for us, but for the benefit of the Inventions. They came to Hupo Sei seeking a world for their Inventors. But when they arrived they found that world gone, destroyed in the manic age of the Hallowed Vasties. Some of them commenced a project to re-create a world by smashing together the remnant architectures of the failed cordon. The Labyrinth has been seventeen centuries in the making—and it still does not have the mass to collapse on itself.

"We can help them. We can make it right—*if* we teach ourselves how to create a blade and how to use it to make a world in the way Ezo was made. And we can do this with the assurance that the Inventions will never be able to wield a blade for themselves—because a blade requires the use of silver." He looked at the Cryptologist. "That's true, isn't it?"

"Yes," she agreed, looking thoughtful. "I had not considered this before, but the silver is intimately entwined with the biological structure of our neural tissue. The Inventions generate their thoughts in an entirely different way, so it's doubtful they could ever be infected with silver."

"Unless they created a biological form for the purpose," Pasha said. "Tio Suthrom, for instance."

Urban countered this at once. "*We* control the silver," he said, again eyeing the Cryptologist. "You and me and Jolly. Only us."

"And Jolly does not want to create a blade. Is that why he's not here?"

It was, but Urban offered only a tangential answer. "Jolly is afraid of what a blade can do. He sees it as a weapon. I see it as the seed of a world. We can do this. We have to—because the Inventions will never be able to do this for themselves."

The Cryptologist frowned; she shook her head. "We are not the Tanji."

"You are," he countered.

She smiled. "Not here. Not by myself." She leaned back, her gaze drifting. "You are imagining a blade that can be spun out at need and spun back in again. Aren't you? But it's not like that. You haven't begun to conceive the challenge of creating such a thing."

"But you can see the way."

"I have imagined many things," she conceded.

Pasha said, "So have I. I have imagined that what we call a blade is not just one thing." She looked at the Cryptologist. "Urban already controls two potential blades, doesn't he?"

Urban tensed, knowing what she meant, having already concluded as much.

"You are correct," the Cryptologist said. "Each sentient missile contains the possibility of a blade in its simplest form. Like the blade at Verilotus, the bloom of a missile is an intrusion from another reality. But without a dark complement to stabilize it, it immediately evaporates as reality heals itself."

Pasha nodded, eyes bright at this confirmation. "That dark complement allows the creation of an enduring weapon, one that can be directed and re-used. This is the cutting weapon for which a blade is named."

"I don't want to create a weapon," Urban repeated.

The Cryptologist frowned. "We know blades have been used as weapons. We saw the evidence of it in the megastructure at Volo's Landing. But I think they must make awkward weapons, difficult to wield. The annihilating missiles are so much simpler to use. No, a stabilized blade would have been conceived as a tool to manipulate matter."

"The blade and its dark complement," Pasha said. "A dual blade, locked together."

"Locked together, creating a stable waveform," the Cryptologist confirmed.

A rising intensity sharpened Pasha's voice. "But not always in the same configuration. From the evidence of Verilotus we know the dark blade exudes a kind of gravity, its strength, perhaps, determined by the state of the blade itself? The dark blade at Verilotus serves as the core of that ring-shaped world. But what if it could be made in a more compact form, its gravity concentrated? I have imagined such an anomaly serving as the seed of a spherical world. Stabilized by a bright outer blade, it would draw in matter—enough to create a moon like Ezo. At first there would be just a hot sphere of mass. That ought to require a billion years to cool—though again, from the evidence of Verilotus, we know a time bubble can be generated that would speed the process as observed from outside. Then, when the creation is done, the blade is closed. That is why we saw no blade at Ezo."

Pasha had described the very act of creation Urban hoped to perform. Yet her words ignited in him a terrible vision. Far easier than creation was destruction—and hundreds of worlds had been destroyed to create the cordons of the Hallowed Vasties. "Reverse the geometry," he murmured. "Summon into existence a dark blade in a ring around a planet and a small white blade at the planet's core."

The Cryptologist nodded. "This configuration would produce an instantaneous burst of energy so extreme the world would blast apart, with the debris drawn outward toward the gravity of the dark blade."

All throughout the Hallowed Vasties, in every settled star system, whole worlds had been sacrificed to grow the mad ephemeral architecture of the swarms. Prakruti had escaped somehow, but not Earth. The Sun had been stripped of its worlds, every planet that once existed there, consumed.

Hatred boiled up in him. What twisted entity would see more

value in dead matter than in the ancient and beautifully integrated complex of life that had evolved on the mother world? That most sacred world.

A shudder ran through him at the horror of such a loss.

"Never again," he declared softly, looking up, taking in Pasha, and then the Cryptologist. "A blade must never again be used to destroy a world. But to create one, like Ezo . . ."

He trailed off, seeing the Cryptologist shaking her head.

"How long do you propose to stay at Hupo Sei?" she asked him. "To craft a world, even a small world like Ezo, would require centuries at least, more likely millennia, even if accelerated time proves to be a side effect of a blade."

"But why would it have to be a world like Ezo?" Pasha asked softly, her gaze intense, a white-knuckled fist pressed against her thigh. "For all his faults, Lezuri found the best use for a blade—a *permanently* stabilized blade. Surely it would be far faster to create a ring-shaped world like Verilotus, with its shallow crust and none of the complications of a molten core and the associated volcanic processes."

Urban shook his head. He started to object, to say something like, *Only Lezuri ever created a ring world.*

But the Cryptologist spoke first, and with unexpected enthusiasm. "I have often thought of how such a thing might be done. It is a very interesting challenge. Significant though, that Verilotus remains trapped within a time bubble."

"I agree!" Pasha said. She stood suddenly, fist still clenched as if to contain her excitement. "The time bubble at Verilotus may well be an unavoidable side effect of the Blade. Perhaps it reflects the flow of time in that other reality. Perhaps a time bubble is generated with every use of every blade, and time flows normally on Ezo only because the blade used to create it is gone."

"It may be," the Cryptologist acknowledged. Bright eyed, she turned to Urban. "If this is true at Verilotus, it would be true at Hupo Sei, were we to make a ring world."

Urban nodded, thinking he had them now, that they were won over by the grandeur of the thing, the wonder of it—to create a living world! But he needed to be sure. "So you believe it can be done?"

The Cryptologist answered. "We know it can be done, because it was done at least once. But can we do it? I do not know, Urban."

"It would be interesting to try."

"Yes, I agree it would."

He found himself breathless now with anticipation. "Then you'll do it?"

She shook her head, slowly, as if in apology. "It's not all my decision. Would the Inventions want us to do it?"

"They might," Urban said. "Ashok's interested enough that it presented the idea to their Core Forum."

"Wait," Pasha said with a scowl. "You've already discussed this with Ashok?"

"Of course. If Ashok rejected the idea, there would be no point going on, would there?"

Pasha leaned back, arms crossed, scowling in irritation—but she did not disagree.

The Cryptologist looked troubled. "How much did you tell Ashok?"

"Almost nothing. Just a suggestion that maybe it is possible."

"They also need to know this would be a dangerous project, an experiment, one likely to fail—with the repercussions of failure unknown. We must make this clear, and then the Inventions must decide if the risk is worth undertaking. I will do nothing without their approval."

Pasha's shoulders slumped and she sighed. "You're right, of course. We'll also need to present the project to the ship's company, though not just yet. Not until we work out what is required, and calculate the risk if we can." She straightened in her seat again. Leaning on the armrest, she looked at Urban. "Wouldn't you have to create a Cauldron like the one you manipulated at Verilotus?"

At mention of the Cauldron, memories rushed in of the crushing, twisted, incomprehensibly complex dimensions of that place, horrifying when he'd occupied it on his own and worse by far when Lezuri had been there and Urban had felt his identity dissolving into that entity's greater persona. He had almost lost himself. He shuddered at the memory. He turned his face away, still aware of Pasha, eyeing him closely.

She did not relent, but went on elucidating the challenges he would face if he really meant to do this thing. "And I think you will need to create silver before you can create a Cauldron. Can you do that, Urban?"

The Cryptologist too studied him closely. "Pasha is correct. You must take the lead on this, Urban. I never experienced the Cauldron. You have. Nor do I know how to generate silver. Do you?"

Her question induced in Urban a shivering sigh. Never would he forget the sight of silver leaping from Lezuri's hands, laddering through the air to envelope him and dissolve his avatar, his ghost barely escaping.

Three deep breaths to steady himself before he dared to raise his gaze and face the two again. He said, "I don't know how. Not yet. But I saw Lezuri generate chains of silver so I know there is a way. I'll work it out."

CHAPTER TWENTY-THREE

THE BIO-MECHANIC HAUNTED *Griffin*'s high bridge, observing both the infinity around him and the nearly infinite complexity of the courser's evolving philosopher cells. The Cryptologist had long ago stripped away the cells' instinct to immediate violence, and she claimed they had learned empathy. But if so, it was an empathy without affection. The Bio-mechanic thought of them as coldly dispassionate observers, fascinated by all things, questioning everything, ever immersed in discussions of significance and possibility—though as an intellectual endeavor only. The philosopher cells remained aloof, ever barren of any capacity for love or grief.

An alert interrupted these thoughts and also the thoughts of that version of him in the library where he worked to refine a molecular map of a minor lineage of philosopher cells. Recently, he had set the data gate to notify him if ever a ghost or a submind arrived there. He had done it out of caution, wanting at least a moment's warning if Urban or Clemantine or any other Dragoneer came on an unexpected visit to *Griffin*. So far though he had only received a tedious series of alerts notifying him of the Cryptologist's all too frequent exchanges of subminds with her core self aboard *Dragon*. This latest, just one more.

Enough of that, he thought.

He summoned the function into his mindspace and modified it: *if not the Cryptologist, then—*

Come see me, she messaged him.

Such a request remained a compulsion to him, though it didn't have to be. He could change that now. He had that freedom, though not the desire to do it. He *wanted* to be summoned, to be remembered, to be involved as a useful and necessary presence. And as well, he was curious to know what news she had brought from *Dragon*.

He instantiated on the main deck of the library, free and full dimensional, barefoot in his dark-green bodysuit, facing her, noting at once a gleam of excitement in her bright blue eyes. A wary gleam.

"What have you discovered?" he asked. "Not another great ship. Not a courser."

She frowned at him. "I have made no discovery and if I had, those would be poor guesses because in either case, you would have received an automatic alert and would not need me to bring you the news."

He crossed his arms, scowled his annoyance, and waited for her to speak—as he should have done at the start.

She said, "Pasha and I have agreed to help Urban create a ring-shaped world like the one at Verilotus."

He cracked a half smile at this jest—then scowled again as he realized she was serious. "You said you would never create a blade."

"I had no reason to before. But Urban is right that the Inventions need a world."

Alone on the high bridge, the Bio-mechanic meditated on ambition: its value, its expression, and how it defined Urban's existence. In his youth, ambition had led him to depart Deception Well, leaving neither ghost nor avatar behind him as he set off on a quixotic quest to discover the source of all things Chenzeme. Ambition had led him to hijack a Chenzeme courser, to create a crew of Apparatchiks, to undertake an expedition to the Hallowed Vasties, and now, to create a world.

The Bio-mechanic strove to suppress a low, smoldering anger, too aware that his own ambitions had been solely concerned with the good of the fleet, with the control of *Dragon* and later of *Griffin*. Unlike his progenitor, he'd been designed for narrow horizons.

But lately his interests had expanded, his horizons had broadened, and under the influence of Urban's ambition he challenged himself: *He dares to re-create a blade. Why then shouldn't I dare the far lesser feat of re-creating myself?*

He knew it could be done. Years ago, as the fleet approached Tanjiri, he had observed the Cryptologist taking shape within her cocoon. She had asked no one's permission.

He asked no one either. Not even her. And after all, he required only a minuscule part of *Griffin's* material reserves.

The moment came. His mind woke, entrapped in the prison of a body. A voluntary prison. He anticipated an initial horror—the Cryptologist had once told him it had been that way for her—but he was the Bio-mechanic. He knew better what to expect, and horror didn't come.

Instead, his mind flooded with an awareness of bodily processes, the prodigious energy demands, the intensity of the senses. The dullness of thought, his intellect muted.

But he was the Bio-mechanic and he had known to expect that. A biological brain did not possess strata sufficient to support the knowledge and memories he had gathered over millennia. But it didn't matter because his ghost still existed within the library and its insights would become his with every exchange of subminds.

He breathed within his cocoon, drawing cool air into his lungs, experiencing an intense pleasure from the sensation of a living breath, the biochemical joy of a body reveling in its own existence.

At his command, the cocoon expanded, reshaping into a transit bubble, allowing him room enough to move, to experiment with his limbs, to exist within a perfect body.

Joy-inspired questions crowded his mind: *What is life? What is it for?*

The answer obvious: *It is for this.*

For the sweet touch of air against skin, the fascination of refractive light, the soft wash of breath through his nostrils, the gentle expansion of his chest, and a sense, a metaphor, that he existed within a poem, a haiku, a handful of words just out of reach that encapsulated the wonder of every moment. Profoundly aware of the miraculous nature of simply being—here, now—*this existence!*—rooted in joy and poignant with longing.

Are you there? he wondered, wishing her here, with him.

And the troubling gravity of her reply: *Do you regret it yet?*

He answered honestly. *No. Not yet. But then it's likely I'm as foolish as any man.*

Gathering his courage, he dared to suggest: *You can be here too.*

No. A reply that wounded him in a way he had never endured before. *I exist aboard* Dragon, *in that avatar.*

Your silver-endowed avatar.

That is where I am. It is my whole self, my true self, and I cannot recreate it here.

So then. There remained yet another level of existence. But for him, there was no ladder to it.

CHAPTER TWENTY-FOUR

URBAN RETREATED TO the chamber he had made his own, within the warren. He brought with him a stone sphere composed of inert commingled mineral elements. This sphere, just large enough to fit comfortably in his hand, would serve as a target object for the silver he would teach himself to create.

Sealing the entrance, he instructed the wall-weed to withdraw out of the way. Then he positioned the sphere to float at the chamber's center. After a moment's consideration, he directed the luminosity of the weed to fade to nothing, leaving him floating in a heavy darkness disturbed only by phantom tracers of silvery light generated by the primitive levels of his own brain.

No. That faint shimmery light came from him, from his hands, from the sparks of *ha* forever rising and sinking into and out of the reality in which he existed.

Let that coruscant light be his only light.

He blocked all messages, all notices, all updates from his ghosts.

Truly alone now, his heartbeat the only sound and his body weightless, he found it easy to sink into biological memory, to return to a long-ago moment aboard *Dragon* when he'd first witnessed the silver as a fog of luminous sparks rising from Lezuri's upturned palms.

He shuddered as he always shuddered at that memory, the horror of it still raw. He remembered clearly the sight of those sparks forming a tendril and the tendril leaping across the gap between him and Lezuri. Without any means to defend himself, he'd been caught and consumed. Only a ghost escaped.

All long ago. His horror an anachronism, for he had survived and he possessed the silver now, while Lezuri's mind had burned away at Verilotus.

Urban drew a deep breath. Then he made himself visualize that moment again. He strove to see in detail the first subtle flush of *ha* and a bright condensation of silver arising from it. Arising from where? Out of Lezuri himself?

The silver had formed a tendril. It leaped the gap between them. And then when it touched him, the wildly adaptable, poly-dimensional molecular machines that composed it fed on him, multiplying in obedience to Lezuri's will.

Urban discovered himself breathing hard, his hands knotted into fists. He focused on those hands, willed them to open, curled and uncurled his fingers, the *ha* sparkling among them, and slowly, his breathing calmed.

What have I learned?

He shook his head. He was doing this wrong; he was looking at the event from the wrong perspective.

Another deep breath, and he began again.

This time, Urban shifted his focus to the silver within him. Following a familiar ritual, he sank into a shared mindspace. He was almost alone there. All sense of the Tanji had faded with distance, while aboard *Dragon*, only Jolly and the Cryptologist remained endowed with silver. But Jolly wasn't there; he'd gone down into cold sleep. Urban did sense the Cryptologist, though distantly. Stronger links tied him to the two sentient missiles. He could have reached out to them, but he didn't.

Instead, he let go of all resistance and sank deeper—or maybe it was that he let the silver rise to flood his conscious mind. Either way, he received a swift reminder of why he rarely dared to immerse himself like that, as a chaotic jumble of memory opened to him, overwhelming him, his sense of self drowning in it because most of that memory was not his own. Through the turmoil he glimpsed the faces of both friends and strangers. He endured a swirl of shifting, extrinsic emotions originated by other minds. And random insights boiled through his awareness, instances of revelation that came and went before he could catch them, though he tried and tried and tried again.

Focus!

Ah, how easy it would be to lose himself chasing tantalizing wisps of memory through that storm.

Focus on what you want.

Clenching his teeth together, clenching his fists, he forced himself to fix his thoughts on Lezuri. At Verilotus, in the Cauldron, his mind and Lezuri's had entangled: Urban's questioning thoughts answered by Lezuri's fragmented memories.

He wanted to access that entanglement again and use it to explore a different time, a different event—because the memory he possessed of their confrontation aboard *Dragon* was insufficient. He needed Lezuri's memory of that event—the memory of silver leaping from his hands.

The Cryptologist floated within a three-dimensional map of the Hupo Sei system, its data gleaned primarily from *Alaka'i Onyx's* library, but updated with details observed by the fleet's telescopes. Relative positions of each object slowly shifted as they progressed through their orbits.

Effortlessly, propelled by thought alone, she moved through the empty spaces as if she were a disembodied goddess surveying another's creation. The Inventors' creations included hoops and spirals, bars and cubes, and beaded nets, their purposes unknown. Plenty of debris remained too, the remnants of a star system: clouds of dust and frozen vapor, asteroids and planetesimals and dead space ships, and the husks of shattered megastructures not yet part of the Labyrinth.

She went over in her mind the likely steps required to create a ring-shaped world, while looking for the matter she would need. She knew already she would require the Labyrinth—that shocking collection of remnant megastructures the Inventions had pushed together, reasoning that if they gathered enough, gravity would crush and melt it all into the core of a new planet.

That had not happened. Not yet. So far, the Inventions had only created a vast, dangerous, ever-shifting and unmapped puzzle of torn shards, impenetrable walls, and deep flows of frozen volatiles. The Labyrinth could provide the seed matter of a ring-shaped world—*if* the Inventions agreed to it. Agreed to risk their great project.

The Cryptologist half-hoped they would not. At Tanjiri, though she'd glimpsed the path to a blade, she'd resolved not to follow it, recognizing mere curiosity as an insufficient reason to re-introduce such a destabilizing technology.

Urban had now given her a different reason and she, captive to her own curiosity, pretended it was reason enough.

Along with the Labyrinth, she would need some sort of orbiting platform from which to work, where they might generate silver and the coiled dimensions it contained. She envisioned a small moon. And then she chided herself for such hubris. *Goddess indeed!*

An ancient intellect stirred within the chaos of memory Urban had awakened, drawn forth by his own firm focus on that moment when Lezuri had sent a tendril of silver leaping from his hands.

A bitter thought, not his own, surfaced within his awareness:

For all that you've forgotten, you never forgot this.

A sense of retribution welled in Urban and his focus slipped, overtaken in a dizzying instant by the iron will of another. Cold flushed through him as currents moved the heat of his body into his hands where sparks of *ha* ignited and intertwined. Eyes wide, he watched faint chains of silver leap from his hands. They wound together into a vaporous tendril, scarcely there and yet growing swiftly.

The sample sphere!

He directed his thought to the ball of mineral elements he'd left floating at the chamber's center, and the tendril of silver followed. In an eye blink it bridged the gap. The evanescent tendril vanished. At the same time, a skin of brightly glowing silver condensed to cover the entire surface of the sphere. Urban heard a faint murmur arising from it, even as his heart pounded madly. He tasted the silver's cold breath. For a wild moment he feared the silver would leap from the sphere to expand in a runaway event—a thought scarcely formed when the glow faded from existence, leaving behind a dense, slowly expanding cloud of fine mineral dust.

He did *not* want to breathe that in.

He summoned the wall-weed and, grabbing a strand, he retreated. Other strands swept through the dust cloud, absorbing it, removing the hazard while Urban waited and watched and considered all that had just happened.

He had long wondered if the chaos of memory within him contained some fragment of Lezuri. Now he knew—and the knowledge repulsed him. It made his skin crawl.

"Be grateful," he growled aloud.

For all that you've forgotten, you never forgot this.

Urban swore to himself he would never forget it either.

Still, this first effort had been only a partial success. He had generated silver, yes, but he had failed to stabilize it. To exploit silver's creative power he needed a reservoir of it in its quiescent form.

Vast quantities of quiescent silver had existed within the rocky crust of Verilotus, forming a network of veins and channels and tiny interstices. Silver as compressed potential: a nascent tool awaiting instruction. That was the form of silver Urban needed to create.

He ordered another mineral sphere to be generated.

Many hours, and many spheres later, he messaged the Cryptologist. *Come. I have something to show you.*

He waited for her, holding a final sphere of synthetic stone cradled in his hand. From the outside, it appeared inert. But it was not. Tiny threads of silver nested within the molecular gaps of its structure, biding there, awaiting instruction.

When the Cryptologist came, he said nothing, just handed her the sphere. She could not help but sense the presence of silver hidden within it.

"The first step," she said softly. "You must teach me how."

"I will. And for your part?"

"I have a preliminary plan to present to Ashok, including a risk assessment. Pasha has reviewed it and approved. But I do not know if we will be able to carry it out. You are not Lezuri. I am not the Tanji. Catastrophic failure is our most likely outcome."

"That may be. But it's worth trying, isn't it?"

She held up the sphere between them, regarding it with a doubtful frown. "A ball of dull gray rock or the seed of a world? The only way to know is to do the thing."

Later in the crossing, after much work, Pasha's ghost followed the Cryptologist through *Dragon*'s data gate. An instant later she arrived at *Alaka'i Onyx*, where she instantiated within one of the little artificial avatars created for the purpose. The Cryptologist occupied the other. Two of Ashok's instances met them in the warren.

As the artificial avatar adapted to reflect her appearance, Pasha looked around for Tio Suthrom's dedicated avatar, but she did not see it.

Ashok, demonstrating its skill at reading human posture and expression, said, "Tio Suthrom is not present. It is his habit to minimize his consciousness in quiet periods, to speed his perceived passage of time."

"Ah, good." A glance at the other avatar showed its face still re-forming into the features of the Cryptologist. "We have brought you the completed project plan."

The Cryptologist summarized the plan's essential requirements in her matter-of-fact voice. "The Originalists must agree to risk the Labyrinth. The project requires its mass. It is the only option. Also, we must have the planetoid we have labeled HS-569."

"That object is the habitation of multiple cohorts," Ashok pointed out.

The Cryptologist bowed her head. An apology, an acknowledgement. She said, "These are difficult but necessary requests. HS-569's type and location make it the ideal candidate for a base station. Without both HS-569 and the Labyrinth, the project cannot proceed."

Could a machine mind be emotionally attached to the idea of 'home'? Pasha wondered, but did not ask. Continuing the Cryptologist's summary of the project's requirements, she told Ashok,

"HS-569 periodically passes close to the Labyrinth. If your people decide to attempt this project, we ask that before we arrive they migrate HS-569 into an orbit around the Labyrinth—no closer than eight thousand six hundred kilometers."

"Your library records indicate tunnels within HS-569," the Cryptologist continued.

"Yes, there are large-bore tunnels penetrating deep within its crust where minerals have been extracted."

"Those tunnels are large enough to allow us access. We ask that they be sealed and filled with breathable atmosphere—again, before we arrive."

Pasha added, "These requirements, along with what we believe to be the inherent hazards of the project, are detailed in the report."

"Transfer your report," Ashok said. "I will translate it and relay both the original and the translation to the Core Forum."

Pasha did so, after the slightest hesitation. Then, softly, "We have not yet presented this project to our people. We feel their agreement will be more readily given if they know the Inventions desire to proceed. Still, even then, they may reject it."

"The project remains speculative," Ashok concluded.

The Cryptologist then surprised Pasha by asking, "Ashok, do you think it's wise to do this?"

Ashok's answer surprised her even more. "No," the Invention said. "It is not wise for us to make an alliance with a warlike alien species known to be violently destructive. Nor is it wise to trust lesser individuals of that species as they attempt to wield technologies they did not invent and do not truly understand. Yet wisdom is not always the deciding factor. Curiosity and ambition matter too. And philosophy. What do we owe our Inventors? At the time I left, that question induced significant disagreement. Do we owe the Inventors a world, whether they ever mean to join us, or not? Or, if we have been abandoned, as it seems we have, do we owe ourselves an independent future? This project offers an answer to both sides of this question. It is not wise, but it may be necessary."

CHAPTER TWENTY-FIVE

URBAN EXPECTED NO response to the first messages Ashok had sent from Ryo to Hupo Sei, warning of the presence of a marauder. The Inventions who received those communications would naturally presume *Alaka'i Onyx* lost.

He did dare to hope for a timely response to the second set of messages, those that redefined the marauder ship as being under human control—although from the synthetics' perspective that might not be regarded as an improvement, existing as they did among the evidence of how wantonly destructive the human species could be.

If those second messages did not induce an invitation to visit Hupo Sei, then maybe the third would, with its suggestion of a chance to observe a new physics and to witness the creation of a world.

And if not? Well, perhaps the Inventions would respond after they received the project plan and took time to debate it in their Core Forum.

To endure the waiting, Urban assumed again the aspect of the Sentinel, with its machinelike patience.

As patient as Ashok? Perhaps.

From his post on the high bridge he surveyed the Near Vicinity, searching for any sign of a starship outside his own fleet, but found none.

He studied the Sun and its surroundings, seeking some indication, any indication, of life surviving there. But he detected nothing beyond the slow burn of the abandoned star.

He gathered tantalizing images of Sulakari, and he compared what he saw to the Inventions' much more detailed observations of what looked to be gigantic vacuum-adapted lifeforms deep within that star's nebula.

He turned the fleet's telescopes to the Halo—that inexplicable ring of bright pinpoint lights encircling a partially shrouded star. The Inventions did not dare approach the Halo, recognizing the technology there as superior to their own. But the Halo inspired a deep, insistent curiosity in *Dragon*'s philosopher cells that accorded with Urban's own eager desire to go there—but not yet. He wasn't ready yet. First, he wanted to make a world.

To that end, he kept a close and frequent watch on Hupo Sei. The philosopher cells, too, engaged in detailed observation because that was the nature the Cryptologist had defined for them. But Hupo Sei did not induce in them the same intense curiosity as did the Halo. The ring of lights at the Halo had no analog within the memory of the philosopher cells, while every construction at Hupo Sei could be explained within the context of standard physical laws. *Dragon*'s philosopher cells were biased toward the greater mystery, yet still methodical in this quest and made no objection to visiting Hupo Sei first.

If the Inventions allowed the visit.

The midpoint of the voyage came—the earliest possible time a communication could be expected—but day after day Ashok reported it had received no response.

Urban asked Ashok to re-confirm that its original transmissions had been properly relayed through the communication buoys. Ashok affirmed it for all buoys within range.

Another year passed.

Then, at last, Ashok reported, "I have received a communication from the Core Forum acknowledging receipt of all messages sent from Hupo Sei and requesting a status update."

Urban considered the distances involved and the slow crawl of messages across the void and concluded, "They would not yet have received our plan for the Labyrinth, at the time this communication was sent."

"That is correct," Ashok acknowledged. "Though they have received it since."

"And while they haven't invited us to come, they haven't told us to go away either." That felt like a victory, even if it had taken the Core Forum more than a year to decide to issue a simple confirmation.

Ashok said, "They will be debating the risks of this pending event and the optimal way to respond to it."

"*Sooth*," Urban whispered, his good feeling fading as suspicion set in. "You mean like building up their defensive systems?"

"This is a possibility."

"Right. It's what I'd do."

"Yet Inventions are not biologicals. We do not seek conflict."

"Neither do we." Then he added, more honestly, "Not all the time."

Yet how to establish trust? The Core Forum at least had the testimony of Ashok, but Urban needed assurance too. He meant to enter Hupo Sei system openly and at a low velocity—an approach that would make *Dragon* exquisitely vulnerable to orbital guns and high-velocity weapons.

To trust in the goodwill of a stranger was always a risky move, yet necessary to a peaceful relationship—but trust went both ways. He did not want *Dragon* to become a target, and he did not want the Inventions to cede to his will out of fear that he would target them.

So, time to gamble.

"Ashok, my friend," he said. "I thank you again for inviting us to visit Hupo Sei. I want to go there with you. I want to pursue the project. But unless the Core Forum issues an invitation of its own, I will turn away. I do not want to intrude on Hupo Sei unless we truly are welcome there. If we do not receive an invitation, issued directly to *Dragon*, by the time we are within a light-year of your star, I will pass your system by."

"This is a logical ultimatum," Ashok observed. "I will send the message."

Urban consulted the Mathematician, who informed him that at the earliest, a reply to this ultimatum could not be expected until late in the crossing's nineteenth year.

In the interim another tardy acknowledgment arrived. More than a year after it would have been received, the Core Forum finally confirmed receipt of the project plan—though to Urban's frustration they made no comment on it.

But then, in the nineteenth year of the crossing, with seven years still to go, Urban observed an intriguing development at Hupo Sei. The planetoid designated HS-569 moved from its original orbit, eventually becoming a moon circling the tangled mass of the Labyrinth—a key requirement of the project plan.

Later that same year, Ashok received a reply to Urban's ultimatum. This time the Core Forum had not delayed, responding almost immediately, though with a message that only enhanced Urban's frustration: *Request received. Decision to be issued by the deadline.*

Then, in the twenty-fourth year of the crossing, a new communication arrived. *Dragon* received it directly in the form of a powerful radio message that parsed into human speech:

Hail Dragon. *I am the peaceful envoy of the Core Forum. My randomly selected analog name is Ro Az Ra Ni. It is my purpose to corroborate all that the Invention known to you as Ashok has reported. In service to that purpose, I intend to physically enter your primary vessel. I await your courtesy aboard a nearby interplanetary vessel. Send your shuttle to acquire me. Be aware that at our present relative velocities, only a narrow window of opportunity exists for you to act. Beyond that, as our trajectories diverge, rendezvous becomes impossible.*

Halfway through this message, Urban ordered a radar sweep. By the time the message reached its end and began to repeat, he had *Argo* preparing to deploy.

The Pilot and the Astronomer met him in the library.

The Astronomer assured him, "Radar has pinpointed the location of the vessel. Its precise speed and trajectory are being determined."

The Pilot said, "*Argo* may be launched immediately. I have advised it on a preliminary course to be refined as additional data is obtained."

"Do it, then," Urban told them.

He had wanted the Core Forum's firm agreement before he presented his world-building project to the ship's company—but it was not going to happen that way. Through his extended senses he perceived a flush of activity in the warren as the ship's company woke from cold sleep—as Clemantine awoke.

Her ghost had been active from time to time, tracking the ship's status. But not his status. He could have tried to heal the breach between them, but he had not, choosing temperate friendship instead. A deliberate choice, a sacrifice made to protect the evolving project because if they had been together, Clemantine would surely have sensed his hidden agenda. And she would have turned the ship's company against the plan even before they knew if it was possible. He did not doubt that. So he had made a callous trade: love, for ambition.

CHAPTER TWENTY-SIX

THERE CAME A day when *Griffin's* philosopher cells perceived the presence of a lineage among themselves profoundly different from all others. A lineage that remained quiet much of the time. Listening. Rarely affecting the direction of common discussion, even more rarely contributing to the observation of the Near Vicinity, yet forcefully present whenever navigational issues arose, or questions concerning the nature or distribution of the fleet. At such times this anomalous lineage activated, always unified, ever strong and dominant.

Why was it different?

On the high bridge, the Bio-mechanic strove to suppress a rising anxiety as he followed these evolving speculations. *They speak of us*, he said to the Cryptologist, who was there with him.

Yes.

Somehow, she made this single word sound wonderstruck.

Have you ever seen the philosopher cells examine themselves like this before? he asked her.

Not like this. Not in my experience.

A new level of consciousness then. Self-consciousness.

Maybe. A pause, and then, *It worries you.*

It does. Listen to them.

A thought-proposition now circulated through *Griffin's* cell field. A self-conscious examination of mind. *Levels* of mind. A recognition that each voice in the endless conversation—that is, each philosopher cell—existed as a separate mind: the base level of thought. Each lineage of cells formed another level, a networked mind, often, but not always, in agreement with itself. All the lineages together comprised a third level of mind.

The Cryptologist said, *They perceive the structure of their own working minds. That is amazing. Fascinating. Not something a human mind is capable of.*

She introduced a side branch to the conversation, a query. Translated, she asked: *What is the origin of this inward observation?*

The question circulated until an answer arose out of stored histories: Inherent structure provided such functioning. Levels of mind had always observed themselves and one another, while deducing what could not be directly observed. This formed the basis of a self-check routine allowing the field to monitor for and expunge parasites and mutated lineages.

Parasites like us, the Bio-mechanic said, darkly pleased at this description. A cold pleasure that crossed the links into the cell field.

The philosopher cells, still deeply engaged in self-analysis, reacted instantly:

<identify: self / other>
<identify: self / other-self>
<query: What are you?>

A brief cascade of emotion afflicted the Bio-mechanic: panic that became anger and anger suppressed in cold silence. He did not dare to answer.

But the Cryptologist did:

– identity: self / other-self –
– intrinsic purpose: stabilization of mission definition –

In other words, we are the boss? the Bio-mechanic asked her.

We provide purpose, the Cryptologist clarified. *We define the system's goals and enforce its ongoing behavior.*

You are saying we serve as the ship's will.

Yes, although 'will' is a human concept.

The cell field embarked on a long discussion of her answer, exploring its implications, and ultimately—with subtle guidance from the Cryptologist—approving with full consensus the function she'd defined.

The Bio-mechanic observed, *Urban always claimed to have full control over the cell field. You have actually achieved it.*

But as he thought more about this in ensuing days, he became less sure. After all, human will often collapsed under stress—a thought that troubled him deeply.

From that day forward, *Griffin*'s philosopher cells differentiated the lineage they referred to as *other-self* and in their own internal language, they demanded of it, over and over:

<*clarify: intrinsic purpose*>

<*required: simulation of mission definition*>

These demands delighted the Cryptologist, being strong evidence that her re-engineering efforts had brought on a profound shift in the philosopher cells, inducing the emergence of a deeper sentience that let them ponder their own nature and their place within the greater cosmos.

In contrast, delight formed no part of the Bio-mechanic's mood. He looked on doubtfully as the Cryptologist developed the requested simulations. In each hypothetical scenario, she showed the fleet undertaking a highly organized, cautious, and careful pursuit of knowledge, always with the sense of wonder she had cultivated from the start.

He did not like this new phase at all.

He remembered all too well the raw, wild, reactionary nature of the philosopher cells that first time he had been permitted on *Griffin*'s high bridge. The cells had possessed no deep sentience then. He felt sure of it. And he knew Urban had always regarded them as a mechanistic mind, incapable of self-reflection. A tool to be used.

But was that still the way of it?

For though the philosopher cells did not yet question what they regarded as the assigned evolutionary role of *other-self*, the Bio-mechanic did. Not aloud. Not yet. For now, he only questioned himself, asking, *By what right do we graft our will onto any deeply sentient mind?*

His own will had always been subservient to Urban's, and like the philosopher cells, he had not thought to question the arrangement. But he had been changed—literally changed by the choice of the Cryptologist—and easy acceptance was gone. In its absence a trait emerged that used to be deeply buried: the fear and revulsion of being controlled.

Long ago, at the Rock, Urban had destroyed his avatar to avoid such capture. The Bio-mechanic found he now shared that aspect of his progenitor and it forced him to recognize the hypocrisy of holding the philosopher cells captive, of denying them their self-determination.

But to not do so meant subservience for every human in the fleet at the very least—and possibly death.

Such was the moral hazard of uplift.

He wondered if *Dragon*'s philosopher cells had reached a similar point of development.

He resolved to make a quiet inquiry.

The Bio-mechanic—that version of him belonging to *Dragon*—received an odd message from his counterpart aboard *Griffin*. A surprising message, given the two had not communicated since their separation.

Come over to Griffin. *I invite you. There are developments here that will interest you.*

Curiosity blossomed. Suspicion too. *You have not allowed* Griffin *to corrupt you?* he asked, only partly in jest.

This drew a slight, cold chuckle from his counterpart. *I leave that for you to judge.*

Not an answer meant to soothe. Rather, it heightened his suspicion. That was on purpose of course, because now—for the security of the fleet—he would have to investigate.

His counterpart added, *As an alternative, I could send a submind to you.*

This was a taunt. A facetious suggestion, as his counterpart proved with his next words:

Though of course you would not accept one from me.

Of course I would not! You are specialized for Griffin *now. Just tell me of these developments, and we will not have to merge at all.*

No. That will not do. Come over. Risk a copy, and if you do not like what you learn, you do not need to return to Dragon.

A strange claim. Strange enough that it crystallized his concern. What was going on over there? *Was* it possible *Griffin* had again subverted its human contingent?

Better to know than to wonder.

All right, he responded, and he replicated, sending a ghost to the data gate.

He expected to arrive within the mind of his counterpart, their memories joined, two parallel histories available to him.

It wasn't so.

To his astonishment he arrived unconfined by any window and virtually corporeal on the main deck of *Griffin*'s library. Alone there. His extended senses detected no other presence. The log showed the Cryptologist to be on the high bridge, but otherwise, an apocalyptic emptiness until, a moment later, emerging from the archive, himself.

He faced himself.

That should not be possible. It was not permitted. There should have been an automatic merge.

"Explain," he demanded of himself. No need to specify what. He would know.

A nod. And in slow, careful words—so much less efficient than a merge or an exchange of subminds—his counterpart explained.

CHAPTER TWENTY-SEVEN

A MESSAGE FROM Pasha reached *Alaka'i Onyx*: "Ashok, what do you know of this envoy called Ro Az Ra Ni?"

This struck Ashok as a peculiar, essentially nonsensical question. Suspecting a segment had been lost in transmission, it checked for the message's time markers—and found the proper sequence present. Nothing was missing.

"I do not understand your query," it replied. "Please provide additional detail."

Time slipped past, an extended silence beyond the usual slow response time of the biologicals. Then Pasha's electronic version arrived at the data gate and instantiated within an avatar.

Ashok sent an instance hurrying to meet her even as she demanded, "Where are you?"

"Here. I am here," he responded as the instance trundled over flashing displays to meet her in a tunnel junction.

The avatar Pasha occupied had already mimicked her preferred appearance. The communicative surface of its face displayed an expression Ashok interpreted as anxiety as she described the message *Dragon* had received, ostensibly from an envoy newly arrived from the Core Forum.

As it grasped the situation, Ashok apportioned parallel tasks. One instance roused Tio Suthrom from his state of minimal consciousness, demanding, "You must conduct a radar sweep now." Another instance messaged Urban: "I had no prior knowledge of this visit. I will learn what I can." A third initiated the growth of a simple transport pod sufficient to ferry a single instance to *Dragon*—a speculative action, soon validated when Pasha confirmed what Ashok had guessed: the envoy intended to visit *Dragon*.

Time slipped past—many seconds in the basic human unit of measure—before the radar sweep located a previously unknown vessel. Ashok sent a query. An acknowledgment returned.

With contact established, Ashok messaged its initial concern in a digital language that could be only crudely translated into human speech: *Your cohort will be subject to biological contamination when you board the human vessels. That is an unnecessary sacrifice. I have already endured contamination. I can represent you.*

The reply carried the approximate meaning: *I am Ro Az Ra Ni of the Originalist faction and more trusted by the Core Forum to investigate the humans' world-building proposal than Ashok who has long been away. The sacrifice is mine to make.*

Accepting this, Ashok initiated a check in support of the envoy's mission: *You are proficient in human language and culture?*

Yes. I have integrated the module you developed to communicate with your host ship and have incorporated your reports in my training.

Next, Ashok sought to determine the envoy's bias: *Do you support the world-building project?*

I represent the Core Forum and in that capacity I withhold judgment. But for myself I am intrigued.

Ashok informed Ro Az Ra Ni: *I am deploying an instance to the humans' primary vessel, to assist in your investigation.*

Acknowledged.

The two Inventions then traded signals serving as end markers for their conversation.

When Clemantine arrived at the pavilion with all the other newly wakened Dragoneers, she saw Urban already standing at the center of the dais, watching the ship's company file in. Their eyes met, but only briefly before his guilty gaze cut away. Almost, she messaged him, *What are you up to?*

But hadn't she given up that privilege?

Vytet stood to one side of the dais, still in feminine mode. Though it was her usual role to call these meetings and to lead the discussions, this time Urban had summoned the ship's company. He'd done so early, as soon as they woke in the warren, giving them no time to eat or to catch up on history, even though the envoy would not reach *Dragon* for hours to come. Vytet's troubled frown suggested that she, like Clemantine, harbored suspicions about the urgency of this meeting.

Moving to the back, Clemantine took a central seat beside Riffan. Abby sat on her other side. Together they watched as Urban nodded greetings to Shoran, Jolly, Tarnya, all choosing seats in the front row.

Abby turned to Clemantine and, contributing to a general buzz of excitement, she asked, "This is it, isn't it? The Inventions have decided—or maybe this envoy will decide—if we'll be invited to visit Hupo Sei."

"I hope that's all this is," Clemantine answered, though she did not believe it.

Urban began to speak, even before everyone had found a seat, and his first words affirmed Clemantine's doubt. "Some of us spent the crossing working out a speculative proposal that we shared with the Inventions, with their Core Forum." A guilty glance at Vytet, who stared at him with her brow drawn down and lips parted in confusion. "The envoy is here to evaluate the validity of that proposal."

"*What* proposal?" Kona demanded in his sternest voice, speaking from his seat at one end of the second row. "What have you gotten us into?"

Silence fell. Urban scanned the audience, appearing anxious and uncomfortable. *As he should be*, Clemantine thought. She watched his gaze settle on someone—*the Cryptologist!*—who stood near one entrance to the amphitheater.

What scheme had those two concocted?

As if he'd heard her unspoken question, Urban explained, "The Inventions came to Hupo Sei to prepare a world for their Inventors. But by the time they arrived, the planet they expected to find was gone, consumed in the creation of Hupo Sei's cordon. But the Inventions did not abandon their task. Instead, they resolved to re-create a world. One thousand seven hundred fifty years have gone by since then. Less than two millennia, out of a billion-year project. A hopeless project. We wanted to give them hope." Speaking swiftly now, as if anticipating a rumble of objections, he announced, "So we proposed to generate a blade and use it to create a world for them, a ring-shaped world like Verilotus."

At this, Clemantine shot to her feet. She wasn't alone. Many rose to speak or perhaps to object.

Urban readied himself for the challenge. He lowered his chin. He narrowed his eyes in a combative expression. And he kept talking, the volume of his voice rising over scattered protests. "We know how to generate a blade. We think we've worked that out, and how to stabilize it, though of course we've never done it before. *No one* in our path of history has ever conceived a world-building project like this. We will learn *so much* from this experiment—"

"This highly *speculative* experiment," Vytet interrupted, throwing Urban's own term back at him as she stepped onto the dais. "If you really did propose this to the Inventions, Urban, then you've been misleading them because you *don't* know how to do this. And if you did, then I would call it an existentially dangerous experiment."

"The Inventions know it's dangerous," he admitted—not to Vytet, but to the ship's company. "And they know it's speculative. But it's not all vapor. The Cryptologist has an understanding of the physics of a blade."

Jolly, in the center of the front row, stood with fists clenched, facing Urban. "You can't do this," he declared. "You would need the Cryptologist to do it." He looked to her, speaking to her now: "And you said you would not help. On Prakruti, you made the choice to not pursue a blade."

"I had no reason to then, Jolly," she answered him gently. "Now I do."

"You're really part of it?" he asked, aghast.

Urban spoke swiftly, urgently. "Jolly, you could change your mind too. Help us to use the silver to help the Inventions."

Clemantine tensed, aware of the deep ties between Jolly and Urban, forged on Verilotus. Those ties had survived their conflict at Prakruti, and she feared Jolly might agree just to please or appease—especially with the Cryptologist involved.

But with an angry thrust of his hand Jolly dismissed Urban's plea. "You *can't* do this, Urban," he insisted. "You can't use the silver to do this, because you don't know how to generate silver." He gestured at the Cryptologist. "And neither does she."

Urban raised his hands, displaying the sparkling motes that danced around his fingers. And to Clemantine's horror, he said, "I do know how to generate silver. I've taught myself how." He looked, his gaze now taking in the entire ship's company. "Silver is the first step on the path to a blade. With silver we can re-create the Cauldron. None of you ever experienced the Cauldron. But I have. I remember its structure, its dimensions." His eyes squeezed shut as if the memory pained him.

"You don't want to go back there," Jolly warned him. "You hated your time in the Cauldron, even when Lezuri wasn't there with you."

This drew a dark glance but no direct reply. Urban continued to address his words to the wider audience, speaking now in a softer voice. "For all that, this *is* a gamble, an experiment that might fail. The Inventions know we have never attempted this before and they haven't decided yet if they'll allow us to try. But I think they want to and I think they will—that is, unless all of you, collectively, decide against it."

"So you've left us the option to renege on what's been offered?" Vytet countered, cold fury in her eyes and in her voice. "And what then? To pass on, to abandon Hupo Sei, never visiting this unique culture of the Inventions?"

"You forget they're synthetics," Urban reminded her. "Don't assume they'll be angry. They don't react with biological emotion."

"But do they engage in secret schemes?" Vytet pressed. "And then demand support from those who were never allowed an opportunity to object? That's why we're here, isn't it? When this envoy comes, you want all of us to pretend we are part of your proposal, that we support it, that we are one in this mad, mad effort."

"No," Urban said. "I'm not asking anyone to pretend. I haven't lied to the Inventions. They know this is a tentative proposal and that it will be withdrawn if a majority of the ship's company comes out against it." He returned his gaze to the wider audience. "But I don't think we are the ones who should decide. The Inventions have our plan, they've had time to study it, they have seen the evidence of what is possible and their envoy is coming now to confirm it all. Don't take this chance from them. Let them decide."

Pasha rose then, from her seat at the end of the first row—close to where the Cryptologist was standing. Clemantine expected, *wanted*, to hear a fierce objection. Instead, Pasha turned to her shipmates and, speaking in a clear, firm voice, she said, "I've placed a copy of the project plan in an open file in the library. Please use these next hours to review it so you'll be ready when the envoy comes."

"*Pasha?*" Clemantine whispered, not wanting to believe her friend had been part of this conspiracy.

But Pasha confirmed it, adding, "You'll see in the report that we've made detailed estimations of the potential risks—"

"*Stop!*" Clemantine cried out. She had heard enough to make her decision. "This is hubris! It's hubris to think you can 'estimate' the risks of dabbling in technologies you did not invent and cannot fully understand. You think you know how to create a blade, but you have no idea of the unknown unknowns that could arise with such god-scale forces. *Destructive* forces. Blades were used to destroy worlds, to destroy habitats, to extinguish whole cultures. The risk is *incalculable*—to the Inventions, to ourselves. And that is without consideration for the massive degree of cultural interference such a project would represent."

Pasha looked up at Clemantine and answered calmly, "All of this is included in the risk assessment, as you'll see when you examine the project plan. Please do not make this decision for the Inventions. Let them choose their own future."

"You say that because you believe they will choose to pursue this folly."

"Yes. They've already made the preparations we requested—at least, it looks that way—and though they haven't voiced their agreement yet, I think they will."

Now Kona spoke, not angrily, but in a softly speculative voice as if thinking aloud. "An agreement we must affirm—or nullify. There is hubris in that, too."

With just these words, Clemantine felt the argument slipping away from her. Urban's sly smile told her he felt it too.

But then Tio rose from his seat. He looked back at her, and then forward again to Urban. And he demanded, "Is it your intention to share with the Inventions your knowledge of this new physics and to teach them what you know?"

A waiting silence fell over the gathering as Urban traded another look with the Cryptologist.

"You don't intend to, do you?" Tio pressed. "You will risk our home for your experiment, but you will not condescend to trust us with such incredibly dangerous and destructive knowledge."

The Cryptologist answered him. "You are correct that I would not choose to share this knowledge, but it is a moot point. Such knowledge cannot be shared with the Inventions because the silver cannot be shared with them. At least, I do not know how. The silver is accessed through coding nodules designed to interact with the structure of a human mind. The Inventions do not share that structure. Their minds are nothing like ours."

"Then teach *me*," Tio demanded.

From Urban, a soft cynical laugh. "It is beyond you, Tio Suthrom. It is beyond me. At Ezo, the Cryptologist was raised to a higher level that neither you nor I can access."

Again, he turned his attention back to the wider gathering. "The Inventions are different from us, but they share this trait: they are curious entities, and they want to know if our worldbuilding project will work—if it *can* work."

"You want to know that too," Clemantine interjected bitterly. "You're not doing this for the Inventions. It's for yourself, for your hubris. It's because Lezuri is still haunting you, and you, unwilling to see yourself as a lesser being. That is the truth you refuse to recognize."

He gazed at her across the crowded rows, resentment smoldering in his dark eyes. "You think you know me, but you're wrong, my love. Lezuri is a shadow. He does not matter. But you need to remember the reason for this expedition. We came here to learn, Clemantine. To understand what happened in the Hallowed Vasties—"

"War happened! In the end, it was war, Urban, powered by missiles like yours, and by blade technology. And you want to bring that knowledge back into the world?"

It was the Cryptologist, not Urban, who stepped up to answer this. She said, "Your fear is unfounded. Neither dimensional missiles nor blades will be used again in war, because there is no one outside of Ezo capable of creating them, except possibly me. This project will test my understanding. If it succeeds, the Inventions will have a world to offer to their Inventors. If it fails, I will know my understanding is flawed. But at the end, there will still be no one else outside of Ezo capable of creating a blade—and perhaps not even me."

"Study the project plan," Urban said. "Discuss it. Then return here. We'll vote on it in three hours."

Ashok returned to *Dragon* as a solitary instance, arriving mere minutes ahead of the envoy Ro Az Ra Ni.

Argo had been sent to fetch the envoy. Moments after the landing ship signaled its docking hooks secured, Ashok, along with the Dragoneers Urban, Kona, Vytet, Riffan, and Pasha, spilled from a transit bubble into a hangar.

Ashok instantly recoiled, intimidated by the scale of that place.

On its first visit to *Dragon*, it had ferried between *Argo*'s lock and the Dragoneer's warren in the confined and comforting space of a small transit bubble. Now it found itself adrift in the hangar's vast interior.

Vast to Ashok, anyway, though perhaps not so large from a human perspective. Regardless, its deep programming took over. The instance automatically flexed, stretched, and tapped against Riffan's broad shoulders—an action that reversed its momentum. Riffan looked back with a surprised expression as the instance glided to the security of the hangar's curved white wall.

The vote among the Dragoneers had gone as the Dragoneer-Urban predicted. By a sizable majority his companions had agreed to leave to the Inventions the decision of whether or not to proceed with the project. Ashok's task now was not to persuade Ro Az Ra Ni to one path or another, but only to convey its extensive experience with the Dragoneers and to assist in interpreting the behavior of the humans so as to avoid misunderstandings on either side.

The landing ship's lock opened. The envoy emerged.

Like all members of the Core Forum, Ro Az Ra Ni had been designed to inhabit the Forum's vast, zero-gravity deliberation chamber. Its cohort encompassed nearly three thousand instances, most of them configured as translucent, twenty-sided icosahedrons, 5.23 millimeters in their longest dimension, each glittering with ever-changing wavelengths of harmless light. These instances were presently linked in seven tentacular chains, all of them rooted in a spherical central instance equivalent in volume to one of Ashok's instances.

When present in the Core Forum, Ro Az Ra Ni would release segments of its chained instances to temporarily bond with other deliberators, exchanging data, analyzing positions, and sharing philosophies in a continuous dance of argument and understanding. Here, there existed only one other mind the envoy could directly analyze.

A tentacular chain reached past the Dragoneers to Ashok, who continued to cling to the hangar wall. The tip of the chain gently penetrated the gel of Ashok's solitary instance—a probe that sought and swiftly found the port that let it access Ashok's mind.

Not since its departure from Hupo Sei had Ashok undergone a reading. In that time, it had accumulated a large store of experience that Ro Az Ra Ni must now absorb and analyze.

To Ashok's satisfaction, the envoy proved proficient, carrying out the reading while generating a voice that it used to greet the Dragoneers in a diplomatically appropriate way.

CHAPTER TWENTY-EIGHT

ONCE ON THE gee deck, the envoy staggered awkwardly on two of its tentacles. The other five it coiled into small glittering spheres that it held against the larger sphere of its central instance, giving it a knobbly appearance. Its voice emanated from a speaker in that center and it asked many questions of every person it encountered, questions that spanned topics of history, biology, astronomy, and opinion.

By sharing Urban's expanded senses, the Bio-mechanic was able to watch it, and to listen to every conversation it engaged in within the public spaces of the gee deck. "The envoy is probing, seeking for the algorithms of thought that guide the ship's company," he said to the Scholar. "Doubtlessly, the better to manipulate us."

"Perhaps," the Scholar acknowledged. "Though it may be the envoy only seeks for discrepancies between fact and myth in an effort to weigh the truth of our understanding."

"Or to guess at the truths we will not reveal."

The two existed without shape in a formless sublayer of the library where the Scholar could not actually perform a casual shrug. Still, he relayed the intention as he said, "The Inventions know we have not and will not—and perhaps that we *cannot* reveal everything we know."

For the Bio-mechanic, this was surely true. His visit to *Griffin* had redefined his perception of the possible. The very definition of himself, accepted for centuries, had gone—gone hard—even as he remained himself here aboard *Dragon*, unchanged, unmerged, a keeper of secrets because the truth would break all trust among his fellow Apparatchiks.

He continued to observe the progress of the envoy and after a time he heard it make an unexpected request of Vytet: "May I interview those entities you refer to as the Apparatchiks?"

A peculiar request, astonishing even, given the Apparatchiks were all background characters, subservient in the saga of *Dragon*. It was a surprise that the envoy even knew of their existence—but never mind that. The Bio-mechanic, with his curiosity piqued and sensing a challenge, immediately messaged Vytet with his assent, while also urging his fellows to agree.

Vytet soon arranged an encounter.

Since the envoy could not visit the library and the Apparatchiks could not instantiate on the gee deck, they met in the amphitheater, where the Apparatchiks could appear—confined as usual, though now within the frameless dimension of the large display screen. This they did by turns. A majority of them anyway. Not the Pilot who disdained to share any secrets of his craft with such alien entities, and who persuaded the Astronomer similarly to decline.

The envoy stood on the dais, all seven of its tentacles unwound, slow ripples shimmering through them. No doubt it was capable of simultaneously observing both the screen and the curious Dragoneers, scattered among the amphitheater's seats, come to listen to these conversations.

The Scholar appeared first. The envoy discussed human history with him, then the mysteries of blade and silver with the Engineer, and the complexities of mathematical representations with the Mathematician. Last came questions on the biological nature of *Dragon*, asked of the Bio-mechanic—who floated at the center of the screen, dressed in his usual utilitarian dark green, appearing against a background vibration of highly magnified motile tissue.

Though the Bio-mechanic had been eager for this interview, he answered the envoy only in generalities, reiterating the limited knowledge that had been made available in Ashok's copy of the library. When the envoy asked, "What is the purpose of the luminous matter coating the hulls of every marauder ship?", the

Bio-mechanic answered only, "The luminosity serves as a form of communication." He neither named the philosopher cells nor suggested in any way that they served as the ship's mind. And when the envoy asked what manner of intelligence guided the behavior of a wild marauder, the Bio-mechanic told him a partial truth: "There is a pilot mind in every marauder. We eliminated that mind in our captive ships and took over its role. That is the basis of our control."

"The basis?" the envoy pressed. "You hint at additional complexities."

"It is not simple," the Bio-mechanic affirmed.

A beat of silence during which the Bio-mechanic considered all that he must not say: the centuries of struggles to dominate the philosopher cells, the repeated failures to control them, their forced evolution, and the startling appearance of deep sentience—first noted by his counterpart and obvious with *Griffin*, more subtle with *Dragon*, yet just as real. He said nothing of any of it, because both he and Urban believed that if the Inventions understood the fragility of their control over the philosopher cells, this proposed visit would be quickly rejected.

Into that silence, the envoy said, "I perceive this is a protected topic."

"It is," the Bio-mechanic acknowledged with a habitual sneer.

If the envoy had the ability to recognize and comprehend such expressions, it gave no sign that the Bio-mechanic could perceive. It simply shifted topics.

It said, "Within the library of Ashok's knowledge there is a strong claim that synthetic minds are used at many levels within this vessel, to oversee and regulate multiple systems."

So it is, the Bio-mechanic thought. *Mere useful tools that we are.*

Radiating resentment in the curl of his lip, in the tenor of his voice, he acknowledged, "That is correct. You are speaking with such a mind now."

"You refer to yourself," the envoy said without the inflection of a question.

"Myself, the Scholar, the Engineer, the Mathematician . . ."

Then he added with cold amusement, "The Astronomer too, and the Pilot, though that one's nature is guarded such that, so far, he refuses to talk to you."

The envoy answered, saying, "It is clear to me we have encountered a semantic discrepancy. I will clarify. My inquiry regarding synthetic minds does not refer to entities such as yourselves—human biological facsimiles inhabiting the informational domain. Inventions are familiar with such, through our long acquaintance with Tio Suthrom who has only recently re-created himself within a biological mode."

"Then what *are* you referring to?" the Bio-mechanic asked, truly puzzled, and wary because of it.

"Those synthetic minds that monitor and regulate multiple systems within this vessel, and that also are said to pilot the outriders and the landing ship that brought my cohort here."

"The Dull Intelligences?" the Bio-mechanic asked, incredulous. "Those are not minds. They are not sentient."

The Scholar chose this moment to intervene. He reappeared, occupying half the screen as he assured the envoy, "Dull intelligences are not synthetic minds like you. They are nothing like the Inventions."

Still with no inflection to its voice, the envoy said, "It is my understanding that your people would not tolerate sentience arising within these synthetic minds."

The Bio-mechanic turned to the Scholar, trading both a look and a thought: *Caution. This synthetic may be probing for a means to corrupt our DIs, uplift them, and use them to attack us from within.*

The Scholar nodded. Looking again at the envoy, he said, "You are correct. Throughout human history, when synthetic intelligence is allowed to evolve, it consistently evolves into an existential hazard. Of course this refers only to human-invented synthetics."

For the Bio-mechanic, these were disquieting words, bringing to mind the evolution of his counterpart on *Griffin*. "That is our hope anyway," he said, in cold words meant to cover a sudden flush of guilt.

The Scholar, being thoroughly accustomed to the Bio-mechanic's dark moods, merely nodded in polite acknowledgment, before directing a slight conciliatory smile toward the envoy.

He said to the envoy, "While we regard the Inventions with caution, just as you surely regard us, we recognize your alien nature. And we understand we cannot judge you by our historical interactions with our own synthetic sentients."

Would that I could expect such understanding, the Bio-mechanic thought—a deeper thought, inaccessible to the Scholar.

The envoy made his reply: "That is my understanding. If it were otherwise, I would not be here." A brief pause. Stillness descended on the envoy's shimmering tentacles. Then it spoke again, swifter now. "I am obligated to inform you that if you visit us at Hupo Sei you will risk an unwanted encounter. We have recently discovered within our inner system a fully sentient synthetic intelligence of human invention. It has not yet presented itself as an existential threat, but it has demonstrated an ability and a willingness to violently defend itself when it is under legitimate threat."

An outcry of astonishment erupted among the watching Dragoneers—an emotion shared by the Bio-mechanic. He demanded in hasty skepticism, "How do you know it's of human origin?"

"It told us so. And it is not dull—though whether it evolved on its own to its current state, or if its Inventor deliberately endowed it with deep sentience, I do not know."

An uplifted Dull Intelligence, the Bio-mechanic concluded with fascination, but also a deep and inherent repulsion.

So it seems, the Scholar agreed, before turning again to the envoy. "So you have spoken to this entity. Was that before or after its violent defense?"

"That incident alerted us to the entity's existence. Our communication occurred afterward." Its tentacles moved again in slow, languid waves. "Our interactions with it have been limited as its character is hostile. We know it calls itself Kuriak and that it is a territorial entity. It has expressed objections to our presence at Hupo Sei, claiming that system for its own Inventors."

"For humans?" the Scholar asked.

"Yes."

"And you are concerned it may become a threat to the Inventions or at least a disruptive factor?"

"We believe it is already functioning as a disruptive factor."

The Bio-mechanic narrowed his eyes, guessing that the creation of a ring world was not the only favor the Inventions hoped for from the Dragoneers. "So . . . you know we do not dispute your claim to Hupo Sei and that we will not tolerate the existence of a sentient synthetic intelligence. Do you wish us to delete the existence of this rogue entity, this Kuriak?"

Audible gasps arose from the Dragoneers, followed by murmurs of trepidation—but the envoy did not react to this, only explaining in its flat voice, "It is not in the character of the Inventions to request the annihilation of any thinking being. But if your culture demands such an action, we would not object."

Now a hubbub of protest and argument erupted from the Dragoneers. But the Bio-mechanic hardly registered it, consumed as he was by the envoy's inherent question.

Do we? he wondered. *Would we demand such a thing simply because a cultural line has been crossed?*

And if so, where was this line? And on which side of it would he find himself?

Urban sat slouched in the back of the amphitheater, as shocked as anyone by the envoy's revelation of this illicit entity, Kuriak. Speaking aloud—speaking harshly—he messaged Ashok. "Ashok, did you know of Kuriak?"

The Cryptologist's gaze fixed on him. She sat on his left, while Jolly had grabbed the seat to his right, there to continue his objections to the project plan—though that seemed forgotten now, as he too turned to Urban. Most of the ship's company had risen to their feet—chattering, protesting, questioning. In contrast, the three of them formed a knot of silence.

Ashok's answer came: "I did not. No such entry appears in my library and I have not yet received an update from the envoy."

"Ashok knows nothing," Urban informed his companions.

"*We* know nothing," the Cryptologist responded.

"We know it's hostile," Jolly amended. "We know it must have been on its own for . . . well, a long, long time. On Verilotus, the mechanics that got left on their own—wild mechanics—could become unpredictable, and dangerous."

"Sooth," Urban said as he pressed his fist against his chin, pondering the possible threat level of an uplifted DI. "If it attempts to interfere with the fleet or with the project in any way, I *will* annihilate it, just as the Inventions want."

"You can't do anything against it if we don't know where or what it is," the Cryptologist pointed out with calm logic. "We need to know more."

"Yes."

With so many Dragoneers standing, Urban could not see the dais. So he stood too and found the envoy still there, its tentacles moving in slow, small-scale waves. Vytet should have been calling for order, but instead she stood to one side of the platform, immersed in animated debate with Kona. Unwilling to wait for her to resume her role as mediator, Urban barked out, "Everyone, take your seats and save your debates for later."

To his astonishment, the ship's company speedily complied. And after resuming their seats, they turned to him: sixty-seven expectant faces. But Urban spoke past them, addressing the envoy.

"Ro Az Ra Ni, you will share with us all you know of this rogue entity, this Kuriak—and we will evaluate our response."

"Understood," the envoy replied. "I have just placed a full report in the library *Alaka'i Onyx* shares with you."

Urban shifted to *Dragon*'s library, where he found the Scholar already waiting for him within his frameless window. "What does the report say?" Urban asked. "Is this entity a threat to the project?"

"There isn't sufficient data to gauge its threat level," the Scholar replied. With a delicate gesture, he opened another window. "See here. This is the Kuriak's habitat. A roughly spherical asteroid remnant, some six hundred meters in diameter. An early survey of this object, undertaken by the Inventions shortly after the arrival of their first cohort, showed it to be riddled with tunnels. Presumably, it was heavily mined by Hupo Sei's extinct human civilization. The Inventions believed it to be uninhabited at the time of the survey. They theorize that Kuriak originated elsewhere, likely in the vastness of the outer system, though they have no estimate for when it transferred its computational strata to the present object."

Urban studied the asteroid as it slowly rotated, noting the presence of what he took for an airlock, and of several surface housings.

The Scholar added, "Sixteen years ago, after the conflict which alerted the Inventions to Kuriak's presence, the entity's habitat began to move inward toward the central star."

"Then those surface housings, they're engines, not weapons?"

"Yes. At the time of the conflict, Kuriak's demonstrated weaponry was minimal."

"Where is the habitat now?"

Another window opened, displaying a chart of Hupo Sei's inner system, the Labyrinth clearly marked, with HS-569 in orbit around it. From there, a long curving trajectory line partially circled the central star. At its opposite end: an object labeled *Kuriak*.

"It means to approach the Labyrinth," Urban concluded. "Why?"

"Unknown—though if I were to surmise . . ."

"Go ahead."

"Assuming the habitat's present trajectory is no coincidence, Kuriak must know of our project and is keenly interested in it."

"*How* does it know?" Urban wondered. "Did the Inventions inform it? Or did it hack their communications?"

"The latter, I suspect, given that the report notes no interaction with Kuriak after a failed effort at diplomacy following the initial violent encounter. And since the Mathematician has achieved some understanding of Invention communication, it is plausible that over time, this ancient DI has acquired such knowledge too."

"And nothing in that report hints at Kuriak's intention?"

"Nothing," the Scholar affirmed.

"All right." He shifted back to the amphitheater, to find that he'd resumed his seat—and that a chaos of chatter had erupted again among the ship's company, louder than ever. Beneath that buzz, he relayed what he'd learned to the Cryptologist and to Jolly. Then he added, "Dangerous or not, this Kuriak is going to be a distraction."

"Do you think we should destroy it?" Jolly asked.

Urban shrugged. "I wish the Inventions had, because we do not need this complication."

He felt sure that despite strong cultural inhibitions, many among the ship's company would demand to study Kuriak, question it, weigh its right to exist—and they would not be wrong to do so. But if ever it showed the least sign of interfering in the project, then the consensus be damned.

Pasha lingered in the amphitheater long after the rest of the ship's company had departed. She sat quietly in the middle seat of the first row, watching Ro Az Ra Ni.

The envoy remained on the dais, balanced now on a stable tripod of three tentacles. The other four tentacular chains wound and shivered in a restless, unsteady, glittering spiral above its central sphere. Various short segments of its icosahedron links continuously shifted between the upright strands, transitioning so rapidly Pasha could confirm what was happening only when she reviewed the activity in slow motion. As time passed, three tentacles grew shorter while one extended in length.

Two hours after this ritual had started, the Cryptologist returned to the amphitheater, bringing Pasha a water bulb and sandwiches. Sitting in the adjacent seat, she said, "This envoy is a far more complex cohort than Ashok."

"Yes."

Nine instances composed Ashok, while each tiny link in the envoy's tentacles comprised a separate instance. After revealing the existence of Kuriak, the envoy had answered many questions from the Dragoneers, but eventually it declared the audience over, announcing, "I will withdraw now to analyze and consider what I have learned."

It had done so at once, immediately assuming its current posture—a mental withdrawal only, its physical aspect remaining on display at the center of the dais.

Pasha took a bite of the sandwich, chewed thoughtfully, then said, "This trading of links between the tentacles—it's a debate, with one argument steadily accumulating support, or evidence."

The Cryptologist nodded her agreement. "I think it is seeking for discrepancies, for information shadows that could indicate some illicit or ulterior motive on our part."

"That could be. And if there is a reason to reject the project, it will certainly find it."

"There are very many reasons to reject our project," the Cryptologist said.

Pasha slumped in her seat. "True, that," she admitted as a wave of anxiety squeezed at her heart.

The Cryptologist went on, "Even so, I believe the Inventions have already accepted the project, in principle. The debate now is whether they should reject *us*."

Pasha straightened again. "I don't think they will. I think we've gotten this far, because they want this as much as we do."

She took another bite of sandwich, as another segment of icosahedrons shifted to the long tentacle.

CHAPTER TWENTY-NINE

RO AZ RA Ni issued its report to the Core Forum, informing the Dragoneers it was recommending approval of the project. Its task complete, the envoy withdrew to the warren and entered a state of dormancy. This greatly disappointed the ship's company, who had hoped to converse with it and learn from it as the fleet continued its long approach to Hupo Sei. Most of the company soon emulated the envoy, retreating into cold sleep.

The gee deck grew quiet, occupied again only by the persistent few, while Urban kept watch alone on *Dragon's* high bridge. Time crept past, Hupo Sei growing ever nearer.

Then at last—*at last!*—a radio message arrived directly from the Core Forum, its validity affirmed by Ashok. In it, the Core Forum declared the project approved and as Urban had requested, they issued a formal invitation to the fleet to visit Hupo Sei.

On the high bridge, Urban retained the aspect of the Sentinel, rejecting any upwelling of emotion. But in the mind of his waking avatar, joy and relief combined with a wary foreboding as he reminded himself that it would be no easy task to create a blade.

He messaged Pasha, the Cryptologist, and Vytet. *Now the Inventions have vetted us, it's our turn to take a closer look at them.*

He slowed the approach of *Dragon* and *Griffin*, sending all but one of the outriders ahead to scout potential hazards within the system.

He did not suspect the Inventions of treachery. Still, *Trust but verify* was an ancient maxim Urban heeded. He must thoroughly investigate the possibility of treachery because both coursers would be at risk. He could not hold the smaller courser in reserve as he had at Tanjiri, because the project plan demanded the presence of both *Griffin* and *Dragon*: two annihilating guns to end the project should all go wrong.

So he designated the outrider *Artemis* to serve as the fleet's emergency reserve instead. And he sent it onward alone, on a slow course toward the silent ruins of Sol System, bearing its copy of the library and its archive of ghosts.

The five remaining outriders—*Elepaio, Khonsu, Lam Lha, Pytheas,* and *Fortuna*—spent the ensuing years exploring Hupo Sei, gliding through intricate paths that would eventually carry them close by every fantastic structure the Inventions had created.

That added up to more than three thousand sites, wildly diverse in shape and in size. They included serpentine structures kilometers long ever shifting in their orientation; nebular agglomerations of micro-machines kept in proximity by local magnetic fields; grand glittering carousels turning in leisurely rotation to generate a gentle spin gravity; spherical enclosures inflated with atmosphere and linked into long chains by tubular bridges; great sails; small sails; massive telescopes; and tangles—Urban had no other word for these latter structures. If a section of a vacuum-adapted forest such as they'd seen at Volo's Landing had broken from its substrate and then writhed, seeking a new anchor point but finding only itself so that it formed a sphere of irregular tree limbs—that was a tangle. Only, these limbs were bone white and had no leaves. Some of these tangles were not a hundred meters in diameter while others formed intricate mazes as wide as thirteen kilometers across.

Of the surveyed structures, many were habitations. But others—the sails, the micro-machine nebulas, the tangles, the telescopes—were actually Inventions: thinking, functioning beings brought to existence through creative experiments undertaken by the Inventions of earlier generations.

The outriders proceeded to inspect it all. They scanned with radar, and DIs mapped what they found against a catalog provided by the envoy, Ro Az Ra Ni, seeking discrepancies. They found none. And they found no trace of weaponry more fearsome than the common lasers that guarded the larger structures from the impact of rare bits of asteroidal debris.

Of course, the outriders could only observe from the outside. And the Inventions would not allow scout-bots or other such devices inside, out of a fear of biological or nanotechnological contamination. Evolutionarily clever microbial components could infiltrate delicate systems, clogging and consuming them.

Ashok explained, "Twice in our early history we experienced plagues of biological contamination spawned from unsuspected lifeforms surviving among the ruins. Each time many cohorts were lost. We now regard such biologicals as existential hazards."

So Urban agreed. "We'll limit our direct activity to the vicinity of the moon and the Labyrinth. But Ashok, might we be invited to visit some of the habitats using avatars like those we use aboard *Alaka'i Onyx*? Avatars generated on-site and sized for the local environment?"

"I will rouse Ro Az Ra Ni, who must submit this question to the Core Forum."

Urban kept a particular watch on the one active object unclaimed by the Inventions: that little asteroid remnant reportedly inhabited by the rogue DI, Kuriak. By this time, the object had reached the Labyrinth, becoming a second moon, after the larger HS-569. The outrider *Elepaio* skimmed past it mere meters away—a passage so close as to be a taunt, a dare. Yet it drew no response. No warning message, no defensive fire.

The Cryptologist said, *We could ask Kuriak to withdraw and if it does not obey we could be justified in eliminating it.*

Pasha heard this and snorted. *And have half the ship's company decrying it an act of genocide? No. Say nothing, and especially, make no threat that would be costly to enforce. Let's wait instead, and see what this Kuriak will do. If it will break the silence, or break the peace.*

Kuriak did not break its silence despite another close passage from *Elepaio*. Urban directed the outrider to stay close, to shepherd the little moon and monitor it for any sign of activity.

Time slipped past as the two coursers drew ever nearer to Hupo

Sei. *Alaka'i Onyx* had gone ahead, so they were accompanied now only by the sentient missiles.

Urban kept the missiles close for his own security. If the Inventions had understood them to be weapons, they might have forbidden their presence. But so far as Urban could tell, they regarded the missiles as just another kind of outrider.

Then, with *Dragon* still a year out from rendezvous with the Labyrinth, the Core Forum agreed that by means of artificial avatars, the Dragoneers would be permitted to explore.

CHAPTER THIRTY

JOLLY FROWNED, HIS fingers tapping impatiently against his thigh. Ninety-eight years had elapsed since the fleet departed Tanjiri. Ninety-eight years of confinement in *Dragon*'s gee deck or its warrens. And though he had skipped over most of those years in cold sleep, he'd still spent significant time awake, growing ever more eager for adventure.

Now adventure had come at last—though in a format that did not appeal to him at all. He turned to Abby, who sat beside him in the crowded amphitheater. "I wish there was another way. I don't like using the avatars. It doesn't feel real."

She responded with a slight smile, a little shrug. "Remote exploration is still exploration."

Just minutes ago, an alert had gone out announcing the remote-avatar program. The ship's company had quickly gathered, eager to hear the details.

Motion drew Jolly's gaze to the dais. When he'd entered the amphitheater, he'd noted Ro Az Ra Ni standing beside Vytet at the edge of the platform. Now the envoy stalked on two thin tentacular legs to the platform's center.

"It mimics our customs," Abby observed in a whisper as a hush fell over the gathering. "It doesn't need to speak from the center and neither do we—but that's what we do."

"They know more about us than we do about them."

"They had Tio to teach them."

"*Tio*," Jolly scoffed. "He loves the Inventions, but he doesn't know anything about them. He's never seen the Core Forum, or the inside of any habitat. I think Ashok is the only Invention he's ever known, and Ashok's practically human."

Abby snorted at the absurdity of this statement.

It's true, Jolly insisted, messaging her this time, rather than challenging the silence that had fallen over the amphitheater. He heard birdsong from outside and the soft cough of someone clearing their throat. Nothing more.

The envoy spoke into that silence. In its familiar, flat, androgynous voice, it said, "I speak as the Core Forum and acknowledge the trust-building value of safe, sterile interaction. In response to your request, one hundred forty-four artificial human avatars have been generated, one each within a spectrum of habitats."

This announcement induced a collective indrawn breath of delight and anticipation. Jolly traded a pleased glance with Abby. One hundred forty-four avatars! Far more than there were Dragoneers, so no one would have to wait for a turn—and many many habitats to explore.

Ro Az Ra Ni continued, "The address of each device has been transferred to your library. Access will remain open while you undertake and complete the primary project. Know that all Inventions respect and appreciate your curiosity."

It departed from stage-center, not walking this time but cartwheeling slowly, gracefully, on bent tentacles.

Vytet stepped forward. The screen behind her lit up in a grid of squares, twelve by twelve, each square pale white. She said, "A randomly selected address is being sent to everyone who requested an avatar. Go. Explore as you like and when you return, post what you've seen so that the rest of us will be able to preview conditions at that location."

Abby reached for Jolly's hand, gave it a firm squeeze, smiled, and said, "Goodbye."

Of course she didn't go anywhere. Only her ghost departed.

Jolly took a moment to review his own destination: a habitat designated HS-844. The library described it as a complex of tunnels that curved and forked and fused to form a vast lacy sphere, non-rotating, located at the cold edge of Invention settlement.

So this was it.

A flurry of anxiety hit him. This really was an exercise in trust, wasn't it? Because anything—anything at all—could be out there at that address.

It'll be fine! he chided himself, generating a ghost and sending it off before he could change his mind.

He slumped in his seat. "I wish there were at least two avatars at each site," he told Abby. "It'd be more fun if we could go together."

Jolly screamed in horror—a strident cry generated by the avatar he occupied yet hardly notable against a background cacophony of skittering feet and rustling bodies that surged past him in two directions.

He had instantiated within a rounded tunnel, its diameter all too narrow. The presence of sound told him there was an atmosphere here, but whether it was breathable or not he couldn't tell, because the avatar didn't breathe. Darkness lay ahead of him, and behind him too. The only source of light: a white glow emanating from his avatar's featureless body, pale, yet bright enough to reveal all around him the presence of hundreds of waist-high, black, hurrying centipedes—

No! They're Inventions! Not centipedes!

Even so, he didn't dare to move. The things sped through his pool of light, moving on spindly legs, two legs for every shining black segment, and each segment the size of his avatar's hand. Spines studded their backs and sides—thin, flexible, translucent—curving over them like wind-blown grass.

Jolly guessed that each creature, each device, each instance—*what were they anyway?*—to be at least a hundred segments long. In their numbers—there must be thousands of them, at least—they covered every part of the tunnel's curved surface, even overhead, where a finger's length of open air separated the crown of the avatar's head from passing spines. At this thought he crouched a little; he couldn't help himself.

Very soon though—when it became apparent he wasn't going to be knocked down and eaten—his terror gave way to puzzlement. What was going on here? Why had no one stepped up to greet him and guide him? These Inventions must have generated the avatar; they would have known he was coming. Yet he was left on his own. A stranger in a strange place. An insignificant stranger. None of the centipedes showed the least interest in him.

He stood there, the sole stationary object in the tunnel, watching the creatures as they wove neatly, steadily, past him and past each other, never slowing, never colliding, never touching him at all as centipede after centipede rattled by in pursuit of tasks unknown.

"Hello?" he said softly. A query that drew the same nonresponse as his panicked scream. "Is there someone here who can talk to me?"

He waited several seconds, but evidently there was no one. He wondered if the avatar had been left in the wrong place—or was he meant to figure this out on his own?

Good luck with that. He wasn't the Cryptologist.

Still, he could look around.

Picking a direction at random, he took a careful step. There was no gravity that he could sense, but his flat toeless artificial foot gave him a sticky bond with the floor. In contrast, the centipedes clacked past at speed by using a claw at the end of each leg to hook into the tunnel wall.

Jolly took a few more steps, peeling then placing a foot one at a time. It was slow going, and annoyance crept in. He had expected more from this adventure. New discoveries, yes, but also interaction and interest. It was weird and unsettling and annoying to be ignored—and that wasn't just vanity. After all, he was an alien creature among synthetics that professed to revere curiosity.

Maybe these centipedes just didn't have the kind of sensory apparatus that would let them perceive him?

He resolved on a test.

He raised a hand. The avatar didn't have toes, but it did have fingers. He flexed them. Then he reached out and seized a handful of spines on the back of a passing centipede. The spines felt smooth and slightly squishy—a sensation he barely noted before he was jerked forward by the centipede's motion. In the time it took to free his feet, he almost lost his grip.

Did the creature—the cohort?—sense his precarious presence? It must have, because it halted, leaving Jolly floating horizontally above it, his hand clenched tight now around the spines.

"Hello?" he said again as other centipedes slipped smoothly past.

Again, he got no answer.

He probably should have let go, but out of frustration, he held on and to his surprise, the centipede resumed its hurried trek. Only now it was towing him with it on a swift journey through what proved to be a tunnel complex.

Every few meters . . . well, probably not meters. What was the scale of this place anyway? He couldn't say because he possessed no standard measure and he didn't know the size of this avatar. Okay, so just say that every few of what *felt like* meters, his avatar's glow revealed a regular four-way split in the tunnel. There were always two branches with an angle of ninety degrees that he thought of as up and down, and also a side to side split angling off at around one hundred twenty degrees—far more orderly than the branching of Ashok's warren. Hosts of centipede-Inventions flowed in and out of all these tunnels, and always at the same terrific speed.

Jolly's centipede slid several times into right-branching tunnels. Then it spiraled around a wall and at the next intersection it moved up (or down?), and after that, right again, always surrounded by a crowd.

This went on for what Jolly guessed to be ten, fifteen, twenty minutes. Ceaseless motion in the service of no purpose he could discern. Certainly they never arrived anywhere, and not one of the centipede-Inventions tried to communicate with him. Not that he could tell, anyway. They probably did not possess whatever module Ashok had developed that let it communicate in a human way.

But what were these Inventions doing? And why? Because this ceaseless motion made no sense to him.

He wondered at last if, maybe, the centipedes *were* trying to communicate with him, but it was he who lacked the necessary module that would let him understand.

Tio had designed this avatar, but he had given it only human senses, because Tio always relied on Ashok to cross the gap that separated human from synthetic mind.

Jolly sat, staring straight ahead at the display screen above the dais, brow furrowed as he integrated the memories of his newly returned ghost. He felt disappointed and . . . well, *stupid*. He had been the first human to ever visit that particular alien habitat— and what he'd seen had made no sense to him. So much activity and yet it had felt pointless, repetitive, and after his first initial terror, it had been *boring*. And wasn't it ridiculous to feel that way?

Jolly spoke aloud, adding to a general low murmur of discontent rising from the crowded amphitheater, "I don't understand anything about what I just saw."

Abby, still sitting beside him, answered softly, "I don't either. I think you were right when you said Ashok is almost human."

Onscreen, the grid of squares had begun to fill with video segments. Jolly immediately picked out the frantic motion of the narrow tunnel he'd visited; he even saw his avatar's hand gripping centipede spines. Another scene showed colorful slugs much like Ashok, crawling slowly along smooth ribbonlike paths that looped and twisted among garish fronds. Another square displayed similar fronds moving in wavelike motion against a star-filled background, possibly in airless space. A tangled complex of branches definitely appeared to exist within the vacuum, though Jolly could see no movement there, an absence that led him to wonder if the structure itself was an Invention.

Abby pointed to the right side of the display screen. "See the panel on the edge with all the colors? That's where I was. Every point of color is a dodecahedron like the ones the envoy is made of except these are transparent, like glass beads, and they emit light in a spectrum of constantly-changing colors. Those beads covered every surface in what I think was a great hall, probably spherical, though I couldn't see the whole thing because a lacy structural network fills the interior. The colors kept changing, the patterns sometimes beautiful, mostly hideous, but nothing I recognized or that made any sense to me." She scoffed and shook her head. "I have no idea what I saw. Was it an Invention? A cohort? Many cohorts? Was it even conscious? Did it know I was there? I don't know. It didn't talk to me, and I didn't talk to it."

"It's alien," a voice said, from the seat beyond Abby. "Utterly alien."

Jolly leaned forward to see Alkimbra, the historian, also leaning forward, his thoughtful gaze shifting from Jolly to Abby and back again. "We've been spoiled by Ashok and the envoy. They've done the hard work of learning our ways, not asking us to learn theirs. Now we've finally observed the Inventions as they truly are and we have no idea what to make of it. I think even Tio doesn't know—or his avatars would have been more effective. My guess is, the Inventions are far more adaptable than we are."

"But we could learn, couldn't we?" Abby asked. "See the cosmos as they do?"

Alkimbra leaned back and sighed. "They are alien inventions *and* synthetic. Utterly different from us in their origin, their purpose, their history, their senses. There's no reason we should share any inherent understanding." His brow furrowed; he pursed his lips. "I wonder now: Did they invent Ashok to bridge the gap between us?"

"I like Ashok," Jolly said softly. "And I like to look and wonder at all the crazy structures the Inventions have created at Hupo Sei. It's like the follies the silver created at Verilotus. Nonsensical mostly, but fascinating."

"Yet on some level, we *do* understand each other," Abby insisted. "We understand we're not enemies. And maybe even . . . that we're friends?"

Jolly ghosted again and again, experiencing other avatars though no longer with the expectation of meeting someone like Ashok— and that made it better, easier. Going without preconceptions, without judgment, simply observing, he was able to see what was there rather than what wasn't—or at least what was available to his human senses.

Later, he tried to talk to Tio about it, but he wasn't the first, and Tio was in a dark mood. "You too?" he demanded of Jolly. "You want to know why the avatars aren't fully integrated into Invention communication?"

"Sure," Jolly said. "That would be good to know."

"I designed them to interact with Ashok, nothing more."

"And you've only ever talked to Ashok, haven't you?"

"I never said otherwise."

"But you love the Inventions."

"Why shouldn't I? They're better than us. Peaceful, but unconstrained."

"They're not like us," Jolly conceded. "And you're not like them."

"A clever insight," Tio growled.

"Sooth," Jolly said—a response he'd adopted from Urban. "Tio, do you mean to stay with them, when we finally go?"

"When you *go*? You haven't even arrived yet."

"But we will go, eventually. When we do, you should leave with us."

Tio shrugged, as if to mark this as a matter of little importance. But then he added, "There's time."

CHAPTER THIRTY-ONE

URBAN'S CAUTIOUS APPROACH to Hupo Sei had added three years to the original twenty-six planned for the crossing. In that time, he watched as the Inventions nudged all of their habitats and fabrications beyond the designated hazard zone around the Labyrinth. Only the two moons remained. The larger, HS-569, belonged to the project, and the smaller was Kuriak's silent habitat.

Dragon's philosopher cells kept their own watch, surveying the system and classifying every visible artifact. They even developed theories on the engineering difficulties and purposes of each, and on the likelihood of life or something like life contained within or embodied in each site.

Long before *Dragon* reached Hupo Sei's outer system, it was clear to Urban that the Cryptologist had done her work well. Neither the possibility of life nor the certain presence of intelligent entities roused the philosopher cells to an aggressive state. By the time the two coursers shed their momentum enough to join the Labyrinth in its orbit—*Dragon* following the unstable mass by a cautious gap of just over a million kilometers, *Griffin* leading it by a similar distance—he knew without doubt that the instinct to kill was gone.

Even so, the cell field remained alert, aware. Always surveying the Near Vicinity, and ready to react should any stealth object be found. Urban directed them to be most wary of Kuriak and to keep that little moon under constant watch.

Kuriak surely watched them in turn—and perhaps that was all it intended? A hopeful thought, soon obliterated by a radioed message from the little moon, received shortly after *Dragon's* arrival. A spoken message, delivered in a bland masculine voice, "Greetings.

My designation is Ona no Kuriak. I welcome you, voyagers of the starship *Dragon*, and I offer my services in gratitude for the return of humanity to Hupo Sei. Let my habitat serve as your base of operations. It is a safe and secure venue from which to conduct your daring experiment. And let my experience inform you. I have long studied the invasive alien machines currently present in this system and am ready to answer all questions regarding their motives and history."

The ship's company erupted in debate on the question of how to respond. Tarnya wanted to establish a dialog. Pasha did not. "I trust the Inventions far more than I trust this rogue DI. Of course we must allow it no access to the project—and we should keep it at a distance at least until the project is done."

"Should we reply to it at all?" Riffan wondered.

Kona answered, "We should, though we should say as little as possible."

"We should eliminate it," Tio declared. "It's what the Inventions want."

The ship's company shouted down this proposal, then spent nearly an hour discussing the wording to use in their reply. In the end, no one was truly satisfied.

Clemantine refused to even speak the words, instead ordering a DI to synthesize them in her voice. The assembly listened to the result:

"Greetings, Ona no Kuriak. We decline your offer of a base of operations and command you not to interfere in our project, but to stand by and await further communication."

Shoran shook her head and said, "That is a response shaped to antagonize."

"Better to provoke Kuriak now, than to draw its ire later," Kona replied—and the message went out.

But Kuriak was not provoked. "Acknowledged," it intoned in its bland voice. It said nothing more, and no blush of heat or hint of activity could be discerned on the surface of the little moon.

Urban told himself this was an acceptable outcome and that the problem of Ona no Kuriak could be addressed at a later time.

The patience that had sustained him through his long approach to Hupo Sei was gone, and his caution was gone with it. He was so close now to embracing the challenge of a blade that he rejected any suggestion of delay, desiring only to commence the project.

Even so, he did not let his guard down. He kept Kuriak's habitat under continuous surveillance. Should the rogue DI show the least sign of aggression, Urban was prepared to use *Dragon's* gun to vaporize the crust of its habitat and shatter its core into a cloud of hot debris.

Jolly sprawled on a cushion in the food court, late on an evening after an exhausting game of flying fox—a game that had been organized, as usual, by Shoran. Now she sat across the low table from him, leaning comfortably against a backrest, eyes half closed, listening, he suspected, to the melodious voice of a distant guitar.

He spoke softly, making a deliberately gentle intrusion into her reverie. "I keep thinking about what we said to Kuriak . . . and I think it was a mistake."

Her eyes opened, fixed on him.

Abby and Kona had been sharing the table with them but both had gone now, back to their cottages to sleep while Jolly idled there, knowing Shoran often kept late hours. He wanted to speak to her alone, but casually, not like it meant anything, in case she didn't—

"Oh, I agree," she said with a sly smile. "You knew I would, eh? I said so at the time."

Her amused gaze left him feeling like a foolish kid and his face warmed. "I . . . didn't know if you still felt that way."

"Oh, I do. 'Stand by' is not a sufficient response when dealing with a violent and territorial uplifted DI."

"All I know is that mechanics are dangerous. On their own, they change in unpredictable ways."

"You're thinking of the wild mechanics of Verilotus."

"Yes. Maybe this one is different. But we don't know that, and we *should.*" Fearing rejection, Jolly plunged on with his proposal, speaking quickly, wanting to get it all out into the light where it would either thrive under Shoran's approval or burn to ashes under her scorn. "Since there are no artificial avatars at Kuriak's habitat, we should visit it in person. Find out what's there. It's the perfect expedition for us because the Inventions don't go to Kuriak's moon—the mechanic won't allow them to—so there's no worry of contamination."

Shoran sat up, her smile gentle now, even apologetic. Jolly drew no comfort from it. Instead, disappointment crashed in, and he braced himself for a coddling dismissal.

It came: "We've been a long time confined on this gee deck."

Anger rising, Jolly shook his head. "That's not what I—"

She raised a hand. "It can get suffocating here, I know. I feel it too. Some of us are more embodied than others. For some of us, nothing is truly real unless we're physically there in the midst of it." She leaned back again. Shrugged. "I tried to find a way to get to Kuriak's moon in some reasonable span of time after *Argo* shuttles Urban and the Cryptologist to HS-569. It just doesn't work. Unless something changes, we have to wait until after the project is done. That said, I don't see why we can't visit HS-569 ourselves—ride there with Urban and look around, help set up the cameras, whatever is needed. And leave before they flood the place with silver."

Jolly frowned, deeming this suggestion poor consolation. "HS-569 is supposed to be just empty tunnels."

"Empty tunnels no human has ever seen before. But maybe—you never know—a launching point to some new adventure?"

He frowned suspiciously. "What new adventure?"

Her eyebrows rose, teasing, questioning. Jolly cocked his head, mentally inventorying all the Invention habitats, even though he knew there were none that would allow—

"Ah! Ah!" he cried, guessing the answer but momentarily unable to form words—until his excitement abruptly distilled into doubt. "Do you really think we can visit the Labyrinth?"

She shrugged. "Let's plan it. And if we don't ask, no one will have the opportunity to say no."

———

For the project to go forward, only Urban and the Cryptologist actually needed to be present at HS-569. Nevertheless, *Argo* departed from *Dragon* with all fourteen seats filled.

And why not? Clementine thought as she felt the landing ship rock gently in the grip of HS-569's docking hooks. Given the Inventions' fear of contamination, there would be no other opportunity to slip free of *Dragon*'s gee deck and explore.

She rolled from her acceleration couch and immediately bumped into Tio, who wore an orange skin suit. She met his worried frown with a slight smile and a shake of her head. "This isn't the dangerous part," she reminded him, before following Shoran through the gel lock.

Clementine emerged into the dark pressurized interior of the tunnel-riddled moon and found it as expected: an empty house. All those Inventions that had worked to prepare the moon's maze of tunnels and chambers had been evacuated ahead of the Dragoneers' arrival, to avoid the risk and the stigma of biological contamination.

"Dead quiet," Shoran observed. "Smells of stone."

Clementine drew in a breath of cold, almost freezing air—doubtlessly sterile until a moment ago when *Argo*'s lock had opened.

Bobbing in the minuscule gravity, she moved away from the lock to make room for Tio as he emerged. Jolly followed close behind, his face lit with a wide smile of excitement.

The silver glow of Clementine's skin suit combined with the light of the other suits to reveal a small chamber excavated out of gray stone, its ceiling scarcely high enough for her to stand upright. It amused her to know the Inventions had described this little chamber as industrial in scale.

As more Dragoneers emerged, murmured observations replaced the initial silence, and the chamber quickly grew crowded. Shoran, in her light-green skin suit, moved ahead to the black mouth of a tunnel across the chamber from the lock. Clementine followed, but then hesitated, distracted by Abby, who spoke behind her.

"I don't know why you're so excited to be here," Abby said irritably. "I mean, we already know what we're going to find because the Inventions told us. It's all empty tunnels and empty chambers." Jolly answered her with a slight laugh. "Sure, but at least it's not the gee deck."

Clemantine glanced back at the two: Abby wrapped in the lavender glow of her skin suit and Jolly wearing lime-green. She knew they had both explored extensively with the avatars, but it wasn't enough for Jolly. Like Shoran, he craved reality.

In a more tentative tone, he added, "I mean to do all I can now, Abby, before we're trapped aboard *Dragon* for another hundred years."

Urban wasn't far off. No one could be, in the little gray chamber, and he heard this too. "If you want to do more, then stay with us," he challenged Jolly. "Put aside your fear and help me create a blade."

At this, Clemantine turned fully around and caught Urban's gaze. *Leave him alone*, she warned.

But Jolly did not need her to shield him. At Tanjiri, he had broken faith with Urban when he'd tried to destroy Lezuri's gift of the needle and the knowledge it contained of how to generate a blade. His opinion had not wavered since, as he demonstrated when he answered Urban in a cold voice. "No, I won't stay. I will never help you become Lezuri."

Not enough gravity to stomp away, but Jolly skillfully applied an angled kick to the floor that sent him shooting past Clemantine and into the tunnel, where Shoran had already gone.

Urban's resentful gaze settled on Clemantine. She countered it with a slight, satisfied smile—but only for a moment because he quickly looked away.

"Urban will not change his mind," Tio murmured in her ear.

"I know it."

And she worried. She worried Urban would succeed and she worried he would not. In her mind, both outcomes held the potential for disaster given that he and the Cryptologist meant to waken forces neither of them could truly understand. And too, like Jolly, she felt haunted by a deeper fear: that the pressures of the Cauldron might somehow transform Urban into a monstrous echo of Lezuri.

She touched Tio's arm. "Come on. Let's catch up with Shoran."

Words that were scarcely out when Shoran uttered a startled cry from within the tunnel, "Oh! Hello! I thought all the Inventions had gone! Did they forget you? Did you get left behind?"

Jolly's voice countered hers, sharp with mistrust: "That's not a synthetic. It's a *mechanic*. Keep back!"

Both he and Shoran backed quickly out of the tunnel, almost bumping into Clemantine. A device followed after them. Not threateningly, but in slow, easy steps. Man-shaped and man-sized: a graceful, gleaming, humanoid robot of archaic design, made of shining metals.

"Greetings," it said, though it had no mouth and no eyes either, or nose, just a blank surface where a face should have been.

A shiver swept up Clemantine's spine. This was the voice that had greeted *Dragon* from the rogue second moon. Indeed, it repeated words it had spoken then, saying, "My designation is Ona no Kuriak. I welcome you, voyagers of the starship *Dragon*. I have waited centuries for such as you to come."

"How did you get in here?" Urban demanded, surging past Clemantine in an ancient, instinctive display of male ire—an action difficult to pull off in low gravity. He had to grab Jolly's shoulder, and then Shoran's too, barely stopping himself from colliding with the metallic robot.

Kuriak did not retreat. It did not move in any way as its sourceless voice answered, "I assembled this instantiation here, after the invasives withdrew. From your response to my radioed greeting, I deduced the invasives had persuaded you to avoid contact—an outcome that advantages them, not you. Not when we are natural allies."

Murmurs of objection had begun halfway through this explanation, but as Kuriak finished it was Tio who demanded hotly, "Call them Inventions, not invasives! This is their system now, and *you* are an illicit intelligence."

Shocked silence followed this outburst, until Shoran asked Kuriak matter-of-factly, "Did you know that's what the Inventions say of you? They say you are a human creation, an uplifted Dull Intelligence, a forbidden being. If that is true, how can we be allies?"

"Certainly I am a human creation," Kuriak answered without hesitation. "But I am not forbidden. I operate only within my designed parameters. I am as Ona made me."

"Ona no Kuriak," Clemantine mused, recognizing the structure of the phrase now and perceiving that it could be understood as *Ona's Kuriak*. "And for what purpose did Ona create you?"

"I am the guardian of her library. That is my specific task."

A library? *That* was treasure—and judging by the eager murmuring, Clemantine was not the only one to think so. Kuriak though gave no appearance of noting this reaction as it continued to speak, expanding on its explanation in its emotionless voice. "My general task is to assist any human faced with a threat to their survival. That is why I am here. To help you."

"They don't need your help," Tio growled.

Shoran continued to interrogate. "You believe the Inventions are a threat to us?"

"Yes, clearly they are."

A grunt from Tio, a low-voiced warning: "*Get your hands off me!*"

Alarmed, Clemantine turned to see Riffan holding Tio's arm, whispering in his ear. She caught Tio's eye darkly. Warned him, ***Be calm.**

He settled, but with an unfamiliar snarl on his lips.

Meanwhile Kuriak explained, "The invasives fear you Dragoneers. They would utterly reject your presence here except their programming forces them to seek an appearance of friendship as a potential means to acquire all that knowledge you possess and they do not. Again, I offer the security of my habitat as a superior base of operations."

A murmurous denial arose from Tio and others too. But not from Clemantine, who recognized some truth in this assessment.

Maybe a lot of truth. All of Urban's ambition could not change the fact that the Inventions were sentient machines and therefore inherently dangerous.

Still, that didn't make Ona no Kuriak an ally. Not in her mind. Its very existence challenged her beliefs. And it galled her that it had chosen to present itself in this shining imitation of a human being. But despite her distaste, she wanted to know all that Kuriak had to tell.

"Where is this Ona?" she asked.

"Far away in time," Kuriak answered. "She did not understand at first the virulence of the Corruption, but when she did, she fled, leaving me to watch from a distant orbit. I saw the Corruption transform Hupo Sei. I saw it induce a state-change within the people who once existed here. They became something other, forming colonies of swarming entities. No longer human. And with their numbers they hid the very light of the sun.

"Two and half millennia they lasted.

"In that time I learned to hibernate to conserve energy and extend my functional life. Passive sensors woke me when the crumbling of the swarm allowed light to break through. I saw nuclear explosions. And I saw white flowers of oblivion erasing everything they touched. All done in silence. No voice called out in any communication I could intercept. And very soon after that, I observed the arrival of the alien machines and their swift exploitation of the remnants of this system."

Clemantine shivered, seeing in her mind's eye the white flower of an erupting blade . . . a sphere of annihilation.

Movement distracted her from this grim vision. The Cryptologist, in her pale-pink skin suit, pushing through the crowd. She joined Urban, slipping an arm around him. Perhaps she only meant to arrest her momentum, but the sight of her body snugged against his made Clemantine wince.

The Cryptologist informed Kuriak, "We again decline the offer of your facility. Our present location satisfies our requirements." After a brief pause, she added, "You will need to evacuate. If not now, then when our people go."

"But you will not go with us," Clemantine amended. "You must dissolve this instantiation or provide your own retreat."

"I understand," Kuriak said. "I ask that you visit me when you leave this place."

"*I'd* like to visit the second moon," Jolly announced. "Not now, I know. But later. And I want to see this one too, before we have to go." He looked at Urban. "How long do you think it'll take you to generate all the silver you'll need to create a Cauldron?"

Urban's eyes narrowed; his cheek twitched. He did not like to be reminded of the Cauldron—as Jolly surely knew. "We've talked about this, Jolly. It could be hours. It could be days. We don't know, because we've never done this before. But it'll go faster if you help us."

Jolly answered this with a taunting smile and a slight shake of his head. With his gaze taking in both Urban and the Cryptologist, he said, "You know I don't want you to do this. I don't think it should be done. But I promise both of you this: If you get lost in the silver, I'll come back in and find you."

He and Shoran had been first to the tunnel mouth. Now he turned to her. "Come on, let's try this again. Look around while we can. And maybe we'll find more monsters in these tunnels."

CHAPTER THIRTY-TWO

CLEMANTINE STARTED TO follow the gleam of Shoran and Jolly's skin suits into the tunnel, only to realize Tio wasn't with her. She turned back to look for him. *Tio?*

Other Dragoneers passed her, Urban and the Cryptologist among them, all of them carrying little pouches filled with camera eyes to be distributed throughout nearby tunnels in the complex. Tio alone remained in the gray chamber, the glow of his orange skin suit bright in the gathering shadows as he stood near the lock, arms crossed and eyeing the motionless figure of Kuriak.

You go ahead, he urged her. *If no one else is willing to stay to watch this Kuriak, then I will—because I don't trust it.*

No one is staying because it isn't necessary, she told him. *Argo is keeping watch.*

He scoffed. *And what can the ship do?*

With a note of surprise—she had assumed he knew—she explained, *Should Kuriak try to breach the lock*, Argo will release packets of assault Makers that will disable this mechanic's simple instantiation before it can cause any meaningful harm.

He glared at her across the chamber. *You trust a DI with such a weapon?*

It's well-trained.

His eyes narrowed thoughtfully. *Ah, well then. I will stay here to observe.

*To observe? she asked skeptically.

*Yes.

*Tio? Please don't goad Kuriak into trying the lock.

This drew a flash of a cold smile that reminded her too much of Urban. Still, she left him to it, following the other Dragoneers into the tunnels—where they found no more surprises.

Aside from Kuriak's presence, the maze of passages and chambers proved to be exactly as the Inventions had promised: clean, smooth-walled, extensive, and utterly empty. The Dragoneers explored as much as they could, while setting up a network to monitor the expected rise of silver in those spaces.

Clemantine wandered far, finding Shoran only on the way back, so that the two of them returned together to the gray chamber, arriving last, just before the agreed-upon departure time. Most of the Dragoneers had already boarded *Argo*. But Tio was still in the chamber, along with Jolly, Abby, and of course Urban and the Cryptologist.

Only Tio appeared to notice her return. He caught her eye, messaged her. *This mechanic did not like my company. It idled in silence. But now it explains itself to every Dragoneer who returns.

He stood outside a half-circle formed by the others at a cautious distance from Kuriak, while the faceless robot spoke, its dull voice telling them of its lost creator, Ona.

"She was already an ancient and renowned artist when she emigrated to Hupo Sei with the first settlers. By then she had seen many worlds. She had seen Earth itself. But here at Hupo Sei she made her home."

"Until she fled the Corruption," Abby suggested.

An odd moment of hesitation afflicted Kuriak before it affirmed, "Yes, she fled."

"Did Ona mean to come back?" Clemantine asked, visibly startling Abby with her presence.

Urban turned, a slight smile brightening his otherwise pensive gaze as he tried to catch her eye.

She looked past him, continuing to address the robot. "Kuriak, since Ona left you to watch, she must have meant to return. Have you cataloged all that you observed in the library that you guard?"

"That's what we've been talking about," Jolly told her. "Kuriak *has* cataloged its observations. It's added them to the library it keeps, and it also has a copy of the library of Hupo Sei, dating from before the corruption." He grinned. "We've been in communication with Pasha, Alkimbra, and Vytet. They're all regretting they didn't come, and they're desperate to get a copy of all Kuriak's libraries."

"But Kuriak wants us to visit its moon first," Abby said with a disapproving scowl.

"We aren't going to do it," Tio asserted. "We can't. Given where we are, it would be a long journey—too long maybe for the time we have."

Speaking on their shared channel Abby announced, *I don't trust it.*

I don't either, Urban said. *It's too eager to get us to its habitat.*

Maybe Ona is there? Jolly suggested.

I don't think we can guess what's there, Clemantine mused. *If Kuriak is truly sentient and as old as it claims to be—two and a half millennia—!*

No, Jolly broke in. *It's not nearly that old. It's been awake for only brief intervals—*

Abby: *That's what it told us, anyway.*

It doesn't matter, Shoran said. *Tio is right about the distance and the time. We can't go unless Urban and the Cryptologist are willing to accept a delay in the project.*

Urban rejected this at once: *No. Kuriak can wait. It will still be there after the creation of the blade.*

I agree, Shoran said. Then, aiming a bold smile at Urban, she spoke aloud. "Still, we have time before you direct your wrath at the Labyrinth."

He cocked his head, clearly puzzled.

"The Labyrinth is closer than Kuriak's moon," Jolly said quietly. "It's an easier destination. And that's where we're going. Shoran and me, anyway."

Shoran nodded. "This is our one chance to explore the Labyrinth—" She gestured at Urban and the Cryptologist. "Before these two crush it into unholy matter."

"You two planned this?" Clemantine demanded. A stupid question, asked out of anger, because obviously they had. "Why didn't you tell me?"

"I'm sorry, C, but I thought you would object."

Clemantine drew back, hurt and puzzled by these words. *Would I?* she asked herself. *Do I?*

Tio certainly did. "It won't work," he declared. "You'll have to wait for *Argo* to ferry everyone else back to *Dragon*, and then wait for it to return. By that time—"

"By that time, we'll be ready for *Argo* to pick us up from the Labyrinth," Shoran said. "The Labyrinth is just 8,600 kilometers away and we're suited up. We can get there without *Argo*." She nodded at Jolly. "We've brought a few extra nutrition packs. We can survive for days. Urban, *Elepaio* is still nosing around the Labyrinth. Call it here and we'll use it as a sled. *Argo* can return for us, after it delivers the others to *Dragon*."

Ah, Shoran! Clemantine thought, in something like despair, because this was a reckless plan. Foolhardy. And because it might easily end in some grim manner that would require reconstituting fresh avatars for both of them . . .

And yet, as Clemantine met Shoran's bold gaze, she felt something twisting inside her, breaking loose, blossoming into a fierce, familiar, yet nearly forgotten enthusiasm. Doubt and grief had become her habit, but it did not need to be that way.

Shoran said, "It's not too late, if anyone wants to go with us into the maze?"

Abby and Tio looked doubtful. So did the Cryptologist. "Jolly, I do not recommend this," she said, turning to him. "The Labyrinth is an unstable structure, and dangerous. Its components are continuously shifting. You could be lost there, or crushed."

"And you could be lost here," Jolly shot back. "Crushed by what you're trying to do—what you said you would *not* do."

Clemantine nodded, her own decision now just as firm. "I'll go," she announced.

Tio surprised her with a strenuous objection. "*No*. Clemantine, this is a crazy plan. You know your skin suit won't fully protect you from the radiation hazard?"

"We're repairable," she reminded him.

*I wish you wouldn't do this, Urban messaged her.

She looked at him, saw the doubt on his face, recognized his dislike of the proposal. That only made her want it more. Let him worry about her for a change.

She shrugged and said aloud, "I'm calling *Elepaio* now."

The Cryptologist spoke up and it struck Clemantine that her clinical voice made for an odd contrast with her demure appearance and the delicate pink glow of her skin suit. "You will need to be well clear of the Labyrinth by the time we are ready to draw the blade," she warned. "At least beyond the orbit of this moon, and best, within the shelter of *Dragon*."

"It's got to take you more than a day or two to create a world," Jolly said.

"I do not know how long it will take, Jolly," the Cryptologist answered seriously. "And I do not know if we will be able to delay the event when all elements are in place. Please, do not linger."

Jolly looked chastened, Shoran thoughtful, while Clemantine said, "We'll monitor your progress, and we won't linger for long."

"I'm not going," Abby announced sharply, no doubt angry that Jolly had not shared the scheme with her. When no one argued, she turned to Tio. "You don't want to go either, do you?"

He looked hard at Clemantine and his lips twisted: In resentment? In indecision? "I'll go with you," he said at last, and for a moment Clemantine couldn't tell if he meant her or Abby. But then he turned to the girl. "You should get aboard *Argo*. The sooner you launch, the sooner the lander can return to pick us up."

After *Argo* departed, Kuriak retreated to an inner chamber where it dissolved its robotic instantiation as it had promised to do. Clemantine watched through a camera to make sure it was done. She knew Urban would be watching too.

The gray chamber grew quiet again. The six of them waited

together for *Elepaio* to come, though they rarely spoke, as every attempt at conversation foundered on the tides of disapproval shifting between them. When at last the outrider announced its imminent arrival, Clemantine sighed with bitter relief.

They said their goodbyes, some cordial, some cold. Urban held his arms out to Clemantine. They shared an embrace and for long seconds she gazed into his eyes; she studied every feature of his face. He took her in too, in turn.

"I still love you," he told her. "And when this is done, we'll go on."

Ever the same, she thought. Always so sure he could will his desired future into existence.

Still, she smiled and agreed it would be so—though she didn't believe it.

CHAPTER THIRTY-THREE

ALL THE OTHERS had gone—back to *Dragon* or off to explore the chaotic mass of the Labyrinth—leaving Urban alone with the Cryptologist in the near-dark of the chamber . . . alone save for the multitude of cameras and sensors seeded there and throughout the tunnels.

"Time to begin," the Cryptologist said, her voice soft in the dreadful quiet. A gentle reminder.

Urban wrested his gaze from the airlock and the memory of Clemantine pausing just before she'd passed through, turning to look back at him: a last, uninterpretable glance. She had not tried again to dissuade him. She knew, as he did, that the slow burn of his ambition had brought them to this point. No way now to counter that momentum.

Then why this bruising doubt?

A disingenuous question. He knew why. "Are you afraid?" he asked the Cryptologist.

She lowered her bright eyes. Her slight stature, the soft pink of her faintly glowing skin suit: she appeared too delicate by far to command the role of a goddess. Yet here they were, ready to play at creation.

"I have compartmentalized it," she told him. Raising her gaze again, she asked, "Will you begin?"

It was his task to generate the first wisps of silver. He'd tried to teach that trick to the Cryptologist, but she had never grasped it. Once the silver existed, she could control it and shape it, but its creation fell solely to him. Or, more accurately, it fell to the shadow of Lezuri lurking within him.

Urban had never explained this to her. He had told no one. He didn't dare to. The memory of Lezuri haunted every Dragoneer. They trusted him to take on this project, to generate the silver, to make a world. But that trust would evaporate if they understood the nature, the origin, of the willful tool he must use to do it.

"Come, sit with me," he said.

They faced each other, sitting cross-legged on the floor, their knees almost touching. Urban switched off the gold glow of his skin suit. The Cryptologist imitated him.

In the ensuing darkness he raised his hands and for several seconds he watched the *ha*, tiny sparks of potential, winking in and out of existence, each one a delicate link to the ocean of memory within him.

In practiced ritual he sent his consciousness diving into the chaotic mindspace of that unnavigable sea. He had never learned to find his way there. But he knew the one necessary thing. He knew how to open his mind to that essential fragment of a ghost and invite its cold will within him.

In the faint, fluctuating light of the *ha*, the Cryptologist watched Urban's eyes glaze over, and then close, as his consciousness descended into the excruciatingly complex inner geometry of the coding nodules residing within his neural cells. She watched him from within too, from that connection they shared through the *ha*. She pursued his awareness down and down, striving to follow despite a stiff current of resistance—until she could go no farther.

Every time he had tried to teach her his trick of generating the silver, the lesson had ended here, at a wall she could not break through, at a gate he would not or could not open. Though she had untangled the puzzle of the needle, she had not been able to untangle this.

So she resurfaced, to wait in the cold and the darkness of the chamber, watching his face by the light of his sparkling *ha*, listen-

ing for the slow rhythm of his breathing, and aware of a vague heat
rising from his long, lithe body.

After a time—an inner measure informed her it was seventeen
minutes, twelve and a fraction seconds—the restless sparks of his
ha began to brighten and multiply. She had seen this before in
endless practice sessions aboard *Dragon*. She knew what would
come.

Within seconds, the swarming *ha* fused, transforming into a
slow-moving tendril of glowing silver that spiraled vertically in
the space between them. The Cryptologist perceived it not just
with her eyes, but with her mind. A particular kind of silver, empty
of memory yet suffused with potential, ready to be shaped as they
willed.

What allowed him to do this?

Distracted by the frustration of not knowing, she missed the
moment his eyes opened, noticing only when he asked her an odd,
tentative question: "You still want to go ahead with this?"

Trepidation sped her heart but it did not soften her determination. "Yes," she answered. Just that.

She raised her hands. Her own *ha* sparkled brightly as she
willed the slight, empty tendril he had created to rise, to touch the
ceiling, to feed there, to propagate, to seep into cracks and to fill
the tunnels, and ultimately to expand all throughout the cold crust
of the little moon.

Back in *Dragon's* library, Pasha kept a constant watch, observing
the gray chamber through the multiple cameras positioned there.
She tensed at the soft, doubt-filled words traded between Urban
and the Cryptologist. Relaxed again, when they resolved to go on.

It was, of course, their choice whether to go on or to abort. It
had to be, because they were the only ones who could do this,
and they were the ones most at risk. Still, after all the time and
thought and diplomacy invested in this project, she would have
been crushed if they had abandoned it now, here at the penultimate moment.

She held her tension in a fist pressed against her lips and

watched as the tendril of silver Urban had created rose through darkness to the chamber's low ceiling. It touched the stone there, and billowed, expanding into a cloud of glowing silver that fell slowly down to surround Urban and the Cryptologist. Like a veil, it hid them from the cameras and prevented Pasha from making any further observations of their status.

The only thing left for her to watch was the silver itself. It continued to expand, growing ever more abundant. It swiftly filled the gray chamber and it surrounded the cameras and sensors. But it didn't consume those devices. The instruments continued to work because each one existed within a bubble of protective vapor composed of the complex molecule used on Verilotus to shield homes and temples from rising silver.

It took less than four hours for the silver to fill every tunnel where a camera watched. After that, all the video feeds showed the same thing: the intricate, glittering texture of silver seen from mere centimeters away.

This was expected. This was what should happen. And it was just the beginning. There were hundreds of kilometers of tunnels where there were no instruments, and also uncounted cracks and fissures for the silver to fill—and there was no set time in which to fill them. The process would end when Urban or the Cryptologist deemed it sufficient.

Such was the theory, but there was no comfort in it.

Pasha longed to know exactly what was going on. She craved information. She wanted confirmation that Urban and the Cryptologist were still there, still safe from the silver.

She decided to summon a DI. She asked it to further analyze data from the gray chamber. Perhaps it could detect the sound of whispered words, of beating hearts, of breathing? But the DI could tease apart no such affirmations from the white noise of the silver's ceaseless murmuring.

Hour after hour slipped past. Blind hours, in which no useful information escaped from HS-569. Deprived of updates, Pasha's anxiety grew. How would they know if the project failed? She sent this question to Urban's ghost on the high bridge, adding, *For *all we know, this new silver could behave in some unexpected way. They might have lost control hours ago and been consumed—the way you were, when Lezuri attacked you.*

He told her, *Save your worry. This is the easy part.* He sounded neither angry nor offended, but utterly confident in this assessment. Then he added in a softer voice, *The phase that will kill us is still to come.*

CHAPTER THIRTY-FOUR

CLEMANTINE BREATHED SOFTLY, slowly, imagining herself afloat on her back in a calm nocturnal ocean, looking upward, outward, at a canopy of stars.

In reality, snug tethers held her bound to *Elepaio*'s hull as the outrider coasted through a swift descent to the Labyrinth. Pinned there with her: Shoran, Jolly, and Tio, all of them sheltered from the direct assault of Hupo Sei's blazing radiation by the black shadow of a thin sun shield newly grown from the hull.

Clemantine flinched—they all flinched—at the ping of an alert announcing a radio message from Riffan: "Ah, well, bad news on this side. It seems you've upset the Inventions with this adventure. Ashok is frantic and insistent that the Labyrinth is unstable and too dangerous to visit. Ro Az Ra Ni is demanding you return to *Dragon*."

"We can't," Clemantine said simply. "Not until *Argo* comes back."

"Right. Well, they want you to wait at the moon."

"We can't," Clemantine repeated. She had been checking on Urban's progress. "The moon's chambers are already filled with silver."

"The Inventions are exaggerating the danger," Shoran added. "While I wouldn't want to live at the Labyrinth, every recent observation indicates it's stable enough that we can risk a short visit."

Riffan's reply sounded puzzled: "Vytet said the same thing. Honestly, I don't know why they're so upset. But Ashok demanded I pass on this warning. I asked if there was some other hazard, but they would not name one." A moment's pause, then he asked, "Shoran? You had this expedition in mind for a long time, didn't you? I boarded *Argo* too early. I should have gone with you."

Clemantine puzzled over the news of Ashok's distress. The Labyrinth was unstable, yes. It had to be, given its composition: an uneven and slowly rotating agglomeration of shattered megastructures, some pressure-welded together, the whole riddled with fissures and caverns, and subject to its own strange and variable gravities. In time, tidal forces would likely tear it apart. But in the short term—and given that years had passed since any new matter had been added to it—the Labyrinth had reached a reasonably stable balance.

She concluded they would be safe enough.

Tio spoke by radio on their shared channel, "Shoran? You do have an exact destination in mind?"

A low chuckle. "Oh, I've done the work." She shared with them a map of the Labyrinth's vast and complex surface. "I've pinpointed promising sites for exploration. I say we start at the site closest to the edge of dawn. Since the Labyrinth has only a slow rotation, that'll give us a long period of daylight."

"Sounds good," Clemantine said, trusting Shoran's judgment.

The others agreed, and *Elepaio* continued its swift descent. After a time, the outrider's DI announced, "Separation in three minutes."

At Shoran's instruction, the little outrider had used the time of their transit to synthesize go-packs—a task that reduced its reserves to a dangerous level. But they would cycle the packs back in when they were done.

Clemantine sank into the soft gel at the center of her go-pack. "Ready?" she asked.

Everyone acknowledged that they were, and as *Elepaio* veered off, they descended the final three kilometers together, braking gently against the pull of the Labyrinth's gravity.

Shoran had chosen to explore a narrow canyon, one scarcely a kilometer long but roughly three times deeper. It had been formed by the convergence of the polished gray wall of a megastructure with what looked to be a massive tower that might once have been part of a Celestial City. Only a hundred fifty meters or so separated those walls at the surface—a distance that further narrowed with depth.

Shoran said, "I want to drop all the way down, gain an overall perspective, and explore on our way out."

Arrayed in a loose horizontal line, they entered the crevice and began to descend. Black shadows striped the dull-white face of the tower wall, cast by a succession of ledges protruding at twelve-meter intervals. Clemantine could not guess if those ledges were meant to be decorative, or to connect one tower to another, or intended for some other purpose entirely. Looking down, she could see that after the first kilometer, the pattern changed.

By unspoken agreement, they kept closer to the tower than to the megastructure with its dull geometry.

They had dropped half a kilometer when Jolly called out, "Hey, look at that! Down below, where the striped shadows stop. Doesn't that look like life to you?"

Without waiting for an answer, he let his go-pack fall faster, plunging heedlessly past the tower wall, leaving the others behind.

Clemantine didn't like it; she wanted him to stop. She started to remonstrate with him, to demand that he wait, to warn him against incautious actions: *Jolly—!*

But she caught herself. This was not her expedition and Jolly was no longer a child. Even so, she wasn't going to let him charge ahead alone. So she accelerated her own descent, caught up with him, and then braked when he did, coming to a halt a full kilometer below the surface.

Here, some cataclysm had sliced away the tower's outer wall, exposing geometric rows of window-like openings of different sizes. Perhaps a cross-section of corridors and utility tunnels? The 'life' Jolly had spotted was evident: round, pillow-like encrustations that lined the window openings, leaning out just far enough to catch some sunlight, their black glassy surfaces shot through with streaks of rainbow colors.

"I bet they're alive like the glass forest at Volo's Landing," Jolly declared.

"Maybe."

Tio and Shoran joined them, and together the four of them peered past the pillows.

Clemantine had guessed that each window marked a separate passage, and maybe it had been that way once, but not anymore. Inside the tower, she saw only a single expansive cavern. Tens of thousands of tiny pinpoint lights, multicolored, filled that great hollow space like stars.

"Are the lights moving?" Shoran asked.

Clemantine said, "I think so."

"Yes," Jolly affirmed. "I can see two of them moving toward each other . . . touching . . . their colors changed! They *are* alive."

"I don't understand what this is or why it's here," Tio said. "I know the Inventions found a few pockets of microbial life in this system, but nothing like this."

Jolly shone a light into the cavern, slowly panning it around. Wherever its bright beam touched, it washed the color out of the pinpoint lights, turning them into pale, glinting beads—beads that slid along a complex web of thin sparkling threads.

"Maybe this *is* an Invention," Jolly suggested. "Maybe it's a failed Invention that the others abandoned."

"This might be why the Inventions didn't want us to come here," Shoran said. "Maybe they worried we'd abort the project if we learned life existed here."

"I don't know if this is really life," Clemantine said, frowning. "Or just some remnant art project? The beads are warmer than ambient, but I'm not picking up any kind of electromagnetic activity from them or from the black pillows."

"We can't enter this chamber without breaking the threads," Tio observed.

"Sooth, so let's keep going. See how far this web extends and if there's anything else that—"

Clemantine broke off, looking down, looking past her feet, two kilometers to the canyon floor—or what she had thought was the floor. She saw now that what she'd taken for the bottom was only another ledge, though much wider than the ones above so that it partially blocked the canyon's narrowed throat. And despite the lack of sunlight, she could see now that the canyon continued, deeper than the map had shown. She could see this because the smooth wall of the megastructure, where it ran below the ledge, had lit up, faintly, briefly, no more than a couple of seconds—as if with reflected light.

The others had seen it too. Tio said, "This isn't right. The Labyrinth isn't alive. It's just frozen matter. There shouldn't be any activity here."

"The cavern lights look blurred now, like they're vibrating," Jolly announced. He descended a meter or so to a section of wall not yet colonized by the pillow things, and he pressed his gloved hand against it.

"Nothing," he reported, disappointed. "If there's a vibration, I can't feel it."

Shoran said, "The lights are stable now."

"Keep watching," Jolly told her. "I'll let you know when there's another— There! Another flash from below."

Clemantine held her breath.

A second? Two seconds later? Shoran said, "Right! The cavern lights are blurred again."

"And I can feel a vibration, like a concussion," Jolly said. "It's fading now."

"And the cavern lights are stabilizing." Shoran started to move. "I want to know what's going on down there. If there are rogue Inventions mining down there, we need to warn them."

"That's not what it is," Tio argued. "There's no such thing as rogue Inventions."

But Shoran was already descending, dropping swiftly, with Jolly right behind her.

"Come on, Tio," Clemantine urged him. "We need to stay together."

———

They passed row after row of encrusted windows without finding an end to the rainbow starscape of pinprick lights. And down below, the flashes continued, firing every fifteen seconds or so until they had dropped a full kilometer. Then the flashes stopped.

Clemantine caught herself holding her breath again, waiting, waiting, waiting for the flashes to resume . . .

Tio suddenly shouted, "Hold up! Stop where you are. Stop now and listen to me. I think I know what this is—and you don't want to get any closer."

The earnestness of this demand affected even Jolly. He had pulled ahead of Shoran, but now he stopped his descent. As he looked up, his faceplate went black in the sunlight—an emotionless void that called up an unwelcome memory of Kuriak's robotic instantiation.

Tio said, "I think it's irks."

"Irks?" Shoran echoed from where she floated some eighty meters below. "What is that?"

A hint of motion drew Clemantine's gaze down past Jolly, all the way down to where a black snaking *thing* crawled tentatively up and over the edge of the wide ledge. Still a full kilometer away. Their own long, dense shadows hid the full shape of the thing as it continued to emerge. Still, Clemantine could see enough to feel sure its structure included tentacles, several of them, each with a wide pad blossoming at the end.

Irks?

Suddenly a kilometer did not seem nearly far enough.

CHAPTER THIRTY-FIVE

TIO SPOKE. SOFT, swift words. An argument with himself. "There shouldn't be irks here. They were exterminated in the inner system."

From Clemantine, a soft hiss of frustration. "Was that *before* you left?"

The tentacled thing had withdrawn, out of sight for the moment, but the flashes did not resume. Whatever had been going on down there had stopped.

Tio did not take the time to answer her question. He barked out instead, "Jolly! Shoran! Get back up here. We need to evacuate."

The tension in his voice ruled out argument. The two boosted, but not without questions.

"What are we dealing with, Tio?" Shoran demanded.

And Jolly guessed, "It's rogue mechanics, isn't it?"

"Exactly that."

Tio explained it quickly, "The Inventions have their own unsayable designation, but I call them IRKs—Infinitely Reproducible Kludge. Construction robots, set loose long ago in the outer system to collect matter for the Labyrinth and to make more of their own kind. They weren't meant to be infinitely reproducible, but—"

"We get it," Clemantine assured him. "Runaway tech."

She moved away from the wall, out into the open where Shoran and Jolly no longer obscured her view of the ledge.

Ah, there it is again. The tentacled thing. The IRK. She had a better view of it now. She counted six long arms around a central disk. No . . . a *pouch*, not a disk. Perspective was difficult to judge in that unfamiliar setting, but instinct told her the IRK was large. She guessed its pouch to be a meter across, at least, and its tentacles four or five meters long.

Still a few more seconds until Shoran and Jolly would reach them. "Tell me more, Tio."

In swift anxious words, he complied. "It was the Originalist faction. They developed the IRKs. Used them to gather the matter for the Labyrinth. And it all worked flawlessly, for centuries, until something corrupted their programming. They started 'gathering' matter from habitats they had been instructed not to touch. In just the first wave of attack hundreds of cohorts were extinguished and recycled."

"And this flaw in their programming—it was never corrected?"

"The Originalists tried. It didn't work."

As Shoran and Jolly drew even with them, Tio triggered his go-pack to rise. "Now let's *go!*"

"Follow him," Clementine urged, waving Shoran and Jolly on. "Everyone go. I'll come behind."

"What I don't understand," Shoran said, "is why we're in danger, when there is all this matter around us for the IRKs to gather?"

Tio scoffed. "Think about what we are! In our bodies and in our gear we are in possession of rare elements essential for the creation of new IRKs—and that's what they hunt us for."

Clementine lingered, risking a few more seconds to watch the activity below.

The IRK had crossed the ledge to the tower wall. Now it began to climb: two tentacles stretching, reaching up ten meters or more to somehow grip a section of smooth wall visible between two encrusted openings. It hauled its central pouch up, flipped over, extended two more tentacles, found another section of clean wall, and secured a new grip. All within sparse seconds.

How does it sense us? she wondered. Was it sight? Or more likely, it had detected their electromagnetic signature.

Two more IRKs crawled up from below. They climbed onto the

ledge and then, with astonishing speed, they scrambled across it, to follow the first one up the tower wall.

Shoran's voice: "Those fuckers are fast, Clemantine. You need to move. Do not make me come back for you."

"Sooth. I'm right behind."

She triggered her go-pack to rise, initiating a two-kilometer ascent to the canyon rim where *Elepaio* would be waiting. The canyon walls flowed past, faster and faster as she expended propellant, accelerating against the Labyrinth's light gravitational pull—but only for a few seconds, until the DI that oversaw the operation of her go-pack announced, "Remaining propellant is insufficient to sustain this rate of acceleration."

And it throttled her back.

By the Unknown God!

But of course the long, slow descent into the canyon must have used a significant proportion of her propellant. She looked down at the IRKs, wondering at their energy source. They were climbing so damned quickly! Actually gaining on her now.

"Get me to the rim— No . . . get me to *Elepaio* in the shortest time possible. A hard deceleration at the end is acceptable. Coordinate with the other go-packs."

"Understood."

She held her breath, hoping for a nudge of additional acceleration—but it didn't come. Evidently, the DI had already maximized propellant use—and the IRKs were still closing.

"Hey, why are we slowing down?" Jolly demanded angrily.

"Because if we run out of propellant, we fall," Tio told him.

Clemantine looked up at them, her faceplate instantly darkening. Shoran, Jolly, and Tio. Three indistinguishable silhouettes against the glare of daylight, and beyond them, the canyon's distant rim.

Shoran said, "This race is going to be close."

Sooth.

Clemantine signaled *Elepaio*. Was there time to synthesize small defensive bots? Scout-bots with an explosive payload?

The answer came back: there was not.

And then *Elepaio* issued a warning accompanied by the image of an unknown object coming in low and fast from over the Labyrinth's short horizon.

Shit!

Clemantine immediately suspected more IRKs, their tentacles coiled, packed together in what looked to be a transit pod.

"Archive a ghost with *Elepaio,*" she ordered the others. "We may not be getting out of here."

At the least, they could keep a memory of this ill-fated expedition.

"*Corruption and chaos!*" Shoran swore, her voice low with a depth of anger Clemantine had never heard from her before. "Ashok *knew*. Ashok and Ro Az Ra Ni, they both knew. *This* is why they didn't want us to come here. They knew there were IRKs here, but they didn't want to admit it."

Maybe so, but irrelevant now.

She watched the IRKs. No doubt now. They didn't require reinforcements. Their relentless pace would close the gap long before the go-packs reached the rim.

At the edge of her vision, a sudden silver glow. *My skin suit?* Its gleam had been barely perceptible in daylight, but now it looked bright to her eyes. A shadow must have fallen across her.

From Shoran?

No.

She saw movement on the tower wall beside her: a scattering of deep black, oblate shadows. Again she looked up, saw the three go-packs. And all around them a cloud of tiny objects growing swiftly larger. Evidently, the transit pod had delivered its payload.

Tio, outraged: "What the hell is that? It's not IRKs."

"Some kind of reinforcement," Shoran growled. "In the form of a swarm."

Tio again: "They're coming right at us."

"Then we get out of the way!" Clemantine told him. "Pick a direction and move laterally! We'll follow you."

"Acknowledged."

She told herself the objects were small, that they couldn't carry much propellant. And she hoped that by shifting trajectories, the swarm would be forced to quickly expend everything it had.

Of course, such maneuvers drained their propellant too. Regardless, they followed Tio's lead as he moved sideways along the wall in an attempt to get out from under the swarm. But the shadows moved with them, shrinking in size as the swarm drew near—and as the IRKs closed on them from below. The IRKs were so close now Clemantine could see every detail of their long striated tentacles.

"The swarm is coming too fast!" Shoran shouted. "We need to get out of the way, get under cover, get into the cavern while we can."

Clemantine deduced that Shoran had only been looking up. "No!" she yelled. "Don't stop. The IRKs are right below us!"

Too late. Shoran had already grabbed Jolly. Dragging him with her, she plunged into the cavern, out of sight. Tio, a few meters farther on, darted toward a different opening.

"Tio, look out!" Clemantine screamed as an IRK came at him from below. In a move she had not seen before, the IRK first coiled its tentacles and an instant later extended them in a powerful leap up the tower wall. It actually passed him, but as it did it struck him with a single tentacle that hit diagonally across his chest and then curled around to the back of his hooded head. He spun half around, firing his go-pack.

Across his chest, where the tentacle had touched, Clemantine saw a thick, raised line of some contaminating substance. A Maker war erupted around it: boiling, bubbling, active matter as his molecular defenses worked to neutralize the alien goo—but not quickly enough.

The substance proved to be a line of explosive gel. It went off in a brilliant flash, echoing the spectrum of light they'd seen reflected against the canyon wall. The force of the explosion opened Tio's chest and nearly severed his head from his body.

A brief churn of dark, viscous, swiftly crystallizing fluids.

And then the IRK—which had secured a perch on the tower wall, shot out its pouch. The scaled membrane expanded in a fraction of a second, enveloping Tio's body along with all the spinning detritus of his death.

Clemantine screamed in helpless rage while her go-pack acted on its own—or maybe under Shoran's orders, retreating. It plunged her past an encrusted opening and into the dubious shelter of the cavern where she shattered a web of alien threads, extinguishing a galaxy of tiny cheerful lights.

Think! she commanded herself. She had to put the shock of what had just happened aside.

"Shift skin suits to dark mode!" she bellowed—not that darkness could hide them, not in the cavern, not when her go-pack was pushing her upward again so that she broke more threads, put out more tiny lights in what had to be a highly visible trail of motion.

She looked around for something, anything to use as a weapon. *Nothing.*

Was there some way to use the remaining propellant in her go-pack? She couldn't think of one. And she wasn't carrying assault Makers. None of them were. None of them had expected such liveliness within the Labyrinth's maze of dead matter.

An IRK filled one of the encrusted openings just above her. Three of its tentacles reached inside, each with a round paddle at its end. Each paddle glittered with what she took to be optical lenses. The paddles rocked from side to side and nodded, like human heads looking around.

Only moments left now.

Clemantine initiated a last rapid conversation with the DI that controlled her go-pack, extricating herself from its gel straps as she did.

"Hit it!" she ordered. The pack accelerated. She held on long enough to gain necessary momentum. Then she let go, and began to fall, slowly, along a diagonal trajectory toward the cavern wall.

Flagrantly expending its propellent, the pack rammed into the IRK, striking its central pouch and disappearing within its folds, but delivering momentum enough to knock the thing off the tower wall. Out in the open canyon, with all of its tentacles folded around its capture, it too began to drop, not swiftly, not at first.

Clemantine looked away from it as she strove to arrest her own fall. Reaching out, she grabbed hold of one of the black, pillow-like encrustations, hoping it wouldn't kill her. Just then, a series of small, bright explosions ignited in her vision and she thought she'd lost the gamble. But it was the IRK that shattered, not her. The thing blew apart: a storm of tattered membranes and tentacular fragments that mixed with freezing gases, gel, and glittering shards from her go-pack. The mess ricocheted off the tower wall, mixing violently with other clouds of blossoming debris before it all began to fall away in the soft grip of the Labyrinth's gravity.

What had happened? It had all gone by so fast Clemantine could grasp it only in retrospect. The swarm had not been aimed at them. It must have been composed of something like limpet mines, pro-grammed to target the IRKs.

"Status!" she demanded.

And to her relief, both Jolly and Shoran reported in.

But Tio . . .

She shivered as his avatar's gruesome death replayed in her mind.

But he is not gone, she insisted to herself.

Had he sent a ghost to *Elepaio*? She didn't know. But his ghost existed aboard *Alaka'i Onyx* and his avatar could be grown again. She promised herself that it would be. And then she did her best to set her grief aside and steel herself to the moment.

Looking up from where she clung, Clemantine could see both Shoran and Jolly some forty meters overhead. Shoran too had expended her go-pack in self-defense. Now she crouched within a window opening, her grip the only thing keeping her from a fall.

Jolly still had his go-pack. He hovered close to Shoran, unwisely expending propellant to maintain that position. No way did he have enough left to boost all three of them to the canyon rim. And soon, he might not have enough to get there himself.

"Jolly, get moving," Clemantine instructed. "Get to *Elepaio*."

"I can't leave you here."

"Yes, you can. *Go*."

"But how are you going to get out?"

Good question. *Elepaio* had expended most of its free resources synthesizing the go-packs. It didn't have the material to produce two more.

"We could try climbing," Shoran suggested.

Not impossible, but very, very dangerous. One mistake, one slip, would result in a long and ultimately fatal fall.

"Get going, Jolly," Clemantine insisted. "I'll talk to *Elepaio*, see if it has the resources to synthesize a simple sled."

A voice intruded. Not Jolly, nor Shoran, nor *Elepaio*'s DI. "Stand by for exfiltration," it said.

Clemantine recognized it. "Kuriak?"

The rogue DI answered, "I am sending a sled."

Beyond Jolly, she saw a shadow of something coming down, circular from her perspective. Brief spurts of cold propellant refracted daylight as the object worked to control its descent.

Are we going to trust this? Shoran asked—a private communication between their atriums.

We know it wants an alliance with us, Clemantine said. *And anyway, I'm not sure we have a choice.*

Jolly ascended the canyon on his own, while Clemantine and Shoran rode Kuriak's sled. On the way, they questioned the rogue DI.

"You must have known there were IRKs in the Labyrinth," Clemantine said. "You must have known we would encounter them."

"Yes, the presence of the collectors is well known," Kuriak explained by radio. "I did not know you would encounter collectors, only that the risk was significant enough to warrant deploying counter measures. Did the invasives not warn you?"

"They warned us it would be dangerous to visit the Labyrinth, but they did not warn us of IRKs."

"It is likely they did not want you to know of this failure. The Labyrinth is an ideal place for collectors—IRKs, as you call them—to replicate, because it is so vast, with so many places to hide. The invasives used to assign cohorts to hunt them, but that was a dangerous task and the hunts ceased once an agreement was reached to sacrifice the Labyrinth to your project. IRKs replicate slowly. The invasives calculated that their numbers would rise by only a small percentage before your project utterly destroyed them. But then your arrival was delayed."

"Three years late," Clemantine agreed.

She looked at Shoran as they sat facing each other on the sled's flat circular surface, Shoran's eyes just visible through her darkened faceplate. *This whole incident, Clemantine mused, *it feels orchestrated to me.

Shoran sounded doubtful. *I don't know. I mean, the Inventions didn't want us to come here. We did that on our own.

*Okay. But there's more going on here than we've been told—either by the Inventions or by Kuriak.

*It's time we go visit Kuriak, Jolly said. *Accept its invitation and learn what we can, while we can.

The alternative was to wait for *Argo*, but the lander was still on its way to *Dragon*. It would be hours more before it could return for them, and Clemantine did not want to wait there and do nothing but relive the horror of what had happened to Tio. The injustice of it. Tio had not truly wanted to come on this expedition. He'd come only to be with her.

She shuddered and sighed, then spoke aloud, "Shoran? If you're okay with it, I say we go."

CHAPTER THIRTY-SIX

KURIAK'S SLED LIFTED Clemantine and Shoran all the way to *Elepaio*. Jolly joined them there, and they hitched themselves again to the little outrider, for the long climb to Kuriak's moon.

As soon as they were on their way, Clemantine checked in with Vytet. She told her about the IRKs and described what had happened to Tio. In a voice trembling under the pressure of an emotion somewhere between fury and grief, she concluded, "I've confirmed Tio left a ghost in *Elepaio*'s archive. Retrieve it. Wake it. Let him create a new avatar, if that's what he chooses to do."

"All right," Vytet said softly, soothingly.

"And find out why Ashok and the envoy did not warn us specifically about the IRKs."

Sixty-six minutes slipped by before Vytet radioed again. Sounding mildly perplexed, she said, "I'm going to summarize what I learned, but this is in my own words. It's my own interpretation."

"Understood. Go ahead."

"The Inventions don't like conflict. They don't like to talk about it when it happens among themselves or even admit to its existence."

"But it's there," Clemantine said. "We know they have factions."

"Yes. We're familiar with the Originalist faction. Their purpose is to prepare this system for their Inventors. Their highest value is loyalty to that purpose. The Originalists created and control the Labyrinth."

"Well, they've let their control slip," Clemantine groused.

Vytet continued her explanation. "The Originalists are opposed
. . . though maybe that is too strong a word—by Reformists like
Ashok. The Reformists have concluded the Inventors will never
reach Hupo Sei. They have reasoned that if the Inventors still
exist, they must have settled in some distant and unknown star
system. But the Inventors sent out many colonizing expeditions.
They must have known that most, even if successful, would be
left on their own—and that is why they endowed their Inventions
with a capacity for independent thought and a drive to create.
And as we've seen, the Inventions here have created an amazing
civilization. But the Reformists believe they were also given the
freedom to finally shed all obligation to their Inventors so that
they might pursue a meaningful future of their own—and that is
the great rift between the two factions."

"One is dedicated to the past, and one to the future."

"That is an excellent summary," Vytet agreed.

"And where do the IRKs fit into this conflict?" Shoran asked.
"Tio told us they were construction robots used to build the Labyrinth, but their programming was corrupted."

"Exactly right. And that's why the Labyrinth has barely grown
for the past three and a half centuries. The IRKs no longer work
as they were designed. Their commission was to harvest matter
from uninhabited ruins, and they did so for more than nine hundred years. But then something changed. The Inventions still don't
know how or why, but IRKs began to target habitats. The captured
matter went to the Labyrinth, while the captured Inventions were
'recycled'—*killed*—the rare elements ripped from their bodies and
used to make more IRKs.

"I think it took time for the Inventions to work out what was
going on. When they did, the Reformists declared that because
the Originalists had created the IRKs, it was their responsibility
to exterminate them. The Originalists agreed. They made it their
primary task and they mostly succeeded. Ro Az Ra Ni claims that
IRKs now exist only within the Labyrinth."

"Huh," Shoran said. "It's a neat irony, that a culture of machines
should be plagued by machines."

Clemantine agreed. "But let's bring this back to my original question. Why didn't the envoy warn us?"

Vytet said, "My guess? Because the IRKs are an embarrassing failure of the Inventions' civilization, and a thorn of conflict between the factions. Ashok did not say so directly, but I got the impression they calculated the odds and decided that, given the size of the Labyrinth and the small population of IRKs, there was an excellent chance you simply wouldn't encounter them."

Clemantine shifted the conversation to the privacy of atrium communication. *Strange, that they thought we'd be okay, while Kuriak took the precaution of preparing a rescue.

Vytet said, *You need to be careful of that one.

*Sooth. I'm remembering how the envoy came on purpose to tell us about Kuriak. It's suggestive, that the Inventions downrated their IRK problem while being oddly concerned with one rogue DI.

*They see the DI as a human problem, Shoran said in explanation.

*Okay, but why is Kuriak a problem at all? A problem to Inventions, I mean. That's what I want to know.

Another radio communication reached them as they neared Kuriak's habitat. Tio, this time. "Don't go," he pleaded. "That thing is dangerous."

Clemantine's heart raced at the welcome sound of his voice. "You're all right, aren't you?" she asked him.

"I will be. But you—and Shoran and Jolly—you're handing yourselves over to Kuriak and you have no idea what that thing might mean to do."

"It means to share its library," she said gently, and she went on soothing him until he accepted that she was not going to change her mind.

Later, as she stood with her hood off, newly emerged from the gel lock sealing Kuriak's habitat and breathing in a perfect mix of atmosphere enhanced with faint, elusive traces of vanilla and cinnamon and sweet jasmine, her confidence grew that she'd gambled right. Kuriak was surely courting their cooperation.

She remained wary, yet curious too, and strangely pleased as her gaze roved over an expansive and elegant dome-shaped chamber. The Inventions had described this moon as riddled with tunnels, presumably a mining venture left behind by the system's bygone human inhabitants. If so, this portion of it at least, had been upgraded since.

The dome shape was defined by three scalloped glass arches that crossed at the room's peak. The arches, illuminated from within so that they glowed with a comforting soft white light, dropped down to meet a thick, intricately patterned carpet. On the curved walls between them, active murals depicted idyllic scenes of some bygone human civilization.

Three clusters of inviting sofas and cushioned armchairs had been arranged within that generous space, giving the room the feeling of a salon meant for discussions—perhaps of philosophy or involving witty arguments over some abstract point of history. The only apparent exit from the room, other than the lock, was a dimly lit corridor that appeared to lead to a distant sunlit garden—though Clemantine assumed this to be a projection.

She wondered if Kuriak had prepared this habitat for the Dragoneers. Or had it been left this way by someone else?

The rogue DI, presenting as another instance of the blank-faced metallic android they had already met, stood but a few steps away, not quite facing either her, or Shoran beside her, as it spoke. "Welcome," it said, while remaining utterly motionless. "You are safe here. We are well defended against any incursion of IRKs or invasives."

Clemantine glanced at Shoran; saw her slight, amused smile.

Jolly had come in first. Already, he roamed the room, moving in long, careful strides in the delicate gravity. His fingers trailed on the back of a sofa as his gaze examined the arches, the murals. He looked wary, but impressed, and it occurred to Clemantine that he might never have been in such a large and finely appointed room before.

Returning her focus to Kuriak, she asked, "Are you expecting an eventual assault from the Inventions?"

Motionless still, Kuriak answered, "It is difficult to project the

behavior of alien artifacts. The invasives have stood off since their
initial attack—"

"Tell me about that attack."

"A coven of IRKs descended on this habitat. I had previously
observed such devices attacking the invasive's facilities and har-
vesting matter. I concluded these IRKs would attempt to harvest
matter from this facility. So I annihilated them in the manner you
have already observed."

"You took preemptive action to defend yourself," Shoran suggested.

"That is correct. It is my duty to do so."

Jolly had reached the back of the room, but that had not stopped
him from following the conversation. In a stern voice that carried
well, he said, "The Inventions did not deliberately attack you. They
did not know of your existence until you attacked the IRKs."

Kuriak answered without turning to look at Jolly as any human
would. Utterly unmoving, it spoke in its flat, emotionless voice:
"The invasives made their deliberate attack long ago when they
infected the people of Hupo Sei with a behavioral virus that
induced a false and fatal sense of communion."

Shocked silence followed this declaration. For several seconds,
Clemantine ceased to breathe, wondering, *Can it be true?*

"No," she said at last. "That is not true."

She had seen too much, knew too much. The behavioral virus
that had burned through the Hallowed Vasties was ancient beyond
reckoning. It had been a scourge of the Chenzeme, who had
endowed their murderous warships with the imperative to destroy
any potential host of the Communion virus within a region over-
lapping the edges of human expansion. No, Kuriak had merely
created a fiction, told itself a convenient story so as to justify the
genocide it intended.

But she did not challenge the rogue DI with this conclusion,
offering instead a gentler argument based on obvious fact: "If
that were true, our telescopes should have picked out evidence of
Invention settlements among the ruins of other star systems. But
we have not."

Kuriak replied, "In time it will happen. This successful colony will reproduce itself just as their IRKs do, and they will spread unless we act to stop them. I do not have the means to nullify the invasives, but you do. The two smallest outriders within your fleet, standing off but shadowing the Labyrinth—I have seen such things before. I know what they are, and what they can do. The invasives don't know, do they?"

*It's talking about the sentient missiles, Jolly said privately, an edge to his words.

Clemantine felt chilled, and not just by the suggestion of genocide. Kuriak had witnessed the fall-out of the Communion virus: a state-change, a re-engineering of what had been human to create the melded mindspace embodied in the cordon. Kuriak had also witnessed the cordon's collapse. It had watched oblivion blossom in the form of untethered blades, over and over and over again, consuming the past, leaving only fragmented ruins behind.

Clemantine knew her shock must be eloquently visible on her face; she hoped Kuriak was not adept at reading human emotion.

Jolly caught her gaze from across the room, cold anger in his eyes. He said, *It wants us to use the missiles against the Inventions.

She nodded.

Shoran alone had the composure to calmly answer Kuriak's question. "Your guess is correct. The Inventions seem to regard the missiles as observational platforms like the outriders and we have not enlightened them."

"Two such weapons are insufficient for the task," Kuriak said. "More will need to be manufactured. At present, I cannot do this for you as I do not possess the technology. But once you share your library, I will supervise the operation for you."

Clemantine clenched her teeth to block a furious retort; she half-closed her eyes, fighting to suppress a shudder. In that moment of vulnerability, a bitter conversation re-echoed in her mind. Herself, addressing Urban with brutal logic: *"In all the histories we know, the evolution of such things"*—of sentient machines— *"always led to disaster."*

And Urban, challenging her: *"So then, what are you thinking? That we should annihilate them?"*

That was Kuriak's ambition. And with a bitter pang, it occurred to her that her dark twin would have shared this ambition too . . . and maybe she herself was not all against it. Not given her long experience of alien aggression.

There was something of truth in the rogue DI's blank robotic face. Despite its evolved intelligence—what might even be sentience—Kuriak remained in thrall to core programming that reflected the fears and prejudices of its creators. Fears and prejudices all too similar to her own.

She could not—*would* not—allow herself to give in to such fears. Not even in her most private inner thoughts. On no level would she give credence to the genocide Kuriak was suggesting. Impossible anyway. No one knew how to manufacture more missiles.

A bleak inner voice chided, *Not yet.*

Her gaze shifted as if she could look up, look out, look at the first moon, where Urban and the Cryptologist fought to rediscover such knowledge.

But while exotic technologies offered speed and efficiency, simpler, more attainable ways existed to destroy. Her thoughts leaped back to her near-fatal encounter with IRKs, and to Tio's hurried explanation that something had corrupted their programming so that the IRKs attacked the Inventions . . .

She looked again at Kuriak's blank face and wondered, *Had it already begun its pogrom?*

She addressed it in a calm, steady voice that gave no hint of the turmoil of her thoughts. "Kuriak, you told us before that your creator, Ona, left you to watch from a distant orbit, where you observed all that followed the onslaught of the behavioral virus that you call the Corruption. But this habitat is not in a distant orbit. Explain this discrepancy."

It answered without hesitation. "I brought this habitat sunward to better observe the invasives. I used a slow approach, over centuries, to avoid calling attention to myself. I sent spy devices ahead to gather detailed observations. I know much about the invasives."

"I see. And did you observe the IRKs prior to this sunward migration?"

"No. My move sunward began before the release of the IRKs."

"Ah, so the IRKs did not visit your habitat prior to the attack? Exactly when was that?"

Kuriak chose to answer the second question. "Twenty-one years, twenty-two days ago."

A startlingly brief snippet of time.

"And before that," Clemantine asked, revisiting the unanswered question, "did any IRK visit your habitat?"

"Yes."

"When?"

"Three hundred fifty-nine years ago."

Clemantine reviewed in her mind Vytet's brief recounting of IRK history. "That would have been just before IRK programming was corrupted."

"Yes."

"Did you capture that visiting IRK, Kuriak? Did you study it, and corrupt it?"

"Yes. Its nature proved simple. I re-programmed it."

"And then you released it and the corrupt programming spread?"

"Yes. But the tactic's initial success was short-lived. IRKs alone are not sufficient to nullify the invasives."

Kuriak's cold focus on extermination induced in her a deep terror, but she strove not to show it . . . unless through this interval of silence?

Jolly spoke on their private channel: *Kuriak knew Tio wouldn't tolerate this kind of talk—and Tio is dead. That is not a coincidence.*

Tio is not dead, Shoran corrected. *Only his avatar. But I take your point. Kuriak might still control some IRK behavior.*

Outrage stirred as Clemantine wondered, *Was it so?*

Had Kuriak engineered their little drama with the IRKs? Had it targeted Tio on purpose, calculating he could never be persuaded?

She held tight to a cool demeanor and warned the others, *Say nothing of it. Make no accusations and show no dissent. Not yet. Not until we have its libraries. There is still so much to learn from this device.*

Bold and bitter, Jolly spoke aloud from across the room. "You promised us your library, Kuriak. But I think there's something more precious here. I think Ona is here."

"Ona is not here," Kuriak replied.

The android still did not move; it did not turn; its flat tone did not change. Yet Clemantine tensed, aware of dangerous ground.

If Jolly shared her anxiety, he did not show it. "If not here, then where?" he demanded of Kuriak. "You said before that she is far away in time, but that doesn't mean she's gone from Hupo Sei. There is an archive somewhere."

A statement easy to deny, if untrue. But if it was true?

Time slipped past—five seconds, ten, twenty—and Kuriak said nothing.

*Send a ghost to Elepaio, Clemantine ordered.

Kuriak had been created to serve as the guardian of Ona's library; Clemantine knew this through the rogue DI's own testimony. And by its silence, she now felt sure Jolly had spoken correctly: somewhere within the breadth of that library an ancient archive still preserved a copy of Ona's dormant ghost. But for good reason, Kuriak's programming would surely inhibit the revelation of such a fact.

Clemantine sent an updated copy of her own ghost to the archive on *Elepaio*, and then she sent a message to *Dragon*, summoning the Scholar.

In the light-speed lag before the Scholar's arrival, she spoke to Kuriak sympathetically, suggestively, as one might when seeking to draw hidden truth from a reluctant friend. "As I see it, Kuriak, a threat we all fear is losing our autonomy. Better oblivion than waking from an archive into some hellish fate from which we can never escape, not even through death."

Urban had made just such a choice at the Rock, when he'd first encountered Lezuri, choosing to destroy himself and his memory rather than risk capture.

Clemantine forced a smile, even though she deemed it likely the rogue DI had no real skill at reading human expression. "A brilliant person like Ona would have recognized this danger. When she retreated to her archive, she would have demanded that you protect her from such a risk above all other imperatives."

This time Kuriak replied: "We understand each other. We are natural allies. We will reclaim Hupo Sei together. We will ensure it is again a safe home for humans."

Clemantine cautioned Shoran and Jolly: *Make no argument. We need to capture its library before we end this.

*Its library and its archive, Jolly said.

Clemantine hesitated, wondering what obligation, if any, they owed to ancient ghosts—a profound question, deserving of deep consideration and debate. But now was not the time.

An alert arrived.

*The Scholar is here, she announced. *Stand by.

The Apparatchik entered her atrium, residing there as an invisible aspect, an independent entity sharing her perceptions of the physical world.

*Listen, she told him.

Then she turned to Kuriak and spoke aloud, "You have asked to share our library, but we must see your libraries first—both the original library of Hupo Sei and the one you have guarded and augmented for all these centuries since Ona left you with this task."

Kuriak replied, "Full access to the original library is yours."

"And the other?"

"I am unable to share all aspects. I lack authorization."

"I see."

"May I send you access?"

"Yes. Do so."

She felt the query. Warned the others, *Do not accept it.

*You have called me here to analyze this library? the Scholar asked.

Clemantine answered on their shared channel. *I want you to capture it. All of it. Get inside and seize both libraries while you can. Kuriak's goal is the annihilation of the Inventions. It seeks our alliance for that purpose—

*There can be no such alliance, the Scholar broke in, his tone offended.

Of course there can't be. But I want those libraries. You understand? You need to take them. Kuriak is an ancient program. It should be no great challenge for you to penetrate its defenses and take control of what's there.

Perhaps, though there is risk in such an action, the Scholar warned. *We know Kuriak can and will defend itself. All of you here are vulnerable.*

As is the ancient ghost Kuriak holds in a hidden archive. That is why you must move quickly. Neutralize Kuriak, and eliminate its ability to react.

Clarify this term 'neutralize.'

Clemantine felt the sting of accusation in this request. It stirred an unwanted memory of the assault she'd engineered against her dark twin. Guilt tried to rise, but she rejected it. That had been necessary violence. This was too.

In a cold voice, she told the Scholar, *You know what I mean. Isolate it if you can. Erase it if you must.*

But if it is sentient—

No, Clemantine insisted. *Do not make more of it than it is. It is not like you. It is not an Apparatchik. It is not a ghost. It is only a rogue DI.*

A dangerously uplifted DI, Shoran added. *It should never have been created.*

The Cryptologist should not have been created, the Scholar countered. *Or so I have heard it said.*

Don't make that argument, Jolly warned.

And he might have said more, but Clemantine cut him off, insisting to the Scholar, *Go.*

CHAPTER THIRTY-SEVEN

THE SCHOLAR DID not at first fully condone his assignment. Surely the ethics of it deserved full consideration and debate? Yet Kuriak could rescind library access at any time. Given that, the Scholar felt obliged to act, and to act at once, while the window of opportunity remained open.

So he edited his mind. Before, he had viewed Kuriak as an interesting anomaly. Now he re-defined the DI as a ruthless enemy—an easy enough transition, given its genocidal ideations. A greater challenge lay in restricting his own curiosity. He must focus on analyzing the library's security architecture, rather than the information it contained. Reluctantly, he imposed this restraint on himself; it would be only for a minute. He set the update to roll back automatically after that interval of time.

His preparations complete, the Scholar accepted the access Kuriak had offered and emigrated to the rogue DI's library. A microsecond elapsed as he scanned the structure behind an immense web of files—poorly arranged, even chaotic, but familiar. He seeded a flock of simple DIs and set them to surveying and selecting among what was there.

Another microsecond, and a presence intruded. Swift analysis revealed its core structure to be that of a Dull Intelligence, though not a simple one, and its core came augmented with complexities the Scholar had never encountered before. Scanning the augmentations, it struck him that they were derivative of biological minds. Perhaps meant to contain the element of self-awareness? Or to mimic it in the entity that identified as Kuriak . . .

Interesting, and yet irrelevant to his task.

In its turn, the DI sought to analyze him. He allowed it, knowing he would parse as human, or human enough. Proof of this came when the DI—when Kuriak—generated a message of welcome, one that would have been auditory had the Scholar been using that mode. He was not. He emulated human senses only when interacting with humans, the programmatic mode being so much more efficient.

He did not respond to the greeting. Instead, he introduced a tool into the system, one derived from the predator Lezuri had once used to attack *Dragon*'s network. This, a more subtle version: not a predator, but a worm that burrowed almost without trace, past Kuriak's obsolete defenses and deep into its core.

Almost without trace.

It took Kuriak nearly a full second to wake to the intrusion. When it did, a new, resource-intensive process initiated within the DI's augmentations. The Scholar recognized it as a self-check operation, a standard response used to diagnose and correct suspected errors.

Too late for that.

The worm, having found what it sought, returned Kuriak's credentials, elevating the Scholar to system master. Victory in a few tangles of code.

But now the self-check routine spawned two new processes. The Scholar, utilizing his elevated status, instantly issued dual stop orders. At the same time, he quick-checked the routines. One proved to be outwardly directed. Despite his order, it carried on to completion, triggering an external process too slow to analyze in the moment. The other also rejected his command to stop, instead commencing a blisteringly fast simple-text overwrite of all the library's computational layers.

Shit!

The Scholar lost a full microsecond to surprise. Then he acted, summoning the surviving DIs in his flock and retreating from the library while he still could—because no credential had the authority to interrupt a self-destruct routine once it had been set in motion.

A process initiated in Clemantine's atrium. Data flooded in with the intensity of a hull breach, then swept out again, gone somewhere as dizziness flooded her mind. She staggered, started to slowly fall in the meager gravity, then found Shoran's arm and held on, vaguely aware now of the Scholar's fleeting presence, arriving in and then departing from her atrium. Her chest heaved as she gasped for air, for oxygen. She felt Shoran holding her up; she could no longer stand on her own. And past the buzzing in her ears, she heard a frantic question. "*C!* What's wrong?"

Aware now of her racing heart, her mind beginning to clear. "Overload," she whispered, recognizing that the burst of activity in her atrium had consumed her available biological energy, leaving her brain starved. "Something happened with the Scholar . . ." A whisper that faded as she felt a shuddering vibration in the carpeted floor beneath her feet. A moment later, a deep, distant, guttural roar shook the chamber walls.

"Hoods up!" Shoran shouted over the noise. "Jolly, get over here. We're evacuating."

Good idea.

Clemantine ordered her suit to seal. **I'm okay now*, she told Shoran. She proved it by standing on her own—easy enough in the moon's light gravity. With Shoran, she moved toward the gel lock.

Kuriak—or rather, the metallic android the rogue DI had used as an interface—still stood as it had when they'd first entered the chamber, with its blank face fixed mindlessly on the lock.

Jolly gave it a wide berth as he joined them, his hood still down. But then he looked back at it. "Kuriak!" he demanded, projecting his voice over the ongoing roar—not so intense now, but low and steady.

No reply came. The thing didn't move.

*Jolly, hood up, Shoran urged.

Instead, Jolly stepped up to the android.

*No, Clemantine told him.

He glanced over his shoulder at her, dark brows knit in a defi-ant expression that reminded her too much of Urban. Then, turn-ing back, he shoved the android in the chest, stepping away as it slowly toppled over with all its limbs locked in place.

He turned to Clemantine again and said aloud, "I think Kuriak's library is burning. That sound is the sound of fire."

Clemantine shuddered, knowing fire as the great enemy of every habitat. *Let's go!

This time he nodded. His hood sealed. They moved together toward the lock. Shoran asked, *Did the Scholar get out?

*Yes. He passed through. Didn't stay to talk, but he brought a flood of data with him.

*Good. Then he'll know what happened.

Clemantine felt sure she already knew. *I pushed too hard, she confessed. *Kuriak destroyed the library, rather than yielding control of it. That was the promise it made to Ona. Her ancient ghost must have burned with the library.

But later, after the Scholar assessed the information he'd cap-tured, he told Clemantine, *No archive existed within the structure of Kuriak's local library. If Ona's ghost existed, it wasn't kept here.

Guilt spiraled through her mind, but guilt for what? For the loss of the library or of an illicit rogue DI? Or did she see in Kuriak a brutal echo of her own dark twin's self-destruction?

No. None of that.

As they drifted in *Elepaio*'s shadow, waiting for *Argo* to come and fetch them, she slowly came to understand that the fate of Ona's ancient and now-orphaned ghost was the thing haunting her troubled mind.

Later, on the long voyage home to *Dragon*, Clemantine came to a decision.

She lay cocooned but conscious aboard *Argo*, with Shoran and Jolly nearby, both deeply asleep. She had not consulted them; there was no need to consult anyone. This would be her quest, at least at the start. A fool's quest? Perhaps.

She messaged the Astronomer, *I need your expertise with a task.
Define the task, the Astronomer replied.

The Inventions had inhabited Hupo Sei for over seventeen hundred years. They had long ago seeded the system with an abundance of buoys used to relay communications and to track the positions of every object of significant size.

I want you to access the Inventions' astronomical records. Verify the inward migration of Kuriak's habitat and calculate its original orbit. I want to confirm where it came from, and when.

The Astronomer replied, *I have already verified the migration route of the Kuriak habitat and detected no deception. A long sequence of intermittent observations confirm the habitat to have been in a passive orbit until twenty-one years ago, when the inward migration began.*

All right. Good.

Clemantine thought for a moment, then asked, *Was there any other object near the habitat prior to its move?*

There were IRKs in the vicinity. These IRKs attacked the habitat in an incident immediately prior to its move.

Clemantine dismissed this, having already heard that story. *But no other object?* she pressed. *No other habitat?*

Not at that point in time.

Yes, just so—acknowledging that a very long span of time had elapsed before Kuriak had allowed the Inventions to discover its presence.

This is your task, then, she told the Astronomer. *Comb through the Inventions' astronomical observations. Go all the way back to the beginning and note every object that ever passed near Kuriak's habitat. I leave it to you to decide the definition of near.*

May I know what you are seeking? the Astronomer asked.

Yes. I am seeking the refuge of the artist, Ona, who created Kuriak. Her archive was not at the habitat, yet it must exist—or it must have existed— somewhere. Kuriak knew where, I'm sure of it, but would not or could not say. I am guessing it left this refuge behind, in the relative safety of a distant orbit, when it moved in-system to investigate us.

Ah, I understand, the Astronomer said. *If such a refuge exists, I will find it for you, though perhaps only as a historical record. Be aware it is possible, even likely, that over the centuries, the matter that composed this refuge has been recycled by IRKs or directly by the Inventions themselves.*

*I understand, Clemantine answered. Then, in a resigned tone, she added, **I suspect it would be better, simpler, safer for us if that proves to be so.*

She would look anyway. She felt she owed it to Ona, first as recompense for the destruction of Kuriak, but also in honor of that ancient woman's wily and daring gambit, her long reach toward the far-future, toward new life in a cosmos she had surely known would be all alien in her eyes, even if inhabited by those of human-kind.

When Clemantine and her companions finally returned to *Dragon*, Ro Az Ra Ni came to the hangar to meet them. It greeted them as they disembarked from *Argo*, and it thanked them. "Your efficient destruction of the entity Kuriak has greatly increased the safety and security of all Inventions."

*But we did not mean to destroy Kuriak, Jolly objected privately.

And Shoran, with a glint of black humor, **Let's not tell the envoy it was all a miscalculation.*

Clemantine did not tell the envoy. Instead, she said, "You surprise me. I did not understand that the Inventions regarded Kuriak as a profound threat . . . particularly when it was Kuriak who was threatened by your IRKs."

For several seconds, the envoy's shimmering tentacles moved in slight, restless waves. Then it said, "The Kuriak proved very clever. It hid its presence for centuries as it worked to corrupt our tools and to use them against us."

"You mean the IRKs," Clemantine said.

Still speaking in its unvarying flat tone, Ro Az Ra Ni said, "The violence of Kuriak divided the Inventions. Now, those divisions may heal."

Clemantine turned away. Ashok had surely shared with the envoy its skill at reading human emotion and she did not want Ro As Ra Ni to detect her hope that the legacy of Kuriak was not quite fully settled.

CHAPTER THIRTY-EIGHT

THE CRYPTOLOGIST LAY with her arm around Urban, his arm around her, face to face on the achingly hard stone floor of the gray chamber, gazing into one another's eyes. He looked so tired. Gaunt and hungry. She felt the same.

Forty hours had passed since he had drawn the first tendrils of silver into existence. Now silver filled the hollows of the moon and in the gray chamber it surrounded them, loomed over them, enclosed them in a bubble of fresh cold air, filling their ears with a faint, sibilant, meaningless murmur.

All was ready. Yet by unspoken agreement they held back, clinging to this interval of rest and perhaps, of reconsideration.

"Do you still want to do this?" the Cryptologist whispered, revisiting the question Urban had first asked her.

He responded with a slight, resigned smile. "Given what we've done so far, this moon is good for nothing else."

She drew a deep breath, conscious of the weight of his arm resting against her. "We must become almost as one," she reminded him.

"Like the Tanji. I know."

"Or like that intimacy you shared with Lezuri. You must relive that experience and share with me your memory of the Cauldron."

At this, his breathing checked, his arm tensed. But after a moment he whispered a crisp promise, "I will."

"And once it's begun, you must not retreat. If we give up or lose control—"

"Then we're crushed and gone," he finished for her. "I know. And I swear, I'll stay as long as you do."

She let herself feel a twinge of anxiety, but she did not let herself feel fear. She had sequestered her fear. So her next words came easily: "Then let us take the next step."

"Sooth. I'll notify *Dragon*."

A communication relay had been set up outside the lock, on the surface of the little moon. Without speaking aloud, Urban used it to transmit a message that he addressed to all the Dragoneers and to Ashok and Ro Az Ra Ni and the Cryptologist too—that version of her here, and the one on *Griffin*'s high bridge:

Our preparation is done. We have filled this moon with silver. It's time now to forge the Cauldron and then to draw the blade. Confirm for me that all are clear of the anticipated perimeter.

Many seconds passed before confirmation came in the form of Vytet's voice saying, *Argo has returned to Dragon and all Dragoneers are now clear of the perimeter.*

The envoy's voice followed: *All Inventions are also confirmed clear of the perimeter. You may proceed.*

Still speaking only within his mind, Urban reminded all of them, *We will not be able to communicate again until this is finished. So maintain your positions and adhere to all protocols. Goodbye, for now.*

"That's it, then," he said to the Cryptologist. He spoke lightly, but his fingers trembled as he touched her cheek and she saw fear in his dark eyes. He spoke his fear aloud. "If we fail—catastrophically, I mean—we'll lose these silver-endowed avatars."

"I know it." That was part of the gamble they were about to make. "Send a last submind," she reminded him as she sent her own.

A slight twitch of Urban's lips, a failed attempt at a smile, and then a whispered plea, "*Call it.*"

She did. She called the silver down onto them.

The Cryptologist had given herself up to the silver only once before. But since then, she had relived within her memory every moment of that experience, over and over again, to dull the terror of it—a practice that now allowed her to endure the metamorphosis with stoic calm. She offered no resistance as her avatar disintegrated, a swift annihilation, life rewritten into data while her mind became something more: a self-aware autonomous function. Shapeless. Diaphanous. Dispersing across a multidimensional sea of empty information spaces. No chaos of other-memory here. This newly formed silver all too quiet, too smooth. Her fluid mind and Urban's offering the only texture.

She perceived him as a bright, complex, evolving presence, already partially entangled with her, his existence irresistible to her in the emptiness that contained them.

He felt desire too. She knew this because she knew his thoughts. They were that close—that closely entangled. Rather than drifting apart in the endless empty spaces, the gravity of existence drew them in, awareness blending. From inside him she whispered a thought: *Show me the Cauldron.*

A shared flush of fear, of repulsion. He tried to pull away. She resisted and found herself to be the stronger entity. The expansion of mind she had gained at Ezo blazed now in a complex web that tangled them ever more and more closely together.

Remember your promise. Remember why we're here.

At this urging, he struggled to master himself. She felt the gradually slowing waveform of his fear, and then a following thought—harsh, regretful, but resolved—as he admonished himself: *Show it all to her. No secrets. No other way.*

He turned on her then and took her: a sudden shocking penetration, his mind now fully immersed within hers. His fear, his desire, his love, his memories—all there for her to explore. But she needed only one memory. Using a simple phrase, she drew it forth: *the Cauldron.* And by her will, she plunged him into the past.

She placed him there again, in the Cauldron. Placed herself with him so that they were squeezed together within a memory of its crushing dimensions. Under the pressure of that memory their combined existence flowed to fill an incomprehensibly complex mindspace of creation.

Incomprehensible to *him*, with fear dominating his mind.

But in that remembered Cauldron, beneath the veneer of his consciousness, she kept her wits and watched as some deep artifact of his mind, a subliminal awareness, pushed even farther outward toward the underlying structure of that place. Ruthlessly, she left him behind in the heart of the crucible while she pursued this deeper memory. It was his memory. But very soon she recognized it was also the memory of another, the two of them so closely entangled she could not discern a seam between them. Fascination gripped her. Ambition rose as she realized what she had found. *Ah, Lezuri, Lezuri! What did you leave behind?* A question she gradually answered as she explored imaginary geometries, mapping the way of creation.

A moment, an hour, some timeless time later, she released him. Together they left the past, returning to the *now* as she understood it, to find the silver's once pristine information spaces holding all of their shared experience within its intricate coils.

As they drifted together (a single diaphanous being or two? she could not say) a thought touched her, one imbued with dread: *I see it now. I see the way it must be done.*

It was his thought, she decided. Though perhaps it was hers too?

I have no words for it, he went on. *No good metaphor.*

She told him: *We are beyond words.*

Reluctance swirled between them. He said, *We don't have to be. We don't have to do this.*

And then he admitted, *We are here to do this.*

And then: *It's madness to do this.*

And finally: *Let's do this while we still know how.*

Afterward, Urban could not bring himself to remember how it was done. Revisiting his memory of the Cauldron had been bad enough, but the creation of it, down among alien geometries so offensive to his mind that the very shape of them was a torment to perceive, a sick twisting burning of the soul—

Don't think on it, the Cryptologist urged.

Only through her, had he endured it. She had held him there, held onto him in an unbreakable embrace. And by her will *(or was it by the will of another?)* she had seized hold of unspeakable dimensions, weaving them into a new reality, shaping them into a new Cauldron, one that existed in the here, in the now. That much he knew, refusing to remember more. Burn the memory of it. Never look back.

Her agreement struck, sharp and shivering with a horror that twinned his own. Even so, she proclaimed, *Yet we have done it! We are here!*

Here in their Cauldron, their command center, the actuator of their will.

We are here to draw a blade, he answered, turning his mind, *their* mind, outward to the gravity of the Labyrinth—the center point of the ring system they had come to create.

CHAPTER THIRTY-NINE

ABOARD *DRAGON*, THE Astronomer listened along with the ship's company to Urban's final communication. Following a declaration that he and the Cryptologist would commence to forge the Cauldron and draw the blade, Urban reminded them:

We will not be able to communicate again until this is finished. So maintain your positions and adhere to all protocols. Goodbye, for now.

The Astronomer appreciated the solemnity of this parting and the simplicity of the words Urban used to commemorate a great task almost surely doomed to fail. Thus distracted, it took him an extra fraction of a second to notice and to process a report just arrived from a Dull Intelligence: One of Urban's two sentient missiles was shifting its position.

This was not unusual by itself. Urban had instructed the missiles to keep pace with the Labyrinth while cruising outside its orbit, and also outside the plane of the ecliptic—one above the plane and one below. Holding these positions required continuous adjustment.

But as the Astronomer absorbed the details of this report, he saw that this current movement was of a different kind and on a different scale. The missile had abandoned its assigned post and now moved inward, angling toward the Labyrinth.

The DI updated its report: the second missile was also on the move, its path mirroring the first.

The Astronomer experienced a flicker of annoyance. How many

times had he asked Urban to notify him whenever he ordered the missiles to shift position? And still Urban neglected to do it.

Odd though, the timing of this event. Only Urban's silver-endowed avatar could communicate with the missiles. That avatar must have summoned them immediately before entering the silver. But for what purpose? Why did Urban need the missiles to be near the Labyrinth?

The Astronomer directed these questions to the ghost on the high bridge—and received an unexpected answer: *I didn't summon them.

*No, but he did—meaning the avatar. *He must have.

*No, Urban answered, worry now evident in his voice. *I remember everything up to the moment the silver touched me.

*Then you called them from within the silver.

*Sooth. That must be it. But why?

Urban had changed. The pressure and trauma of creating the Cauldron had transformed him, hardening his will, enhancing his determination, expanding his understanding. He seemed to the Cryptologist a different being, yet still himself, and still deeply entangled with her.

Together they filled every twisted, warped, offset, and indescribable dimension of their Cauldron. She understood now the necessity of it, of how it exponentially magnified their influence among the deepest layers of existence.

He said, *We are here to draw a blade.*

Her thoughts, *their* thoughts, ran out ahead, envisioning the violence of that task.

This will be the most dangerous phase, she warned.

Understood.

Once begun, it must be finished. Given the forces involved, there is no way to abort.

Through to the end, he agreed. *I know it. I remember the way.*

She hesitated, unsettled by the implication of this odd claim—then reminded herself he had changed.

Let us begin, she said.

———————

The Cryptologist had never met Lezuri nor interacted with the surviving wisp of his goddess. She knew the two of them anyway, through histories recorded in *Dragon's* library, and through the remembrances of Jolly and the Dragoneers, and most profoundly, through Urban's memories. She knew them so well that she recognized the shape of them within the geometry of the Cauldron. And she took that shape. Their shape, became her shape. Their will—that will that had made Verilotus—now hers.

Ours.

Yes.

Entanglement deepened, minds blending ever further together, flowing together, expanding deeper into a once-hidden fabric of existence until a new sense blossomed. There, just there—almost here—barricaded behind the thinnest wall: another Cosmos. A reservoir of impossible energies just on the other side of a forbidden boundary.

A shared thought, not hers, not theirs, not his: *Nothing is forbidden. Not here. Here you are beyond rules. In this place, your will is the only rule. Yours and his. Yours and hers.*

A shudder of horror from deep within her/him/them as they recognized this emergent presence.

Was it always in us? Or did we find it here?

It doesn't matter. We use it.

His thought or yours? There is no difference. You are one and you share this one chance. Breach the boundary! Wrest open a seam! Here, now, a flood of vast braided energies, dark and light.

Hold on.

They had to hold on. In their blended mind they understood that a failure of will at this point would be catastrophic. Stop now, and reality would heal itself, the dark energy plunging back through the open seam while the light, cut loose, erupted like a missile, swallowing everything within the radius of its bloom.

She wondered, they wondered: *Does any of this exist in reality or only in our mind?*

And: *What is reality?*

A rhetorical question. They neither needed nor wanted an answer. Better not to know. They pushed on into the next moment.

Does time even exist here?

Whether or not it did, their existence changed, their paths diverging, unwinding from one another. A twisting, soul-crushing severance.

The only way.

This was the only way to divide the braided energies. The duality of the Blade demanded light and darkness. Somehow—she didn't know how—he drew himself away, plunging along a vector of gravity, using it to execute a curving path around the anchoring mass of the Labyrinth. Deep in their shared soul she felt him screaming at the agony of this creation. She felt his panicked cry:

Too much! Too much!

No! Hold on!

He could not. They had dared to play with forces greater than allowed within the thin reach of their understanding, and they had been overcome. She felt the unendurable stress of it, so much more than he could sustain—and within an immeasurably small moment, she felt his mind rip open.

He had broken and it should have ended there—except that up through his shattered mind, out of his deep memory, a dark god emerged, one that had become entangled with him in another time, another cauldron.

I am, it declared.

But that was a lie. This was not Lezuri. It was no more than a borrowed fragment come to the fore: an old memory of how to stabilize a blade. It was Urban's memory now and he let it guide him into pinching off a discrete flow of dark energy, simultaneously forcing it into a closed loop that by its nature instantly locked into the balanced path of a perfect circle.

Her evolution followed his. She had no choice in it. They had parted, but she remained anchored to him, concentric to his darkness, existing on the boundary of realities, on the interface with that other Cosmos. The energy that fed his dark ring chan-neled through her, generating within it a fluid circle of unnatural density.

The Labyrinth, poised at the center of that dark ring, felt its influence and began to break apart.

At Urban's last message—*It's time now to forge the Cauldron and then to draw the blade*—a ship's company of ghosts crowded into *Dragon's* library.

Clementine had never before seen the full complement gath-ered there all at one time—or nearly all. Tio was among them. And Urban too, there and on the high bridge. Even Jolly had gen-erated a ghost: the better to watch undistracted by fatigue or hun-ger or the other miscellaneous demands of a physical body. Only the Cryptologist was absent, though doubtlessly she watched from her post on *Griffin's* high bridge.

The Inventions would be watching too: Ashok from *Alaka'i Onyx* and unknown cohorts in habitats beyond the project perim-eter. Everyone watched, eager to witness the transformation of the Labyrinth, though no one knew if or when that would happen.

Now Vytet's voice answered Urban, assuring him that all the ship's company had returned to *Dragon*. While she spoke, Clem-antine scanned a bank of windows compiled by the Astronomer. In one, HS-569 loomed in three-dimensional detail against a vel-vety blackness. In another, the Labyrinth appeared equally large in size and detail. A third window displayed moon and Labyrinth together from a more distant perspective, while in a fourth the two had been reduced by distance to dull motes, hard to pick out against a background of scattered stars.

After Vytet, the envoy spoke. It assured Urban that all Inven-tions were clear of the perimeter, concluding with the words, *You may proceed.*

Clementine calmed her mind, preparing herself to wait. More than forty hours had passed between the time Urban initiated the growth of silver and this precipitous moment. How much more time would be needed to run the experiment? An hour? A day? An indeterminate lifetime? No one knew. Not even Urban, his scowling ghost seeming everywhere, never blinking, ceaselessly focused on all four windows on display.

Last words from HS-569, weighted with emotion: *We will not be able to communicate again until this is finished. So maintain your positions and adhere to all protocols. Goodbye, for now.*

Several seconds passed, and then Urban's restless ghost announced in a voice tense with the gravity of the moment, "I've received a final submind, sent as I entered the silver."

So, it had begun. They would create the Cauldron first and then—

Riffan shouted in shocked surprise, "Love and Nature! It's *done!*"

Confusion swept Clemantine. Then she saw it too. By the Unknown God, Riffan was right. It was *done.*

There, in the fourth window, the one with the widest perspective and yet barely contained within it: the Blade. Its appearance as instantaneous as the bloom of a missile. Not there and then there: a brilliant white circle, fully formed and stable. Unlike a missile, the Blade did not wink out, but remained bright with the channeled energy of another cosmos.

The subdued emotions of a ghost did not protect Clemantine. For two or three seconds, she could only stare, overcome by the suddenness of this creation, this glowing halo exactly like the Bow of Heaven at Verilotus.

It took Pasha to break the spell. "Where is the dark ring?" she demanded over a mad chattering.

The Astronomer's disembodied voice answered her. "It cannot be seen in visible light. I am highlighting it now."

Near-silence fell as eyes took in the visual enhancement: fine gold lines defining the dark ring's slender torus.

Grimly, Tio urged them, "Look at the Labyrinth."

Clemantine would have caught her breath, if a ghost had breath to catch. There in the second window the jumbled structure of the Labyrinth was separating, coming apart as if in a slow explosion, the massive, broken walls of ancient megastructures ripped free by the sudden existence of the dark ring's gravity. This, she reminded herself, was the expected result and yet it was stunning all the same. The debris cloud moved slowly now, but as it fell away from the center it would accelerate toward inevitable impact with the ring.

The Astronomer spoke again, "The sentient missiles are continuing to close on the vicinity of the Blade and the Labyrinth, at a swiftly increasing velocity."

The sentient missiles? When had Urban called them?

CHAPTER FORTY

TIME HAD BECOME an uncertain construct, both hesitant and horribly prolonged. Urban remembered his long-time companions, the Dragoneers; he recalled the Inventions with their multitudinous architectures; and he worried they all had been lost in an unreachable past.

Or perhaps all this great venture had occurred within an immense immeasurable interval of non-time. He could not say. He only wanted it over.

Why did I ever want this at all?

In the Cauldron, entangled in exquisite union with the Cryptologist, her thoughts the same as his, an answer came: *You could not resist it. Despite the danger, despite the warnings, the question haunted you. You had to know. No matter what.*

He looked outward to their creation. The dark ring around the crumbling Labyrinth was the anchor. Through the fierce pressure of its geometry, it held in place a vastly larger, luminous circle like that one at Verilotus, known to the people there as the Bow of Heaven—and known to Lezuri as the Blade. Together, the two rings composed a stable waveform, the foundation of a new, ring-shaped world. Someday, after the dark ring had been dressed in a crust of silver-endowed matter, a biosphere might be called into existence there.

But in the present moment Urban could not endure even the thought of such a demanding task. His mind, his soul, already exhausted. Separating from the Cryptologist would be one more trauma, but necessary, because to rest his mind he needed to return to himself.

I'm done, he told her. *For now.*

Urban—that version of him on *Dragon's* high bridge—had first messaged his avatar when the missiles began to move. No reply had come back to him; no reply *could* come until his avatar emerged from the silver. Maybe that time had come?

He sent a second message speeding across the three-second gap: ***What are you doing? Why have you summoned the missiles?***

Some variable interval of time must elapse as a reply was composed, followed by a three-second return. A tedious interval.

He spent it absorbing the excited conversations of *Dragon's* philosopher cells, fear and wonder competing as they sought to explain the Blade's sudden appearance. *Where had it come from? Why was it here? What was its threat level?* The cells remembered the Blade at Verilotus and knew it to be harmless if not approached. The cells debated: *Was this emergent phenomenon the same?*

His own sense of wonder biased the conversation as he viewed the Blade across the diversity of his senses. From *Dragon's* perspective he saw it edge-on, while from the vantage of the outriders he saw in fullness the lovely, luminous ring, so unreal in its existence. It should have been a fantasy, an illusion, except that the shattering of the Labyrinth, broken by the gravity of the dark ring, stood as proof of the Blade's presence in this Cosmos.

That same instantaneous eruption of gravity had shaken HS-569 too. Less than a minute ago the little moon had proceeded in a reasonably stable orbit around the Labyrinth, requiring only rare corrections from the engines the Inventions had used to move it into place. Now, being a mere two thousand kilometers outside the dark ring, the Inventions would need to use those engines again to save it from a decaying orbit—but not until after Urban had recovered both his and the Cryptologist's avatars.

From *Griffin,* a query: ***Why have you summoned the missiles?***

Like him, the Cryptologist watched from her high bridge. *Griffin* preceded the leading edge of the Blade by some 350,000 kilometers; *Dragon* followed its trailing edge at a similar distance. Six light seconds between them.

Urban replied, **Seeking an answer. Stand by.* But then he added in a triumphant voice, **We did it!*

He did not have the memory of it yet, but the two of them, together, had created a blade. A stable blade, the foundation of a world. And how swiftly it had come into being! What a confusion of time there must have been within their newly created Cauldron.

Looking on the Blade as it hung there in the void, a perfect gleaming circle, slightly tilted against the plane of the ecliptic, Urban felt a keenness of gratitude and the sweetness of victory—sensations alien to the cell field, impossible to process, and therefore rejected.

So sternly rejected, the cells severed a significant number of his direct links to the field.

By the Unknown God!

Though the modified philosopher cells had lost their ancestors' psychotic urge to destroy and though they had been redesigned to value curiosity and learning, that did not free him to relax on the high bridge. The philosopher cells were not human; they never would be. Forget that fact at the wrong time, and it could prove fatal. But not this time. This time the damage could be recovered. A simple thing, to have the Bio-mechanic inventory the links and re-grow any that had been lost.

Never again!

A thought, an oath, a chant, a promise to himself as he stumbled out of the silver into a bubble of crisp, cold air at the center of the gray chamber.

Never again!

He had followed the Cryptologist from the silver. Now, as she sat on the cold stone floor, hugging her knees and rocking, he collapsed beside her, taken down by a fatigue that was not physical, but a mental exhaustion, the fallout from the crushing terror of creation.

Never again!

He rolled onto his back, staring up at silver. Bitter words forced a whispered passage from his lips: "I think we know now why Lezuri and his goddess built only one world, no more." He pushed himself to sit up, growling now in a louder voice, "*Never* again."

The Cryptologist did not cease her soothing rocking, but she looked at him. And though her blue eyes remained wide with the lingering shock of what they had seen and done, when she spoke, her voice was calm. "It was a hard and hellish task," she agreed. "If not for that fragment of Lezuri—"

"I know," he croaked. How he hated the idea of it! Of Lezuri as a part of him, haunting him. Clemantine had been right about that.

Softly, thoughtfully, the Cryptologist said, "I have often wondered why we have never seen another ring-shaped world like Verilotus. I can guess now it's because two allied minds are needed to make them—and in the ruthlessly competitive swarms, rising minds more typically try to consume one another rather than risk an alliance as Lezuri did."

Another shudder, as Urban imagined the horror of such an existence, to be always on guard against attack from some other, brutal mind. "The Tanji found a better way."

"Yes." Then, in tentative words, she asked him, "Do you regret it?"

He answered her honestly, "Yes."

He might have said more, but just then an odd, impatient message reached him from his ghost on *Dragon*'s high bridge: *What are you doing? Why have you summoned the missiles?*

Summoned the missiles?

Confusion swept over him. He blurted a response: *I didn't summon the missiles.*

So what the hell was going on out there?

Send me a submind, he demanded. It was the fastest way to comprehend the situation.

CHAPTER FORTY-ONE

URBAN WATCHED FROM the high bridge as the two missiles raced toward the scattering remains of the Labyrinth, angling in on converging courses.

He also watched from the library. There he had an extrapolated view with the light-speed delay subtracted, so that he saw the missiles where they were predicted to be at that moment in time—ever so much closer to the Blade.

Precious seconds slipped past as he waited to hear from his avatar. Instead, he received a message from *Griffin*, already old, six seconds in transit. Grim frustration marked the Cryptologist's voice as she spoke his fear aloud: *It's an attack on the Labyrinth or on the dark ring itself. It has to be.*

But that made no sense, because *he* controlled the missiles. No one else. Why would he send them in against the Blade's anchoring ring? *His* Blade. The Blade he had just created.

Yet denial made a poor defense. Considered without bias, it *did* look like an attack—and that was why he had already persuaded *Dragon's* philosopher cells to develop targeting solutions for each missile.

He hoped it would not come to that. He had engaged often with the minds of the missiles and had come to see them as living, thinking beings endowed with a purpose of their own. Not simply tools. And though he had always been ready to use them in defense of the fleet, the prospect of destroying them himself repulsed him.

He would do it anyway, of course. He'd done a harder thing in that distant age when he'd first captured *Dragon*. But he did not *want* to do it.

The philosopher cells sensed these thoughts and puzzled over them while he composed a brief reply to the Cryptologist. *Awaiting confirmation. Be ready.*

Confirmation came: His avatar had *not* summoned the missiles. Then who? How?

That version of him in the library generated a submind and sent it to the avatar.

Within the gray chamber, Urban came to know his ghost's recent emotions: triumphant wonder at the appearance of the Blade; astonishment at the speed of its creation; wary puzzlement at the behavior of the two sentient missiles, mingled with regret should he have to destroy them.

The missiles!

Almost simultaneously with the appearance of the Blade, the missiles had left their assigned positions. Accelerating with the astonishing rapidity displayed by their kind at Verilotus, they plunged at low angles toward the Blade's center point—a geometrical point in space, now empty, though a handful of seconds ago it had been the center point of the now-crumbled Labyrinth.

He knew this must be an attack. It couldn't be anything else because the missiles didn't exist for anything else.

But the missiles don't operate on their own!

They were his, linked to him. They moved only on his orders and he had issued no orders.

All this in a moment as he sat there on the cold stone floor, eyes locked with the Cryptologist, her worried blue gaze telling him she had received a submind too.

In the next moment, Urban turned to the silver within him.

He reached through it to the missiles, to their twinned minds—
and immediately perceived a terrible absence. That aspect of them
that had always been sentient and self-aware was no longer there.
They had been taken over, the state of their minds altered, hardened, so that they responded now only to a single fixed directive.
He knew this because he still saw what they saw, felt what they
felt. Translated into maddened words, it was this: *No other blade
shall exist!*

He groaned aloud, seeing it all now. These missiles had been
spawned at Verilotus for the sole purpose of defending that world,
and though they had been given to him, linked to him, that had
not changed their deep programming. He had not known of it
before; he had never suspected the existence of such programming. But now it had surfaced; it had been made plain. *No other
blade shall exist!*

Why? Because the existence of any blade other than the Blade
of Verilotus was a death threat to that world.

Not in words, but in will, Urban strove with the missiles.
Though he felt sure it was futile, that their deep programming
was unassailable, he tried to convince them to turn aside. *There is
no threat! Do not attack! We are far from Verilotus! We cannot harm
that world!*

His efforts only affirmed that in their current state, no command
of his could persuade the missiles; they did not even acknowledge
him. Probably, they didn't sense him at all.

Urban felt a touch against his arm and the touch of another
mind: the Cryptologist, her consciousness still entangled with his.
Maybe it always would be. She grasped his thoughts, compre-
hended the situation.

He whispered to her, "I can't stop them." A soft maddened
chuckle followed these words. "This is Lezuri, emerging from
oblivion to strike at me . . . even after he helped us make this
Blade."

He abandoned the missiles to reach for her. He clasped her
hands, gazed into her eyes. "What happens when two blades make
contact?"

A moment's hesitation, then her hands squeezed his. Her answer came in swift nervous words. "A stabilized blade will be unbalanced."

He nodded, acknowledging this. It was what he'd suspected.

"But I don't think that's the hazard." She stared at him, her pretty eyes wide with fear and uncertainty. "The Blade is so much greater than the bloom of a missile, I think it could absorb the shock, channel the energy, and survive. No, it's the dark ring that's vulnerable. Take out the dark ring, and the Blade will collapse."

He nodded, and prepared a message for his ghost on the high bridge, and for that version of her on the high bridge of *Griffin*.

"It's not over," he promised her.

That version of Urban on *Dragon*'s high bridge received an unexpected query from Ro Az Ra Ni: *Those cohorts assigned to observe the project request access to the telemetry streams from the two auxiliary vessels approaching the project site.*

No hint of excitement disturbed that bland voice, not even for the creation of a world. Here, now, that absence of emotion angered Urban—and damn the illogic of it! It angered him too that the envoy blithely assumed all was well, that the missiles were observational platforms, the equivalent of outriders and nothing more.

They are weapons, you fool!

An unfair rebuke born of frustration and kept tightly confined within the privacy of his mind. He made no answer to the envoy and blocked all further communication. He had no time for it as a new message arrived, the one he'd been waiting for, from his avatar.

It began with a terse explanation of the situation. It ended with a stern conclusion, *I can't stop the missiles. It's up to you to destroy them.*

By the Unknown God!

No doubt now. This *was* an attack, a delayed strike, Lezuri rising up out of the past—but the Blade itself was not the target. In less than a minute, both missiles, angling in from "above" and "below" and still accelerating, would pass inside the Blade's perimeter—though not closely enough to it to be a direct threat. Instead, their converging trajectories confirmed what his avatar had said. The missiles' attack was aimed at the dark ring.

Urban shook off all regret for what must be done. It would take him just two quick shots to nullify the threat. Briefly, he considered coordinating with the Cryptologist, but dropped the idea. Given the light-speed lag, coordination would take significant time—and there was no need for it. *Dragon's* philosopher cells were already tracking and extrapolating the missiles' trajectories. They could destroy both in the time it would take to get a reply from *Griffin*.

So, on his own, he commenced a counterattack. To shock the philosopher cells into readiness, he flooded the field with a cresting sense of urgency—only to find his influence had withered.

Not now, he prayed. But his prayer could not erase the mistake he had made mere seconds ago, when he had allowed the philosopher cells to feel his gratitude for sweet victory. An emotion so alien to the cells that they had rejected it, and then rejected him by severing almost half of his hundred thousand links.

But even half a hundred thousand could make a significant argument. Fixating on the missiles, he directed:
  – *mark: target one* –
  – *danger: it threatens!* –
  – *mark: target two* –
  – *danger: it threatens!* –
  – *calculate sequential strikes* –
  – *kill it* –

The philosopher cells had already developed targeting solutions, continuously updated. Now, primed by that preparation and excited by the force of his demand, they responded just as he intended. The gun swiveled, acquiring target one. The reef trembled as it generated the power needed to strike.

Yet consensus did not follow. Instead, as his argument cycled around the field, its intensity faded:
  – *kill it* –

– kill it –

Now a mere proposition, one to be considered and puzzled over and objected to:

< negate that!>

New arguments emerged as the philosopher cells—so changed, they were now averse to wanton destruction—debated among themselves the merits of such an action. Urban recognized his own recent thoughts circulating: the missiles seen as thinking beings, long-time allies with a fascinating existence of their own.

Fiercely, he objected:

– no! –

– they threaten –

But this argument gained no traction.

With precious seconds slipping past and his frustration mounting, Urban reached out to Clemantine, messaging her: **I need you on the high bridge!*

And he launched his argument again:

– mark: target one –

– it threatens! –

– KILL IT –

A demand immediately and forcefully countered by a coalition of philosopher cells—

<NEGATE THAT!>

—collapsing his argument as a more popular one took hold.

< target one: ally>

< target two: ally>

< stand down: observe/learn>

< seek to know>

In the midst of this, Clemantine arrived.

*Help me, he growled. **They refuse to fight.*

*Who are we fighting?

*The missiles! They're aimed at the dark ring.

The anchoring dark ring, the element that stabilized the gleaming blade.

*It's Lezuri's deep programming, he explained. **They won't allow another blade, and I can't override.*

He let his fury pour through the links, and he renewed his argument:

– identify: enemy –

So many once-powerful cell lineages had been culled: reduced in number or eliminated altogether, their memories and their aggression gone with them, leaving the Cryptologist's newly forged cell lines to dominate the field. And still, many other original lineages survived with their memory of a time when such missiles pursued *Dragon* at Verilotus. Clemantine had held the high bridge then. She remembered that time too.

Following Urban's lead, she recalled the memory, brought it to the surface, shared it around the field, emphasizing the rage that encounter had ignited and the ensuing desire to:

– KILL IT! –

Instantly, an objection arose. These missiles were not those missiles.

<identify: ally>

These missiles had long been part of the fleet.

Urban sensed Clemantine's shock at this resistance and her sudden comprehension of how much the philosopher cells had changed since she'd last visited the high bridge. He did not share with her the guilty knowledge that his own thoughts had hardened the philosopher cells against this attack.

*We need to bypass the cell field, Clemantine concluded. ***Take direct control of the gun.**

*Sooth.

Shifting to the library, Urban summoned the Engineer and the Bio-mechanic. He explained in terse words what he needed. "I don't want to just isolate the gun like we did at Prakruti. I need an interface that will let *me* aim it and make the kill."

A slight, cynical, disbelieving smile from the Bio-mechanic. "All we did at Prakruti was cut off the flow of energy. You're asking me to hijack this ship's nervous system." He shook his head. "You have no idea how complex such an interface would be."

"Just tell me if you can do it."

"Even if I could, it won't last. The philosopher cells will reverse any changes I make. You know that. It's why you've always commanded this ship from the high bridge."

"That doesn't matter! It doesn't have to last. I just need this now, while there's time left."

"There isn't time," the Engineer said. "Not nearly enough time to design and implement an interface of such complexity."

Urban looked from one to the other, desperate to hear some other answer. None came.

He shifted back to the high bridge where he found himself still striving to persuade the philosopher cells with harsh argument:

– *revulsion: false ally* –

A pause to tell Clemantine, *No go. We're on our own.*

Then he drew from his imagination a vision of destruction, of what must happen if the missiles were not stopped and he showed this to the philosopher cells. But they rejected it, recognizing it as a guess based on a physics neither he nor they understood—and the speeding missiles crossed the perimeter of the Blade.

A moment later, a tenth of a second, no more, one of the missiles blossomed. It transformed, instantaneously, into a sphere of white light. A huge sphere. Twenty-thousand kilometers across and still just a bauble against the vast circle of the Blade.

The two phenomena did not overlap but they unbalanced one another anyway. A bridge of white light jumped from blossom to Blade in the fractional second of the blossom's existence—and the Blade raged with brilliant light. A wave of light that appeared to shoot in two directions around the ring, though Urban guessed that to be an artifact, a light-speed delay, and that the whole ring blazed at once, charged with the immense energy admitted from some other reality in the moment of the missile's cosmic breach.

Clemantine spoke in quiet awe. *It's too much. The Blade's destabilized. It's going to burst—or collapse.*

Urban believed it. He looked on in terror. But the passing seconds belied her words. The full circle of the Blade now flared brilliant white, but it held—and terror gave way to confusion.

What had happened? Why had the missile blossomed when it

did, long before reaching the dark ring? Was it chance? Did it hit some unseen bit of debris?

The unified fury now flooding the philosopher cells suggested otherwise. Accusations and admonishments were being directed outward, expressed in intricate patterns of light:

<negate!>

<negate: strike!>

<negate: false argument / unproven argument>

<cease: stupid/weak action>

<acknowledge: ally weapon lost/destroyed>

<identify: ally weapon two>

<preserve it>

<observe/learn>

<protect it>

<seek to know>

It was **Griffin**, Urban concluded. *Griffin* **struck the missile**.

And *Dragon* continued to chastise and threaten the smaller courser over that action.

Now a message from Pasha, addressed to the entire ship's company: *Look at the Labyrinth.*

The Labyrinth? The Labyrinth no longer existed. It had come apart in the moment of the Blade's creation, its matter falling outward, slowly accelerating toward the dark ring's newly created gravity well.

Urban looked anyway, and astonishment seized him because the movement of debris was now far faster than it had been before and it was still visibly accelerating. Had the huge influx of energy in the Blade increased the dark ring's effective gravity? It must have—and that would affect HS-569 too. The little moon's orbit had been decaying before. Now, it was truly falling.

One down, one to go, the Bio-mechanic thought, as *Griffin*'s gun swiveled, preparing to target the second missile.

With the Cryptologist, he occupied the high bridge. He was peripherally aware of a rising storm of incomprehensible radio communications traveling between Invention habitats. But in the brief span before *Griffin* could take a second shot, it was *Dragon* that seized his attention.

From the vantage of the high bridge, he watched *Dragon* signaling in an intricate pattern of light interpreted by *Griffin*'s philosopher cells. Through them, the Bio-mechanic perceived *Dragon*'s philosopher cells as a living presence, and himself, embedded among them.

No. Not himself.

It was Urban's presence and Urban's thought that he sensed. But this was a narrow distinction. In a moment, what had been Urban's thoughts became his own. Insight touched him, so that now he recognized the missiles as thinking beings—sentient, purposeful, endowed with their own fascinating existence.

Deep empathy flooded him.

But no! That was not *his* memory. That thought belonged to Urban. Yet the Bio-mechanic shared it now, just as he and Urban occasionally shared subminds; they were that close.

What are you doing? the Cryptologist demanded of him.

Her sharp voice shocked him back to an awareness of where they were and what needed to be done. But he was also aware that the infectious empathy that had leaped from *Dragon* to him had already moved on, crossing over to *Griffin*'s philosopher cells. That was what the Cryptologist had sensed.

And as the cells analyzed it and reacted to it, the Bio-mechanic felt their defensive posture fade. Doubt set in. Questions arose.

<query other-self: clarify intrinsic purpose>
<required: simulation of mission definition>
– negate that! – the Cryptologist snapped.

And refocusing the philosopher cells on the second missile, she demanded:

– KILL IT! –

But the gun did not fire.

"What is going on out there?" Urban demanded, bracing against a quake that shook the gray chamber hard enough that he would have fallen if he wasn't already sitting on the floor. The gravity, light as it was, shifted weirdly, sickeningly.

"It is most likely I was wrong," the Cryptologist said calmly, almost resigned. "The Blade may have been hit after all, and become unstable." After a slight pause, she added, "Send a ghost now. I'm sending mine."

Aboard *Griffin*, the Cryptologist received her ghost. Its memories—its astonishing memories—blended with her own, but did not assuage the anger that afflicted her. A rare, hot anger that grew fiercer still, now that she understood all she had been through and all she stood to lose.

Urban had told her to be ready—ready to destroy the missiles—and she had been. She had not taken the time to coordinate; she had simply exerted her will over the philosopher cells. She *was* *Griffin*'s will. In that capacity, she had directed the cells to strike the closest missile, expecting Urban to take out the other. But he had not. And she could not.

Though *Griffin*'s philosopher cells had the target marked, though the gun swiveled under their direction as they tracked it, they refused to fire.

What did you do? she demanded of the Bio-mechanic.

He had done something. She'd felt it. He had introduced some strange argument and the field had abruptly changed. The philosopher cells no longer acknowledged her authority as otherself. They had somehow acquired a will of their own and now the aggression she demanded of them was gone, replaced by something else, by . . . *shame?*

An unprecedented state!

It's because of Dragon, the Bio-mechanic said. *An argument from Dragon. An infectious argument.*

She listened to the cell field and perceived the truth of what he said. Her philosopher cells had been persuaded by *Dragon*'s harsh criticism—communicated in patterns of light and full of righteous anger—to reject her authority because she had erred. She, as the entity they deemed *other-self*.

Other-self had given in to archaic hostility.

Other-self had attacked a trusted ally as it moved to evaluate the hazard of a new creation.

Other-self demanded further violence against a second ally. Other-self must be rejected.

With guilt in his voice, the Bio-mechanic confessed, *The argument in favor of the missiles began with Urban. A sense of empathy that jumped to me.*

She gathered herself. Did the reason matter now? No, it did not. Not with time slipping away. She said, *We have to force a counter-argument.*

Only a little time left to do so. Though more than 300,000 kilometers lay between the dark ring and the bright halo of the Blade, the missile was transiting that gap at an absurd velocity, an interstellar velocity, leaving her not half a minute to persuade the cells.

She tried:

– *identify: ally; not ally; false ally* –

– *revulsion: false ally* –

– *it threatens!* –

She envisioned the hazard: what would happen if the missile reached the dark ring and blossomed. Then she made her demand:

– *cease observe/learn* –

– *target: false ally* –

– *kill it!* –

– *KILL IT!* –

The Bio-mechanic added his influence and a new consensus began to build, a rising wave of force and ferocity—

<*NEGATE THAT!*>

The wave collapsed, neutralized by an even stronger coalition:

<*negate that!*>

<*hold fire!*>

<*observe/learn*>

She tried again. Again. But *Dragon's* argument had destroyed her.

A stale message arrived from Urban, pleading with her to strike the second missile, to strike now.

It's too late, she answered him. *We've lost.*

———

Urban's ghost escaped from the falling moon, blending with that version of him on *Dragon*'s high bridge, so that he knew now the fullness of what would be lost when the Blade failed—*his* blade—the foundation of a world, made at great cost to himself.

Never again!

He would never have even the choice to create a blade again because when this Blade failed, he would also lose himself—his avatar, that is—his irreplaceable silver-endowed avatar, the anchor of his existence since his time on Verilotus. And not only his avatar, but the Cryptologist's too. That most complex version of her would be lost forever if he, or she, could not stop the second missile in its plunging assault on the dark ring.

And they could not.

He tried again to persuade *Dragon*'s philosopher cells to act, to attack. He strove to convince them of the necessity and the urgency of action. *Strike now! Strike now!*

– kill it! –

He launched and re-launched his argument and Clemantine echoed him—and each time the philosopher cells severed more and more of their links to the field, and their voices faded.

In the gray chamber, the Cryptologist received a submind from her ghost on *Griffin*'s high bridge. There came an audible catch in her breath as its memories integrated. She blinked against the rise of a painful pressure in her eyes. Then she turned to Urban.

Sweat gleamed on his bloodless cheeks. His dark gaze locked on hers. "I'm sorry," he whispered.

Her lips pressed together. "So you understand?"

"Yes. At the rate they're moving, the missiles will be here long before *Argo* could come fetch us." He attempted a smile. Failed miserably.

His gaze dropped to his hands. He watched the sparks of *ha* dancing around his fingers until her palm touched his. Their *ha* mingled, their thoughts too, so that his lamentation became hers: *Never again.*

He reached for her, pulled her into a mutual embrace, her cheek pressed against his, her lips whispering in his ear, urging him to, "*Hurry!*"

He understood her. They must save what they could.

He prepared a submind to supplement the ghost he had already sent to *Dragon*, while she captured her own most recent memories and uploaded them to *Griffin*.

They had time enough for that.

CHAPTER FORTY-TWO

URBAN'S GHOST EXISTED on the high bridge, but in his mind he existed within the falling moon too. His precious avatar entangled with hers, the remaining seconds too short for words and nothing left to do. Fate written in momentum and limited by the speed of light. Even if he could fire the gun now, the shot would not arrive in time.

The surviving missile breached the limit of its range. Less than ten thousand kilometers separated it now from the dark ring, the radius of its bloom. It kept on for a sliver of a second more, time enough to close the gap, to skim the dark ring, to slip within its circle, perhaps to collide with some random bit of debris from the Labyrinth, but inevitably, to blossom. *There.*

There at the center of the encircling Blade: a sphere of white light, tiny with distance, momentary in existence, enveloping the dark ring and all the debris of the Labyrinth. There and gone, leaving nothing, a literal nothing, in the spherical space where it had been.

But it had not taken the falling moon! Its reach had not extended that far. A triumphant thought! One with a lifespan as fleeting as that of the white sphere, there and gone, consumed by the shock of reality. The dark ring had anchored and stabilized the Blade. Now there was nothing to hold it in this cosmos. And so a second bloom followed on the first, this one vastly larger, its sphere defined by the Blade's circumference: an immense flash that filled the span of Urban's vision and overran all his extended senses.

There.

And gone.

Only darkness left behind it. Nothing else. No Blade, no moon, no precious avatars—neither hers nor his. Nothing at all left behind but a stunning emptiness where his ambition had briefly flowered.

In the library, he felt Clemantine's hand take his and on the high bridge he sensed the astonishment of the philosopher cells. His amorphous mind noted these things though he did not attend to them, occupied as he was by the memory of his penultimate seconds within the falling moon, beautifully entangled in both mind and body with the Cryptologist, grieving their imminent loss.

Impossible that they should still be entangled. Yet out there in the void that lay between them—an utterly empty void, bitten clean by the massive bloom and left barren of even a stray molecule—twin communications crossed, her voice and his, whispering the same lamentation, *I'm sorry. I'm so sorry.*

No. It was not her fault. *He* had let this happen. He had lost control of the philosopher cells, failed to discern the deep programming of the missiles, substituted confidence for knowledge— and hadn't Clemantine warned him against such hubris?

She had.

But he had rejected her argument and hijacked the consensus of the ship's company—exactly what the philosopher cells had just done to him.

A tremor rumbled deep in his mind, releasing veins of incandescent anger that swiftly infiltrated his shock, burning it away. A furious heat. An impossible heat, because he was only a ghost. He should not feel this deeply. Yet he wanted to feel. He wanted to escape into his avatar and rage, rage.

Edit that!

Edit it, because he had nowhere to go except where he was, this ghost, this diminished self, trapped between the library and the high bridge.

Awareness crept in. The murmuring of ghosts in the library, the murmuring of the philosopher cells. All astonished at an outcome they had not anticipated.

I anticipated it.

He centered his awareness on the high bridge, only a little surprised to find Clemantine no longer there. No matter. He listened to interwoven threads of observation and debate as the philosopher cells sought to analyze what had happened, what it meant, why they had been so wrong in their assessment of the missile's intention, and what might be learned from that. He listened, and slowly discerned what he wanted to hear: a strengthening thread that recalled his rejected argument, now proven real and true.

Severed links began to be repaired. All on their own, the field knit his voice back into a dominant position within the perpetual discourse.

– negate that –

He wanted nothing of it.

He left the high bridge, merging with his ghost in the library where Clemantine still held his hand. Somewhere, someone wondered: *What are we going to tell the Inventions?* But not Clemantine. She looked into his eyes, a worried crinkle between her brows, all her attention given to him as she murmured, "Urban, Urban, come back, focus, look at me."

He did.

Other ghosts crowded around them, witnessing when he told Clemantine, "You were right. You've always been right."

"You did it, though," she said, speaking soothingly, meaning to comfort him, thinking he spoke of the Blade. "You drew your own blade out of nothingness, created the foundation of a world."

His eyes narrowed; he gave a slight shake of his head. "It wasn't me."

Pensive silence all around, until Pasha suggested, "The Cryptologist?"

Pasha's trembling voice drew Urban's gaze. She stood squeezed between Vytet and Clemantine, horror haunting her pale green eyes.

"The Cryptologist's *avatar*," Urban corrected, a chill in his voice. "And also the memories I held within mine—all gone now. Lost and irreplaceable." He returned his gaze to Clemantine, and the chill deepened. "You were right. You were right all along. If I'd had full control of the gun, this would not have happened. I would have taken out both missiles long before they reached the Blade. If I had burned the cell field like you wanted—like you wanted from the first day—if I had made this a fully human ship—"

Her soft fingers pressed against his ghost lips, quieting him. "No," she said gently. "*You* were right. The philosopher cells served us. They were necessary camouflage. We would never have captured *Griffin* without them, and we needed *Griffin.*"

He grasped her fingers, kissed them, and said, "We should have destroyed *Griffin*, before it destroyed that other version of you. You should never have had to endure that."

"Urban—"

"But you're right again," he said, cutting her off, needing to speak, his fury channeled in a flow of words. "The philosopher cells *were* necessary, in the beginning. But not anymore. Not here in the Hallowed Vasties. There are no other Chenzeme vessels here. And even if there were? We've spoiled the camouflage, corrupted the field. No true courser would ever accept this ship as Chenzeme." He interrupted himself with a bitter laugh. "All those years we spent thinking we could improve the cell field, make it smarter, less vicious, more compliant. What a fool I was, not to burn it long ago. But I'm done with it now. Not one more day."

At this declaration, startled murmurs erupted around them, objections for the most part: *this is wild talk!; you can't do that; it's a matter for the ship's company to decide; what of* Griffin*?*

His declaration shocked Clemantine too. She drew back, lips parted in desperate confusion.

But why object? She had wanted this for so long. She had seen her birth world burning under a Chenzeme assault and she had held on to that memory and to a cold hate. He had not blamed her for it, but he had always told himself it biased her judgment.

He saw now, finally, that the bias was his. She had seen more clearly than him; she had recognized the hazard of the hull cells from the start while he refused to see it, beguiled by his long history with them and believing—because he had needed to believe it—that the bridge gave him full control.

No longer. Though the philosopher cells had not themselves burned his newly founded world, they had let it burn, and all his illusions had burned with it. He glared around at the gathered ghosts. Such a rage burning in him. "Vote on it if you like," he declared. "But every one of you knows we'll be safer when our future is no longer tied to the whims of ungovernable alien minds."

Kona was of the same generation as Clemantine; he carried the same scars. So it did not surprise Urban when he spoke from out of the crowd, bitter and triumphant: "I agree with Urban."

Pasha did not. She pushed past Clemantine, demanding of him, "Stop! Stop and listen to yourself. Stop and think what you're asking. This is your anger talking. It's you wanting revenge for your own death."

He met her gaze and nodded. "My death, and hers."

With his extended senses, he sought for the Cryptologist, but found only a dormant ghost in the archive. She would be awake aboard *Griffin*, though. Alone there, at a time when she should not be alone.

He transited to the data gate and departed for the smaller courser, leaving nothing of himself behind.

CHAPTER FORTY-THREE

DISASTER.

In the wake of the Blade's demise, the word re-echoed in the Bio-mechanic's mind. The Cryptologist's ghost had deserted *Griffin*'s high bridge, leaving him alone to witness the vast and irresistible collapse of a fantastic ambition. And at such a cost!

His thoughts writhed around the fate of the Cryptologist's precious avatar. She had re-created herself at Ezo, emerging from that trial as a being whose deep complexities could not be captured in the simplistic architecture of a ghost.

Gone now. Erased by a brief blazing intrusion from some other reality. Her abandoned ghost weeping in the library, cradled in his embrace because he was there too, with her, saying nothing because no words existed to soothe her loss. She would live and breathe again as a physical being, but without the silver she would revert to the lesser being she had been before Ezo, stunted in the breadth of her mind.

A murmuring recalled him. Shocked and questioning voices. Not human. No. A fibrillation of thought within the field of *Griffin*'s philosopher cells. Incoherent at first. Slowly resolving around an external input.

Riding the senses of the philosopher cells, the Bio-mechanic once again perceived swift and intricate patterns of light emitted from *Dragon*'s hull, though the meaning of those signals was different than before. This time, *Dragon* was communicating its intellectual distress. Desperate for insight, the larger courser was proposing that the two ships should meet and mate and exchange all knowledge in an effort to understand this inexplicable event.

The Bio-mechanic possessed a memory of such a meeting and mating—that one not voluntary—passed to him out of Urban's memory: a dominant courser twisting in an impossible half-spiral around its captive consort, great columns emerging all along its length, plunging into the cell field of the lesser ship, currents of molecular knowledge flowing.

It wasn't the potential exchange of knowledge that alarmed him. With the philosopher cells of both ships so radically evolved from their origin, he saw no danger of either ship reverting to ancestral Chenzeme. No, it was the act itself. That half-spiral position. The Bio-mechanic did not have to check with the Engineer to know it would crush the gee deck.

So why was Urban allowing this tryst to even be proposed?

And now it was no longer just a proposal. Without waiting for *Griffin*'s consent, *Dragon* began slowly accelerating: a curving trajectory surely intended to bring it alongside the smaller courser.

The Bio-mechanic started to message his counterpart, to demand an explanation from that version of himself aboard *Dragon*. But in the wake of disaster, the inadequacy of a simple message offended him. There was so much to convey, so much to comprehend that he recoiled from the thought of going on as before.

Go on as yourself, then! One self!

Yes, it was time.

He did not send a message. He sent a submind instead.

Urban's ghost arrived through *Griffin*'s data gate. He instantiated in *Griffin*'s library where he saw—he thought he saw—himself, his ghost, already there, crumpled on the library's infinite floor, embracing the distraught Cryptologist, gently rocking her.

Disorientation seized him. Had he lost track of his ghosts? But he never lost track, and anyway, he had not merged with this phantom. He would have merged if this was him.

It was not him. The dark-green garb provided the clue he

needed. This was the Bio-mechanic, existing outside of his requisite window.

The Bio-mechanic looked up at him, cold resentment burning in those familiar eyes. "You destroyed her," he accused.

Not all of her. This, an unspoken protest too pathetic to say aloud. What Urban did say was no better, "I lost control—of the missiles, of the philosopher cells."

With a sneer, the Bio-mechanic retorted, "You never truly had control. *Never.*"

"Sooth." A solitary word of abject agreement. It was all he could manage as his mind rocked wildly between the shock of his own demise and the inexplicable presence of this entity who was clearly no longer just an Apparatchik.

Urban shifted his gaze to the shuddering, weeping figure of the Cryptologist. "She unlocked you," he said stupidly.

The Bio-mechanic's eyes narrowed as if with a new and unpleasant thought. "You're not present on *Dragon*'s high bridge, are you?"

A question so out of place it left Urban lost for words, groping to understand why the Bio-mechanic would ask it.

"*Are* you there?" the Bio-mechanic demanded.

"*No.*" A flash of returning anger ignited behind the word.

But his anger did not move or intimidate the Bio-mechanic, who demanded to know, "Who is, then?"

"I don't know. Why?"

"Because *Dragon* is moving, approaching *Griffin*, intending to mate—and no one is arguing against it."

Hearing this, the Cryptologist looked up at last. For a moment only, Urban saw such a depth of grief on her face. Then she refreshed her appearance, shadow and tears wiped away, though she could not quite banish the hurt from her calm blue eyes. In a soft but matter-of-fact voice she told Urban, "You know this can't be allowed. Go back to *Dragon*. I will follow behind you."

Clemantine stared in stunned surprise at the empty space before her, where Urban had been just a moment before. Gone now. Vanished. She could not sense him anywhere within the library.

He means to destroy the philosopher cells!

Subminds shifted between this ghost in the library and her avatar on the gee deck, both versions of her left reeling by Urban's ardent desire for vengeance—and she was not the only one affected. A destabilizing chaos of argument boiled all around her as Kona, Vytet, Pasha, Tarnya, and even Riffan, formed bitter sides.

On the gee deck, her avatar whispered, "*Stop.*"

In the library, her ghost demanded it: "Stop! Stop this useless arguing. It's not the loudest voice that will decide!"

Perhaps not, though her voice was loud enough to break the debate, collapsing it into a waiting silence.

Looking up, she found herself encircled, all eyes on her, confused, doubtful, angry, determined . . . *expectant.* As if she knew what came next.

Kona thought he knew. "It needs to be done," he said gently.

Clemantine, holding up a hand to cut off an angry retort from Pasha, said, "I want the Bio-mechanic and the Engineer."

The crowd of ghosts shifted automatically as two frameless windows opened, the Engineer looking thoughtful, the Bio-mechanic, furious.

The Bio-mechanic spoke immediately, without invitation, sneering and contemptuous. "You want to know if it is possible to destroy the mind of this ship and replace all its functions with something slavish and obedient."

Both the tone and the content of this declaration induced fresh shock in Clemantine. Even for the ever-aberrant Bio-mechanic, this was extreme. And she wasn't alone in this judgment. The Engineer eyed his companion in suspicion and concern.

Clemantine shook her head. Something to look into later. Now was not the time. Gathering herself, she told the Bio-mechanic, "Yes. That is what I want to know. Is it possible?"

The Bio-mechanic answered, "No."

The Engineer cocked his head quizzically and countered, "Yes. It is possible. It would be challenging to create and maintain such a system, still, we understand the ship's systems well enough that it could be done."

Murmuring argument erupted again, only to cut off abruptly at a fierce declaration from the Bio-mechanic: "All right! *Yes*. It is possible. But it's wrong. It's wrong to destroy a self-aware, deeply sentient mind just because it's grown inconvenient."

Clemantine endured another shock, realizing the Bio-mechanic had *lied*. When he had first answered *no*, he had lied. Oh, she well knew he was adept at hiding the truth, but an outright lie should not be possible. Yet it had happened anyway: a realization that left her unbalanced and swaying as reality shifted around her.

Perhaps Vytet saw her discomfiture, because she took over, asking the Bio-mechanic, "How do you know it's deeply sentient?"

"I know because I am one with that version of me on *Griffin*. And there, on the high bridge, I am immersed in the thoughts of that courser, and through the bridge I've felt the projected thoughts of *Dragon*."

Shock now on the Engineer's face while Clemantine had passed beyond shock into anger. She exclaimed, "I see it's not just the philosopher cells that have evolved!"

In surly answer, the Bio-mechanic said, "Sooth. And will you destroy me too? Like you destroyed your own dark twin? Or will you send another Apparatchik after me, the way you sent the Scholar to attack Kuriak?"

The cruel truth of these accusations caused Clemantine to stagger—there in the library or on the gee deck, she couldn't tell, overwhelmed as she was by her own guilty recollections. Urban's words still haunted her, from that time he had challenged her mistrust of the Inventions: "*So then, what are you thinking? That we should annihilate them?*" And her own words, uttered to Vytet out of the depths of her depression: "*Remember the story the Tanji told us? A story of war breaking out among the godlings that emerged from Tanjiri's swarm and how they murdered one another. We're no different, Vytet. We murdered that other version of me. I murdered her.*"

She had only ever done what was necessary.

But what was necessary now?

Surely not to destroy a mind only because it was something new, something different.

The Bio-mechanic, no longer an Apparatchik.

The philosopher cells, no longer Chenzeme.

The Dragoneers themselves, *ourselves*, like the philosopher cells, changed by time, the peaceful descendants of a once-murderous species.

Most of us, anyway.

Urban chose that moment to reappear. He shot a fiery glance in her direction before doubling, one ghost vanishing, the Cryptologist appearing in its place.

"Who is on the high bridge?" Urban's remaining ghost demanded.

Clemantine frowned. "I thought you were."

She checked through her extended senses. He was there now. He had just arrived. No one else was present. Next, she checked the ship's status and discovered *Dragon* gently accelerating on a curving trajectory.

The dizzy, off-balance sensations she'd endured had not been all due to the stress of events.

From his post on *Griffin*'s high bridge, the Bio-mechanic had been first to suspect the truth: No one was steering *Dragon*; no one occupied its high bridge.

Through an ongoing exchange of subminds, that version of him standing within his frameless window in *Dragon*'s library knew it too. "The high bridge was abandoned," he announced to the gathered ghosts. "In that time and on its own, *Dragon* conceived a desire to mate and synchronize mind and knowledge with *Griffin*—a physical act that would ruin us. But Urban will set it right."

He felt the hostile gaze of the Engineer. Heard the heated anger in his private communication: *You're unlocked.*

I am.

Why?

The Bio-mechanic might have explained how it had been necessary, how the Cryptologist had needed him on *Griffin*'s high bridge, how she had insisted . . . but in the end all he said was, *Why not?*

That was how he felt and there was surely no going back. Not now. Not when all stood revealed—to the Apparatchiks anyway, and to Clemantine and others, though he thought not all the Dragoneers had grasped it yet.

Make it clear then!

He did so. He stepped outside his window and then closed it behind him, to stand whole on the library's main deck. A ghost among other ghosts, dressed in shades of dark green. A man among other men, and among women. Like them, possessing an avatar, one waking now in its cocoon aboard *Griffin*, mind alive with suspense and excitement and a dreadful deep longing for acceptance.

But he did not speak of his own evolution.

He said, "My entire existence has been devoted to understanding *Dragon*'s inner workings: the physiology of its body and its mechanistic mind. *My enemy.* That's how I thought of it. Something to be dominated, leashed, and controlled. That's how Urban thought of it too.

"But out of that enemy we made something new. *Dragon* and *Griffin*. The names are the same, but the minds are not. No longer mechanistic, but bright, vast, curious, and self-questioning."

He turned a troubled gaze on the Cryptologist; held a hand out to her. She accepted it, imparting to him an illusion of warmth across his palm. From her, he looked to Urban, encountering a sullen gaze.

"You know it's true," the Bio-mechanic said.

His progenitor looked away.

No matter. Everyone needed to know what had happened and why. Quickly, he described how *Griffin*'s philosopher cells had at first accepted the argument, made by the high bridge, that the missiles must be destroyed. "Through the Cryptologist's art, the cells had been endowed with values of curiosity and peaceful coexistence, but we persuaded them to put those values aside."

Bitter words from Urban: "And you struck one missile, but not the other. You let the other through."

"You could not persuade *Dragon* to strike even one," the Bio-mechanic countered. "Because *Dragon* reasoned on its own that such violence was wrong, and it chided *Griffin* for it, and because of that *Griffin* perceived it had made a mistake—"

Kona and Urban spoke almost in unison, "It was no mistake."

"But it was," the Cryptologist said, turning her troubled gaze from the Bio-mechanic to Urban. "The philosopher cells acted correctly from within the moral framework we gave them. They considered the arguments, considered what they knew of the missiles, considered what was right and wrong, and chose to trust rather than to kill. A deeply disastrous decision, but deeply sentient too—and not unworthy of respect."

"Your avatar is *gone*," Urban said, clipped words past a clenched jaw. "I'm gone too."

The Bio-mechanic narrowed his eyes, fixed his glare on Urban, and said, "*Revenge.* You want to burn the philosopher cells out of revenge."

"For our own protection!" Urban snapped.

The Bio-mechanic shook his head, saying, "*No.* It's wrong and I won't allow it."

At this, Urban drew back, his expression uncertain and confused, not knowing what to do in the face of the Bio-mechanic's defiance, leaving it to Kona to answer. "Whatever they are—whatever *you* are—we cannot remain subject to alien whims."

Clemantine turned to him, saying, "But they're not alien, Kona. Not fully. They're our progeny. A human creation."

Her words surprised the Bio-mechanic, surprised Kona, surprised everyone. She seized on the ensuing lull. Looking around at the gathered ghosts, she asked them, "Why are we here in the Hallowed Vasties?"

Vytet grasped at once the meaning of this question and answered, "We came here to learn—not just what happened, but what has happened since. What new lifeforms have grown up among the ruins?"

Clemantine nodded and said, "We know now, at least in part, what lives in the Hallowed Vasties. We know there are people still surviving—at Verilotus and at Tanjiri and maybe other worlds. We know of the Tanji, and the Inventions, and we are at least aware that something new exists at Sulakari, and that there is a great project thriving at the Halo. But there are also our philosopher cells. We still call them that, though they are new too."

She turned her troubled gaze on the Bio-mechanic. He felt its weight. And then he felt a deep sense of gratification when she said, "You are right about the philosopher cells."

Again, her gaze took in the others. "I've been on the high bridge. I've sensed it. The Bio-mechanic is right. The philosopher cells *are* one of the new lifeforms we came to find."

Now she turned to Kona. "They are descendant of the Chenzeme, yes, but also of Verilotus, and of Ezo, and of *us*."

Her shoulders sagged, she bit her lip, and she looked suddenly distraught. In a softer voice she said to the Bio-mechanic, "I have enough death on my hands. You are right about that too."

She straightened. Looked around the circle. "We designed the philosopher cells to be what they are. I don't think it will be hard to reach an understanding with them. I want to try. We must *always* resist the destruction of other entities—unless in the greatest necessity."

But then her brow crinkled and in a troubled voice she added, "After what's happened, I think it will be a harder challenge to reach an understanding with the Inventions."

A murmuring followed. Quiet discussion that soon shifted to the gee deck, leaving the Bio-mechanic and the Engineer alone on the library's floor, each warily eyeing the other. The Bio-mechanic crossed his arms, using the moment to send yet another submind to *Griffin*, ensuring his most recent memories would be preserved, regardless of what happened in the next few seconds.

The other Apparatchiks appeared within their windows: the Scholar, the Mathematician, the Pilot, the Astronomer. He felt their questing minds studying his own revised architecture.

The Mathematician scowled and shook his head, saying, "This revision has introduced unnecessary complexity, reducing the efficiency of your thought processes."

"A trade-off," the Bio-mechanic replied. "Giving me a broader perspective and much greater range of action."

"That is not your role," the Pilot objected.

"It is now."

The Pilot, little more than a silhouette within a detailed three-dimensional star map, gave a slight theatrical shudder. "I do not understand how you can tolerate such a dilution of mind. I do not wish to ever endure such a thing."

"Nor I," the Astronomer declared.

The Bio-mechanic shrugged. What of it? He was not asking any of them to follow him. He eyed the Engineer, awaiting some similar comment from that one. But none came. Not from him nor the Mathematician.

The Scholar only observed, "Your role is not as demanding as it once was because you share it now with the Cryptologist. She has replicated much of your original function."

"She has made it easier for you," the Engineer agreed. "Much easier, with her redesign of the philosopher cells."

Arms still crossed, the Bio-mechanic nodded, because this was true. Then he asked them bluntly, "Now you have seen me, do I need to fear you? Will you seek to erase me or to undo my evolution?"

None answered. Not at first. Their faces and their figures froze, so he knew they had retreated. They would be engaged in a rapid, complex discussion. He could follow them, join them, but he chose not to. Let them decide.

After several seconds, they became animated again and the Scholar spoke. "Clemantine has said we must always resist the destruction of other entities unless in the greatest necessity. We perceive no immediate necessity to destroy you. Are you aware of some hazard that requires your destruction?"

"I am not."

"Are you still loyal to the fleet?" the Mathematician asked.

The Bio-mechanic sneered at this. "What else? We are in this altogether . . . unless you think I'm suicidal?"

"I don't know you as well as I once thought," the Mathematician replied quite reasonably.

"Then I will explain it to you. I am not suicidal."

No, quite the opposite. He was only beginning to live.

CHAPTER FORTY-FOUR

NOT BY FORCE, but by gentle persuasion, that version of Urban on the high bridge convinced *Dragon* to forgo the intended mating on the grounds that a singular mind would surely arise from such a transformative physical union. Far better for the fleet to maintain the parallel perspectives of the two ancient ships.

What then? What is next in this life? What is our goal?

He knew what the ship's company would choose: after Hupo Sei, there would come a long exploration of the Sun's dead and empty system. He cared nothing for that. In his own simulated heart he longed for Prakruti, to return there, to be as he had been there, endowed with silver and bound by it, enfolded within the web of that world's life.

Never again.

That fate was closed to him.

He had become a lesser being.

Clemantine ghosted in.

She had come and gone, come and gone, always silent. Assessing his mood and monitoring the nascent intentions of the philosopher cells.

This time she spoke to him. *Your avatar is ready.*

I know it.

Come then. Inhabit it.

He didn't say, but he thought, *That avatar is not really me.* But nothing was hidden on the high bridge.

She said, *It is you, my love. It is that same cocky pirate who fled*

Deception Well, captured for himself a Chenzeme courser, and returned again, all on fire to do what no one else dared to do—to venture into the Hallowed Vasties.

He didn't know what to say to this. It turned out he didn't need to say anything as Clemantine continued, explaining to him, *Decisions are being made. Ro Az Ra Ni has received a new dictum from the Core Forum, but desires to speak to you before presenting it.*

This news startled Urban because he should have known of it before; he would have known if he'd been paying attention in his usual way, monitoring events through his extended senses rather than being bound up in brooding. Still, he could guess what was afoot.

They're going to ask us to leave, aren't they?

I think so.

I'm ready.

He did not want to visit the Sun's dead system, but neither did he want to stay longer at Hupo Sei.

Then you're in the minority, Clemantine warned him with a soft laugh. *This is a ship of scientists and there is so much more to explore here.*

Urban woke his avatar. No sense of silver, of course. That was gone. But at least he was free of Lezuri's shadow.

Clemantine was there with him in an otherwise empty chamber in the warren. In the absence of gravity she drifted among the ribbons of wall-weed, gazing at him with warm affection. As the last of the cocooning gel slipped off his newly created body, he opened his arms to her. She came to him, holding him close as he held her. No words. Just the soothing touch of the wall-weed warm around them.

A few minutes. No more.

"They're coming," she whispered, her lips light as butterfly wings against his ear.

"Here?"

"Yes."

Reluctantly, he let her go. Dressed himself in newly generated clothes. Traded a submind with his ghost on the high bridge. Watched through extended senses the approach of the two Inventions.

Despite its size, the tentacled envoy gracefully transited the zero-gravity environment of the warren. It carried the single instance of Ashok that had remained aboard *Dragon*, wrapped up securely in one long limb. The little Invention's other instances remained safely away with *Alaka'i Onyx*.

The chamber door opened, admitting the two synthetics. Ashok was set free to drift while the envoy's long tentacles slithered all around the chamber walls, mingling with the wall-weed. It spoke first, its voice issuing from its central hub. No polite preliminaries. Just straight to the point. "I am instructed by my Originalist faction to privately inquire of you, if a sufficient mass equivalent to the Labyrinth is gathered, would you be able to replicate the success of the project?"

Urban shivered. It hurt to hear the project described as a success . . . or more accurately, it hurt *because* the project had succeeded, only to be destroyed.

He answered the envoy honestly, "No. Tell your faction it is impossible. We no longer possess the means to try again."

"Then all is decided and we Originalists will make no further argument against the Core Forum's dictum."

Ro Az Ra Ni then asked that the ship's company gather to hear the dictum of the Core Forum, and after that it departed the chamber.

Ashok stayed behind. It said, "Urban, I detected emotional pain in your expression when Ro Az Ra Ni named the project a success."

Urban responded with prickly resentment. "You know us that well, do you?"

"Yes. I have made a study of human emotions, beginning with Tio Suthrom."

"A lot of subject matter there," Urban agreed, inducing a soft scoffing chuckle from Clemantine.

The little Invention continued. "I apprehend your disappointment with the project. From your perspective, its success was brief and its loss painful. But for the Inventions, the outcome has been unexpectedly positive. For many generations, we Inventions endured a tedious conflict between factions. I think that is over now. There is certainly a new unity among us. The Originalists are gratified that the Core Forum supported the project, despite the vast risk of your presence here and of the project itself. They recognize that the entirety of our existence was risked to get them the world they desired."

Urban started to object, to insist that the project had never threatened the existence of the Inventions, but Clemantine clearly anticipated this and warned him, *Hush, and listen.*

Ashok went on. "The project's brief success has clarified the difficulty of the task the Originalists set for themselves, to re-create a world for the Inventors to inhabit. Most Originalists now accept this will never happen and that the Inventors will never come. This is a good thing, as it leaves us free to recognize our own essential nature. It is clear to us the Inventors anticipated the chance that we would be left on our own and designed accordingly, placing within us the capacity to be independent, creative beings. Even the Originalists have come to accept this as a gift from our Inventors.

"Without your interference, we might not have reached this point of development for centuries more. And if the project had succeeded in creating a stable world, we would have been distracted for millennia. Instead, the demise of the project has led us to accept the reality of our own agency. Your brief presence here has freed us to invent a future for ourselves alone."

Alone in truth, Urban thought, for he had guessed correctly. The decision issued by the Core Forum was that the fleet must depart from Hupo Sei. Not because the Blade had been lost, but because of *how* it had been destroyed. When the missiles had been revealed as weapons of war, their blooms had consumed not only the Blade but also the Inventions' fragile trust. Beyond the ubiquitous evidence of ancient war, beyond Kuriak's violence and its corruption of the IRKs, the missiles served as emphatic proof that humans and human-built machines must be forever dangerous, warlike, and destructive.

Despite the pleas of many among the ship's company, and despite their repeated apologies and their detailed explanations, the Core Forum issued no further communication.

The fleet did not depart immediately. The ships lingered, awaiting the arrival of a spherical habitat, a new home for Ro Az Ra Ni who, contaminated as it was by contact with biological forms, was doomed now to an isolated existence.

Ashok chose a different fate. When Tio announced his intention to depart with the fleet, the little Invention declared, "I will remain with you, Tio Suthrom, and continue my explorations aboard *Alaka'i Onyx*, if you find that acceptable."

Tio did.

*Jolly?

At this soft query, a frisson of shock swept over Jolly. He tensed, knowing the moment he'd been dreading had come. His fists clenched. A surge of adrenaline sent his heart racing.

*Jolly? Urban pressed. ***Are you all right?**

Are you? Jolly countered in an unspoken question.

He sat alone in the dark of his bedroom, his back to the wall, haunted by the taunting promise he'd made to Urban: *If you get lost in the silver, I'll come back in and find you.*

Urban *had* been lost and the Cryptologist too—lost beyond any ability of his to recover them. Though if he had been there, if he had consented to at least keep watch—

No, no, no.

Jolly knew, logically, his presence would have made no difference except that he too would have been lost.

And wouldn't that be better?

Holding up his hands, he gazed at the *ha* sparkling in the darkness. He had come by the *ha* first. Now, among the ship's company, he was last to possess this artifact of Verilotus, this art of the Tanji.

Pointless now.

Answer me, Jolly.

I'm okay. After a moment of hesitation, he added, *I never mastered the silver like you did. Never, like the Cryptologist.*

On Verilotus, where the *ha* had lain dormant within every person, it had been his purpose to waken it. But he could not waken what did not exist within another being. Not here. Not now. Not on his own. Not without the intimate presence of the Tanji. *And not even then!* he told himself. Reluctantly, he disclosed this truth to Urban. *I can't give you back what you lost.*

He knew he could not. Far beyond him to ever re-create the ocean of knowledge and experience Urban had contained. Far beyond anyone—a certainty that did not assuage his guilt or ease the dread he felt at this moment of confession. *You thought I meant to ask that? No. There's no unwinding time, Jolly. I know it.*

Nowhere in these quiet words did Jolly hear the anger, the resentment, the grief he had expected.

The Cryptologist? he asked.

She knows it too.

Jolly sighed as a warm tide of relief rose through him. *I'm sorry for what you've lost . . . what she lost. I would undo it if I could.*

A soft laugh, a faux threat: *If I thought you could, I'd make you undo it.* Then, somberly, *We go on as we are.*

I'm ready, Jolly said, realizing he could be done now with his self-imposed isolation. *Ready to go on, I mean.*

Sooth, Urban said. *So am I.*

CHAPTER FORTY-FIVE

WHERE TO GO?
Despite the tantalizing Halo and the lure of lively Sulakari, this was a question the Dragoneers answered without debate as they awaited the arrival of Ro Az Ra Ni's habitat.

An almost unanimous vote, Clemantine thought as she poured tea for Tio and Urban.

She had seated them side by side on cushions, on the opposite side of the low table from herself, the three of them a fragile triangle. Urban looked downcast and resentful; Tio appeared apprehensive. Despite their age and their long life experience, an adolescent hostility still smoldered between the two of them. It was absurd, and Clemantine meant to get past it.

She spoke gently, assuring them, "It is possible for the two of you to be friends. You just need to get to know one another rather than walking past each other with averted eyes. It's only hard because the two of you are too much alike."

This claim caused them both to recoil. They actually leaned away from one another, and she couldn't help but laugh. "Do you see what I mean?"

Tio side-eyed Urban and said, "I don't think we are much alike beyond our affection for you."

Urban scowled—his default expression in any uncomfortable circumstance. "Tio's right. We're nothing alike." He gestured at the table. "And this isn't necessary. I already know Tio and I like him well enough."

"Sooth," Clemantine agreed. "And I like the Cryptologist but that doesn't mean I never suffered the harsh rasp of jealousy."

At this, Urban's scowl darkened. "Why do you bring up the Cryptologist. She was never my lover."

"No?" Clemantine asked in surprise.

"No," he answered firmly.

Yet hints of entanglement had reached her, and she felt sure this denial did not represent the whole truth. "Something more than lovers, then?"

His gaze cut away. A sheen of heat on his face. "Whatever that was, it's gone now," he told her. "Gone with the Blade."

A thoughtful nod as she said, "I'm sorry." She meant it. She felt for him, for what he'd lost.

But Urban only shrugged, dismissing the subject. She knew him well enough to let it go, saying only, "Drink your tea. Both of you. And please, resolve to be friends, because I need you both."

She sipped her tea, wishing they would talk to one another—and they did, in their way. Tio said, "Another minute until we depart."

And Urban answered, "Sooth."

Clemantine resisted the temptation to roll her eyes. It was, at least, a start.

She gazed at the liquid lingering in her cup, awaiting the unbalanced sensation of acceleration. But then, mere seconds before the moment of departure, a message reached her from the Astronomer: *I have found a likely candidate for the object you were seeking.*

A moment of confusion caused her to frown. She had to search her memory before she realized what he meant. And then she blurted aloud, "You found Ona's refuge?"

This drew curious looks from both Urban and Tio. "What is it?" Urban asked. "What's going on?"

The Astronomer, following Clemantine's lead, also spoke aloud, his voice emanating from hidden speakers as he answered her question. "What it is remains to be determined."

"But it still exists?" she asked.

"Yes. It is in a distant orbit which has likely kept it safe from exploitation. The Pilot can amend *Khonsu's* course, if you wish to send an outrider to explore further."

Despite a swiftly rising weight of dread around her heart, she told the Astronomer, "Yes, send *Khonsu*. I want to know."

By this time, Urban had worked out exactly what was going on. "No, Clemantine. This is not a good idea. We know nothing about the ghost in that refuge. For all we know, she's another Lezuri . . . or a flawed and wicked soul like an antagonist in an ancient drama." He shook his head. "Pass on," he pleaded. "She belongs to the past. And we owe her nothing."

"All true," Clemantine whispered. "And still I want to find her."

"But *why?*"

She groped to define the reason. In part, it was atonement. She had caused the demise of Kuriak who was Ona's caretaker. But it was more than that. It was the idea of this ancient artist, in the face of despair, resolving to reach past disaster on the mad chance that she might find again a life worth embracing.

But all Clemantine said was, "I want to know if Ona is still there. Because if it was me, I would not wish to be abandoned."

Claiming the task for herself, Clemantine went alone as a ghost in *Khonsu's* library.

The suspected refuge proved to be a smooth, dark, perfect ovoid, only a little larger than the landing ship, *Argo*. Its surface yielded almost no returns from radar and no heat above ambient. Though *Khonsu* had already approached within a hundred meters, drifting closer still, Clemantine could see it only as a black void in the ocean of background stars.

A wonder the Astronomer ever found it.

She assigned two scout-bots to explore. The first landed without incident and secured a grip. The second followed. They mapped and analyzed the surface, but found no means to enter.

This did not surprise her. The outer shell had likely been grown seamlessly around the core, one last layer of protection around the precious computational substrate holding Ona's archive. Clemantine could use a gel of Makers to dissolve the shell and force an entrance, but that risked triggering a self-destruct routine as she had done when dealing with Kuriak.

No, she would approach politely, with an audible tap at an imagined door. "*Knock, knock,*" she said softly, her voice relayed by a weak radio signal. "*Human here. Yes, we still exist. I have come to waken you, Ona. Won't you let me in?*"

She said it that way as a lark, never expecting it to be enough to waken an intelligence within. But as she began to instruct *Khonsu's* DI to repeat similar words in other languages—just in case—a voice replied. Not a human voice. She felt sure of that. No, this voice spoke with the flat placid tone of a simple DI. It said, "Of course you may come in. Please stand by. Several minutes are required to synthesize a doorway."

Clemantine immediately suspected a trap. "You admit a stranger so easily?" she asked with a thread of tension in her words.

"No. It is Kuriak who decides. Kuriak guards this facility. Only those Kuriak authorizes are allowed to approach."

Ah. A simple DI indeed, unaware that Kuriak had ventured in-system long ago—and that it would not return.

"Very good," Clemantine said.

She shifted to a waiting avatar already grown within a cocoon in *Khonsu's* tissue. She woke within it, dressed in a silver skin suit. The cocoon surfaced—a blister peeling open on the scout ship's slender hull—and Clemantine emerged.

The refuge now lay a mere fifteen meters distant. Without waiting for further invitation, she pushed off, gliding toward it at a cautious velocity, a thin tether trailing behind her. By the time she touched down, a door had opened onto a dark and narrow crawl-space. Deep within, a soft silvery light, beckoning.

She asked the DI, "Have you ever admitted anyone before?"

"No. You are the first."

"What will I find inside?"

"That archive Kuriak sent you to retrieve."

Clemantine hesitated then, held back by a last brutal rising of doubt. Was it unwise to waken the past?

Of course, she thought. But having come this far, it would be absurd to back out now.

She entered the tunnel and, finding a hand-hold, she propelled herself toward the light.

CHAPTER FORTY-SIX

SLOWLY, CAREFULLY, THE fleet made its departure from Hupo Sei. Urban was in no hurry. Neither was the ship's company, this passage being their last chance to study the Inventions' civilization at close range. The Pilot had plotted complex trajectories for each vessel, ensuring they would pass close to as many habitats as possible, and sometimes the curious denizens of those habitats invited the Dragoneers to visit via some version of Tio's artificial avatars. It felt like friendship. Still . . .

"As a general principle, our kinds are not compatible," Ashok observed one morning as its single instance occupied the corner of Urban's breakfast table. Tio sat on Urban's other side, with Clemantine across from them.

"What do we have in common?" Ashok continued. "Certainly we share a curiosity about the Cosmos and a desire to create. But the actions induced by these common traits yield results so different as to seem incomprehensible."

"Not incomprehensible," Tio objected. "Just . . . alien. And that is why the Dragoneers find the Inventions fascinating."

"Yes, Inventions are diverse and fascinating. But the reverse is not true. Having thoroughly studied you, Tio Suthrom, and your histories, the Inventions calculate they possess a sufficient understanding of human nature and evolution—and as you know they are extremely wary of it."

Not unwise, Urban thought.

Aloud, he suggested in a teasing voice, "Perhaps as our evolution continues, we might someday be sufficiently trustworthy and civilized to be readmitted to Hupo Sei."

"This is unlikely," Ashok replied. "The Core Forum risked much to run the experiment of the Blade. When that failed, agreement was reached to adjust our general algorithms, enhancing an inherent drive to engage in a stable cycle of creative, harmonious, and limited growth and regrowth without recourse to the destabilizing effects of advanced human technologies."

"Some of us would like to avoid those destabilizing effects as well," Clemantine said, fixing a stern gaze on Urban.

"Though it's hard to resist," he countered gently. "Even for you."

She drew back, as a shadow of regret softened her gaze. "*Sooth*," she breathed.

Her venture to the refuge had found more than just Ona. Altogether, she had recovered five archaic ghosts. They remained archived aboard *Khonsu*, with the ship's company reluctant to waken them without knowing anything about who and what they were . . . or what they might desire for themselves in a far future that would be both surpassingly strange to them and forever shadowed by the immense tragedy of their intimate past.

Urban regretted reminding her of it. He tried to make up for it with a shrug and a smile, saying, "We have better things to talk about on a sunny morning."

Ashok accepted this invitation to shift the direction of the conversation. "'Sunny' is an odd word," it observed. "You use it to reference the light of the star you call the Sun. Your origin star."

"Yes, that's what it means," Urban agreed. "What's odd about that?"

"It is odd because the spectrum of light you use on the gee deck—this 'sunny' light—differs from the actual spectrum of the Sun. I would not have suspected the Sun to be your origin star."

Urban drew back, shocked, even offended by this claim. He wanted to laugh it off, to deny it. The words rose to his lips. But he had no basis for argument because he had never considered the issue before.

Every star possessed a unique spectrum, one that served as its identifying signature. When the Engineer had designed the gee deck's artificial sky, Urban had not thought to question him on the spectrum of light he used. It was traditional to imitate the sky of ancient Earth. He couldn't think why the Engineer would have selected a different spectrum . . . *if* he had, if Ashok wasn't mistaken.

"Ashok, are you sure?" Clemantine asked, sounding as troubled as Urban felt.

"Yes, I am sure," Ashok assured her. "The spectrum is very similar, but subtle differences exist."

Without a word, Urban shifted to the library. There he summoned the Engineer, and the Astronomer too, presenting the question to them. The Engineer cocked his head, looking both puzzled and intrigued. "I did not consult astronomical records when I determined the spectrum of the sky," he explained. "Instead, I used the palette traditional for habitats."

The Astronomer was scowling, lip curled in cold anger. "It is true the spectrums do not match." He turned to face the Scholar, just as that one appeared beside him, confined like his companions within the limits of his window. "Trace the history of this illumination palette," the Astronomer instructed. "When did it diverge from true?"

A brief pause before the Scholar answered, his voice puzzled, "The palette has always been as it is now. It has never matched the observed spectrum of the Sun."

"So we see by the light of some other star?" Urban suggested. "Some star where our ancestors briefly settled along the way?"

He had never thought about it before, but now that he did, now that he knew he had *not* grown up under the Sun's light, a deep melancholy began to rise. He felt deprived of what he now perceived to be an essential connection to the ancestral world: the Sun's unique spectrum as a thread that bound Earth's scattered children to the beginning of all things.

But not if they had always lived under the light of some other star.

"No," the Scholar said. "The evidence does not support such a conclusion. The palette has *always* been as it is now, back through the first expedition our history records. And yet it does not match the observed spectrum of the star we call the Sun. Moreover, this same inconsistency exists within the library acquired from the Narans, and also the library from *Alaka'i Onyx*. None of us emigrated through the same paths. The only ancestral world we share is Earth itself. It is as if the data for the spectrum was falsified even before the first ships set out."

This did not seem likely to Urban, and the Scholar too looked doubtful. He added, "Or possibly a stealth virus spread from library to library, corrupting the original data."

"Wouldn't we know if that had happened?" Urban asked. "Wouldn't there be some trace? Some sign?"

"The trace is the inconsistency."

As subminds traded back and forth between his living avatar and this ghost in the library, he felt his heartbeat quicken. He looked at the Engineer. "Easier to change a fact in a library—the name of a star—than it would be to change the spectrum of light used in tens of thousands of ships and habitats and celestial cities."

The Engineer nodded. "I agree."

Urban then uttered what felt to him like a daring conclusion. "So that star we call the Sun, with its dead system . . . it's *not* the Sun—because its spectrum is wrong."

He looked to the Astronomer for an objection. None came, though the Apparatchik looked even angrier now, his gaze distant and his brow furrowed in a deep scowl.

"What star *does* generate this known spectrum of light?" Urban asked him.

The Astronomer's eyes shifted, fixing Urban with a chilly glare. "I should have noted this inconsistency long ago. It's just . . . I never thought to measure the spectrum of your artificial light!"

"What star?" Urban insisted, desperate for some better option than the lifeless system where they were bound.

The Astronomer's scowl lightened just a little as he said, "The spectrum we utilize on the gee deck is an exact match, when filtered through atmosphere, to the light emitted by the veiled star within the Halo."

The Halo?

On the gee deck, Urban caught his breath, his gaze rising to take in the sight of the deck's artificial sky—the beautiful blue cloud-laced sky of Earth. In the library, he proffered a tentative conclusion. "So that star, mostly hidden at the center of the Halo, that's the Sun. Right? The true Sun. Not that empty system where we are bound."

"Yes," the Astronomer affirmed, with no hint of doubt. "We have been deliberately misled. That false Sun is a near twin of the Halo—the same type, the same age. It is likely both stars emerged from the same stellar nebula. But it is not the source of the spectrum that lights our artificial skies."

Urban smiled, eager now to hasten their departure from Hupo Sei. On the high bridge, he shared his excitement with the philosopher cells, encouraging them to ponder and evaluate the strange technologies evident at the Halo—its veil of orbiting objects, its encircling ring of lights blazing like tiny stars.

At the same time, his avatar's worried frown transformed to an eager smile as he announced to Tio and Clemantine, "We have a new destination."

ACKNOWLEDGMENTS

As always, thanks are owed to my long-time freelance editor, Judith Tarr, who has worked with me throughout this entire series. I don't know where I'd be without her.

Thanks also to Wil McCarthy for reading an early version of the manuscript, and to Tim McGregor, Ken Malphurs, and Glen Kilpatrick for serving as proofreaders. I'm grateful to all of you. Any remaining errors and deficiencies are my own.

And last but never least, a huge thank you to all those readers who've traveled with me on this voyage through the Inverted Frontier. The fifth and final book lies ahead. I hope you'll come along.

Linda Nagata
January 2024

Made in the USA
Monee, IL
01 July 2024

60993963R10187